HOME

ALSO BY MATT DUNN

HOME

Matt Dunn

Published by Lake Union Publishing, Seattle

www.apub.com

Amazon, the Amazon logo, and Lake Union Publishing are trademarks of Amazon.com, Inc., or its affiliates.

ISBN-13: 978-1503948396
ISBN-10: 1503948390

Cover design by Lisa Horton

Printed in the United States of America

For Dave and Nic. For old times' sake.

1.

'Read 'em and whip?'

It's taken me a week to come up with these four words – well, three-and-a-half words, technically – as the tag-line for a series of new *Fifty Shades* rip-off S&M novels, but thanks to the slightly patchy mobile phone reception I always seem to get driving along this particular section of dual carriageway, as if I'm entering a zone where the modern world hasn't quite got a firm foothold yet, it's hard to tell whether Marty, my boss at the ad agency, likes them. Though given how he's felt the need to call me on a Sunday, not to mention his sarcastic tone, I'd guess the answer's 'no'.

'Yeah,' I say. 'You know, with "whip" instead of "weep", like when you're playing poker and you've got a good hand, so you put your cards on the table, then say . . .' My voice tails off, and I realise I need a clever question to get Marty to put *his* cards on the table, but after a long and awkward silence that lasts a whole traffic-light change, 'And?' is all I can come up with.

'It's not up to me, Josh. It's up to the *client*. And seeing as you're not coming to the pitch tomorrow . . .' There's a heavy disappointment in his voice, and I'm sure it's put on for my benefit, as if he wants me to be in absolutely no doubt that I'm letting him down by choosing to take my dad to hospital to finally find out what's wrong with him rather than attend Monday's client meeting.

'Okay. So . . . ?'

'So hurry back, Josh. Remember, holidays are for people who don't like their jobs. Or don't want to keep them.'

'Marty, it's *one day*. And it's hardly a holiday.' I think about explaining how it's technically 'compassionate leave', but I'm not sure Marty would understand the first of those two words, and I'm too scared he'll ask me to do the second if I try.

'Hmm. Well, you're driving, so I'll let you go. I'll call you *mañana* with the lowdown.'

'Actually, could you, you know, *not*? I'll be a little busy tomorrow.'

'Ah. I forgot. The big consultant appointment.'

For a moment I wonder whether I'm imagining the inverted commas I've heard round those last two words, but surely even Marty's legendary insensitivity wouldn't extend to my dad's illness?

'That's right.'

'No probs. I'll ping you the deets in an email instead.'

I cringe a little at the idea of being 'pinged' some 'deets', but know it's my own fault for working at a hipster ad agency based in Shoreditch.

'Sounds good.'

'Then we'll talk about it on Tuesday.'

'Sure.'

'When you're back in the office,' he adds, for effect.

'Right.'

'You will be on email, I take it? Or is carrier pigeon a better way of . . .'

'It's Derton-on-Sea, not some third-world country,' I say, although when I play the sentence back in my head, I sound like I'm trying to convince myself of that fact.

'Yeah, right,' says Marty, although I doubt he has any real idea what it's like this far outside of London. People like him can't survive without 24/7 access to the latest mocktail juice bar, artisan cupcake café, pop-up falafel stand, or whatever the current trendy way to waste your money is.

At the sound of his 'Laters,' I click off my hands-free, put my foot down, and remind myself that at least I'm going to a place where no-one says 'laters', or if they do, they never pronounce the 't' so it doesn't sound quite so precious. I'm doing eighty, but the dual carriageway is clear, and in any case, there's little chance of being caught speeding going in this direction, as the police always set up their radar on the other side of the road. People only normally break the speed limit in their haste to *leave* Derton.

As if on cue, just as I pass the sign that says 'Welcome to Kent's Sunshine Coast', the rain starts, so I slow back down to the speed limit as I cross the bridge over the river Der – a name I always snigger at like a five-year-old. Not that it's much of a river any more – it dried up years ago, much like the tourist trade the town was originally built on. Back when I left, it was only people who couldn't afford a bargain-bucket flight to the sun who'd come here for their holidays (why would you, when for the same money as a donkey ride in Derton, you could ride a camel somewhere, well, *nice*?), and even then it was more likely to be day-trippers taking the cheap two-hour coach from London, like the one I happily let overtake me a few miles ago.

I reach the final roundabout before Derton proper starts and circle it a couple of times, readying myself for what the next twenty-four hours might bring. *You'll never break free from Derton-on-Sea* is what we used to say at school, before the few of us with any ambition did exactly that.

And as I flick the indicator and steer the car towards the coast, a tiny, niggling part of me is worried that might well be true.

⁓

My mum and dad live in a three-bed red-brick semi a three-minute walk from the seafront. It's a large house by London standards, but pretty average for Derton, and as I park the BMW next to the Rover my dad hasn't been well enough to drive for the best part of three months, the usual feeling of nostalgia hits me. They've been in this house for thirty-six years, since my mum was pregnant with me, in fact, when they moved down from London in search of a better quality of life, which makes it pretty funny that I headed in the opposite direction for exactly the same reason as soon as I could. And although (once they're gone) I'll be glad to never have to come to Derton again, my being here today – and the irony's not lost on me – is an attempt to delay the first step along that particular road for as long as possible.

I switch off the engine and climb stiff-legged out of the car, then retrieve my overnight bag from the back seat. While I've crammed in a couple of changes of clothing *just in case*, not bringing a suitcase is my way of trying to convince myself that this is just a short-term engagement, a temporary solution: come here, make sure my dad's on the road to recovery, and get myself on the road back home to London as soon as possible. But as Mikayla, my girlfriend, delivered as a parting shot this morning as I left the rented shoebox of a flat in Hoxton we've shared for the best part of three years, sometimes there's nothing as permanent as a temporary solution.

I head up to the porch and reach for the bell, but before I can even press the button, my mum makes me jump by throwing the front door wide open. She seems to get greyer – and shorter – every time I see her, though given recent circumstances, the 'greyer' part isn't a surprise.

'Josh!' she says, giving me a look that's part 'pleased to see you', part 'welcome to the madhouse', then she envelops me in a hug that lasts so long I fear we're in danger of missing tomorrow morning's appointment.

'Hi, Mum.'

'I heard the car,' she explains, though I know she's probably been watching out for me for the last hour or so, then she takes a step backwards and looks me up and down. 'How are you?'

It's a good question, given the mixed emotions that being back home always brings, but under the circumstances, I know there's only one appropriate answer. 'Fine. How is he?'

'Today's a good day.'

I smile encouragingly. Ever since my dad suddenly fell ill, there've been bad days or good days depending on how his health has been. And even though his range can be pretty wide, her definition is always binary.

'And how are you?'

'Oh, you know.' My mum makes a face, which – *depending* on whether it's a bad day or a good day – might mean anything from 'at my wits' end to 'surviving,' and right now I take it to mean the latter. 'Thanks for coming, Josh. I know this isn't easy for you.'

'He's my dad,' I say, as convincingly as I can, and because she knows the truth – that actually I'm here for her, rather than for him – she gives me a look of such gratitude that it almost breaks my heart.

∽

My dad's made a special effort today given my arrival, which means he's actually dressed in clothes he could go outside in, as opposed to the normal 'paisley pyjamas and towelling dressing gown' combination he's taken to wearing on a daily basis since this *thing*, whatever it is, knocked him for six. Not that he goes outside much – or goes anywhere anymore, seeing as he can hardly walk ten feet without stopping for a breather. As usual (given that it's five minutes to midday), he's glued to today's episode of *Catch Me If You Can*, my parents' favourite TV quiz, on every day, and a show that occupies a special place alongside *Countryfile* and *The Antiques Roadshow* in their 'programmes if you call while we're watching we won't answer the phone' list. When I walk into the front room, he glances momentarily up from the TV.

'Hello, son,' he says. He's a lot thinner than the last time I saw him, and while he didn't have any hair to lose, he has grown a thick, grey beard. Though I understand from the series of increasingly desperate phone conversations I've been having with my mum recently that this is because even shaving's become a bit too much for him nowadays, rather than any oldest-hipster-in-town fashion statement.

'You're looking very . . . distinguished,' I say, giving him a brief pat on the shoulder, trying not to recoil at how bony it's become. We're not big on physical affection, my dad and I – though to be honest, that's probably because we're not that big on each other full stop.

'Thanks.' He scratches at his chin. 'Itches like a bastard, though,' he says, causing my mum to tut at his language from where she's filling up the kettle in the kitchen.

'I bet.'

He nods towards the television. 'This'll be over in a minute.'

'Sure,' I say, not expecting the fact that I've been driving for the best part of two hours to come and see him to be enough for him to miss even a minute of his precious viewing schedule, so I pull out a chair and take my usual place at the dining table, cursing under my breath as I knock my knee on the sharp corner of the table leg. I've eaten upwards of five thousand meals sitting in this exact same spot, yet

I still do this every time I sit down, and while you'd think I might have learned by now, there are some things that apparently never change.

By the time my dad finally clicks the TV off and turns round to face me, the pain's subsided into a dull ache, though I know I'll have a bruise there tomorrow.

'So . . .'

'So?'

He places the TV remote on the table next to his chair – a table, I notice, that's crammed with boxes of tissues, bottles of tablets, and a book called *Chemo-nly When I Laugh*, and though I do my best not to let it show in my face, the thought that he might have cancer chills me.

'How's the big bad world of advertising?'

My dad doesn't believe mine is a proper job – he thinks there's some dishonesty to it, as if what I do forces people to buy things they don't want.

'Oh, you know. Pays the bills.'

'That's good,' says my dad, though he can't resist adding a begrudging, 'I suppose.'

'Yes. It is.'

'What are you working on at the moment?'

'Just a campaign for some books.'

I stare levelly at him, reminding myself to ignore the inevitable snarky comment about them being someone else's and not the one I've been threatening to write for what seems like forever, but when he smiles, I can't help myself.

'What's so funny?'

'Nothing. I'm just delighted that after all these years you're finally putting that English degree you were so keen to leave Derton to study to good use.' He shakes his head. 'Still, what is it you're always telling me? Advertising's where Salman Rushdie started? Though I doubt he did it for as long as . . .'

7

'Books, eh?' says my mum, from where she's hovering nervously in the doorway, as if ready to step in between us like a referee at a bad-tempered boxing weigh-in. 'Anything we'd like?'

I hesitate, not sure my parents are *Fifty Shades* kinds of people, and even if they were, it's the last thing I want to think about.

'Probably not.'

'And how's . . . Mikayla?' says my dad, after a moment.

'She's . . . She sends her . . .' I can't quite bring myself to lie on her behalf, mainly because the arguments Mikayla and I have had about me even coming here today are still too raw. 'You know.'

'That's good of her.'

'How are you feeling?' I say, keen to change the subject.

He does a couple of gentle arm and shoulder stretches. 'Fine, considering. I get the odd twinge, but on the whole . . .'

His eyes flick briefly towards my mum when she tuts again, but my dad's always been like the knight in that old Monty Python film who gets his arm cut off then dismisses it as 'but a scratch'. And if 'the odd twinge' is how he wants to describe how whatever it is that (and we'll find out for sure tomorrow) might just be the end of him makes him feel, well, that's his right, I suppose.

'Pleased to hear it.'

I'm conscious we're nearing the outer limit of our usual conversational pattern, unless I can think of anything new to say that doesn't involve his health, or he can come up with a new, thinly-veiled insult about my line of work, or Mikayla, or even my life choices in general. Instead, he just looks at his watch, and I can't help but notice how loose the strap is.

'You sticking around for lunch?'

'One of Mum's roasts? Wouldn't miss it for the world.'

'Good,' he says, then he reaches for a tissue from the box on the table next to him, coughs loudly into it, and (to another round of tutting from my mum) inspects the contents. 'No lung in there,' he announces breathlessly, and after he's finished laughing at his own joke, he coughs so hard he looks like he's about to pass out.

'Are you all right, Phil?'

When he doesn't answer immediately, my mum hurries anxiously towards him, but he waves her away. 'I'll live,' he replies, once he's got his breath back, and my mum and I can't look at each other. He clears his throat noisily, then adds the tissue to the growing collection in the bin by his chair. 'How about a coffee?'

My mum's already making for the kitchen, but I reach out and put a hand on her arm. 'I'll do it,' I say, relieved to have got through this first encounter without too much of the usual verbal sparring, and for a moment, I wonder whether this visit isn't going to be as painful as I'd feared.

I smile at her as I get up from the table, then – and I can't help thinking it means something – knock my knee again in the exact same place.

2.

The 'tennis player scratching her naked bottom' poster has gone, but otherwise my room's pretty much how I left it eighteen years ago, with my single bed against the far wall, the desk in the corner, and the crammed-to-bursting bookshelf underneath the window, though the matching black MFI wardrobe and chest of drawers that seemed so modern to my teenage self now look like they're only a few years away from qualifying for a spot on *The Antiques Roadshow* themselves. And while I'd have preferred to stay in the spare room in a proper double bed, my dad's in there now, ever since his night-time coughing got so bad that neither he nor my mum got a lot of sleep.

I don't bother unpacking – not that I've got much to unpack – but just throw my bag onto the bed, then head back downstairs. My dad's still in front of the TV, making the most of the Sky Sports subscription he treated himself to when he sold the shop – 'if there are balls involved, he'll watch it, even women's football,' my mum often deadpans, which always makes me smirk childishly. She's in the kitchen, putting the finishing touches to today's roast lunch – a Peters family ritual that even the outbreak of nuclear war probably couldn't interrupt – and the delicious smells coming from the oven are making my stomach rumble.

'Can I help?'

Startled, my mum wheels round, as if she's already forgotten I'm visiting. 'What? Oh, no thanks, love. All under control.'

I gaze at the numerous pots and pans bubbling away and realise that such is my mum's expertise at this particular meal, I've just done the equivalent of tapping a heart surgeon on the shoulder mid-operation to ask if they need a hand.

'Shall I set the table?'

She glances up at the kitchen clock. My parents eat lunch regimentally at one on the dot (and have dinner at six), and any variation to this timetable virtually requires advance written notice.

'Bit early, don't you think?'

I'm about to ask why – after all, it's not like we're planning to use the dining table for a family table tennis tournament between now and lunchtime – but decide against it. My mum and dad have always had their routines, and for some reason, they're just more comfortable when they stick to them.

I peer around the kitchen, looking for a surface to lean against where I won't be in the way, and wonder whether I should go through and chat to my dad, but decide I'd better save what little conversation I have left for while we're eating. And though I suppose I could ask my mum how she's feeling about tomorrow's hospital appointment, I can't really see an upside to starting *that* discussion.

'How about a drink?'

My mum frowns at me. 'A *drink* drink?'

My parents aren't big drinkers, and normally – when I'm here, at least – nor am I, mainly because I always have to drive back to London. But this time (for one night, at least) I'm not going anywhere.

'We might need one, don't you think?'

'Don't take what he says too personally, Josh. It's just that he'd have loved for you to have taken the shop over.'

'Instead of – and I quote – "abandoning the family business for some London literary pipe dream"? I'm sorry, Mum, but a life stood behind the counter of a seafront sweetshop in the arse-end of nowhere was never something I could see myself doing. He's known that for the best part of eighteen years. So why he still feels the need to constantly remind me of it.' I hunt angrily through the nearest kitchen cupboard, but all I find is a half-finished bottle of sherry that looks older than I am.

My mum smiles apologetically. 'I'm not sure we've got anything in. Your dad would only drink it if we did.'

'Not to worry,' I say, already glad of an excuse to get some air. 'I'll nip out and pick something up. Any requests?'

'Red wine,' says my mum, after a moment. 'Your dad's allowed that.'

'By you? Or his doctor?'

She gives me a look. 'Both.'

'Red wine it is, then.'

'There's a shop on the corner of . . .'

'I know, Mum. I used to live here, remember?'

'Okay, clever clogs.' She rummages through the kitchen drawer and removes a handful of change. 'Let me give you some money.'

'Only if you let me pay for lunch.'

She smiles again, then walks over and rubs my arm affection-ately. 'You may not think it, but your dad's pleased to see you, Josh.'

And while I know I should say *I'm pleased to see him too* in reply, I've a feeling the jury will be out for a while on that one.

❧

Raj's corner store (or 'megamart', as he used to optimistically refer to it) is now a Tesco Metro. I'm both saddened and gladdened by this, as Raj's wine selection more often than not put the 'off' into 'off licence'. But despite the reassurance I'm not going to be buying something that'd be more suitable for sprinkling over chips that this new development gives me, it's always a shock when something you've known your whole life isn't there anymore.

I make for the drinks section and pick out a bottle of Rioja, then decide to get two just in case, and I'm just scanning them through the self-service till when the light on the top of the machine starts to flash, and 'Age-restricted item – Wait for cashier' appears on the screen. I grit my teeth in frustration, then a gruff voice from behind me makes me jump.

'Got any ID?'

I spin around to find Gary – sorry, *Gaz* – Marshall, my best friend from school, grinning at me. I haven't seen him in I don't know how many years, and the receding hairline, along with the slight beer belly, are a bit of a surprise. Though not as much as the Tesco uniform he's wearing.

'Hey, Gaz!'

We do a little dance, not sure whether to shake each other by the hand or hug, and in the end, we settle for some mutual shoulder-clapping.

'How are you?'

'Good,' I say.

'You've hardly aged at all. Bastard.'

'I don't know about that.'

'The till would seem to disagree. And I'm sorry, but I'm still going to need to see some ID.'

'What for?'

'Just to prove it's actually you.' He balls his hands into fists and one-two punches me lightly in the stomach. 'I thought you'd emigrated, or something.'

'Sorry. It's just . . . I've had a lot of stuff going on. And now I've got some other stuff going on. Which is kind of why I'm here.'

'I heard. How *is* your dad?'

I shrug. Gaz knows my parents well. 'Not so good.'

'Bummer.' He makes a face. 'Sorry, mate. Though does this mean we might be seeing a bit more of you?'

'Don't take this the wrong way, but I hope not. For my dad's sake, I mean.' I grin guiltily. 'I didn't know you worked here?'

Gaz glances down at his name badge, which – rather unfortunately – has 'Ass Manager' printed on it. 'Living the dream, Josh,' he says, reaching past me to tap an authorisation code into the touchscreen. 'How's London?'

'London is . . .' I struggle for an answer that isn't 'not Derton' as I slot my Visa card into the reader. 'Good.'

'Pleased to hear it.' Gaz narrows his eyes at me. 'Let's go for a beer soon, yeah? Have a proper catch-up.'

'Sounds good. Though I'm not sure how long I'm . . . I mean, I'm planning to head back home tomorrow, assuming . . .' I stop talking, aware that I shouldn't really be assuming anything.

'Oh. Right.' Gaz looks at his watch. 'How about tonight?'

I think for a moment. From *Countryfile* to the news, my parents have a full TV schedule this evening that not even the house catching fire would distract them from, so I doubt I'll be missed. 'Why not? The Grapes?'

'You have been away for a while, haven't you? The Grapes is now a Starbucks.'

I pause, mid-PIN entry. 'A Starbucks? In *Derton*?'

Gaz laughs. 'You'd be surprised,' he says. 'Tell you what. Remember that pub in the Old Town? The Submarine?'

'Isn't it a dive?'

'Ha ha. And no, actually. Well, not any more. They've done it up.'

'The alternative was to knock it down.'

'Yeah, well, it's quite nice now. Maybe even as good as one of your posh London pubs. But without the ridiculous prices. Or the stupid, beardy hipster types.'

'Okay, okay.'

'Sevenish?'

'Sounds like a plan. I'll swing by the flat and pick you up?'

'Sure.'

'You still living in the same place?'

'Same flat, yes. Same place?' Gaz nudges me. 'Wait and see.'

A light above the adjacent till is flashing – an old lady appears to be trying to feed a five-pound note into the credit card slot – and Gaz rolls his eyes. 'Well, I'd better . . .'

'Yeah, me too.' We do our little dance again. 'Right. Well. Later,' I say, stopping just short of adding an 's'.

'Excellent!' Gaz grins. 'It's good to see you, Josh. You and me, out in Derton! It'll be just like the old days.'

'Great,' I say. Though I actually hope it won't.

3.

The Submarine is all polished wooden floors, funky original for-sale artwork on the walls, and a selection of mismatched tables and chairs, some of which Gaz proudly tells me came from his wife Michelle's 'vintage' shop, Second Time Around, round the corner, which apparently does a nice line in 'distressed' furniture. And 'distressed' is a good description of how I'm feeling upon seeing how much the place has changed, especially the menu. Where once you'd have been lucky to get a choice of crisp flavours (and I still remember the momentous day dry roasted peanuts arrived), now there's a chalkboard above the bar listing a range of 'artisan' ales and 'locally caught' sausages (which I can't believe is a phrase anyone's ever so much as tittered at, let alone repeated as they've ordered one), and even a vegetarian section featuring 'Quornish Pasties' (though I have to admit I admire the wordplay on that one). Such is my shock that for a moment I think I must have passed through some sort of teleportation device when coming in through the doorway, as a place like this can't possibly be in Derton – at least, not the Derton I know.

Once I've finally managed to pick my jaw off the floor, Gaz leads me to a booth in the corner, and hands me a laminated card.

'What's this?'

'The beer list.'

'The *what*?'

'You know – like a wine list? But . . .'

'. . . with beer. I think I've worked that out, thanks, Gaz.'

'Well, why did you ask, then?' He laughs. 'What are you having?'

'A heart attack. What's going on?'

'Where?'

'Here.' I wave a hand randomly around to indicate the pub's interior. 'And here,' I say, handing the beer list back to him.

'I told you they'd done the place up.'

'Yeah, but.' I try and think of the right way to ask who from around here wants to drink in a place like this, but can't quite come up with a phrase that doesn't sound rude, and besides, the pub is pretty full considering it's a Sunday night. Fortunately, Gaz seems to read my mind.

'Hey, don't sell the old town short. It's on the way up!'

'It only had the one way to go.'

'Seriously. It's not the same place you left. Derton's almost trendy now.'

'As are you,' I say, admiring the checked-shirt-and-turned-up-jeans combination he's wearing. 'What's all this about?'

'F&F.'

'Effing *what*?'

'F and F,' Gaz says, enunciating carefully. 'It's Tesco's new designer clothing line. They've got it in the superstore. I get a discount. One of the perks of working there. Not that there are that many others.'

'Tesco's do *clothes*?'

'Yup.'

'That fit people?'

'That fit people what?' Gaz makes the 'duh' face. 'Sometimes, places can surprise you.'

17

'You're telling me.' I peer at the label on his shirt pocket. 'What do the "F"s stand for?'

Gaz looks like he's about to tell me, in no uncertain terms, then he grins. 'No-one knows. Like with B&Q or IKEA, they're a mystery.'

'As is what's happened to this place.'

He rolls his eyes. 'When was the last time you went out around here?'

'I dunno. I haven't been back that much. Mikayla . . .' I give him a 'you know what she's like' look, then realise that's a little pointless given how Gaz has never met her. 'My girlfriend – she's a London girl through and through. To be honest, Gaz, on the rare occasions I managed to get her to set foot outside of the capital and come down here, we tended to stay in and have dinner with my folks. She found Derton a little scary.'

'*Scary?*'

'Well, not the place so much.' I lower my voice. 'More the people.'

'The people?'

'The locals.'

'Like you and me, you mean?'

'No. But everyone *except* you and me. I overheard her once describing Derton as an "RAF town". I told her it didn't have an airfield, and she laughed and told me "RAF" stood for "rough as fu—"'

'It's never been *that* bad.'

'Come on, Gaz. There were times you could go up the High Street and think you'd accidentally stumbled onto the *Walking Dead* set.'

Gaz gives me a look, then signals the barman, and I do another double-take at the fact that a place that once didn't have any tables now has table service. He orders himself a pint of something called Bishop's Finger, then turns to me. 'What do you want?'

I scan the list of beers, still trying to take it in. There's not a single name I recognise, and there are even cocktails listed on the back – this in a place where a shandy used to be beyond the mixology skills of the bar staff. 'What's good here?'

'You still drink bitter? Or has London turned you onto that fizzy stuff?'

'Champagne?'

'I meant lager.' Gaz shakes his head. 'You *have* changed.'

I stare at the list for a moment longer, then realise it's just easier to order the same as him, and Gaz sniggers as he tells the barman to 'give my friend the finger', then we have the customary elbowing competition while we argue over who's paying, but Gaz insists, and I feel bad because he works in Tesco's, until I remember I've got no reason to feel superior given how my career's hardly gone as I'd have hoped. So I tell him I'll get the next round, and I ask him how things are, and . . . Well, I won't bore you with the details because Gaz can go on a bit, but essentially he tells me about how he and Michelle have been trying for a baby but they're not having any luck so they're thinking of adopting, and about how well her shop is doing since Derton's started to get busy, and about Tesco's (highlights: the previously-mentioned discount clothing and as much 'past its sell-by date' food as you can carry home; low points: the uniform, and, well, the look on people's faces when they see that you work in Tesco's), and how he sings in a band – 'Nothing serious, like. Just a bit of fun.' Though when I ask him whether it's fun for the audience, he refuses to answer. Then he tells me he still sees a few of the old 'gang' from school from time to time, though apparently I wouldn't recognise them now as Phil Phillips has gone bald, Vik Patel's really fat, and Andy Wilson's had a sex change, and the look on my face at that last piece of news makes Gaz laugh so hard he nearly falls off his chair.

In return, I tell Gaz about my job, and how advertising isn't really where I saw an English degree taking me but it pays the bills while I write my novel, and when he points out that advertising's where Salman Rushdie started I remember why Gaz was my best friend and feel bad for not seeing more of him in the last few years. So I apologise for this, and he tells me not to give it another thought (and looks like he means it), and I realise I'm having a good time, and that makes me feel guilty given what I'm back here in Derton for, but then I remember that while the source of this guilt was telling my mum and dad I was going out to meet Gaz this evening given tomorrow's appointment, they'd almost bundled me out of the front door (though that was probably more to do with the open-ing credits of *Antiques Roadshow* appearing on the TV than any desire for me to catch up with an old schoolmate).

And the beer is good, so we have another, and then another, then Gaz says he's feeling a little hungry, and I'm almost tempted to suggest a kebab like we used to do back in the day before I remem-ber I don't want to feel ill tomorrow (especially around someone who's *really* ill) which kind of sobers me up a little. So Gaz waves the barman over again and we order more beer, along with some of those locally caught sausages (a phrase that now we both find hilarious) and they arrive along with some home-made (!) crusty bread, and they're *good*, as are the two more pints we order to wash them down (which we wash down with two *more* pints), and it's a real shame when I catch sight of the time and reluctantly tell Gaz I have to go, and he calls me a party pooper, then I explain *why* I have to go, and it's his turn to feel guilty, so we drain our glasses and make our way unsteadily out into the night air. And we're walking back towards his place when (and I blame it on the beer) I insist on a nostalgic detour through the old marketplace, and suddenly

I can't believe what I'm seeing: the once-dilapidated buildings have been smartened up, baskets of flowers hang from freshly-painted lamp-posts, but it's what I spot in between what's now a trendy-looking bicycle store, 'BeSpoked', and a shop called 'Florist Gump' that makes me stop dead in my tracks.

'Whassa matta?' slurs Gaz, whose legendary low tolerance to alcohol seems – like most legends – to have become even more exaggerated with time.

'Cupcakes?'

Gaz grins. 'I've ass you not to call me that!'

'No. *There*. Where my dad's sweetshop used to be.'

It takes him a few moments to focus on the sign I'm pointing at. 'Issa cupcake café.'

'Really?' I say sarcastically, given that the words 'Baker's Cupcakes' are painted in a huge red piped-icing design above the window. While I could maybe forgive a pub that sells artisan beers, a cupcake café in Derton pretty much tops the list of things I never thought I'd see here. 'Amazing! Though zero out of ten for the name.'

'Huh?'

'"Baker's Cupcakes". That's like saying "Brewer's Beer". Or . . .'

'Alright, alright,' says Gaz, 'though they're actually d'licious.' He frowns, then his expression goes through a series of complicated changes, finally settling on what looks like mischief. 'Speakin' of delicious, you'll never guess who owns it.'

I stare at him for a moment. 'It's not you, is it?'

'Nah. Course not.'

'Well, how could you possibly expect me to know, seeing as I wasn't even aware it was here until thirty seconds ago?'

He walks over to me unsteadily and puts a hand on my shoulder, though that could be as much for his benefit as mine. 'Now don' get angry.'

'Gaz, please,' I say, wondering what on earth about the owner-ship of this café – unless it's someone like Robert Mugabe, or that Syrian president chap, for example – could possibly make me angry.

'S'Anna.'

'Sanna?'

'Yeah.'

I don't know anyone called Sanna. 'Who?'

'It's Anna,' Gaz says carefully, and my head starts to swim, and it's nothing to do with the beer.

'Anna?'

'S'right.'

'*My* Anna?'

'Uh-huh.'

Even though he and I only know one Anna – the Anna I was crazy about, the 'love of your life' and 'the one you were stupid to let get away', as Gaz often took pleasure in reminding me back then – I still feel a need for a little more information. 'Anna *Coleman*?'

He nods. 'She's *Baker* now.'

'I guessed that, seeing as she owns a cupcake . . .'

'No, her *name's* Anna Baker. She married that . . .' – Gaz frowns as he searches for the most appropriate word, though to be fair, there are quite a few to choose from – '. . . git Ian Baker. F'm school. Theyownit.'

At the mention of his name, I sober up almost instantaneously. Ian Baker: the alpha male in our class at school, the charismatic, good-looking, bigger-than-everyone-else kid who'd charm/smarm/harm whoever got in his way, who regarded the whole of any football game as 'injury time' (even when we were on the same side), and – given how his parents owned the one successful guest-house in Derton – never seemed to worry about what his future was going to hold.

'You're joking? Ian never struck me as a . . . Well, a cupcake kind of person. And *Anna* . . .'

Gaz nudges me. 'S'probably why he used to try and kick chunks out of you during PE. Coz he fancied Anna. And you and she was going out.'

'Thanks, Sigmund Freud. And does she . . . I mean, is she still . . . ?' I'm having trouble formulating sentences, and while I'd like to blame that on the alcohol, it's more the shock of finding out that Anna's still here in Derton. *And* married to Ian.

'A looker?' Gaz makes a face that's more than a little creepy. 'Oh yeah.'

'That wasn't what I was going to ask,' I say indignantly, though it's exactly what I'm wondering. 'But . . . *Ian Baker?*'

'Yup. Though 'cording to Michelle, things aren't exactly rosy in that department.'

'Really?' I say, as indifferently as I can.

''Parently.'

I walk up to the door and peer in through the glass panel. From what I can make out, the shop's been completely remodelled: half a dozen tables now line the back wall where the counter used to be, the shelves where the sweet jars once were are now dominated by a shiny coffee machine, and there's a huge glass cabinet – which I guess is for the cupcakes – right next to the till. I'd say I liked what they'd done with the place. If I didn't dislike one of the people who'd done it.

'She won' be there now.'

'Really, Gaz? Though I think I could have guessed that from the "Closed" sign, and the fact that all the lights are out. Oh, and that it's eleven o'clock at night.'

'Shit!' says Gaz, and I wheel around anxiously, my first thought that Ian is here and wondering who these two drunkards peering

into his shop are, but instead, Gaz is looking at his watch, a pan-
icked expression on his face.

'What's the matter?'

''Part from the fact I oughta be home, like an hour ago?'

'*Ought* to? Or what?'

Gaz stares at me. 'You've met Michelle, right?'

'Point taken.' I grin sheepishly. Even though I've got a hundred
more questions about Anna, I'm just sober enough to realise that
now's hardly the time. 'Come on, then.'

We hurry back along the seafront towards his house, where I
prop him up against the side of the porch, ring the doorbell, then
run back round the corner like a naughty teenager, not wanting
Michelle to see me and blame me for her husband coming home in
such a state. But as I walk the short distance back to my mum and
dad's house, the shame I feel isn't about hiding from Gaz's wife. It
goes back much further than that.

∽

Anna and I were going out for two years, give or take, and I was
crazy about her, and I'm pretty sure she felt the same about me.
Although I say we were 'going out' – when you're that age, and not
quite old enough to go to pubs (legally, at least), and you don't have
much money, or there aren't many coffee bars (as we called them
back then) in a place like Derton so there's nowhere to hang around
in (though even if there had been, no-one at that age actually likes
the taste of coffee, so you probably wouldn't anyway), 'going out'
really just meant not going home. 'Staying out', if you like. So we'd
stay out after school, and hang out together on a park bench, or
meet up on the beach in the least vandalised of the shelters, or ren-
dezvous behind the amusement arcades, where we'd make our own
amusement in a fumbling, sixteen-year-old's kind of way.

And she was gorgeous – even back then, you could tell she was one of those cute girls who'd grow up to be a beautiful woman - and smart, and funny, and kind, and . . . Well, all of those things you could ever want. Too good for the likes of Derton. Too good for the likes of me, probably, so I should have snapped her up there and then. But then I got a place at university in London, and she went to catering college here, and while I could have gone somewhere more local, I was desperate to get away from the place, from the life my dad seemingly had planned out for me, so I 'turned my back on' (my dad's words) the family pick 'n' mix shop and off I went.

And men (well, boys) get a bit stupid at that age, away from home for the first time in their lives, and at a place full of women in a city full of women, especially when they've spent most of their lives somewhere where (and I know this'll sound bad) it was sometimes hard to tell the (wo)men from the boys. I'm not proud to admit it, but I was like a kid in a candy store (I know, I know, even though I had an *actual* candy store waiting for me back in Derton), seeing it as an opportunity I'd be stupid not to make the most of. Though I'd have had to have been a fool to think there was a better opportunity than Anna Coleman.

But most eighteen-year-old boys *are* fools, aren't they? Some still are, decades later. Obsessed with sex. Getting it, having it, bragging (okay, lying) to your mates about it, wondering if you're any good at it, and worrying what's wrong with the girl you're trying to do it with because she's not prepared to have sex with you (though trying not to worry that the reason is actually because there's something wrong with *you*). That's testosterone for you: women (though I'd never dare to tell them) have it lucky – maybe once a month their hormones start affecting their judgement, their moods, their character, but for us guys? It begins at puberty, lasts all month every month, and *never goes away*!

Though in my defence, the girls at college were different. And from different places – different to Derton, at least. They smoked, and they drank, and they had opinions that had been formed outside a small town. They'd been around. (Not like *that*. Well, apart from a couple.) They had interesting friends. Most importantly, and unlike Anna, when I tried to put my hand up their jumpers they let me. And to an eighteen-year-old small-town boy (I'm ashamed to say), these things mattered.

Plus Anna couldn't come to visit, because she was too busy working (every weekend in my dad's shop, would you believe?), and I didn't come back at weekends, because that's when I *wasn't* working, and the last thing I wanted was to spend time (and a large proportion of my precious beer money) on a clanking old train journey to and from the place I'd spent most of my life desperate to escape from. And then I stopped coming home in the holidays. Why would I, when London was available and I could spend my time with my hand up *its* jumper? And Derton stopped being home, which meant Anna and I just . . . Stopped.

I won't say we lost touch. 'Lost' makes it sound like it was something accidental, and ending our relationship wasn't an accident. I even wrote her a letter – I thought it was the best piece of writing I'd ever done – explaining how I felt, asking if she wanted to (but knowing she probably couldn't) come to London with me, and telling her if she wouldn't, then we didn't have a future and (possibly the most cowardly thing I've ever done) gave it to my dad to give to her. But it obviously wasn't my best piece of writing, because she never replied, and in a way, that suited me. Because that meant I could blame her. Didn't need to feel guilty. Especially if I was never going to see her again.

And while there were times I missed her – her smile, her laugh, how she'd light up a room the moment she appeared, or the way she used to stare at my lips just before we kissed as if zeroing in on a target – these just stopped being important enough to make me pick up the phone, so I didn't. But now, especially if things with her and Ian (while I still can't believe she married him, of all people) aren't exactly 'rosy', I'm suddenly intrigued enough to think about doing exactly that.

As I turn into my mum and dad's street, I remind myself I shouldn't be thinking like this. After all, there's the small matter of Mikayla to think about, plus the obvious geographical differences – and who knows what other differences might have materialised over the years. Plus with everything else that's going on at the moment, it's pretty selfish of me to start thinking about my ex-girlfriend – assuming Anna ever speaks to me again, given how I treated her all those years ago. Though I suppose there's only one way to find out.

One thing I do know, though, is that suddenly, being back in Derton doesn't seem quite as awful as it did.

4.

We're sitting in the waiting room in the Oncology Department at Derton General, or Derton-on-Sea Healthcare NHS Foundation Hospital Trust, as nobody calls it, though it might as well be any waiting room, to be honest. They've not made any special provision for the seriousness of the disease that the people sitting here – the ones with the sunken cheeks and grey complexions, as opposed to the ones with scared faces like my mum and me, at least – are probably suffering from. And *suffering* is the right word. I can't think of a place where I've seen so much obvious illness. But that's cancer for you, I suppose.

Though – and I'm trying not to get my hopes up – my dad's actually one of the less ill looking ones, and in fact, seems in positively good form. He's already made a joke about how the 'Waiting Room' sign should have the word 'God's' in front of it, and pointed out that the dog-eared magazines piled high on the table in the corner should be called *Goodbye!* rather than *Hello!*, and while neither my mum nor I have found either of these observations funny, we've smiled politely. It's his day, after all, and if he wants to deal with it with gallows humour, then who are we to protest?

I've a raging thirst after last night's overindulgences with Gaz at The Submarine, and my dad keeps licking his lips, so I check my pockets for change, lean across and nudge him, then point to the drinks machine in the corner, where an inquisitive toddler is in danger of getting his head stuck in the glass flap.

'Anything you want?'

'Not to have cancer,' says my dad, dryly. If he's nervous, he's certainly not showing it, and – though it surprises me to realise it – I find myself admiring his calm detachment. My mum, on the other hand, is doing a good impression of how I used to be on childhood visits to see the dentist, and looking like she wants to be anywhere but here.

'Mum?'

'Hello?' she says, startled, as if I've interrupted her innermost thoughts. 'Sorry. Yes, Josh?'

'Anything for you?'

'What your dad said,' she says, reaching across to give his hand a squeeze, and I have to swallow hard. Fortunately, the screen above the reception desk chooses that moment to announce that it's our turn, and after exchanging a series of looks so lingeringly dramatic they wouldn't look out of place on a Spanish soap opera, we haul ourselves out of our chairs, make our way towards a door bearing a nameplate that reads 'Mr. Stephens', and troop into the specialist's consulting room.

❧

Mr. Stephens is a tall, bespectacled, distinguished-looking man, dressed more like he's off to some high-powered office job than someone who works in a hospital, and as my dad introduces me I have to fight the urge to ask why specialists don't call themselves 'doctor' anymore. Surely they could have come up with something more superior to 'mister'? But I don't get the chance, partly because we have to get an extra chair from the room next door because there are only two on our side of his desk (though after I've carried it in,

Mr. Stephens perches on the edge of his desk anyway, so I suppose I could have borrowed his, although I don't dare point this out), and all the while my mum is peering intently at him, as if she's looking for a 'tell' like poker players do, some clue that the news is good. So far, all my knowledge about what my dad's illness might be has come via the Internet, and I'm hoping today will be a little less scary than Google's pretty bleak diagnosis, but 'I'm afraid . . .' is as far as Mr. Stephens gets, and my mum bursts into tears, maybe because she's afraid too – afraid of the truth, and what it all means. Then my dad is comforting her, his arm around her shoulders, whispering something into her ear, and I'm sitting there like a lemon wondering whether I should be asking a thousand questions, though the only one I can think of is 'How long has he got?'. So that's what I ask, and as soon as Mr. Stephens pushes his glasses higher up the bridge of his nose and takes a deep breath, I already know I'm not going to like what I hear.

'It's hard to say. Lung cancer . . .' He leaves a pause that's almost reverential, as if he's describing a great footballer or an Oscar-winning actor. 'And it's spread.'

'Which means?'

Mr. Stephens folds his arms and regards me over the top of his bifocals. 'It could be weeks.'

'Weeks?' exclaims my mum, a millisecond before I do. 'How many weeks?'

'It's difficult to give an exact number.'

My mum frowns. 'So it could be fifty-two weeks? A year, in other words?'

'I think Mr. Stephens means "weeks" in the sense of "not months", love,' says my dad, softly. 'Or if it is months, certainly not twelve of them.'

'That can't be right.' My mum looks at the specialist, then at me, then at my dad, then at the specialist again. 'Can it?'

Mr. Stephens nods slowly. 'I'm afraid it is. Two, three months, if we're lucky . . .'

My dad grimaces, though that could be because my mum's gripping his arm rather firmly. 'If we were lucky, surely I wouldn't have cancer in the first place?'

'*Three months*? Is there nothing you can do?' My mum's turned even paler. 'Nothing at all?'

'I'm sorry, but any intervention . . . At this stage, it'd probably do more harm than good.'

We sit there in shocked silence, until another question occurs to me. 'What if we went private?'

'Then you'd still get me, and the same opinion, and the same result, I'm afraid. It'd just cost you a fair bit of money.'

'There must be something you can do for him?' asks my mum, desperately.

'We can make your husband comfortable. Apart from that . . .'

'Hello,' says my dad, brightly. 'I am here, you know. Though evidently not for much longer.'

Mr. Stephens smiles. 'Sorry, Mr. Peters. We can make *you* comfortable. Manage any pain. But unfortunately, one day . . .'

My dad stares at him for a moment, then he nods slowly, grabs the arms of his chair, and tries to lever himself upright. 'Well, if that's the case, there's no sense sitting around here and wasting everyone's precious time.'

I'm still a little stunned, so it takes me a moment to realise my dad could do with a hand. I get to my feet, then help him out of his chair and towards the door, though my mum still hasn't moved, which makes things a little awkward.

'Love?' says my dad, after a moment. 'Time to go.'

'But . . .' My mum's showing no sign of wanting to leave, although that could be because she doesn't trust herself to stand up. 'Shouldn't we get a second opinion?'

My dad rests a hand on my shoulder. 'Josh, shall we go?'

'Not from *Josh*,' says my mum, a little hysterically, reaching up to grab the specialist's sleeve. 'Isn't there any other treatment? You read about these alternative therapies. Or maybe an operation?'

Mr. Stephens shakes his head. 'I'm afraid not. Your husband's condition is too far advanced. Any surgical procedure would really impact on the quality of whatever life he has left. And, in my opinion, would have very little chance of making a difference.'

'But you're making advances all the time. Finding new cures. I read it in the papers. *This week*!' She delves into her handbag, removes an article about coffee enemas she's taken from yesterday's *Mail on Sunday*, and hands it to him.

'We are, but . . .' Mr. Stephens passes the page back without even so much as a glance at it. 'If only we'd caught it sooner.'

My mum looks accusingly at my dad. 'You hear that, Phil? If you'd gone to the doctor earlier . . .' She doesn't add 'like I told you', but we both know that's what she means. And while it strikes me as a little unfair to tell someone who's just been told he doesn't have long to live that it's his fault, I don't dare say anything. For all I know, underneath that cheerful exterior my dad could be struggling to hold everything together, and if he *and* my mum lose it, I don't know what I'll do.

'Come on Sue,' says my dad, then he turns to the specialist. 'Thanks, Doc. I appreciate your honesty.'

Mr. Stephens shakes his hand, then opens the door. 'I'll speak to your GP. And anything you need . . . Well, you have my number.'

'And lung cancer's got mine, eh?' He smiles grimly. 'Thank you.'

My dad and I are halfway through the doorway, but it's only now that my mother gets up, though it looks like putting one foot in front of the other takes the greatest of efforts, and she's a little wobbly as she walks towards us.

'Steady, love,' says my dad, miming to me that she's had a drink or two – something fortunately she doesn't see – before taking her by the arm, though it's doubtful he's strong enough to hold her if she falls, so I step between the two of them, link my arms in theirs, and lead them out into reception like we're in some slow-motion Scottish country dance.

As Mr. Stephens shuts the door behind us, my dad makes an 'I'm in trouble' face. 'Well, that could have gone better.'

'For pity's sake, Phil!' shouts my mum, suddenly rounding on him.

'Steady on, love. I'm just trying to . . .'

'Well *don't*. It's alright for you.'

'Pardon?'

'You heard me.'

'I'm not sure I did. How is it "alright" for me, exactly?'

'Weren't you listening in there?' She shakes her head. 'In a few weeks, it'll all be over as far as you're concerned, so you seem to think it's okay to treat it as one big joke, but we're going to have to deal with this, *and* live without you for the rest of our lives.'

'That's hardly . . .'

'It's not funny, Phil. None of this is funny. So stop pretending that it is.'

She's right. It's not. And while she hasn't perhaps explained herself in the most sympathetic of terms, what *is* funny is how I can see exactly what she means. I can tell my dad gets it too, and while I know he's being cheerful for our benefit – and possibly for his – I'm not sure now's the time. Particularly given the way my mum looks like she could burst into tears again at any moment.

'Josh,' he says, quietly. 'Will you give us a minute?'

'Sure.' I check my watch, then realise to my horror they might assume I'm doing exactly what my mum's just asked my dad not to do. 'I mean, you can have more than a minute. I wasn't . . .' I sigh. 'I'll go and bring the car round.'

My dad nods, so I make my way through the sliding doors and towards the car park, happy to be out of that place, and relieved not to be in the middle of their argument. But when I get to the car, there's a parking attendant standing in front of it.

'Everything okay?'

'Lucky you got here just now.' He nods towards the small white printed slip stuck to the inside of the windscreen. 'Ticket's about to expire.'

But as I jump in the car and drive round to pick up my parents, I'm suddenly struck by an unpleasant realisation.

The ticket's not the only thing.

∾

The drive back's an awkward one. I'm staring straight ahead out of the windscreen (because I have to in order to avoid hitting the car in front), my dad is too (possibly because he's silently contemplating what's in front of *him*), and – when I catch sight of her in the rear-view mirror – my mother is doing exactly the same (though probably because if she meets anyone's eyes, she'll burst into tears). In fact, no-one says anything for the entire ten-minute journey, and even when I pull the car into the drive and turn the ignition off, nobody moves.

After a couple of minutes, the absurdity of the situation hits me – well, that plus the fact that I'm desperate for the toilet – so I climb out and head round to the passenger side to help my dad out of the car. But even by the time I've let him into the house – and been to the toilet – my mum is still nowhere to be seen.

'Where's that wife of mine got to?' asks my dad.

I frown, check the kitchen, then peer out through the dining room window. 'She's still in the car.'

'What on earth for?'

'How should I know? But she doesn't look like she wants to come in.'

'Well, go and get her.'

'Yes, sir!' I stop short of saluting him. 'Er . . . How?'

My dad rolls his eyes. 'Just press the button on the remote that activates the alarm. She moves, she'll set it off, bingo!'

'Do you really think that'll work?'

'It used to work with Buster.'

Buster was the dog they used to have, before they had me. I've only ever seen him in photos, back from when they looked happy, posing in front of their old Ford Escort, or out in the garden on a rare sunny day. Then the dog died, and I came along, and . . . Well, they never looked quite as happy anymore.

'Or that she'll find it funny?'

My dad sticks his lower lip out like a scolded toddler. 'S'pose not.'

With a sigh, I walk back outside to the car and knock lightly on the window. My mum looks round with a start, then winds the window down.

'Hello, Josh.'

'Are you coming in?'

'I can't.'

'Why not?'

My mum looks down at her hands, which are clutching a soggy, balled-up hanky. 'Don't you see? Because that'll be the beginning of the end.'

'I'm sorry, mum, but . . .' I clear my throat awkwardly. 'I think we've already reached that point. No matter how long you stay in the car.'

35

'I know, but . . .' She sniffs loudly. 'This might sound silly, but the moment I set foot inside the house, it'll feel like this stupid however-many-weeks countdown has started. But for as long as I'm sitting here . . . Well, I don't have to go in and begin getting ready for . . . You know what.'

I catch sight of my dad peering at us through the dining room window and surreptitiously wave him away, then walk round to the other side of the car and climb in beside her.

'It's just . . .' My mum is staring intently at the back of the head-rest in front of her, as if fascinated by the pattern in the leather. 'He worked so hard in that shop of his, and then when he finally sold it and retired, I thought we'd have time. Together.'

'To do stuff?'

'To *not* do stuff. To just be with each other, without him worrying about work. And now it's all being taken away, *he's* being taken away, and I know it sounds selfish, but I'm going to be left all alone.' She dabs at her eyes with the hanky, though I fear it's long ago reached its maximum level of absorption. 'I can't even begin to think what that means. It's so . . . unfair. Don't you agree?'

I nod, because the thing is, I do. You hear all these stories of people who live to be a hundred and one despite smoking forty-a-day, or who eat like a horse and remain stick-thin, and while that's amazing, how do you explain someone like my dad, who as far as I know hasn't ever smoked in his entire life, never even had one of the candy cigarettes or chocolate cigars he used to sell in the shop, and here he is dying of a disease that millions of chain-smokers miraculously manage to avoid? And while I don't wish death on anyone, surely it isn't fair that one of them is getting away scot-free, while through no fault of his own my dad is fac-ing the day when his lungs simply can't do what they're supposed to anymore?

And I can understand that my mum feels cheated. You marry someone, go through the pain and suffering of having a family, economising, planning for the future, all the tough stuff with the hope that there's a payoff down the line, that the retirement you've saved and planned for will at least give you a good return on your investment. And to have all that suddenly whisked away from beneath your feet like a tablecloth in a magic show . . .

'You've still got time,' I say, putting an arm round her shoulders.

'*Three months*? That's nothing.'

'No, it's *better than* nothing. Imagine if something else had happened – he'd had a car accident, or a heart attack in the shop, and you'd lost him without even having a chance to say goodbye. At least this way you can. Give him a good send-off. Make whatever time he has left the best it can possibly be. For both of you.' I give her a squeeze, and I'm shocked to notice how much weight *she's* lost, how small she is, how I can feel her bony shoulders through her coat, and I suddenly realise there's more than one person who's going to need looking after.

'How?'

I swallow the lump that's rapidly forming in my throat given what I'm about to say, though it takes two goes. 'I'll help.'

'Really?'

'Really. Now come on.' I reach over and open her door. 'At the risk of stating the obvious, we don't have long. So we better get on with it.'

My mum gives me the briefest of smiles. 'I'm glad you're here, Josh,' she says.

Though given the sinking feeling in the pit of my stomach at the knowledge I might be in Derton for a while, I'm pretty sure I can't say the same thing.

5.

I decide my mum and dad could do with a bit of time to talk, and besides, I need some air while I try and work out what all of this morning's news means, not to mention what/how I'm going to tell Mikayla/Marty. The seafront's as good a place as any to think things through, but after half an hour I'm no clearer, plus I'm fed up with battling the unseasonably brisk wind that's whipping in from the North Sea, and in desperate need of a coffee. While I could go to the new Starbucks, I've never been a fan of the big coffee chains, which here in Derton really only leaves a couple of options. And since I'm starving, and it's a while till lunchtime, I decide to go for the option that includes a cupcake.

I first noticed Anna because of her smile, mainly because it seemed to be her default expression, and in a town where most people went about with a scowl on their faces it made her stand out, as did the fact that she was blonde, and tanned from the unusually warm summer we'd had that year, and gorgeous, with a fantastic figure: slim frame, and breasts slightly too big for the rest of her (okay, if you were to look at video evidence from the first time I saw her you'd probably conclude that I noticed that a millisecond or two *before* I noticed her smile). Anyway, after the usual sixteen-year-old's faffing about trying to establish whether she had a boyfriend (and remember, this was back in the day before you could simply log on to Facebook to find that kind of stuff out), I'd plucked up courage (that is, been dared by Gaz) to ask her out.

And to my amazement, she'd said yes, so we'd gone to the cinema to see . . . Well, I can't remember what it was (maybe *Mission: Impossible* – though I might think that simply because that was how I remember feeling about my chances of getting a second date) as I'd spent the whole time watching her out of the corner of my eye instead of the film, and when she'd caught me and asked me what I was looking at, I'd had to admit it was her, because she was just *so beautiful*, a word that even twenty years later I seem to be way too immature to say without feeling like a twat, and we'd never looked back from then on.

Anyway, the reason I mention this is because she looks just as beautiful today. Sure, she's not quite the same, tiny sixteen-year-old, but everything's grown/changed in proportion, like in those morphing videos you see on YouTube, or from the kind of special effects they use in films to gradually turn people into werewolves . . . Okay, bad example. But suffice to say, if my teenage self had had any idea this was how she'd look today, there would have been *no way* he'd ever have let her get away.

And I realise that sounds fickle. Shallow, even. But I reckon back then I'd still have fancied the present-day Anna (and that was when you'd only see words like MILF if you accidentally hit 'Caps Lock' and mis-typed the name of a dairy product), because she positively glows as she rushes around behind the counter, and even from the street, with my sunglasses on, peering through the window while pretending to study/hiding behind the menu fixed to the doorpost, I can't take my eyes off her.

The café is busy, and I feel a sense of pride, which I immediately bat back down. It, *she*, is nothing to do with me now – and she probably *wants* nothing to do with me now. Which is just as well, because I decide there and then that there's absolutely no way I'm going to walk in through the door, buy a cupcake, and see if she recognises me. No chance. I wouldn't even know what flavour to order. And besides, do men even eat cupcakes? Maybe I should call Marty and ask. Plus Ian might be there, and while Anna might not want to see me, I definitely don't want to see him.

But then someone comes out, and I realise they're holding the door open for me, and it seems ridiculous to stand there and say 'no thanks, I'm just looking' (especially given what it is I'm looking at), so instead I leave out the 'no' and 'I'm just looking' parts and walk inside, and before I know it, I'm standing in front of the counter, and then . . .

'Who's next, please?'

'Yeah, can I have a, um . . .'

'*Josh?*'

I look up from the glass case full of admittedly delicious-looking cupcakes I've been pretending to stare at and put on my best 'surprised' face.

'*Anna?*'

'What . . . What are you doing here?'

'I could ask you the same question.'

Anna obviously decides that I have. Or did. 'My shop,' she says proudly, with a sweep of her hand, nearly poking the girl operating the coffee machine behind her in the eye. 'It's . . . Wow! I'm stunned.'

I think you mean 'stunning', I almost point out, though if she is stunned, *I'd* be stunned if it was in a good way, mainly because I think she must still hate me for dumping her back then, but I realise that'd be pretty arrogant, and besides, maybe time has been (as the saying goes) the great healer. After all, what's the half-life on a dumping? Doesn't this many years kind of do it for you? She met someone else she wanted to marry, so what I did to her can't have been that bad, surely, unless she only married him on the rebound . . . Perhaps that's it. After all, according to Gaz things aren't great between them, so it can't have been that much of a match made in heaven, so maybe she *does* hate me, for forcing her into an unsuitable, unhappy marriage, and she's stunned that I've had the audacity to march in here and ogle her cupcakes like nothing's happened. On the other hand, I have to take some comfort from the fact that she hasn't picked up the Victoria Sponge from the cake-stand on the top of the counter and custard-pied me in the face with it. If that's not too much of a mixed metaphor.

'Me too,' I say, worried it's been too long a silence already. 'It's been . . .'

'Eighteen years,' says Anna quickly, maybe a little *too* quickly, as if she's been marking the days off in chalk on her bedroom wall like prisoners do in their cells (in films, at least. I've never been in prison), waiting till she can get her revenge. Or maybe she's just got a better memory – or is better at maths – than I am.

'Eighteen years!' I make a face, intending to convey something about the passage of time (maybe how it flies, or perhaps the 'great healer' thing – my face doesn't seem able to decide, which makes Anna look at me a little strangely). 'How have you been?'

Anna makes a different face, one which is more 'huh?', and I realise it's a bit of a silly question. *How have you been?* is good for maybe a year, two years tops, but there's no global answer to cover the ups and downs that this sort of time period probably includes. Though to give her some credit, she nails it.

'Good. Mostly,' she says. 'You?'

I'm someone who puts sentences together for a living. Wows with words. Amazes with assonance. Well, you get the picture. But standing in front of the woman I've just realised – and this is a biggie – none of the women I've dated since (including the one I've been with for the past three years, which hits me like a slap in the face) have ever matched up to, the best I can come up with is 'Yeah,'

41

which I know isn't really an answer, so I add, 'you know. Mostly.' Though in retrospect I doubt it helps much.

Anna glances around the busy café, as if I'm stopping her from going out and collecting cake wrappers or something, which makes me a little angsty. I shouldn't be here, surprising her after all this time, keeping her from her work like this, especially given this morning's news, and of course there's no way I'll be able to sit here and have a coffee without feeling really awkward, so I do that classic thing of looking at my watch and frowning, which is supposed to simultaneously indicate that I'm busy and running late, thus giving me an escape, and it does the trick because Anna suddenly looks a little perturbed, and while I'd like to think that's because I'm looking like I'm about to go, I realise it's probably due to the grumbling that's building up from a group of pensioners who've formed an orderly queue behind me.

'Won't be a minute, girls,' Anna says to them, which makes a couple of them giggle, then she turns back to face me. 'You better tell me what you want, Josh.'

Christ. Talk about to the point. But what *do* I want? Why did I really walk in here after so long? 'Well, um, I . . .'

'Red velvet are the most popular.'

Phew. She means *what cupcake?* Which, I suppose, is not surprising, given how I have walked into a cupcake café. I peer into the cabinet in front of me. Is this some kind of test? Am I going to wreck my chances by not knowing the first thing about cupcakes, and in doing so prove to Anna that I don't have any interest in her business, and therefore her? Is there a 'man's' cupcake flavour? This throws me even more, though it's my own stupid fault for coming into her shop in the first place.

Unfortunately, there are no 'beer' or 'steak tartare' ones, and although I can rule out half of the cabinet's contents given the glittery things sprinkled on them, it's still difficult to choose. Eventually, after scratching my head for effect, I point at a brown one. After all, brown's a manly colour. Isn't it?

'What flavour's that chocolate-coloured one?'

'Chocolate,' says Anna.

'Right. Of course. Well, I'll have one of those. And one of those ones you mentioned. The red . . .' My mind goes blank as to what she actually said earlier, and while I'm sure she can't have said 'red vulva', it's the only thing I can think of. '. . . things. Thanks.'

'Coming right up!' She picks up a small cardboard carton with two cupcake-sized holes in it and in one, smooth, well-practised action, slots my cupcakes inside, folds the lid shut, and hands it to me. 'Here.'

'Thanks. How much is that?'

Anna smiles again, then reaches across and squeezes my arm, and I know it's silly, but I can't stop myself from tensing what little muscle I have there. 'Have them on me.'

'Er . . .' I shake my head to clear the strange mental picture that phrase has just conjured up. 'Okay. Thanks.'

'You're welcome. So . . .'

'So?'

'This is weird.'

'I know. Cupcakes! In Derton.'

'No, I meant bumping into each other after all this time. Are you just visiting, or . . . ?'

'Yeah,' I say, for the hundredth time, then mentally slap myself. 'I mean, I'm not moving back. God no. Nothing like that. I'm just . . .' I stop talking, suddenly remembering this morning's hospital visit and still not clear about exactly what it means, and besides, the impatient murmuring from behind me is getting louder. 'Listen, I should let you get on,' I say, glancing nervously behind me, where the group of pensioners have bunched together and look like they're about to launch an attack. 'We should have a proper catch-up before I leave, though. Maybe . . .' I swallow hard. 'Dinner?'

I don't know what I was expecting, but Anna's suddenly thunderous expression isn't quite it. 'Julia,' she says, levelly, to the girl at the coffee machine. 'Would you mind taking over for a moment?' Then she grabs my arm – not quite as tenderly as before – and steers me to one side. 'Sure, Josh,' she says, her voice an angry whisper. 'Let's just pick up where we left off, shall we, before you go waltzing back off to London?'

'Um . . .'

'I don't know how you've got the nerve to walk in here after so long, as if nothing's happened.'

I want to tell her that the 'after so long' bit is precisely why I've got the nerve to walk in here. But my suspicions are that she doesn't quite feel the same way.

'Not a word,' she continues, a little loudly for my liking. 'Off you went to college, and then one day . . . Nothing.'

'I wrote to you. A letter.'

'A *letter*? We were going out in the real world, Josh. Not in some re-enactment of *Pride and* bloody *Prejudice*.' She shakes her head in disbelief. 'And what did it say, this mythical letter you supposedly wrote?'

I think hurriedly. Along with the emotional bits, what it also said was why I felt I could never live in a place like Derton, that I didn't want to see out my days as a slave to my dad's grand plan for me by working behind a shop counter (like Anna seems to be now), and that I wanted to see other places and other women. And it would take a PR firm way better than Marty's to spin all of that in a positive light.

'Just stuff,' I say, hoping that if I refer to it dismissively, Anna might decide it's not a big issue. But unfortunately, she doesn't take my lead.

'*Stuff*?'

'About how much you meant to me. And how I thought it was probably best for both of us if we saw other people . . .' I've meant that last bit in a 'to be sure about how we felt about each other' kind of way, but by the looks of Anna's incredulous expression, she hasn't quite come to the same conclusion. And neither have a couple of the pensioners, given how one of them has just muttered the word *disgraceful*.

As a few of the others frantically adjust their hearing aids, worried they're missing out on a real-life version of what often happens in The Queen Vic, Anna glares at me. 'Best for *you*, you meant!'

'Come on, Anna. You were here. I was there. There was no way I was coming back. How was that possibly going to work?'

'You could have at least asked me to come with you.'

'I did! In the letter.'

Anna makes a different face, and this time there's no mistaking that it's the 'yeah, right!' one. 'When you first left, I was so upset I cried for *weeks*, Josh. And then, when you stopped coming home, stopped calling, I didn't know what to do. I thought you were the love of my life, and . . .'

She throws her hands up in the air, as if she's Italian, or something, and I don't quite know what to say next. Not that I don't believe in loves of one's life. More that I think that sixteen is a strange time to meet them. After all, how do you *know*?

'Christ, Anna, we were just kids.'

'Was that why you behaved so immaturely?'

'That's not what I meant.'

'Well, what did you mean?'

'Well . . .' What *did* I mean? 'Um . . . Take books, for example. I mean, every kid loves something like *The Catcher in the Rye*, don't they, because it kind of speaks to them when they first read it – which is usually when they're forced to at school. But read it for the first time at, say, thirty, and it's not going to mean the same thing. Have the same impact. You try getting through it again now, it's hard going. So expecting someone to know they've met the love of their life at that age . . . It's just not fair. Or realistic . . .'

'It felt real to me,' interrupts Anna, quietly.

And does it still? I want to ask. Even though we're arguing, I'd guess that my chances of getting a positive response would be pretty good. After all, she married Ian soon afterwards, and realised that *he* wasn't, and so in an – admittedly limited – field of two, despite what I did, I'm surely still hanging on to the number one spot? But of course, I don't dare.

'Anna . . .'

'You broke my heart, Josh. And there's no coming back from that.'

I open my mouth to protest, but given the way Anna's stomped off into the kitchen and slammed the door behind her, it's doubtful she'd even hear me, let alone hear me out.

With a sigh, I leave my cupcakes on the counter, make my way through what's now a rather hostile crowd of pensioners, and slope out of the shop.

❧

I'm walking back along the seafront trying to analyse what's just happened when my mobile rings, and when I absent-mindedly answer it, Mikayla's customary 'It's me,' snaps me back to reality.

'Oh. Er, hi,' I say, a little guiltily, given how five minutes ago I was trying to ask one of my ex-girlfriends to dinner.

'You sound strange.'

'Do I?'

'*Yes,* Josh.' She sounds irritated, though whether that's because I haven't phoned her yet with an update or simply because I've questioned her 'you sound strange' observation, it's hard to tell. 'Are you on your way home?'

'Not yet.'

'Why not?'

'Well, my dad . . .'

'How is he?'

Shouldn't that have been your first question? I think, then take a deep breath. 'Dying,' I say, perhaps a little coldly.

'Oh.' There's a pause, and then: 'So when are you coming back?'

'I'm not sure. I can't just leave.'

'What?'

'Not straight away.'

There's another pause, perhaps while Mikayla debates whether to ask *why ever not?*, then she lets out a loud sigh. 'So how long are you going to stay there?'

'I don't know.'

'How long has he got?'

'They're not sure. The cancer's pretty advanced.'

'Put a number on it, Josh.'

'Weeks.'

'Weeks?' says Mikayla indignantly, though I suspect she's more in shock about me being away for any length of time rather than my dad's diagnosis. 'Aren't you forgetting something?'

'Huh?'

'The holiday?'

Ah. Unless she's referring to her favourite Cameron Diaz rom-com movie, I'm in trouble. Mikayla and I are – *were* – supposed to be going to Sri Lanka for a fortnight on what her glossy magazines would call a 'save-cation' the weekend after next. And though I *had* forgotten about it, I instantly know there's no way I can go.

'Well . . .'

'We talked about this, Josh,' she says, exasperatedly.

'This is my dad!'

'You don't even get on with him.'

'That's not the point.'

'Well, please tell me what the point is, exactly?'

I ignore her question. Mainly because I'm not sure I've got an answer. 'Trust me, it's not through choice.'

'Yes it is, Josh. And it's the wrong choice.'

I take the phone away from my ear and stare at it in disbelief. As usual, Mikayla's making it all about her. Even *this*.

'This is a bit more important than a bloody holiday, Mikayla. My dad's *dying*. Didn't you hear what I said?'

'We all are, Josh. Just some of us a little quicker than others.' Mikayla's answer trumps mine in the heartless stakes, but then again, she's good at that kind of thing.

'Well, that really makes me feel better. Thank you for those reassuring words. I'll be sure to pass them onto him when . . .'

'Sorry, Josh, but what did you want me to say? That I'm sure he'll get better? Because you know that won't happen.'

Yes, I realise, with a start. *That's exactly what I want you to say.*

'Besides,' Mikayla continues, matter-of-factly. 'You've always had older parents. One of them was bound to die. And sooner, rather than later.'

'D'you know, Mikayla, you should seriously think about volunteering for the Samaritans? Because with your sympathetic—'

'I'm just telling it how it is, Josh.'

My throat is starting to tighten, and all of a sudden I need to end this conversation. 'Listen,' I say, staring at the couple of dog walkers braving the wind on the beach in front of me, 'I'm kind of in the middle of something, so if there's nothing else . . . ?'

'No, Josh.' Mikayla sighs again, even more loudly than before, and I can picture the haughty expression on her face. 'There's nothing else. Oh, apart from Sri Lanka.'

'What about it?'

'I'm still going. And if I don't see you at the airport . . . Well, don't expect a postcard. Ever.'

My jaw drops open, but by the time I start to ask her what that means, she's already ended the call. Though I can probably work it out for myself.

For a moment, I wonder whether I should call her back and apologise, try and salvage something, then it occurs to me that not once did she ask how *I* was. And while I know that sounds like me being selfish, it's what you do, isn't it, when someone you love is going through something like this?

With a sigh, I realise we're over, and the reason we're over – the unreasonable reason – is that I've put someone else before her. Some-one, and I quote, I 'don't even like that much', as if that matters in a situation like this. But as far as Mikayla's concerned, that's a dump-ing offence that's right up there along with infidelity, or not opening her car door first, or forgetting to feed Nino, her Chihuahua, an animal so needy (and yappy) it's put me off dogs for life.

I slip my phone back into my pocket, turn my jacket collar up against the wind, and trudge miserably back to the house, but as I walk, something occurs to me, and it's the tiniest of silver linings to the growing cloud that's hovering above my head: if I'd rather stay in a dump like Derton to look after the dad I don't get on with than spend two weeks on a tropical beach trying to save my relationship with the girl I've been going out with for the last three years, then splitting up is probably the right decision.

6.

It's the following morning, no more than a couple of seconds past eight o'clock, and I'm in my mum and dad's local discount supermarket, pushing a trolley that even the pound I've had to pay to release it from where it's been chained up outside hasn't guaranteed that all its wheels point in the same direction. It strikes me that if you want a trolley (though I can't work out why you would – maybe for the scrap metal, or to use as a go-kart down the long hill at the back of town) paying a pound for it isn't that bad a deal, but perhaps that's because even though I've already been up for the best part of two hours, the lack of proper (non-instant) coffee in the house means my brain isn't quite functioning yet.

Up ahead of me, my mum is working her way through a long list that she's written in pencil on the back of an old envelope and that – I'm amazed at the powers of recall this must have taken – follows the exact order the products are stacked in along the aisles we're methodically working our way up and down.

My dad's decided to stay at home. There's some cricket he's recorded that he wants to watch, though don't ask me who's playing – to be honest, I'd zoned out at the mention of the word *cricket* (in fact, possibly after the first syllable) – another interest of his we don't have in common, and given yesterday's news (plus the fact that he'd probably struggle to make it round the shop without stopping for a breather every two minutes, and he's too big to fit in the trolley's fold-out child seat) he's decided life's too short ('Well, mine is,' though neither my mum nor I laughed when he said it) for shopping.

The place is busy, even this early. I suppose this shouldn't be a surprise given the high number of old people in the town who, along with my mum and dad, seem to get up at some ungodly hour, maybe to make the most of the time they've got left. But it could be they're all here to snap up this week's 'special buy' before they all run out (although five-litre tins of white paint don't seem that special to me, even at £1.99). And while I can initially see *why* everyone shops here given the ridiculously low prices, on closer inspection the cheap name brands actually seem to be mis-named brands that I'm mystified have managed to pass trading standards and copyright checks: Special OK cereal, Alpine muesli, Red Ball energy drinks, and chocolate-covered coconut Bouncy Bars. (I'm making these up, but only just – if you've ever shopped somewhere like this, you'll know what I mean.)

Every so often, my mum looks round to check I'm keeping up, like when she used to walk (a reluctant) me to school, then she stops and – instead of placing whatever item she's taken from the shelf straight in the trolley – reaches *across* the trolley to hand it to me so I can do exactly that for her. Occasionally, she directs me to reach something on a higher shelf or that's heavy. More often than not, her choices are accompanied by, 'Your dad likes those,' and after the tenth occasion, I start to feel a little awkward.

'Mum,' I say. 'Why don't you get something *you* like?'

'Pardon?'

'It's not all about Dad, you know?'

She shoots me a glance as if to say 'yes, it is', as if this is what she's signed up for, and I have to admire how she seems to have adjusted already to the scary situation she's found herself in. But this is what mums do, I suppose. First they have the likes of us, and we generally make their life hell for . . . Well, maybe the jury's still out on that one, given my lack of marriage and provision of the grandkids I know she wants. And then – because on average, women live longer than men – they have to look after the person they always thought would look after them. Though that seems to be coming a few years earlier than she perhaps bargained for.

'What about you, Josh. Anything you'd like?'

I glance up and down the aisle, and I'm just about to tell her that I doubt it but stop myself. Being judgemental about places like this is Mikayla's bag, and while I may not be in Waitrose anymore, I'm not with Mikayla anymore either.

'I'm fine, thanks.'

We head silently along the aisle, until she stops in the middle of the biscuit section and frowns.

'What's the matter?'

'They're out of Mingers.'

I can't help but snigger. 'Pardon?'

'What's funny?'

'*Mingers.*'

'What about them?'

'They're . . . Mingers. It's slang for . . .'

'For what?'

'Well, for . . .' I find myself starting to redden, as if I've been caught doing something I shouldn't in my bedroom. 'Ugly people.'

'Don't be ridiculous,' says my mum, crossly. 'They're your dad's favourite biscuit. Milk chocolate and ginger fingers. We have one with a cup of tea every afternoon.'

I scan the shelf. There is, unbelievably, a label that says 'Mingers', though the section behind it's empty, so I pick up a purple packet of chocolate fingers that in the right light (that is, with it switched off) are probably supposed to pass for Cadbury's, but when I show them to my mum she shakes her head.

'He won't like those.'

'Okay . . .' I put the fingers down and find a packet of chocolate digestives. 'Mc . . . Fitty's?' I say, squinting at the packet.

'He won't want those either.'

'Why not?'

'You don't know your dad.'

She's looking a little distraught, and I stare at her for a second then realise she's right – I don't. Certainly not like she does. And I wonder if I ever will know someone that well. Thirty-something years of marriage, not to mention the time they spent before that dating, or courting, whatever they called it in those days. All of a sudden, I can see how tough it's going to be for her without him, and suddenly I understand how important their routine is – to my mum, in particular. She might not be able to control the cancer, but at least for the next few weeks she can control everything else.

There's a shop assistant in the other aisle – a thin, nervous-looking man about my age – stacking tins of baked beans into a pyramid, so I walk up behind him and clear my throat.

''Scuse me.'

He wheels round, startled, as if I'm the first ever person to speak to him in the shop, nearly knocking the cans over in the process.

'Can I help you?'

'You've run out of . . . Mingers. Or at least, there don't seem to be any left on the shelf.' I smile. 'Which is funny, because in the real world, that's exactly where the mingers would, you know . . .' – my voice tails off, because the assistant's expression suggests it isn't funny at all – '. . . be.'

'They're replacing them. Well, changing the name.'

'What for?'

'Why d'you think?' he says, giving me a look that implies 'to stop idiots like you making fun of it'.

'You don't have any left?'

'Hold on.' He adds the final couple of tins to the beans pyramid, takes a second to admire his work, then sighs, as if the highlight of his shift's now over. 'I'll check the stockroom.'

As he disappears through a heavy plastic curtain in between the freezer cabinets, I swivel round and grin at my mum, who's looking at me with an expression of such hope, such expectation that it breaks your heart, and I realise it's not just that my dad will be disappointed if he doesn't get precisely the brand of biscuits he likes, but more the implication that she'll have failed as his wife if he doesn't. And suddenly, that makes this the most important purchase I've ever made.

'Yeah, we've got some,' says the man, emerging from the stock-room with a cardboard box under his arm. 'Last lot, though.'

'Great.'

'How many packets did you want?'

I nod towards the box. 'How many packets is that?'

'Thirty-six.'

I do a quick calculation in my head. Thirty-six packets, times six biscuits per packet is . . . Well, if Mr. Stephens was right, the box should see him out. And it's shocking, because finally, I realise how little time he has: by the time this relatively small box of inappropriately-named biscuits is finished, so will he be. And the revelation makes my head swim.

'I'll take the lot.'

'The *lot*?'

'Yeah.'

'I'm not sure that's allowed.'

'Why not?'

'Some other customers might want some.'

'But there weren't any on the shelf in the first place. So I'm hardly denying anyone . . .'

'Even so. Besides, these are quite a rarity now. So how do I know you're not just going to sell them on eBay?'

'Listen,' I say, and I can't help fearing it isn't the last time I'll be playing this card. 'My dad just got diagnosed with terminal cancer. These are his favourite biscuits, and there are just about enough in that box to last him until he's in a box of his own. And I know it might be a little unorthodox, but if you'd sell me them all, I'd really appreciate it.'

'Well . . .'

'. . . or you could just tell his soon-to-be widow that she has to go home and explain they won't be having one with a cup of tea together *ever again*.' I finish my speech, and nod towards where my mum is watching intently from the other aisle.

The assistant looks at her, then back at me, and after a moment, wordlessly hands me the box, so I carry it back over and load it triumphantly into the trolley, then my mum and I high-five (or, I go to high-five her, and she looks over her shoulder to see who I'm waving at). It's a small victory, I guess, but right now we'll take anything we can get.

7.

My mum and dad's GP, Doctor Watson, is at the house when we get back. He's a tall, thin man who – according to my mum – always rushes through these house calls as if he suspects he's left the oven on at home. Not that my dad minds – he's never been a fan of doctors. Which is possibly why he avoided seeing one until it was too late.

As he introduces himself to me, I can see my dad grinning over his shoulder. 'Just don't ask him where Sherlock Holmes is,' he says, followed by a burst of laughter that quickly turns into a hacking cough.

'I bet you get that all the time,' I say.

'Surprisingly, no. Your father is the only one. It's actually quite funny. Or at least, it was the first time he said it.'

'So how is he?'

'No real change.' Doctor Watson gives me a thin-lipped smile. 'I mean, he's not getting any better, of course, but as long as he's not in any pain . . .'

'I've got lung cancer, you know, not chronic deafness,' says my dad.

Doctor Watson raises his eyebrows at me, then turns to my dad. 'You're not in any pain, are you, Mr. Peters?'

'Only when I laugh.'

'Well, keep those jokes up and you should be fine.'

My dad grins up at him. 'Touché, Doc, touché.'

'Is there any more he should be doing? Or that we should be doing for him?'

'Not really. Though it's important he keeps as active as he can. Gets out of the house once in a while.' He thinks for a moment. 'Tell you what, I'll arrange a wheelchair for him. That way you can make sure he gets some fresh air. A bit of variety. It can't be much fun for him being stuck at home all day every day.'

I look at my dad, sitting in his favourite armchair, a cup of tea in one hand, his Sky Sports remote in the other, a half-read copy of *The Times* on the table next to him. In the kitchen, my mum is already attending to dinner. 'Don't you believe it.'

'Still, he ought to get out and about, if only for a change of scene.'

'Okay. Thanks.'

'Like the specialist told you, it's important that he's comfortable.' He turns back to my dad. 'Are you comfortable, Mr. Peters?'

'I'm not too badly off. Why, did you want to borrow a fiver?'

As my dad collapses into another laughing/coughing fit, Doctor Watson picks up his bag. 'Walk me out, Josh?' he says.

We make our way into the kitchen, where my mum is mixing something in a bowl. While I'm no expert, it looks like some sort of cake mix, and while I know it's for my dad, I suddenly remember the cakes she used to make when I was growing up, and I can't stop my mouth from watering.

'Tell me,' says Doctor Watson, once we're out of my dad's earshot. 'Is your father always this . . . cheerful?'

'I'm afraid so.'

'Well, that's good, I suppose.'

'You suppose?'

'Sometimes, people with terminal cancer can put on a bit of an act, as if there's nothing wrong, whereas what they're not doing is facing reality. I'm just a little worried that he might be in denial.'

'In denial?'

I've lowered my voice to ensure my dad can't hear, though mainly to avoid his usual Egyptian river joke, but my mum freezes, mid-stir. 'If you're worried that he doesn't know that he's dying . . . Well, you don't have to be.'

'Good,' says Doctor Watson. 'Well, not *good*, but . . .'

She smiles grimly. 'I know what you meant.'

'Because it's important that he knows. That *everyone* knows.'

'He does. We all do. I think he suspected the moment he got ill, and then yesterday, with Mr. Stephens . . .' She sighs hopelessly. 'And there's nothing more that can be done for him?'

Doctor Watson shakes his head. 'We can give him something to manage the pain, but he's going to get weaker and weaker as his lungs shut down, and then, one day . . .' He lets the sentence hang, but even though neither my mum nor I have been to medical school, we can both complete it ourselves.

'And I'm sorry to ask,' he continues, 'but has your husband put his affairs in order? Made a will? Sorted out his finances? It'll make things easier. Afterwards.'

'I'm not sure. But we can do that after lunch, if that's alright with you, Josh?'

'Er, sure,' I say, amazed again at my mum's matter-of-factness. Her husband of nearly forty years is dying, and she's talking about tying up any financial loose ends as if it's as simple as ticking names off her Christmas card list.

'And how are you coping?' he asks my mum.

'Fine, considering. It's had its moments, but I've got Josh here now . . .' She gives me that look again, and I force a smile, even though I want to look away.

'Good, good.' Doctor Watson nods sagely. 'You know there are . . . options?'

My mum looks up sharply. 'What do you mean?'

'If it gets bad. Because it might get bad.'

'What kind of options?' I say, worried he's going to suggest having him put down.

'We could get him moved. To a home.'

'He's *in* a home,' snaps my mum. 'His home.'

'Yes, of course,' says Doctor Watson. 'I didn't mean he wasn't being well looked after here. I meant more of a hospice, where he could get round the clock medical care. And it might be good for you to have a break.'

'Yes, well, I'll be getting a long enough break after he's gone, won't I? So I think I can put up with whatever happens before then.'

My mum turns her attention back to her cooking, indicating that the conversation's over, so I walk Doctor Watson outside to his car.

'She didn't mean to snap at you, I'm sure,' I say. 'It's just . . .'

'Don't worry. Just remember that this disease . . . Well, it affects everyone, not just your dad, and in different ways. And neither of them are – and this isn't strictly a medical term – spring chickens anymore.'

'So what can I do?' I ask, as Doctor Watson climbs into his car.

He frowns up at me as if I've asked the most obvious question in the world. 'Look after them both.'

'I'll do my best,' I say, but as I watch him drive off down the street, I can't help wondering something, and it's selfish, I know, but I can't help myself.

Who's going to look after me?

∽

Marty phones mid-morning, and I hurry outside to take the call, mentally kicking myself for forgetting to ring him with an update. Though it's clear from the outset he's called to give me one and not the other way round.

'I hope you're stuck underground on a broken-down Tube? Either that, or you've had an accident.'

'Er, not exactly.' I decide not to thank him for 'hoping' I've had an accident, or point out that if I was stuck underground, we wouldn't be speaking. 'We had some bad news yesterday, and . . .'

'You weren't the only ones,' interrupts Marty. 'You read my email?'

Ah. The 'deets' he promised to 'ping' me. 'I'm sorry. Things have—'

'The client didn't go for your "Read 'em and whip".'

'Oh. Right.'

'And without you there with some other ideas . . .'

'Sorry, Marty. It's just . . . My dad . . .'

'Listen, Josh,' he says, ominously. 'I know you're going through some . . . stuff at the moment, but I think it's showing in your work. So maybe you should have a bit of time off.'

If it was anyone else, I'd be thanking them for being so understanding, but Marty doesn't do empathy. 'You want me to take some leave?' I ask, wondering whether I should be removing the words *take* and *some* from that sentence.

'If you like,' says Marty, though the tone of his voice leaves me in no doubt that it's what *he'd* like.

'You're sure?'

'Definitely.'

'How long for?'

'Indefinitely.'

'You're . . . firing me?'

'Not firing, no.' Marty lets out a short laugh, which strikes me as a bit inappropriate. 'We just won't be using you for a while. Until you've got your head straight.'

'My head is straight, Marty. But my dad's just been diagnosed with cancer, and . . .'

'That's hardly my fault, Josh.'

I shake my evidently crooked head. I should have known the 'cancer' card wouldn't work with Marty. I tighten my already vice-like grip on my phone, trying to ignore the rising tide of panic building in my chest, as the only way my being here in Derton is going to work is if *I* still can.

'I didn't say it was. Please, Marty. I need this job.'

There's a long pause, and then Marty sighs, as if he's about to grant me the biggest favour ever. 'Tell you what, Josh. There is another project, if you're interested? But you'll have to do it on spec. Payment on results, and all that.'

'Of *course* I'm interested. Thanks,' I say, then realise I've just thanked Marty for effectively terminating my contract and re-hiring me for free.

'Okay. Well, I'll . . .'

'Ping me the deets?' I say, a little too quickly.

'Roger,' says Marty.

And before I can say 'It's Josh, actually', he's signed off with his usual 'Laters,' and ended the call.

❧

On Doctor Watson's advice, we're sitting at the dining table going through finances, which basically means my mum's presented me with the large cardboard box she and my dad keep all their important paperwork in. The session's not had the best of starts, because my dad's suddenly remembered that the pension plan he has stops paying out on his death, and while most normal people would have some sort of life insurance policy, as you'll perhaps have gathered by now, my dad doesn't exactly fit into the definition of 'normal people'.

And while I've never thought of my parents as particularly well off – they've always lived within their means whether it's been a good or bad year – going through the shop's accounts I'm beginning to realise the last few years have all been bad ones. Though while my dad had to go and sell the shop just before Derton seemed to get going again, even I have to concede that was hardly his fault.

After a few minutes of me anxiously rifling through papers and tapping numbers into the 'calculator' app on my phone, my dad clears his throat so he can speak. Which takes a while.

'How's it looking, Josh?' he wheezes. 'Healthier than me, I hope?'

'About the same, I'd say. Though I'm struggling to find where the money you got from selling the shop is.'

My dad reaches over and picks up a bank statement from the pile next to the box, then hands it to me. 'Ta-da!'

'Thanks.' I scan down the column of figures, then do the same again. 'And the rest of it?'

My mum frowns. 'The rest of what?'

'The money. From the shop.'

My dad nods towards the bank statement. 'That's it.'

I peer at the sheet again, wondering whether I've misread it. Apart from one entry of thirty thousand pounds, the rest of it is just their normal outgoings.

'No, I mean the balance of the money you got from selling it.'

My dad clears his throat uncomfortably, though this time it's due to what we're discussing rather than any health issue. 'That's it.'

'The thirty thousand?'

'That's right.'

'Surely that's just the down payment? Or one of the instalments?'

He and my mum exchange glances. 'No,' he says, awkwardly.

'You got thirty thousand pounds?' I say, as my mum beats a strategic retreat into the kitchen. 'For the shop?'

He nods.

'I'm sorry. Perhaps I should have said, you *accepted* thirty thousand pounds.'

He nods again as I look at him in disbelief. 'The question I have to ask – and I'm sorry if it sounds a bit obvious – is "Why?".'

'What do you mean, "Why?"?' He looks a little affronted, but I can't help myself.

'The shop – a business you spent thirty years building up – you let go for . . . Well, the equivalent of a thousand pounds a year?'

'That was the market rate,' he explains, as if it's as simple as that, and his dismissiveness angers me.

'Dad, my *car* cost that,' I say incredulously. 'How could you let it go for so little?'

'What's all this? Someone worried about his inheritance?'

'It's not me I'm worried about.'

'Pardon?'

I lower my voice. '*Mum?*'

He looks at me shiftily. 'She'll be okay.'

'She'll have to be.'

'She's got the house. It's worth a bit.'

I lower my voice to a whisper this time, though I suspect my mum's still listening in given the lack of tea-making noises. 'Yeah, great plan. She sells it, and then lives where, exactly?'

'What else was I going to do with it?' he says, the implication clear.

'Not this again, please, Dad.'

'You're the one who abandoned—'

'It's not fair to expect your kids to take over your business. Especially one that was going down the—'

'Yes, well, life isn't fair, Josh. As I think we can see.'

That hurts. Even though I've been brandishing it freely, it's the first time he's played the 'cancer victim' card, and while he's of course within his rights to do so, it's not really something I have an answer for.

'You can't blame me for wanting to go off and do something different.'

'Yes, well, maybe I wouldn't have minded if you . . .'

'What?'

'Nothing.'

'No. Go on. Say it.'

'Forget about it.'

'You were going to say "had amounted to anything", weren't you?'

My dad just glares at me.

'*Weren't you?*'

'I built that shop up from nothing. The least you could have done was to have shown some interest.'

'In a failing shop in a failing seaside town? That would have been career suicide. Why do you think I went off to university?'

'You could have studied something useful, like business. Maybe come back and—'

'Helped you out? No thanks. Stuck behind a counter in a shop no-one visited all day, watching myself grow old faster than normal, and for what?'

'For self-respect, Josh.'

'Pardon?'

'I worked for myself. I was my own boss. No-one told me what to do.'

I smirk. We both know that's not quite true given Mum's role.

'Whereas you? You went off with all these dreams to study something . . . poncy . . .'

I laugh at his use of the word.

'. . . and all you've ended up doing is writing stuff for other writers. How is that a career?'

'At least I'm following my dream.'

'It's a pipe dream.'

'Maybe. But at least I have a dream.'

As I worry I've just come across all Martin Luther King, my dad looks at me, opens his mouth to say something, then all the fight seems to go out of him.

'You could have stayed and helped,' he says, slumping back in his chair.

'I did help. Every weekend for years. And that was enough to put me off for life.'

'I thought you'd like it. Not all kids are so lucky. Or ungrateful.'

'Yes, well, if you wanted someone to take over the business so badly, why didn't you have another child? That way, you wouldn't be left with the disappointment of this one.'

I've done this on purpose – diverting the issue back to my failings. Because what I've never told him is that the last thing I ever wanted to do was follow in his footsteps, mainly because I saw what it did to him. What it did to *us*. The effort he put into the shop, trying to make ends meet . . . It made him old before his time, and he wasn't that young to start with. And while the other kids at school all had fathers who were around at the weekends, taking them to the park, or the beach, we could never do that. As for summer holidays – well, they never happened. It was the busiest time for Derton, so my dad always seemed to be working doubly hard. It was no wonder I retreated into the world of books, seeing them as my escape – and ultimately, that's what they became. And while I could probably win this particular argument by telling him all that, to remind him he was never here seems particularly cruel. Especially because he's not going to be here for much longer.

'I was offering you a job on a plate.'

'Well, I had different plans.'

'So did we! But then you turned up out of the blue, and . . . Well, sometimes you just have to play the hand you're dealt. Even if it's not the one you wanted.'

I open my mouth and close it again. While I've always known I was an accident, this is the first time it's been referred to without the word *happy* in front of it.

'Anyway, you're the big shot advertising executive,' he continues sarcastically. 'You can help your mum out when I'm gone.'

'Well, I could, if . . .'

'Oh, that's just great.' My dad rolls his eyes. 'She looks after you for thirty-six years, and in her time of need, you can't even spare a few quid to make sure she's alright.'

'I shouldn't have to.'

'Well, you *do* have to.'

'Well, I can't.'

'Why not?'

'Because . . .' I stop talking. I can't tell him that I'm *this far* from losing my job, partly because that would validate everything he's been saying, and partly because I don't want to tell him that the reason I might be losing it is because he got ill, so I've come back here, and now I have to stay. And because I don't tell him, the look he gives me is one I won't forget for a while.

'I never had you down as the selfish type. But maybe you've changed. Maybe that London life has turned you into . . .' He stares at me for a moment longer, then hauls himself up out of his chair, shrugging off my attempt to help him. 'I'm sorry, Josh, that your old dad was such a failure and couldn't amount to much more than your precious car after a lifetime's slaving away, but that was just the way it was. And seeing as you'd buggered off and I had no-one to hand the business down to . . .'

'Dad, for the *millionth time* . . .'

'. . . what was I supposed to do? Nothing much was happening in Derton, and we only had the one offer. Under the circumstances . . .'

I immediately feel guilty. The 'circumstances', as he puts it, were actually pretty dire. He'd just gotten ill, and no-one knew how serious it was, though we all suspected the chances were he wasn't going to set foot in the shop again. And what would I have done in that situation? Maybe the bird in the hand would have been too strong to resist. But just as I'm about to tell him I understand, he raises a hand to silence me and shuffles out into the kitchen, passing my mum, who's carrying a tray full of tea and biscuits. I leap out of my seat to follow him and apologise, but she stops me.

'Let him cool down first, love.'

'I'm sorry, Mum. I didn't think. But *thirty thousand* . . .'

She gives me a flat smile. 'We had it on the market for a while, and there was so little interest. And with the shop shut we weren't making any money, and the rates were going up . . .'

'Why didn't you tell me?'

'You were hardly going to come back and take it over, were you?'

'I could have helped. Some other way.'

'I know, Josh. But by the time we got that offer, we were desperate. To be honest, we'd have bitten their hands off if they'd offered us half that amount. And then, well, Derton started to pick up again. Just our luck.'

She smiles, and I feel awful. 'Just our luck' is the phrase she's always used to describe everything that goes wrong, as if she and my dad are eternally cursed with the 'bad' variety. Though there are some days I believe that too.

'Besides,' she continues, 'we wanted to leave you some-thing . . .'

I don't want your money, I want to tell her. *The only things I want are for Dad to get better, for you both to be around for ages yet, and for me to get back home to London, back to my life.* But like Mikayla said, I know that's not going to happen, and so what would be the point?

I'm angry at my dad for leaving her in this mess. I'm angry at Ian – *and* Anna – for taking advantage of a desperate man, though maybe Anna did that to get back at me, and if that's the case, then I feel responsible too. But I also know I need to sort this out, and fast. My mum's got enough to worry about without this hanging over her head.

I suppose I've got no redress over the sale, although leading a picket outside Baker's Cupcakes strikes me as an option. But that would hurt Anna as well as Ian, and I think I've done enough on that front already.

With a sigh, I get up from the table, squeeze my mum on the shoulder, grab a mug of tea and a Minger, and go upstairs to my room to sulk. Under the circumstances, I'm sure my dad did his best. And sometimes, that's all you can ask for.

8.

My dad's wheelchair arrives today, delivered in a heavy box by a cheerful man with tattooed forearms bigger than my thighs. It's collapsible (so we can put it in the car) and painted bright red (presumably so they're easy to spot if people stick them on eBay instead of returning them), and the 'minimal assembly required' that the wording on the box promises ends up taking me the whole morning, so by the time I wheel it into the lounge for my dad to see it, he's more than a little impatient.

'Ta-da!'

He peers at it sceptically for a moment, but doesn't say anything.

'Well?'

'It's red.'

'*Ferrari* red,' I say, trying to get him at least a little bit excited. 'And it collapses.'

'Like me, nowadays. Which is why I need it, I suppose.'

'D'you want to try it out?'

My dad sighs, then nods reluctantly, so I help him out of his armchair and lower him into the seat.

'So?'

'So what?'

'Comfortable?'

He shimmies around in the seat. 'It could do with a bit more padding. Again, like me nowadays.'

'Anything else?'

He reaches down to adjust the footrests, then fiddles with a couple of levers behind the wheels. 'It's a bit . . . basic.'

'Basic?'

'Yes.'

'What's basic about it?'

'It's just . . . a chair. With wheels.'

We're both still a little tense after yesterday's argument, and while I know I should bite my tongue, I just can't. 'I'm sorry, I didn't realise you were planning to try out for the Paralympics. Or did you have something more like Stephen Hawking's in mind?'

'I'm just saying,' says my dad, glumly inspecting his new mode of transport, and it occurs to me that I might be being a little insensitive. After all, I've been thinking that he'll see the wheelchair as some great freedom device, allowing him to actually go outside whenever he wants, whereas he's probably seeing it as the next stage in his decline, one short step – or rather, roll – closer to the end.

'Tell you what,' I say, with as much enthusiasm as I can muster. 'Let's take it for a spin.'

He gives me a look I've seen a thousand times. 'Where to?'

I shrug, intending to express *the world's your oyster* with the gesture. 'Well . . . How about Tesco's?'

'Tesco's? Be still my beating heart,' deadpans my dad.

I count to ten under my breath, then position myself behind the chair, grab both handles firmly, and push. And push. And either I shouldn't have cancelled my gym membership last year, or my dad – despite appearances to the contrary – has actually got a lot heavier, because for some reason I can't shift him.

'Is there a problem, Josh?' he says, eventually.

'No, I'm just . . .'

'You're supposed to release the brakes.'

'I know that. I was just testing to see if they worked.'

'And now we know the answer to that question, perhaps we can get going?'

I reach down and release the mechanisms I'd forgotten about on both wheels, then steer him through the lounge and along the hall, nearly running my mum over as she comes out of the kitchen.

'Ooh, Phil,' she says. 'That's . . .'

I watch as she struggles for the appropriate word, then put her out of her misery. 'We're just off to Tesco's. Anything you need?'

'Milk,' says my mum. 'We always need milk.' She reaches for her purse, but I wave her away. 'You two have fun, now.'

And my dad and I don't dare meet each other's eyes.

⟨∾⟩

I've never pushed a wheelchair before, and it's actually quite difficult – every kerb, uneven paving stone, or fallen twig becomes an obstacle that requires a combination of technique and brute force to get over. By the time we're halfway to Tesco's, I could do with a breather, but instead, my dad orders me to speed up.

'What do you want to go faster for?'

'I feel ridiculous. Someone might see me.'

'It's not much fun for me either.'

'So tell me why we're doing this?'

'So you can get some fresh air.'

'I could have just opened a window.'

'You don't want to stay cooped up at home, do you?'

'Cooped up? Where I've got everything just how I like it?' He swivels round and glares at me. 'Including a *comfortable* chair.'

'Well, maybe it's good for Mum, getting you out of the house. Give her a bit of time to herself while you get a change of scene.'

'Yes, but . . . to *Tesco's*?'

'Okay. Fair point. Well, where shall we go, then?'

'Monte Carlo? The Serengeti? Though the way you're puffing, I'm beginning to have my doubts we'll make it to the end of the road.'

I glare down at the back of his head, then remember that there's a pub, The Lobster (and after my experience at The Submarine, I wouldn't be surprised if that was on the menu) just around the corner.

'When was the last time we went for a pint?'

'When was the first time?'

'Yes, well, whose fault is that?'

'Let me see,' says my dad. 'Either mine, for not taking you when you were here, or . . . Oh no, hang on. You buggered off when you were eighteen, didn't you? Before I had a chance to.'

'You wouldn't have wanted to.'

'Yes, well, whose fault is *that*?'

For a moment, it occurs to me to leave him there on the pavement and go for a drink on my own, but instead, I do another under-my-breath count (to twenty, this time), check there are no cars coming (shamefully, a part of me wishes there were), and push him across the road, though I take the kerb with a little more speed than perhaps is necessary. It's a relief to see the pub a few yards away, and it's a sunny day, so rather than negotiate the heavy swing doors I wheel him to a table in the garden, stick the brakes on, and strop off into the bar, though my dramatic exit is spoilt a little by the fact that I have no idea what my dad drinks, so I have to march back outside and ask him.

'A pint.'

'Of?'

'Bitter,' he says, as if there's no other possible drink.

'Bitter. Right. Any particular sort?'

'Nope.'

'Coming right up.'

'But not Watneys,' he says, as I turn and make for the door.

'Not Watneys.'

'That's right.'

'Fine.'

'And a packet of crisps,' he calls after me.

'Crisps? Are you sure?'

'What's wrong with crisps?'

'Well, they're not good for . . . Nothing. What flavour?'

'Cheese and Onion. No – Salt and Vinegar.'

'You sure?'

'Maybe one of each.'

'One of each. Right,' I say, beginning to appreciate what my mum's been going through these past few months. Or maybe these past thirty-odd years.

There's a bit of a queue at the bar, and once I finally get served I have to go back because I realise I've accidentally bought Ready Salted instead of Salt and Vinegar, and by the time I get back outside, my dad's nowhere to be seen – and nor is the wheelchair. Frantically I peer around the beer garden in the manner of someone who's lost their child at the beach. Do people steal these things? You hear about cars being pinched with children still strapped into their car seats in the back, but wheelchairs? Maybe Derton hasn't changed that much after all. Perhaps I should have chained him up somewhere. I mean, if those supermarket trolleys require a one-pound ransom, something like a wheelchair . . . Then suddenly I spot him wheeling himself round the corner.

'What the bloody hell happened to you?' I say, once he's manoeuvred himself back to the table.

'Thought I'd try it out for myself, didn't I?' he says, a little out of breath. 'Take it for a spin, like you said.'

'You might have told me where you were going.'

'And what time I'd be back?' He rolls his eyes. 'Now you know how it feels!'

'I was getting worried!'

'About what? In case I hurt myself? Bit late in the day for that, don't you think?'

'Yes, well.'

It's one of those picnic-style tables, and I'm worried it'll be too much effort to get him up and slot his legs through the gap, so I march round behind him, grab the wheelchair's handles and wheel him closer to the table, though I manage to bump the chair's foot-rests against the table leg, spilling some of his beer in the process, then spilling some more when I sit down and – because he's not sitting on the other side – nearly tip the table over.

We sip our beer in silence, then look around the garden, at the pub, everywhere else but each other, until I can't stand it anymore.

'So . . .'

'So?'

'This is . . . nice.'

'Hmmm,' says my dad, examining the two bags of crisps that I've been careful to put where he can reach them. 'Walkers?'

'What's wrong with bloody Walkers?' I snap.

'Nothing.' He looks from one bag to the other, as if he's deciding which one to have as a starter, then picks up the Cheese and Onion, pulls the packet open, and offers it to me. Careful not to abuse his generosity with the crisps *I've* paid for, I grudgingly take a couple.

'Thanks.'

I nurse my drink as I watch him work his way through the rest of the bag, inspecting each crisp as if it's the first time he's ever seen one before popping it into his mouth. Once he's finished, he rolls the empty bag up and ties it in a knot, before tossing it onto the table.

'This is good of you, you know?' he says, picking the other packet up and tearing it open.

'They only cost a pound each.'

'No, I mean you being here. For me.'

'Well, like Doctor Watson said, it's good to get out of the house.'

'Josh, I meant the fact that you've come home. Now.'

I just shrug. Saying *I didn't have much choice* seems a little churlish.

'You must miss Mikayla?'

'Oh, you know.'

'You and her making plans?'

I swallow a mouthful of beer and wave away his offer of another crisp. 'Different ones, it turns out.'

My dad stares at me for a moment, then realisation dawns. 'I'm sorry, Josh. What happened?'

'We're splitting up,' I say, as dismissively as possible, in what's hopefully a 'let's change the subject' kind of way, but sadly, it doesn't seem to work.

'Why?'

'We were just headed in different directions.' *Derton and Sri Lanka, as it turns out.* 'But I think it's for the best.'

'I am sorry. She was a lovely girl.'

'No she wasn't.'

'Me and your mum always liked her.'

'No, you didn't.'

He makes a 'guilty as charged' face. My dad and Mikayla never really got on – not because she's like me or because of any particular argument or perceived slight, but mainly because (*apart* from me) they just don't have anything in common. Putting the two of them in the same room (and that's only happened a handful of times) makes my conversations with my dad look like the Frost-Nixon interviews. Though given how my dad knows nothing about fashion (she designs window displays for Topshop), or shoes (Mikayla's specialist subject – the spare bedroom in our, sorry, *her* flat is a virtual shrine to Jimmy Choo), and Mikayla knows nothing about either sport *or* lung cancer (my dad's specialist subject and my dad's specialist's subject), it's perhaps not surprising they haven't had much to say to each other.

'Are you okay about it?'

I nod, then decide to borrow one of Anna's phrases from the other day. 'She wasn't the love of my life. So no harm done.'

'Well,' says my dad, 'if you want to talk about it . . .'

'Thanks, Dad. I mean, I guess we both knew the relationship had probably gone past its sell-by date, but . . .'

'. . . your mum's good at that kind of thing.'

'Right.'

My dad nods, sagely. 'Still you're back on the market now. Playing the field. Quite a catch, especially here in Derton . . .'

A jobless thirty-six-year-old living with his parents? I let out a short laugh. 'Yeah, Dad. I'll be beating them off with a stick every time I walk down the High Street.'

For the first time in a while, my dad smiles. 'You might be surprised.'

'I doubt it.' I shake my head. 'In any case, I can't think about that at the moment.'

He smiles again. 'Come on, Josh. We both know that that's what men think about *every* moment.'

A plane is flying across the sky, and we're both grateful for the distraction. In fact, we're so grateful that we watch it with the same sort of fascination as if we'd spotted a UFO, until it disappears from view.

'And work's fine, is it?'

'Uh-huh.'

'Only I haven't noticed you doing much of it. Since you've been here.'

'Well, I've been rather busy, haven't I? Running around after you. Taking you to the hospital. Taking Mum shopping. Sorting out everything that you'd normally do,' I say – in my head.

'I've gone freelance.'

'Is that wise, given everything we talked about yesterday?'

I look at him for a moment, then think *what the hell*. 'Turns out I didn't have a lot of choice.'

'Why ever not?'

'Because I came back here.'

'But that's . . .'

'Not fair? Well, there you go. But apparently, if you have a job that's based in London you can't do it if you're going to be based in the arse-end of nowhere for the foreseeable future.'

'Well, I didn't ask you to come back, did I?'

'No, Dad. You didn't. But it's just as well I did, isn't it?'

'Right.' My dad drains the rest of his beer, then puts his empty glass down. 'Well, I better get the next round, then. Assuming you're going to finish that one.'

I picture my dad wheeling himself into the pub, then trying to get himself noticed from his chair. And although I would quite like another drink, I don't want to put either of us through the ordeal – either of him getting it, or us trying to make conversation while we drink it.

'Best not. Don't want to be drunk in charge of . . .'

'Me?'

'Well, yes.'

My dad lets out an indignant snort, then folds his arms and looks at his watch. 'How long shall we give your mum before we go back, do you think?'

I sigh. 'I don't know, Dad.'

'It's just that we're kind of running out of things to talk about.'

'I'd say we reached that point in about 1998, wouldn't you?' I say, exasperatedly, hauling myself off the end of the table and making for the bar.

'Where are you going?'

'To get you another drink.'

'Josh . . .'

'I know, I know. And some crisps.'

'No. Honestly. I don't want anything.'

'Sure?'

'Sure.'

'Well, that makes a change.'

'Right.' There's a long pause, and then: 'Actually, Josh, since you ask, there is something you could get me.'

'I knew it,' I say, wearily. 'Same again?'

'A dog.'

'Pardon?'

'A dog,' repeats my dad.

'A dog?'

'Right.'

'But I don't like dogs,' I say, shuddering at the memory of Mikayla's bug-eyed, constantly-shivering, yappy-snappy Chihuahua.

'Oh. Sorry. I didn't realise this was all about what *you* wanted.'

I glare at him across the table. 'And you want a dog because?'

'Well, it's not for me, really. It's for your mum. Something to keep her company when I'm gone. It occurred to me yesterday. A pug, like Buster. Great personality. So I thought, if we got one now, pretended that I wanted it, then your mum could . . .'

'You don't think she's got her hands a little full at the moment?'

'With me, you mean?'

'Well, yeah.'

'Maybe. But you're here to help her, aren't you? And like you said, you're not working at the moment, so you've got a bit of spare time.'

He's right, of course, and I don't really have an answer for that. And maybe he's right about my mum, too. After all, I'm not going to be here forever, and it's already going to be hard enough to leave her if I am leaving her on her own.

'A pug?'

He nods, then extracts a piece of paper from his trouser pocket. 'I think it would be good for her. I've already tracked one down. All you'd have to do is go and pick it up.'

'Can you imagine what Mum's going to say?'

'You wait till she sees it.' My dad hands me what looks like an advert from the *Derton Gazette* that reads: *Good homes wanted for pug puppies*. 'And anyway, tell her it's for me. Terminal cancer is a great excuse for behaving selfishly.'

I stop myself from asking what his excuse was before he got ill. 'Right.'

'There's an address,' he says.

'So I see.'

'So?' My dad taps the table in front of my glass, indicating I should drink up.

'You want it *now*?'

'Sooner rather than later might be a good idea.'

'Are you worried they'll have gone?'

'No. I'm worried *I* might have.' My dad grins. 'Oh, and Josh?'

'What.'

'Make sure you don't get sold a pup.'

'But the ad says they're *all* pu— Ah. Yes. Very funny.'

My dad shakes his head, and gives me a look. 'And you're the one who's supposed to be good with words?'

And while I'm sure I am, and even though I know thousands, at this precise moment, I can only think of two.

9.

I'm standing in front of a large, rather run-down house on the not-so-nice side of Derton (though to be honest, that definition depends on which side you live in, otherwise it's a toss-up), wincing at the ferocious barking coming from inside and staring at a sign that features the silhouette of an Alsatian. Beneath the picture of the dog, there's a caption that reads, 'I can make it to the gate in 2.4 seconds. Can you?', and as I'm nervously assessing the distance between me and the safety of the pavement, the door is suddenly flung wide open.

'Can I help you?'

The woman is mid-seventies, I'd guess, and as round as she is tall, with a flat face and short, grey-white hair, and when she opens the door fully, I see she's carrying – with some effort – not the Usain Bolt of Alsatians, but a pug so fat that I doubt it'd be able to make it to the gate *at all*.

'I'm Josh. Peters.'

'Peter's what?'

'Huh?'

'Peter was my husband. But he's dead.' She looks suddenly alarmed. 'You're not his long lost son, are you? Because I haven't got any money.'

'No, my name is Josh Peters.'

'So?' she says, eyeing me suspiciously, and I try not to do the same to her, though it's hard to stop myself. If Crufts ever added an 'owners who look like their dogs' category, she'd be the supreme champion.

'I'm here about the dog.'

She tightens her grip on the pug. 'What's she done now?'

'No, not that one. At least, I hope it isn't. I mean, surely that's not a puppy?' I pull the advert from my pocket, though when I show it to her, she stares uncomprehendingly at the scrap of paper.

'Huh?'

'*Good homes wanted for pug puppies*? I've, you know, got one.'

'A pug puppy? Well, what are you doing here? I don't need any more.'

'No, I've got a good home. For . . .' My voice tails off, and I'm thinking of turning round and leaving, but then a look of recognition flickers in the woman's face.

'Oh. Right.' She peers over my shoulder, then up and down the street, and stands aside. 'Well, you'd better come in, then.'

There's not much room in the hallway, and she's still holding the dog, and given its (and her) impressive girth I have to press myself against the wall to get past her, which still puts me within easy reach of the dog's jaws. Though given the way its tongue is lolling out of its mouth, it looks more likely to slobber me to death than anything else.

'First on the left,' says the woman, slamming the front door behind her. She's wheezing loudly, and while at first I assume it's from the effort of carrying the dog, it could also be from the awful smell that hits me when I enter the lounge, which is so bad I almost expect to see the decomposing body of her dead husband propped up in his armchair. I'm beginning to regret coming here, but as much as this house stinks, so does my dad's current situation, and desperate times call for desperate measures.

'Sorry,' the woman wheezes, nodding at the dog as I try and breathe through my mouth. 'She's eaten something that didn't agree with her.'

As I hope it wasn't the last person who knocked on the door, the woman shifts the dog from one arm to another, and goes even redder in the face at the effort.

'Why don't you put her down?'

The woman looks at me, horrified. 'I couldn't do that. I've had her nearly ten years. Besides, it's only a bit of flatulence.'

'I meant *on the floor.*'

'Oh. Yes.' She deposits the pug on the sofa in front of her, then flops down next to it. 'Sit.'

I'm assuming she's talking to me and not the dog, and as I look around the room for a chair that doesn't have some junk piled on it, my gaze settles on a cardboard box on the floor by the window. At first glance, it seems to be full of tiny cuddly toys, but when I look closer, they all seem to be *moving.*

'Is that them?'

The woman beams proudly, as if they're her own offspring. 'That's right.'

I walk over to the box and peer inside, and at once I know I've come to the right place, given the off-the-scale adorable furry bundles that are snuggled up against each other. How could my mum possibly resist these levels of cuteness? I'm having a hard enough time myself.

As I extend my hand towards the box, half a dozen tiny faces turn and blink in my direction, then start snort-whimpering excitedly. 'Can I just . . . pick one?' I say, conscious that the word *how* would fit comfortably in front of that sentence.

'Help yourself,' says the woman, a little off-handedly. 'They're five hundred pounds each.'

I stop, mid-reach. 'Pardon?'

'Five hundred pounds,' repeats the woman. 'Each.'

'But the advert didn't . . . I mean, it said *good homes wanted for . . .*'

'Well, I wouldn't sell them to just anyone.'

'Ah. No. Of course.'

'Well?' says the woman, impatiently.

I reach down into the box and pick up the nearest puppy, which whimpers endearingly, then starts licking its nose excitedly. 'And if my mum doesn't like . . . If we don't get on, can I bring it back? As long as I, you know, keep the receipt?'

I've intended it as a joke, but the woman scowls at me. 'A dog is for life, not just Christmas,' she says.

I decide not to point out that it's June, and place the puppy carefully on the floor in front of me.

'I'll throw in a collar and a lead,' says the woman, and I peer down at the puppy. It's smaller than my foot, and I worry that trailing it around on a lead might actually look a bit, well, silly.

'Plus you'll need a stick.'

'To throw for it?'

'No, to beat off women with. These things are like catnip. But for women.' She brushes a not inconsiderable amount of dog hair from the front of the sack-like fleece top she's wearing. 'You married, are you?'

'Well, no, but . . .'

'Well, you will be soon if you get yourself one of these. Women can't resist cute puppies. Trust me,' she adds. 'It'll be the best six hundred pounds you ever spent.'

'I thought you said five.'

She nods at the puppy. 'That one's six.'

I swallow hard, but it occurs to me that whatever the cost, this isn't a bad idea. Not only will the dog be great company for my mum (and I suspect my dad will get some benefit out of it too in the time that he has left), but in the meantime, while I'm here, it'll be me who gets to walk it. Maybe I could even choose a route that'd take me past a certain café. It might be a help. God knows I could do with some after the other day.

'Could I take it on a test . . . walk? Or maybe even try it for a day or so?'

The woman laughs. 'No chance. He doesn't get his final vaccinations till next week.' She nods at the dog's mother, who hasn't moved from where she's been placed on the sofa. 'You can have a go with this one if you like. I'm not getting any younger, and she doesn't get the exercise she needs nowadays.'

'What's her name?'

'Ziggy,' says the woman.

'Because you take her out for a drag?' I say, realising the old joke might actually be appropriate in this case.

'With a "Z",' says the woman, flatly. 'Not a "C".'

I think for a moment. While the only thing Ziggy might attract is a UN inspector on the lookout for chemical weapons, taking her for a walk might at least give me a good feel for this dog ownership lark. Maybe I'll even take her past Baker's Cupcakes now. Just to see.

'Ziggy? Walkies!' I say, as the dog angles her head at me disdainfully, and as I reach down to scratch her affectionately behind one ear, she silently emits another cloud of poison gas.

'See?' says the woman, hauling herself up from the sofa and cracking open a window. 'She likes you.'

I try and prevent myself from retching, and as I pop the puppy back in the box, I silently pray it's not a case of like mother, like pup, then fix the lead the woman's handed me to Ziggy's collar and make for the door. But walking Ziggy brings a whole new meaning to the phrase 'on the pull', as by the time I've reached the beach, I'm exhausted from trying to haul her most of the way. Pushing my dad in his wheelchair was a breath of fresh air (in both senses) compared to this: she's stopped and sniffed every lamp-post, tree, tuft of grass, and passing dog's backside as if her life depended on it, and I'm beginning to match her constant panting and wheezing from the sheer effort of trying to keep her moving.

I'm also regarding the small, plastic, bone-shaped container that the woman's given me with suspicion, as it evidently contains bags for the collection of any *deposits* Ziggy decides to make, although given the odour in the house, I'm worried I won't be able to get near enough to pick them up. If, indeed, that's even physically possible.

I flop onto a nearby bench, then reach down and unclip Ziggy's lead so she can run free, but instead of going off to sample the smorgasbord of smells that Derton Main Sands must be, she simply plonks herself down by my feet and gazes up at me. Those big brown eyes are cute, I suppose, once you get past the lolling tongue and the excessive saliva, and as I reflect on how that description would sum up how I possibly looked when I saw Anna the other day, a female voice from behind me makes me jump.

'That your dog, is it?'

I have to fight the temptation to look at my watch, amazed it's worked so quickly, convinced that if even this four-legged stink-bomb works, that puppy will turn Anna to putty in my hands. Maybe *this* is what those signs mean that say 'Pick Up After Your Dog'. I pat Ziggy gratefully on the head, then swivel casually round on the bench.

'Well . . .'

'Because it needs to be on a lead,' says the woman, who appears to be dressed – and I look her up and down to make sure, which for some reason makes her frown – in a police uniform.

'Oh. Right.' Even in my thirties I'm still a little afraid of the police, as if they're always going to be able to get me for some small misdemeanour in my past I've forgotten about, and I wonder what other laws I'm breaking right now. Environmental health, probably. 'Actually, she's not my dog.'

'No?' The policewoman eyes the lead I'm holding. 'She's a stray, then, is she? Should I be calling the dog pound? Or have you stolen her?'

I give her a look that does its best to say *who'd steal this*? 'No – I mean . . . I'm just walking her for someone.'

'You've got a funny idea of "walking".' The policewoman squats down next to Ziggy and scratches her affectionately behind one ear, then wrinkles her nose and stands back up.

'It's my first time,' I say, and the policewoman looks at me strangely. 'Walking this dog,' I continue. 'Well, any dog, to be honest.'

'Well, this one certainly looks like she needs the exercise.'

'She does. We were just taking a breather.' I clip Ziggy's lead back onto her collar, hoping she won't choose this moment to make taking a breather somewhat unpleasant, then glance at my watch. 'I guess I'd better get her back,' I say, getting up off the bench and tugging as hard as I can on the lead, but Ziggy doesn't seem to want to go anywhere.

As the dog looks up at me, then squats to do her business, I grimace, then take a bag out from the plastic bone, and the police-woman shakes her head slowly. 'Good luck with that,' she says, beating a hasty retreat.

And whether it's a metaphor for something, or just an indica-tion of what the next however many weeks have in store for me, I'm not sure, but I've a sneaking suspicion I'm going to need all the luck I can get.

❧

I call in at Tesco's to see Gaz on my way back and tell him it looks like I'm going to be around for a bit, and his face goes through a complicated series of emotions during the few seconds it takes him to work out why that is. Then he takes me to one side and tells me if there's anything I need, anything at all, I just have to ask, and I'm so overcome at his selfless generosity after me virtually ignoring him for so many years that it's all I can do to croak out a 'thanks' before hurrying out of the shop.

My mum and dad are watching TV when I get to the house, so I sit down obediently and turn my attention towards the screen, grateful not to have to make small talk. It's *Catch Me If You Can* time, and I'm interested to see what the fuss (in this house, at least) is all about. Ever since I can remember, quiz shows have been the only thing my family have ever been united at. Forget childhood games of football in the park – my dad was always too busy at work (or too tired *from* work) or simply too old to take me on at those kinds of things – but the competition was always fierce when it came to shouting out answers at the TV screen, whether it was *Mastermind* or *University Challenge* or any of the other quiz shows that were on in that post-dinner timeslot. My dad considers himself a bit of a general knowledge buff from the years he spent reading various science and nature magazines in the quiet times (of which there were many) in the shop, and my mum has always been able to absorb facts like a sponge. And I guess I've got a little of that from them, as even now I can't help but join in.

The show's format – as explained by Lesley O'Connor, *Catch Me If You Can*'s perma-tanned host – is pretty simple: a team of four contestants who've 'only just met' have to individually answer general knowledge questions against the clock, then do the same again while being pursued up a ladder (not literally – it's done on a digital scoreboard thing, which is probably just as well, given the age (and size) of some of the competitors) by one of the show's resident 'know-alls', who (according to my dad) seem to be able to pretty much regurgitate any general knowledge fact at will. At the end, anyone who hasn't been 'caught' returns to the team, where they play together against the know-all for a cash prize.

Lesley invites the nervous-looking competitors to introduce themselves, then the questions start – and while I know I should hold back a little given my dad's illness, I'm afraid this competitiveness runs too deep in our family to allow any quarter. And besides, my parents have been doing this for so long, there's no guarantee I'll beat them.

It's an easy first round – the history ones my dad reels off, the arts ones I (not surprisingly) get right, there's an obscure one about plants my mum almost jumps out of her seat to answer, and between the three of us, we pretty much have them covered. As usual, my dad has a little notepad and pencil, which he jots down our relative scores on, and even though he swears it's just to see how we've done that day, I've always suspected he's keeping an actual tally of inter-family results. Particularly since I once found his stash of old notebooks in a large box in the cupboard under the stairs.

Once all four contestants have finished it's onto the competition round, and there's a collective sigh as today's know-all is revealed: it's Mary, or 'The Eliminator' as she's nicknamed (though it 'could be worse', according to my dad). The quicker you answer, the less time the know-all has, and we get so into it that anyone turning up at our front door about now would think we were in the middle of a huge family argument – though when it comes to a question about the first person to reach the South Pole (Amundsen, in case you're interested), they'd be right.

Only two of the team make it back – unlike the Derton contingent, where we'd have a solid three. Sadly, with such depleted numbers, they're unlikely to win, and when they don't, we feel a little sorry for them – or as sorry as three smug people firing off answers from the comfort of the sofa can be. As the programme finishes, Lesley gives a slightly creepy wink and sign-off, and then a message saying: *Think you can do better? Why not apply to be on the show?* appears on the screen.

'You should do that.'

'Huh?'

My dad aims the remote at the television and hits 'Mute'. 'Apply to be on *Catch Me If You Can*.'

'No thanks!'

'Why not?'

'It's embarrassing.'

'What's embarrassing about being on national television?'

'I don't know. Being made to look stupid in front of millions of viewers, perhaps?'

'You might win.'

'Yeah, right.'

My dad makes a face. 'Suit yourself. But it's easy money, as far as I can see.'

'If it's that easy, why don't you go on it?'

I blanch at the inappropriateness of what I've said as soon as the words have left my lips, but my dad just smiles good-naturedly. 'Bit late in the day for me, Josh,' he says, and we both know he doesn't mean the show's broadcast time. 'But you should think about it. You'd make your mum and me proud. And a cash prize isn't to be sneezed at, given the circumstances. Is it?'

And as he turns his attention back towards the television, like most of today's contestants, I can't come up with an answer.

10.

Marty calls this morning, just as I'm getting dressed, to ask how I'm getting on, and while I'm a little surprised at the question, I realise I should dignify it with an answer.

'Okay, I suppose. He's not in any real pain, but it's my mum I feel sorry for. She's watching him get weaker, and there's nothing she can—'

'With the job I emailed you,' says Marty, flatly.

'Oh. Right.' To be honest, I haven't given the project much thought at all given everything else that's been going on. In fact, I'm not sure I can even remember what the book is he's asked me to work on. Possibly because I haven't opened his email yet. 'Well, I've had a couple of ideas.'

'And what might they be?' asks Marty, when I fail to elucidate.

My laptop's on the desk, but it's switched off, and I don't have time to turn it on and check the message. And even if I did, would I really be able to come up with something on the spot? Then again, how hard can it be? Knowing the kind of stuff the agency normally gets involved with, apart from the odd re-launch of a classic, they're usually romance novels, or erotica. And what was that one that had just come in before I left? *The Blind Masseur.* A love story about a French woman and her Cambodian massage therapist, who'd lost his sight in an unfortunate incident involving a chicken and a landmine . . .

'Well?' says Marty, impatiently.

Think, think . . . 'How about "A touching novel"?'

In the silence that follows, I decide I'm quite pleased with that. Off the cuff, it's actually pretty good. Apt. Sums up the book – or at least the third of it I struggled to get through – pretty well. But instead of congratulating me, Marty starts to laugh. Though there's not a lot of humour in it.

'*A touching novel.*'

'That's right.'

'For *Lolita*? A novel about paedophilia.'

Fuck. 'Well . . .'

'I'm hoping your other idea is better . . . ?'

'My other idea?'

'Yeah. You said you had a couple.'

I laugh nervously. 'Not really. Just using the word "couple" as in, you know . . .' As in the 'me and Mikayla are a couple' sense, I remember. 'Okay, wrongly, actually. Besides, how could I top "A touching novel"?'

Marty sighs. 'Josh, do you really expect me to go and tell the client that?'

'That what?'

'Tell the client *that*.'

'Well . . .' I think for a moment. In the absence of anything else, it seems that I do. 'I mean, I know it's a bit controversial, but if you think about it, it's actually quite . . .' My voice tails off as I realise I'm struggling to even sell it to myself. 'Clever.'

'Really,' says Marty, his tone suggesting the opposite.

'It's worth a try,' I say, desperately. 'Controversy. That's what people want nowadays. Conventional is boring. You need something that's going to get you talked about.'

'In a court of law? Come up with something else, Josh. You've got a week. And if I don't hear from you . . . Well, you won't be hearing from me. *Capisce?*'

He puts on a 'Noo Yawk gangster' accent for this last word, and while I don't speak Italian, I've watched *The Godfather* enough times to know what it (and he) means.

'*Capisce*,' I say, then wait for Marty's usual sign-off, but ominously, there's no 'Laters.' And I can't help thinking that means something.

ᖇ

I get downstairs to find my dad in the kitchen, reading the paper.

'Morning, Josh.' He checks my mum's nowhere within earshot, though his voice is getting croaky enough to be little more than a whisper anyway. 'Any progress?'

'With?'

'You know.' He puffs his cheeks out, holds his arms in front of him like a T-Rex, and performs some strange little side-to-side mime that I can only imagine is supposed to be a pug. Though it looks more like he's suffering from a combination of mumps and a bad case of wind.

'Yup,' I say, though I've already decided not to mention the six hundred pounds. My dad's worried enough already about how my mum will do financially when he's gone to be hit with any extra expenses, so I'm just going to have to grin and bear it myself. 'I can pick it . . . Sorry, *him*, up in a week or so.'

'Good, good.'

'So . . .'

'So?'

I sit down at the table and rearrange the two apples and a banana in the fruit bowl so they don't look obscene, trying to work out how to broach the subject. 'I was wondering . . .'

My dad puts his paper down and stares at me. 'Care to do it out loud?'

'I was wondering if there was anything else.'

'Anything else?'

'Apart from this "dog" thing. Anything more . . . personal. People you'd like to see. Any unresolved issues, stupid arguments you'd like to put behind you, that kind of thing.'

'Well, Josh, it's funny you of all people should say that.'

'It is?' I do a double take. Is this about us? Is he finally going to apologise for being a bad dad? If so, while in the kitchen first thing in the morning wasn't exactly when and where I saw this happening, it's better than nothing, I suppose. And better than doing it on his deathbed.

'Yes. Because I was thinking I'd like you to organise my funeral.'

'Your *funeral*?'

'Is that okay?'

'Of course.'

'But . . .'

'But?'

'I'd like it before I die.'

'Pardon?'

'Sort of a farewell party. A wake. But with me actually, you know . . . awake.'

'You want to *be there*?'

'That's the idea.'

'It's a crazy idea.'

'What's crazy about it?'

'Well . . .' It's a good question, actually. 'Who gets to go to their own funeral?'

'No-one. And isn't that a shame? So if we do it this way . . .' My dad grins. 'You know how someone always says "it's what he would have wanted"? Well, this is my opportunity to get exactly what I would have wanted.'

'And what exactly *would* you want?'

93

'Nothing fancy. Just some people over to the house. Or we could have it in the garden, if it's nice. We'll get some food in – those nibbles we had last Christmas from Marks and Spencer's were pretty good – and some drink, obviously. People will need a drink.'

'Especially Mum, when you tell her.'

'And we'll keep it informal. And I want some music.'

'Do you want me to get a DJ?'

'You can wear what you like.'

'No, I meant . . .' I notice my dad's sporting his usual 'got you' expression. 'Yes, very funny.'

'Actually, while I think about it, no-one's allowed to wear black. I want it upbeat. No morose speeches, or tears, or anything like that.'

'So what you're really describing is a *party*.'

My dad thinks for a moment. 'Yes. I suppose it is. And you can invite some people too. Be a good chance for you to catch up with your friends.'

'Dad, the last time I had some friends round was for my sixteenth birthday, and you spent the whole time "accidentally" popping into the room because you'd . . .' I make the 'speech marks' sign. 'Forgotten your glasses, or left your book in there, when really all you were trying to do was check we weren't raiding your drinks cabinet.'

'Which I seem to remember Gary was.'

'Or getting up to any "funny business", as I think you described it at the time. Loudly. And in front of everyone.'

My dad chuckles to himself. 'That's right! And you were so embarrassed you stormed off and hid in your bedroom until every-one left.'

'Quite. So as unmissable as this . . . event is sure to be, I think I'll let you keep it to *your* friends.'

'Suit yourself.'

'And when were you thinking?'

'Well, sooner rather than later, obviously. I mean, I want to be able to enjoy it. And I don't want to look too ill.'

'Trust me, I'm sure you'll look better than most people do at their funerals.'

'Hah! True. So you'll do it?'

I mull it over for a second or two, and decide it's not such a bad idea. Since I've been back, the one thing that's struck me as strange is how few people have actually said anything to him about his illness: not the guy in the paper shop where my dad used to buy his lottery tickets every week without fail, or the postman, not to mention any of his old customers from the sweetshop. No-one's actually come round to see him. In fact, it's been quite the opposite, as if they're scared they'll offend him, or even catch something. Then again, what on earth do you say? *Sorry to hear you're dying?* Last time I looked, Hallmark didn't make a card with that particular message on the front. But I also can't help wondering whether the point of this party is because there are some goodbyes my dad wants to say. And an event like this will sure beat my taking him on a farewell tour of Derton in his wheelchair.

'Fine,' I say, standing up to leave. 'I'll speak to Mum. Clear it with her first.'

My dad makes a 'good luck with that' face. 'Thanks, Josh.'

'Sure.' I get halfway to the door when something else occurs to me, so I head back over and sit down again. 'One other thing.'

'Shoot.'

'Have you thought about your *actual* funeral? You know, after . . . wards. Does Mum know what you want? How you want to be . . . ? Where you . . . ?' For some reason, I'm having trouble saying the words.

'Yes. And I don't want any fuss.'

'Sounds like we're having that beforehand.'

My dad rolls his eyes. 'Cremated, in case you were wondering. Though make sure I am *actually* dead first. You know I don't like the heat.'

'Well, you better hope there's not a hell, then.'

'Very funny, Josh.'

'And your ashes?'

'What about them?'

'Well, where do you want them scattered? Assuming you don't want Mum to keep them in an urn on the mantelpiece so she can have breakfast with you every morning.'

He peers around the room. 'I haven't really thought about it. Here, maybe?'

'What, like some sort of Shake'n'Vac?'

'Not on the carpet. I meant in the garden.'

'And have people tramping your remains into the house every time they walk inside? I'm not sure Mum would be too happy about that.'

'Well, where do you suggest?'

'I dunno. What about in the sea? Isn't that a bit more traditional?'

He narrows his eyes at me. 'Actually, that's not a bad idea. We've had some good times at that beach. I'd like that. Or maybe . . .'

'Maybe?'

A smile begins to form on his face. It's a smile I've seen before. And it usually means trouble. 'What about from the rollercoaster?'

'In Funland?' He's referring to Derton's rather run-down amusement park just off the seafront. (Tagline: 'Where the fun never stops'. Although it *actually* stops every October, when the place shuts for the winter.)

He nods. 'It's where I proposed to your mum.'

'Don't you think the owners might object? Not to mention the other riders, when they get a mouthful of you mid-scream. Mind you, it's hardly the most exciting of rides, so I suppose it would actually give them something to scream about.'

'You'd have to do it surreptitiously. Like they do when they get rid of the earth in *The Great Escape*. You know, take a bit in your pockets each time, then shake it – well, *me* – out of your trouser leg.'

I stare at him for a moment, then sigh. 'If that's what you want.'

'I do,' says my dad. 'Though the other place would have been on the allotment.'

'The allotment?' For years, my dad spent any spare mornings tending to a small patch of ground on the other side of town – another thing of his he'd always hoped I'd take over – occasionally coming back with a handful of misshapen carrots and presenting them to my mum with the same kind of reverence as if he'd just discovered fire. Which would probably have been the best place for them.

He nods. 'Plus it'd be a great fertiliser for the next crop of veg. Though then your mum would probably be all funny about eating, you know, *me*. Then again, the place is looking pretty overgrown now, and some stranger will probably get it after I'm gone, and the last thing I want is to be the seasoning on someone else's roast potatoes. So no, thinking about it, the sea's probably the best option.' He picks up his paper, signalling that the conversation's over. 'Now, if you could go and make a start on my party plans . . . But maybe don't tell your mum just yet.'

I sigh again. 'It's your funeral.'

'Yes,' he says. 'It is.' Then he winks at me. 'Or rather, it isn't.'

11.

It takes Gaz a full two minutes to stop laughing when I tell him the *Lolita* story in the pub over lunch.

'And you get paid for that?'

'Sometimes.'

'How long does it take you to come up with them?'

'Well, that one, about two seconds. But in general, it can take days.'

'For three words?'

'Yeah, well, it's actually more about what you don't say. What you leave out. That's the skill – deciding what message you want to get across, but in the minimum words.'

'Unlike what you just said, for example?' Gaz nudges me. 'Seriously, Josh. How do you do it?'

'I dunno. It's just the way my brain's wired, I suppose. I see words in a different way, so I can put them together to mean something else at the same time. And something like that – well, to condense a novel of tens of thousands of words into just three . . .'

'Hey.' He picks up his glass and clinks it against mine. 'That's why you earn the big bucks in the big city, eh?'

When I don't answer, Gaz looks concerned. 'I'm hoping you don't get paid per word?'

I let out a short laugh. 'Sometimes I don't get paid at all. Marty's hardly the most generous of employers. And with me back here in Derton . . .'

'Ah.' He peers at me over the top of his glass. 'Listen, Josh, and don't take this the wrong way, but are you okay for money?'

I shrug. 'I suppose.'

'It's just that . . . Well, Michelle's looking for someone to work in the shop. Just the odd morning over the summer, if you're interested. And obviously, if you need any time off for your dad . . .'

'Thanks, Gaz. But I don't know anything about furniture.'

He laughs. 'You'll be okay. Nor do any of the people who come in. Doesn't stop them paying through the nose for it, though. I tell you, the only way we'd get more money for old rope is if we were actually selling old rope.'

'Well . . .'

'It might just tide you over. At least until that big – how's it go again? – "small-town coming-of-age novel" you left Derton to write hits the best-seller lists.'

'If that's the case, I might be working there for a while.'

'Get a move on, will you? It's my only chance to be famous.' Gaz grins. 'How's it going?'

'Slowly.'

'You are still writing it?'

'Yeah yeah yeah,' I say, though in truth, I haven't put pen to paper – or fingers to keyboard – for a long time. Since I moved in with Mikayla, now I come to think of it. And certainly not since all this stuff with my dad started.

'And doesn't it bug you?'

'What?'

'Writing all this stuff promoting other people's books, when you really want to be writing yours?'

'It didn't. It does *now*.'

'Sorry, mate,' he says, sheepishly. 'But you know what I mean?'

And the truth is, I do. But how on earth do you write a book about the life you left behind, when it won't quite let you leave it? 'It's just not as . . . easy as I thought it would be.'

'Hey. If it was easy, everyone would be doing it.'

'Haven't you looked on Amazon recently? Everyone is!' I sigh. 'I just thought I could write about Derton when I knew I'd escaped. And I don't seem to have managed that, do I?'

'No?' Gaz frowns. 'So who was it you were running away from?'

'I wasn't "running away" from anyone,' I say, crossly.

'*Escaping from*, then?'

I stare into my beer. 'I don't know. I just thought there must be more to life than . . .' – I wave a hand in the air to indicate, well, *everything* – '. . . this. And I worried that if I didn't go – stayed around, stayed with Anna, and took over my dad's shop – I'd be trapped. Could never leave. Ever.'

'Would that have been such a bad thing?'

I give him a look. 'What do you mean?'

'Just, you know, London. How's that working out for you, exactly? I mean, here you've got family. Friends.'

'Well, *a* friend. And a family that's soon to be reduced by fifty percent.'

'Or increased.'

'Huh?'

'If you get back together with Anna.'

'Where did *that* come from?'

Gaz ignores me. 'And besides, it's more than you had there, isn't it? With Mikayla.'

I glare at him, though possibly because he's got a point. 'I just thought I could do better.'

'Than Derton?'

'Than *me* in Derton. No-one knew me in London, Gaz. I wasn't the one with parents everyone thought were my *grand*parents because they looked so much older than everyone else's mum and dad. There was no school, where all I wanted to do was read – escape into my books – and everyone else wanted to play sport, and if you preferred spending time in the library to spending it on the games field that automatically marked you out as a geek or a weirdo. I didn't have the shame of my dad running the sweetshop on the seafront rubbed in my face on a daily basis, watching him struggle to stay afloat as the tourists stopped coming, spending longer and longer hours there, desperate for business, so my mum and I never saw him. I didn't fit in, Gaz. I hated it here. Is it any wonder I couldn't wait to get away? Derton is the place I was born. The place I grew up. Where my mum and dad live. But it's never felt like home to me. I had a dream, and I wanted to pursue it. London was the place where I could. Derton certainly wasn't.'

Gaz regards me warily until he's sure I've finished. 'All I'm saying, Josh, is look at me. My mum moved us here from Bolton when I was one, and everyone used to take the piss out of me at school because she talked differently to the other mums. And when I was growing up, she always used to refer to going back up north as home, so that's how I thought about it too, even though I never really lived there. Because she refused to let go.'

I shake my head. 'Because this didn't feel like home to her, and that did.'

'It did to me too, though, because I felt different here. And maybe that's my point. That you can never really escape home. Because the word means so many things. Accents. Schooling. Family. London's just somewhere you lived for a while, but Derton will always be your home.'

'Thanks a lot, Gaz,' I say, miserably.

'Don't mention it.'

I take a sip of my beer. 'So don't you feel torn? The pull of those Northern roots? The desire to go back to Bolton?'

'And leave all of this behind?' Gaz makes the same 'waving' gesture I did earlier, then grins. 'No – because it never was *actually* home to me. Derton is, like it or not. But eventually, you realise it is just a word. And I've come to realise something else too – and I only realised it when I met Michelle.'

'And that was?' I say, as Gaz stares at the table.

'That my home is wherever she is.'

'You soft git.'

He reddens slightly. 'I'm serious. You can't be home alone.'

'Macaulay Culkin seemed to manage it.'

Gaz rolls his eyes at my attempt at a joke. 'You need a family, Josh. People to love. To put roots down with. Somewhere. Otherwise . . .' His voice cracks a little. 'There's no point.'

I stare at him, *you'll never be free from Derton-on-Sea* running through my mind. I know what 'home' means, I just don't want it to be here, and that's always been my dilemma. But at the same time, if I think about what I was – to quote Gaz – 'running away from', if it's not here anymore, then do I really need to keep running?

'And what are you going to do when, you know . . .' Gaz looks at me over the top of his pint glass. 'After your dad's . . .'

'Dead?' I shrug. 'Back to London, I guess. Try and get my career back on track. Find somewhere to live. Meet someone who isn't Mikayla and live happily ever after.'

'And it's that good there, is it, that you want to go through all that? Again?'

'There's more opportunity there, Gaz. More people. Which means more women. So statistically . . .'

'There's more competition?'

'Huh?'

'If there were a million eligible women there, then there'd still be a similar number of single blokes. So you'd still face the same competition.'

'I'm not sure it quite works like that. But at least I'd have more choice. More chance of finding someone I could be happy with.'

He laughs. 'And if you found this person, you'd have to pursue her, right?'

'Which person?'

'Say you met someone that you thought was the one for you. It'd be irresponsible not to have a crack, right? To see if things worked out.'

'I suppose.'

He nods towards the pub window, or more specifically, through it and towards the café on the corner. 'Go on, then.'

'What?'

'What are you waiting for?'

'Huh?'

'Might as well have a go at the one right in front of you first, so you can cross her off your list.'

'Gaz, please.'

'So all this bollocks you've been telling me about pursuing your dreams is, in fact, bollocks?'

'No, I—'

'Since I've known you, you've only wanted two things. One was to be a writer – and I think we can say that's still a work in progress – and the other was Anna Coleman, then you blew that. Now you've got the best chance you've ever had to find out whether she's interested in you again, and you're just going to walk away from it?'

'Gaz, I can't. There's just too much going on at the moment for me to even think about Anna,' I say, deciding not to tell him about our recent disastrous meeting.

'But don't you think it'd all be easier to deal with if you had someone? Someone to talk to?'

'I've got you, haven't I?'

'Yeah, but I mean someone who *cares*. What are you waiting for, Josh? The right time? Trust me, there's never been a better one.' He clinks his glass against mine. 'Strike while the iron's hot. And right now, as far as Anna's concerned, your dial's set on "linens".'

I nod, and 'cheers' him back, though more in the hope it'll shut him up. 'Right,' I say, 'linens.' Even though I don't have the faintest idea what he means.

12.

Derton, day fourteen, and the housemates are getting restless. My dad's constant demands – combined with his eternal optimism – are driving me mad, and while he's keen for us to 'spend some quality time', I'm beginning to suspect that's actually best achieved apart. Besides, he and my mum need some time together without me around. Or at least that's how I'm justifying it to myself.

Inspired by Gaz's pep talk yesterday, I'm sitting in a café called Al Cappuccino's that overlooks the seafront, trying to write. I say 'trying to write', but in reality, it's simply that I don't have any other work to do. I haven't had any more ideas for Marty (and, of course, Marty's not come back with any more projects, and I'm way too proud to chase him – though we'll see how long that particular stance lasts). And as for Mikayla and Sri Lanka . . . Well, my laptop and Derton Main Sands will have to do.

I have arranged to go in and see Michelle tomorrow morning about the job, however, and God knows, we could do with the money. And in a moment of rashness (inspired by a quick check of my bank balance), I've even gone online and filled in an application form for *Catch Me If You Can*. But in the meantime, I'm having some 'me' time.

Normally, cafés are good to write in – the background hum of the coffee machine, the clinking of cups on saucers, the murmur of a hundred different conversations, all create an atmosphere that's conducive to putting words down on paper (or in this case, on screen). The only problem is, I can't think of a single thing to write about. My brain's still spinning with everything going on – my dad, Anna, Mikayla, what my mum's going to do afterwards, what *I'm* going to do afterwards – and while it occurs to me that I could actually write about *that*, I haven't the faintest idea where to start. Because how can you begin to write a story when you've not got a clue what the ending is going to be?

And I can't simply listen in to the conversations around me for inspiration (that is, steal ideas/choice dialogue) because no-one's actually sitting around me. In fact, for the last half hour, I've been the only one in here, which has meant the rather over-attentive young waitress has been asking me pretty much every five minutes if there's anything else I want, and though all I really want is to be left alone, saying that might come across as a little rude. Plus I'm feeling guilty, because normally if you're in a big Starbucks or Costa, you can sit there and nurse a cappuccino until the place shuts, but when you're the only customer in a family-run establishment, that's not quite so easy. But she's bored, I suppose. And so, I have to admit, am I.

'Are you sure I can't get you anything?' she says, as if on cue.

I sigh, and cave. 'Same again, please.'

'Which was?'

I have to stop myself from rolling my eyes. It's been the only order she's taken all afternoon. And given the name of the establishment, I'd imagine it's what everyone asks for. 'A cappuccino?' I say, gesturing towards my chocolate-frothed cup.

'Oh. Yeah. Right.'

She's lingering at my table, so I fix a smile on my face and look up. 'Yes?'

'I was just wondering what it was you were doing?'

'Working.'

'And what is it you, you know, do?'

'I'm a writer.'

She casts a scornful glance at the blank Word document on the screen in front of me. 'Really?'

'Yes, really.'

'What kind of stuff do you write?'

I shut my laptop and fold my arms. 'Novels.' Though I decide to leave the words 'descriptions of' off the start of my answer.

'Oh. Right,' she says, raising her eyebrows. 'Would I have read anything you've written?'

I open my mouth to answer, then close it again. It's the question all writers get, and while I suppose it's a fair enough one, how on earth are you supposed to answer it – *that depends on how well read you are*? 'That depends . . .' No, I can't do it. 'No. This is my first book.'

'Wow. Impressive. Books are . . .'

I wait, but when she doesn't complete the sentence, don't dare suggest a word. 'What kind of stuff do you like to read?'

'I don't read much. I mean, I *can* read.' She reaches for my cup. 'Don't get me wrong. I just prefer the telly.'

'Right. So when was the last time you read an actual book?'

The girl thinks for a moment. 'School, probably. But only coz I had to.'

Which is probably why you're working as a waitress in this wasteland of a café, I think. 'Right. So . . .'

'So?'

'My cappuccino?'

'Oh. Yeah. Sorry. Back in a tick.'

'Take your time.'

As the girl scampers off behind the counter, I open my laptop again and stare at the screen, then tab through to my emails. Still nothing from Marty – and that includes my last month's salary, I see, when I check my bank balance again. Then I'm aware of someone standing in front of me, and I'm just about to tell the girl she's the fastest cappuccino-maker ever, but when I look up I'm greeted by the unmistakeable (although slightly rounder-stomached) sight of Ian Baker.

At once, I feel a little dizzy, as the speed at which I'm transported back to being a nervous sixteen-year-old makes my head spin. It's Ian Baker. *Ian Baker*!

'Well, well, well. Look who it isn't,' he says (I'm not kidding, he actually talks like this). There's a smug smile on his face, and while it's not quite the same one he used to adopt before doing something nasty to someone at school (and yes, I can still picture it oh so clearly), I'm instantly on my guard.

'Ian,' I say, as levelly as I can manage, which isn't actually that level when I play it back in my head. I scan the table anxiously for anything that can be used as a weapon – by him, I mean – then wonder if I should offer to shake his hand. After all, it's been eighteen years, and I suppose I should forgive some childish bullying. But as I think about it, I realise that what I should want to do is punch him in the face, or – seeing as I'm sitting down, and he's standing over me – somewhere a bit lower, but a lot more painful. 'How have you been?'

Ian folds his arms. 'Surviving,' he says. 'You?'

'The same.'

'I married Anna, you know?'

And there it is. Fifteen seconds in, and he has to mention it. 'Yeah?' I say, as disinterestedly as possible, though I decide not to add *And how is that going?*

'Yeah.'

'She didn't say,' I tell him, still unable to believe it. In the movies, you always see the good-looking girl going out with the school bully, then the wimpy guy eventually wins her. Ironic that in this case, it seems to have happened the other way round.

Ian stiffens, as if he suspects I might know something, or that I'm trying to imply something. Which, perhaps, I am. 'You've seen her?' he asks, glancing across the street towards Baker's Cupcakes.

I nod, though I decide not to go into detail. 'We've spoken.' Which I suppose is a version of what happened.

'And you know we're still married, right?' he says, frowning at me, though there's a hint of something – menace? Uncertainty? – behind it.

'Is that right?'

'Yes, that's right!' he says, quickly, in a 'matter closed' kind of way. 'So, what are you doing back in Derton?'

'Oh, you know.'

'No, not really.'

The last thing I want to do is tell Ian the real reason I'm back. At school, any chance he got to use something as leverage, he'd take it, and even though I'm sure (at least, I hope) he's changed, I'm still cautious. 'I missed the old place.'

'Yeah?' he says, incredulously.

'Yeah.'

Ian is still standing above me. I don't want to ask him to sit down, and I want to get up and go, but I haven't paid for my coffee yet, plus I've got another on the way – somewhere – so my only choice is to stay here.

'By the way,' he says. 'Don't feel you have to thank me.'

'For what? Picking on me all through school?' I've surprised myself that I've said it, but at least it's out in the open now – though Ian doesn't seem the slightest bit guilty.

'That was just a bit of fun.'

'For you, maybe.'

'Yeah, well, it was a long time ago. Kids can be nasty bastards, eh?'

I look up at him in disbelief as he dismisses six years of torment with those few words. 'Some kids.'

Ian lets out a rumbling laugh. 'I meant thank me for doing your old man a favour.'

I bristle a bit, both at Ian's unashamed cheek, and at the fact that he's referred to my dad as my 'old man' – something he did a lot back in the day. 'A *favour?*'

'Buying that run-down old shop of his.'

'What?'

'Yeah. Though between you and me, I got it for a bit of a steal. He seemed desperate to sell, for some reason. Tell him from me that in future, that's not the best way to negotiate.'

And there you have it. Eighteen years ago, Ian used to steal sweets from my dad's shop, and now he's gloating about virtually stealing the shop itself. And now – unlike then – I just can't let it go. Especially since the words 'in future' have such a short-term feel to them where my dad's concerned.

I shut my laptop and ball my fists under the table. 'You know why he was 'desperate' to sell, Ian?'

Ian shrugs dismissively. 'Didn't ask,' he says, though it sounds like 'didn't care' would be more accurate.

'He has cancer.'

'What?'

'Terminal cancer. It's why I've come back to Derton, to answer your earlier question. Because he's dying. That's why he sold the shop. To get some money for my mum to live on.'

'Ah.'

'Yes, "ah".'

Ian makes the 'what can you do?' face, then, to make sure I've got it, he actually says, 'What can you do? Still, all's fair in love and war, eh?'

The waitress chooses that moment to arrive with my cappuccino, so Ian leans over and gives me a hearty clap on the shoulder, tells me he'll 'see me around' then turns and makes for the café door. And while I'm still stunned by his 'all's fair in love and war' comment, and even though I've never been the vengeful type, if ever there was a reason to get Anna back, I'm watching it walk away from me now.

∽

My mum's in the garden when I get back, tending to the hanging baskets that make walking down the side of the house a dangerous head-banging journey at night. It's always been her haven, something she's lavished care and attention on, though recently, understandably, it's been looking a little overgrown.

'Need a hand?'

My mum looks up with a start. Apart from the odd bit of heavy lifting, or collecting 'three bags for £10' multi-purpose compost from B&Q, I'm usually of little use in this department, but today, she nods.

'You could water the agapanthus.'

'Sure.' I drop my bag on the doormat, fill up the watering can from the tap on the wall, then stand there with a bewildered expression on my face. 'And the agapanthus is . . . ?'

She smiles. 'That big blue thing in the corner,' she says, pointing to a big blue thing in the corner.

'Okay. Great. Thanks.'

I do as I'm told, though I manage to water my shoes as much as the plant. By the time I've finished, my mum is sitting at the cast-iron table under the pergola.

'Your dad used to do that.'

'Soak his shoes?'

She smiles. 'The watering. He used to say he found it therapeutic. You never got into gardening, Josh?'

I pull out a chair next to her, and sit down. 'Not really, despite all the times Dad made me help him on the allotment. I had a yucca plant once. Those things are supposed to be indestructible, but even that . . . Well, you know, I managed to . . . It didn't . . . survive.'

My mum reaches over and squeezes my hand. 'When do you think we'll be able to say that word again?'

'What word?'

'The one you just avoided. The d-word. *Died.*'

'Hopefully not for a while.'

'Yes, Josh. Let's hope so.'

We sit in silence for a moment or two. To be honest, it's the first time I've sat in the garden for a long time, and I'm impressed with the little square of paradise my mum's created. Derton town centre's only five minutes away, the beach is even closer, but here? Surrounded by these ivy-clad walls, looking up at the cobalt-blue sky, you could be anywhere.

'Have you thought what you're going to do?'

'When?' asks my mum, though I'm sure she knows what I mean.

'After. Once he's gone.'

She lets out a long sigh. 'Carry on, I suppose. I don't see any other option.'

'Will you stay here? In the house?'

'As opposed to in the garden?' She smiles briefly. 'Where would I go? And why would I move?'

'Well, because . . . The memories. It might be a little tough. To be reminded of him every day.'

'Why would you think that? Why would anyone think that? The memories – they'll be all I have left, won't they? They're all anyone has, really.' She gazes up at the roof, where a seagull is squawking noisily. 'Josh, you probably won't understand this just yet, but when you've been with someone for as long as I have with your dad, you get into a routine – and that's not a bad thing. Knowing what you're going to do, how you're going to do it, where and when things are going to happen. Sure, it can bug the living daylights out of you from time to time, but for the most part, there's a comfort in that. A security. Just because one element of my life won't be there anymore, why on earth would I want to change the rest of it?'

'Well, because . . .' I hesitate, knowing I'm on slightly sticky ground here. 'You'd still have time to . . . I mean, you might meet . . . You're still young enough . . .' I stop talking, hoping she knows I'm saying this for her own good, to remind her that there's light at the end of the tunnel. 'After all, people are getting divorced and remarried later and later nowadays. So the fact that Dad's life is ending prematurely doesn't, you know, mean yours has to as well.'

'Josh, you don't get it, do you?' She squeezes my hand again. 'When you meet someone, and they're – what is it your generation say, *the one*? – it's different. It changes you. You don't see it as a conveyor belt, where if it doesn't work out – for whatever reason – you can simply say "next" and move on. You and Mikayla . . .'

'Dad told you?'

She nods. 'Your dad and I knew it wasn't what you wanted, knew *she* wasn't *who* you wanted, and I think deep down you knew that too, which is why – and I hope you'll excuse me for saying this – you don't seem too distraught about it being over. But your dad and me? I can't possibly allow myself to even think what's going to happen afterwards, because I can't even conceive of an afterwards without him. He's all I've known for the past forty-odd years – and trust me, some of them have been pretty odd – but I've got used to that. I've been shaped by him. Moulded, like a comfy chair, or a favourite pair of shoes. So anyone else? We're just not going to fit as well as me and your dad did. You and Mikayla – she didn't fit you, and vice versa. Do you know what I mean?'

I don't say anything, but just smile, and my mum peers at me across the table.

'What's so funny?'

'All this time I've thought of relationships being something exciting, whereas you've just compared them to an old pair of trainers.'

My mum laughs, and it's the first time I've heard her laugh since I've been here. 'And forty-odd years with your dad? It's forty-odd years more than some people ever get.' She hauls herself out of her chair. 'So I don't need anything more with anyone else, because I'll always have had that.'

As I stare at her, open-mouthed, I can't help thinking about Anna. The years she spent married to Ian – well, they obviously didn't 'fit' (not that that's an image I want to dwell on). But the interesting thing is, if I'm going to have a chance of a future with anyone – at least, a future like the one my mum and dad have already had, if you see what I mean – then it really ought to start sooner rather than later. If there's one thing this whole cancer bollocks is teaching me, it's that you've got to seize the day. Because you never know what's around the corner. And those people who say 'it's never too late to . . .' then make some glib observation?

They don't know the first thing about it.

13.

The dog arrives this morning, though the word *arrives* hardly does justice to the chaos caused the moment it sets foot (or rather, paw) in the house. And it's not the six-hundred-pound version (cost, *or* weight) – partly because I'm not sure my mum could cope with a puppy (and all right, mainly because of the cost, but hey, I'm virtually unemployed, okay?) – but a four-year-old pug from Derton's animal sanctuary, Paws For Thought, which, even with re-homing fees, has set me back a tenth of the price.

And while I've had to stop the car twice on the journey home wondering what the strange noises I thought I could hear coming from the engine were (which turn out to be normal operating sounds for a pug, apparently), in the (slightly wrinkled) flesh, this big-eyed, snuffling, squashed-faced thing is actually quite endearing. If, you know, you like big-eyed, snuffling, squashed-faced things.

Which my mother evidently does. A lot. Because the moment I bring Wallace (for that's the name inscribed on the metal bone-shaped tag hanging from his collar) into the front room, she rushes over, picks him up, and starts clucking loudly – much to his bemusement (and my dad's and my amusement).

'He's gorgeous! What's his name?'

'Wallace.'

'Hello, Wallace,' she says, holding him so his nose is about an inch from hers. 'Hullo, Wallace. *Hulloo, Wullace.*' Each time she says it, her voice gets more and more Scottish.

'His first name isn't "William",' says my dad, eventually.

Wallace, to his credit, only looks a little scared, though his permanent expression could be interpreted in several different ways. 'Whose is he?' she asks, lowering him gently to the floor, and my dad and I exchange glances.

'Mine,' he says. 'Well, yours and mine, actually.'

My mum frowns. 'I don't understand.'

He nods towards me as Wallace scuttles over and sniffs his outstretched hand. 'It was Josh's idea.'

'Hold on. Don't blame me for . . .'

My dad laughs as he picks Wallace up off the floor and sets him down on his lap, though the effort's almost too much for him. 'Okay,' he wheezes. 'It was mine.'

My mum walks over to where he's sitting and reaches down to scratch Wallace behind one ear, and he snuffles his approval. 'We used to have one of these.'

'Why do you think I told Josh to get a pug?'

'And who's going to walk him, what with everything going on?'

My dad glances across to me. 'Josh said he wouldn't mind.'

'That's right,' I say, in answer to my mum's raised eyebrows. And, it has to be said, Wallace's.

'And afterwards?'

My dad smiles grimly. 'I thought we'd decided we weren't going to talk about afterwards?'

'But . . .' She shakes her head. 'No. We can't. A dog is too much work. Especially now.'

My dad gazes up at her, doing a pretty good impression of Wallace's pleading expression. 'He's a pug, remember? They're no work at all. They sleep most of the day and just need feeding and the odd walk.'

'Sounds like someone else I know.'

'And I always wanted to get another one after Buster got run over. But what with Josh surprising us by arriving on the scene . . .'

'Hang on. Now you're blaming me for not getting one then *and* getting one now?'

'. . . and the shop, it just wasn't practical. And I always thought we'd get one when I retired. And now I have. Retired. And got one. Haven't I?'

My mum's already wearing the expression of someone who knows she hasn't got a leg to stand on, as opposed to Wallace, who – given how comfortable he's looking in my dad's lap – already seems to know he's got four.

'I suppose I should think myself lucky that this is all you've asked for.'

'I'm not dead yet,' says my dad, and at once the atmosphere in the room changes, and I can't help thinking how it's funny how even though you can live with something constantly on your mind, and it almost becomes the norm, all it can take is the slightest trigger to bring it front and centre.

We stand there silently, until Wallace looks up at my mum, nuzzles the hand that, until thirty seconds ago, was stroking him, and whimpers imploringly. 'You see?' says my dad. 'He likes you. And besides, we can hardly send him back. Give him a taste of freedom, then lock him back up again? It wouldn't be fair. Plus it'd be good for Josh, while he's here.'

'Good for *me*? How, exactly?'

'Teach you some responsibility. Good practice, too.'

'Practice?'

'*Grandkids*,' says my dad, as if I'm being completely thick.

As I shoot him a look, my mum folds her arms. 'Where's he going to sleep?'

'Already taken care of,' I say, proffering the bag containing the dog bed I've picked up from the pet shop on the High Street earlier. 'And there's a spot in the kitchen by the back door that'll suit him perfectly.'

My dad nudges her. 'Unless you want him in with you?'

'Over my dead—' My mum corrects herself quickly. 'I mean, no chance.'

'Plus he's a rescue dog, so he's already house trained,' I add, though I don't admit that when the woman at the dogs' home told me that, I expressed my doubt that Wallace could rescue anyone. 'And he's had all his jabs.'

'I wish *I* had,' grumbles my dad.

'Well . . .' My mum's face softens as Wallace gazes up at her, his bright pink tongue flicking out to alternately lick his eyebrows. 'I suppose we could . . .'

'That's sorted, then.' My dad picks Wallace up by the shoulders, holds him in front of his face, and plants a kiss on the top of his head. 'Welcome to your new home, Wallace.'

I look at the cosy little tableau in front of me, and I'm ashamed to admit I feel a stab of jealousy. Wallace has only been here five minutes, and already the three of them look more of a family unit than the three of us ever did. And it's cruel, I know, but there's something I can do about that.

'Wallace,' I shout, jangling his lead. 'Walkies.'

Wallace jumps down from my dad's lap and scurries towards me, the look on his face suggesting he can't wait to go out. And as I clip his lead onto his collar, I suspect it's an expression he'll be wearing an awful lot in this house.

Michelle's a short, roundish woman with an infectious smile, and every time I see her, I'm reminded how lucky Gaz is. Some people spend their lives looking for the ideal woman, whereas Gaz has done the smart thing and found someone who's ideal for him. Together, they're a unit. Stronger. And though I'm a bit jealous of what they've got, it's in a good way.

She's with a customer, so when Wallace and I walk into the shop (having sneaked past Baker's Cupcake Café on the way in) she beams at me from where she's doing her best to persuade him to buy what looks like the kind of soda siphon that everyone threw away when Sodastreams became popular (I'm interested to see she's got one of those for sale too), and so I take the opportunity to have a look around. From memory, this used to be a photographic shop, full of tripods that to us kids looked like something out of *The War of the Worlds*, and expensive cameras on the shelves that the owner used to shout at us for touching. Then no-one needed to buy cameras anymore because we all had them on our phones, and the place closed down, and Michelle came along and (ironically) stocked it with things like old cameras, which people bought to put on their shelves at home.

And I like what she's done here. The walls are painted a simple off-white, the floorboards stripped back to their original pine, and in a clever and economical form of multi-tasking the larger items of for-sale furniture are used to display the smaller ones, all with hand-written tags with prices and (sometimes) years-of-manufacture written on them. And while the collection of objects – wardrobes, desks, old typewriters, lamps – look like they could have come out of your grandma's house (and most of them probably came from *someone's* grandma's), Michelle's strength is picking the ones that are timeless and pricing them accordingly. When I first lived here, these estab-lishments would have been known as 'junk shops'. Now, while the contents are the same, everything's 'vintage' or 'retro'. It's amazing how a few simple words can change how you think about something. And I should know. It's – or rather, it was – my job.

I'm peering through one of those old 3D viewers, looking at scenes of Derton in the fifties (and boy, was it beautiful then) when there's a loud 'ker-ching' sound – Michelle has one of those old cash registers (£250, if you're interested) – and as the man leaves with his purchase, I carefully put the viewer back where I found it, walk over and kiss her hello.

'That's a beauty,' I say, nodding towards the register.

Michelle nods. 'Yeah. The old things are the best. Sometimes they need a bit of a prod, but . . .'

I'm momentarily distracted by the sight through the shop window of Anna opening up the café across the street. 'Sorry?'

Michelle smiles. 'I said you sometimes need to prod the old things. Which is what I can see you're thinking of doing . . .'

'What? Me?' I fight to control the blush that's threatening to cover my entire face. 'I doubt it. Not at the moment.'

Michelle's expression changes into one of sympathy. 'I'm sorry about your dad, Josh. How's he doing?'

'Surprisingly chirpy.'

'And how are you?'

I shrug. 'Fine. It's all a bit surreal, really. We were never that close, to be honest.'

'Why not?'

I shrug again. 'We're just different.'

'And don't you think now might be a good time to put those differences behind you?'

'Hold on. Aren't we due at least another ten minutes of small talk before you tell me to sort my life out?' I must be sounding a bit exasperated, because all of a sudden, a loud snuffling from Wallace – either put out at being ignored, or trying to interrupt what he thinks might be the beginnings of an argument – distracts us.

'This is Wallace,' I say, flatly.

'He's adorable. You're adorable, aren't you?' Michelle squats down and tickles him affectionately on his stomach, and as Wallace looks up at me with a self-satisfied expression, I remind myself not to get too attached to him. He might be staying, but I'm not.

'So, anyway, Gaz said you might need a bit of a hand?'

Michelle nods as I help her back up. 'Though it's just for the summer. Is that okay?'

'I'm not planning to be here longer than that.'

'Oh. Right. Of course. Have you ever worked in a shop before, or do I need to show you the ropes?'

'You sell ropes as well?' Michelle rolls her eyes, so I point across the road at the café, or rather, where my dad's shop used to be. 'Over there. Every weekend. For about four years.'

'You'll be fine, then.'

I nod. It's the same in most shops: 'the ropes' consist of people coming in to buy things, they give you money, you give them the thing and maybe some change. Apart from the odd wrapping/putting in a bag issue, there's not really that much to do. And most of the stuff in here looks too big to wrap.

'In that case, how would three mornings a week suit? Can you open up around ten, and work until around two? I'll come in and join you for the lunchtime rush.'

I look at my watch. It's lunchtime now. 'Was that him?'

Michelle sticks her tongue out at me. 'Just you wait. It gets pretty busy from time to time. Especially at weekends. Derton's a hot destination now.'

'So Gaz tells me.'

'Tenner an hour do you?'

I do a quick calculation in my head. It'll hardly keep me in the style to which I was trying to get accustomed, but (assuming we only ever shop in that discount place) it might just cover the weekly grocery bill.

'Great. When would you like me to start?'

Michelle looks at her watch. 'Now? I've got another house clearance to go and sort through. People just keep dying, and I . . .' She pales suddenly. 'I'm so sorry, Josh.'

'Don't mention it.'

'Would you believe I was trying not to?'

'Seriously. Go and do whatever it is you have to do. We'll be fine.'

'We?'

I look down at Wallace, then up at the heavens. It's started already.

૮૭

My dad's asleep in his armchair when we – I mean, *I* – get back. With Michelle only gone for a couple of hours, apart from having to deal with some drunk I had to turf out of one of the leather arm-chairs who'd 'only come in for a bit of a sit-down' there was little else to do apart from listen to Wallace sleep. Ironically, my dad's making the same kind of noises, but I console myself that at least the loud, rattling sound means I don't have to peer at his chest to make sure he's still breathing.

I unclip Wallace's lead and he runs off into the kitchen, then I tiptoe over to my dad, and study his face. Even in the couple of weeks I've been here, he seems to have grown a little paler and thin-ner, with more flecks of grey in his beard. But then I catch sight of myself in the mirror above the fireplace and realise you could prob-ably say the same about me. Apart from the 'thinner' bit, thanks to my mum's cooking. And it occurs to me how pervasive this illness is. How it doesn't just affect the person who's got it, but everyone around them.

Not for the first time, I wonder how my mum has coped these past few months and feel guilty about not coming here sooner. And as much as I remind myself that his decline is inevitable – and that maybe it's good he's being spared the ravages of old age: the memory loss, incontinence, and loss of dignity (all symptoms of a good night out with Gaz, funnily enough) – I already know my dad's illness is something I wouldn't wish on anyone. Even Ian Baker (though it's a close thing).

And even though it's hard for me to be back here, doing what I'm doing, and for someone I'm not that close to, I need to get over it and fast. Because as tough as I'm finding it, I can only imagine how difficult it must be for him.

14.

After a few days in the shop, it soon becomes evident that the thing that working here gives me (apart from ten pounds an hour) is the ability to watch the comings and goings in Baker's Cupcakes across the street. And over the course of my first few days, I notice the following:

- Anna – always Anna – opens up each morning at around ten thirty. This is good, because the half an hour time difference in our respective appearances means we don't have to mumble an awkward hello to each other every day. I don't know what she does with herself for the thirty minutes before the café opens at eleven, but I'm guessing she's baking, and the idea of her busying herself in the kitchen, perspiring slightly from the heat of the oven, or maybe licking the icing seductively from the tips of her fingers, is one I don't allow myself to think about too much.

- She generally pops out for lunch at one on the dot, returning around half an hour later (though I can't/don't dare follow her, so I have no idea where she goes). And while it initially mystifies me that someone who works in a café should go *out* for lunch, I suppose she can't just eat cupcakes every day. She certainly doesn't have the figure of someone who does, which makes me wonder when the last time she actually ate one was. Maybe being surrounded by something every day puts you off whatever it is. Though I've been here three days, and I'm beginning to understand what people see in all this retro stuff, so maybe not.

- Ian never goes in to see her. And on the one occasion he appears, he gets to within ten metres of the door before muttering something to himself, turning round, and heading back the way he came. I don't know exactly what this means, but I'm filing it under 'interesting'.

- Who do go in are customers. Lots of them. Unlike the average of two an hour we get in here (and the average of two a day my dad used to get). Though I guess the average spend is a lot higher in Michelle's shop than in Anna's – unless Anna's customers are very greedy. Which, given the size of some of her regulars, I suspect might be the case.

- Anna leaves at some time between six and six thirty. She generally goes straight back to her mum and dad's house. Though I only know this because I've hidden round the corner while taking Wallace on one of his evening walks, then tailed her from a distance.

- Every time I see her, I wish we'd never split up.

When you're young, meeting someone new is exciting. There's so much to discover – what they like, what they're like, what they don't like, who they like and don't like. And everything about them that's made them who they are is the result of a million tiny things, different life experiences, which means that everyone you meet is different. An individual. Unlike anyone you've ever known before. And that's what makes finding out what it is you like about them – or don't like about them – fun, because you're matching all that to who and what you are.

Some relationships you win, some you lose. Some teach you to be different, or introduce you to new things. And some – even though the relationship might not last – leave a lasting impression, or change *you* a little bit, so everything you do, everyone you meet after them bears the stamp of what you've been through, good and bad, whether you like it or not.

And then you get to the point where you feel like you've learned enough. You know yourself as a person – what you like, what you don't like – and quite frankly, meeting someone new is exhausting. A chore, even, because you're too comfortable in your skin. Too set in your ways. And so the thought of changing for someone else, taking someone on board – well, it's just a step too far. And it's not because you're obstinate, or a stick-in-the-mud. Just that you know how the world works – your world – so why should you make compromises for someone else? If, indeed, you still can.

I didn't know what I was looking for before I met Mikayla, but the moment I met her, I hoped she was it. She was tall, and tanned, and, well, *polished* was the best word I could come up with to describe her. She'd never leave the house – even to go to the deli on the corner – without make-up and even then would ensure she had touch-up supplies in the huge Gucci handbag that she insisted on carrying everywhere (and that I could hardly lift). She had big (fake) breasts and an even bigger (faker) smile, and the moment I caught sight of both (well, technically all three) of those things aimed in my direction, I was hooked.

We'd met at a book launch in a gallery (ooh, get me!) in Shoreditch that Marty had done the PR for. I'd spotted her across the room and of course had been too nervous to do anything but stare at her from behind what appeared to be large, phallus-shaped glass sculptures while downing glass after glass of the publisher's Champagne, and then she'd caught me staring, and walked purposefully over to where I was standing. (That's always been my method of flirting – looking at someone I find attractive and hoping they're braver than me, and boy oh boy, Mikayla certainly was.) So I'd asked her what she thought of the art, and she'd raised one carefully-plucked eyebrow in response and said, 'You mean, do I like big dicks?', and I'd all but dropped my drink in shock.

And then she'd laughed, so I'd swiped a couple more glasses of Champagne from a passing waiter and asked her if I could buy her a drink, and she'd told me these were free and jokingly called me a cheapskate. Then later, I'd drunkenly asked her out, and she'd drunkenly accepted, so I took her to dinner that Saturday at some fiendishly trendy place she'd heard about in Hoxton that I'd had to beg Marty to get me a table at, and that had been the start of two years, nine months, and three days of the longest relationship I'd ever had. Yet there was always one mystery, one thing that puzzled me for the duration of our relationship. What on earth did she see in me? Though now I know the answer to that.

Because Mikayla regarded me as a project. Like one of the shop windows she dressed every day at work, she saw me as a blank canvas. Someone she could adorn, and transform into her ideal boyfriend. And because I was so desperate to fit in with this new world I'd been introduced to, I let her. So she'd take me round Topshop (well, Topman) after hours, and while at first I thought this was for something rather more kinky, it was really so she could use her staff discount to dress me in suits that suited me, and clothes that, while they didn't always fit me, meant I'd fit in, rather than stand out. And the problem was, the more I fitted in in Mikayla's world, the more

I stood out back home, which gave me another reason to visit even less. It was just easier that way.

But of course, the problem with projects is, what do you do when they're finished? I looked the part. I talked the talk. I knew my way around the smarter parts of London, didn't embarrass myself in restaurants when handed the wine list (and didn't stare in open-mouthed shock when handed the bill). And at that point, Mikayla decided she and I should move in together. And though I didn't want to leave my flat in Elephant and Castle, Mikayla didn't want to leave her Hoxton apartment either. And so, in a move that would set the tone of our relationship, we agreed to compromise (like the time Mikayla wanted to get a Chihuahua, and I didn't, so we compromised and got a Chihuahua) and I moved in with her. And that's when our problems started.

Because back in my mum and dad's day, it was easier. No-one lived together until they got married. Nowadays, most men move in with women because they *don't* want to get married – they see it as a compromise step – whereas most women move in with men because they see it as a stepping stone to exactly that. That's precisely where the mismatches start. Because you're having commitment forced upon you whether you know where you're going or not. And then, you just drift on, either through sheer inertia, or because your different desires tend to balance (or cancel) each other's out, and mostly, because it's so damn difficult to extract yourself. In a way, I should be grateful to my dad for getting cancer – if not, how else would I have split up with Mikayla? And the danger is that this cohabitation, which then results in a sub-standard relationship, can put you off marriage because you're more likely to form sub-standard relationships in the future, plus you're starting everything later, and you're more sceptical of the next relationship you go into.

Whereas, I realise, as I sit here morning after morning, lusting after my ex-girlfriend from behind a large wardrobe, maybe with

Anna and me, the opposite is true. Maybe now, after my Mikayla experience, is the perfect time for Anna and me to get together. We already know we like each other. We've also already had the long-term relationship that hasn't worked out. So we've worked through that. Learned (hopefully!) from it. And won't make the same mistakes again. Though I can't guarantee it.

Because the thing is, I do want to get married. Have kids. Do all the stuff that most normal people do. Most men want that. And while I could have had a version of that with Mikayla, the thing that stopped me was that it just never seemed like it would be much fun. We'd never have seen our kids (assuming we'd have seen enough of each other to have had them in the first place). Plus I always had my suspicions that Mikayla saw having children as just something on her list to tick off, and that she'd see one – a girl, probably, and knowing Mikayla, she'd have probably got what she wanted – as an accessory to dress up and parade around. Much like I was, I suppose. Then it (and she'd probably insist we called it something like Tosca) would be sent for extra tutoring in Swahili, or music lessons to learn to play some obscure instrument like a mandolin, or to boarding school, with no free time to be a child, and everyone needs that now and then – even adults. Like my mum said the other day, everyone wants someone they'd be happy doing nothing with. And I could never imagine myself doing nothing with a woman like Mikayla (personal mantra: If you're not moving forwards, you're going backwards. Which pretty much also describes my technique at the Ceroc dance classes she made us take).

And that's why the idea of starting again with Anna is intriguing. We got on back when we were still forming those all-important, lasting views and opinions of how relationships work, so she's a part of my relationship DNA just as much as I am of hers, like it or not. The only danger will be if we've gone too much of a distance apart in the intervening years, though I have to believe that's not the case.

After all, we're both single (or at least, separated) – which means the relationships we've had since then haven't been right – plus we didn't split up for any negative reasons, but because of circumstances. Nothing went wrong. We just went our separate ways. Which means we should be able to start things off pretty easily.

I try and remember what it was about us that was good because that should all be amplified now. We're more comfortable in our own skin, surely, and more worldly-wise? Plus we know what we're doing – in and out of bed. And we've got more money (well, she has) – which was one of the issues back then. So we could have more fun. And apart from a few wrinkles (sorry, laughter lines) and a couple of grey hairs, we still pretty much look the same. She's still a stunner – I'd notice her now, even if I'd never met her before – and most importantly, she's (virtually) single, which is something I have to think is A Good Thing.

But then again, can I ever forgive her and Ian for swindling my dad out of his shop? More importantly, will Anna ever forgive *me* for leaving (her) like I did? Could it ever work with me in London and her down here in Derton (and Ian wanting to beat my brains out for even talking to her)? And would it be right while my dad's dying of cancer?

It's complicated, as they say. But right now, so is everything else.

15.

In London, I don't know many people who have a garden (or a roof terrace, or even a window box, and Mikayla didn't even have any house plants, though possibly because the withering glances she used to give me on a regular basis would have killed even the hardiest cactus stone dead). And yet – if you include my dad's allotment – my parents have two.

And while the one round the house is really my mum's domain, this muddy, overgrown patch next to the recreation ground that we're walking towards (well, I'm walking/pushing; my dad's being wheeled) has been his escape, his refuge, pretty much ever since I can remember. Most men have a shed at the bottom of the garden – my dad has a whole other garden (with a whole other shed). I say 'has', but ever since he got ill, the allotment's been left to its own devices – and judging by how it looks this morning, its own devices don't include a mower or a spade.

I haven't been here since my late teens, when I used to occasionally get press-ganged (or rather, bribed) into helping dig it over a couple of times a year, and the change from the once-neat beds of carefully-tended vegetables to the Amazonian jungle-like scene that's coming into view is a little shocking. But, thanks to my bright idea of asking my dad if there was anything he wanted to do today, this is how I'm going to be spending my morning off.

'So what are we doing here, exactly?'

'There's some good veg in there. I wanted to get it out. Before . . .' He clears his throat. 'I mean, it'd be a shame to let it go to waste.'

'As opposed to just buying it from Tesco's?'

'Doesn't taste the same, does it?'

No, I want to say. *It doesn't. Because it's not mouldy, or covered in earth, or a funny shape, or half eaten by insects*, which is my memory of most of the stuff he'd bring home. But of course I don't.

It's a foul day (which is probably why Wallace has opted to stay in the car), and there aren't that many people on the neighbouring allotments, but the couple that are braving the spitting rain give friendly waves as – not without some difficulty – I push my dad along the bumpy grassy path that leads to his plot. I position him in the middle, least-muddy part, and fetch the spade and the fork from the shed, which, in contrast to the allotment itself, is perfectly ordered – all the tools clean, hanging in their appropriate places.

'Where would you like me to start?' I say, regarding the unkempt greenery in front of us in a 'painting the Forth Road Bridge' kind of way.

'Doesn't really matter, given that it's in such a state,' my dad huffs, as if that's somehow my fault, then he nods towards the far corner. 'The carrot patch.'

I can't see a carrot patch. I can't see any patches. It's all one big patch, the place is so overgrown. 'Which are the carrots?'

My dad rolls his eyes as I make my way in the direction he's pointing. 'Orange, pointy things?'

'That doesn't really help me when they're buried underground, does it?'

'Just look for a feathery top. And be careful you don't stand on them.'

'Feathery tops. Right.'

I peer closely at the mass of foliage, then reach down and grab the featheriest-looking thing and give it a tug, but it doesn't budge, so I grab it with both hands and pull. And pull. And pull so hard that the feathery top snaps off, and I fall on my backside.

There's a snort of laughter from my dad's direction, and I shoot him a glance as I climb back to my feet. 'You'll have to dig them out,' he says, as I throw away the handful of greenery I've ended up with and attempt to wipe the mud from my jeans. 'The ground's too hard.'

'Fine.' I take the spade and jam it into the ground, then pull up a heavy clod of earth. Along with half a carrot.

'And you might want to use the fork. The spade just cuts them in half.'

'The fork. Right. And you didn't think to make that particular observation beforehand?'

I position the fork next to another feathery thing and lean down on the handle with all my weight, but only succeed in getting the prongs in a couple of inches, and even trying again from a great height doesn't really improve on this. Exasperated, I turn and glare at my dad, only to see him hauling himself up out of his chair and making his way unsteadily in my direction.

'What are you doing?'

'Showing you how it's done.'

'Are you sure you . . . ?'

'I think I can still manage to dig up a carrot from my own allotment.'

I nervously hand him the heavy fork, and ready myself in case he falls, though I'm half tempted to let him if it comes to it. 'Stand back,' he says, then he expertly plunges the fork into the soil, rests one foot on it, then drives it deep into the ground and pulls back with all his weight, and as if by magic, a fountain of bright orange erupts from the soil. Slowly, carefully, my dad leans down, grabs the bunch of carrots by the greenery, knocks the earth off against the side of the fork, and raises them in triumph.

'Now you try.'

I take the fork and copy his movements, and to my surprise, get the same result. And again. And before long, I've got a plastic carrier bag full of (admittedly slightly muddy, and rather misshapen) carrots. And the funny thing is, and maybe it's because I've dug them up myself (or maybe because the effort of digging them up is making me hungry), they *do* look rather tasty.

My dad grins to himself as he makes his way carefully back to his chair. Buoyed up by my success, I grab the fork and move over to where I'm informed the potatoes are, and begin digging them up. And though it's hard work, I can see the reward in growing something yourself. Digging it out of the earth. And – of course – eating it.

'Fun, isn't it?' he says, as I stop for a breather.

'Well, "fun" wouldn't be my first choice of word.'

'You can pass these things down, you know? Father to son, and all that.'

'Won't they go off?'

'*Allotments.*'

'Yes, well, it's very kind of you. But it's a long way to drive just to get muddy while digging up a few vegetables.'

'Especially when Tesco's is just round the corner, eh?'

By the time I've collected a carrier bag's worth of potatoes, dug up a few onions, and – much to my dad's amusement – 'taken a leek', it's nearly midday, and my dad announces that we should get back, so I clean the tools and lock them away, but just as I'm wheeling him back out along the grass, he asks me to stop and spin him round again.

'Everything okay?'

He nods. 'You go and load this stuff in the car. Just leave me here for a sec.'

'I can manage both . . .'

'Josh, *please*.'

It's the first time in a while he's used that word, and his voice has gone a little crackly, and I understand, as strange as it may seem, he just wants to say goodbye. And it's then I realise that you won't just miss people, when you're gone. You'll miss *things*. He's been coming here every week for the last three decades, rain or shine. And that must be a tough thing to bid farewell to.

'I'll be in the car. Just, you know, wave, or something, when you want me to come and get you.'

'Sure.'

I load the vegetables into the boot, then sit in the car with Wallace and watch him. He's not moving, just taking in the atmosphere for perhaps the final time, and while I can't be sure whether there's a tear in his eye, I know for definite there's one in mine.

∾

As we drive back home, he seems a little quiet.

'Everything okay?' I ask eventually, still wanting to add 'apart from the cancer' to that question each time.

He nods. 'Yes, Josh. Just a shame to see the old allotment like that. I've had it for thirty years, you know?'

'Almost as long as me,' I say, stopping short of saying how I wish he'd paid me as much attention.

My dad smiles. 'I always hoped you'd take an interest. But you were always up in your room reading, or out with Gary, or that girl . . . What was her name again?'

'Which girl?'

'You know which girl.'

'Anna.'

'Anna. That's right. Lovely girl. I always thought you and she would—'

'Well, we didn't.'

'Whatever happened to her?'

I want to tell him I don't know, but I can't. 'She bought your shop, remember? Well, not her, strictly. Her husband. Ian Baker. Not that he's her husband any more. I mean, they're still married, but not, apparently, still . . . Anyway, it's now a cupcake café. She runs it. I think.'

I'm conscious I'm gabbling a bit, and he looks at me out of the corner of his eye. 'Have you been in and said hello?'

'Once,' I say.

'And how was she?'

'Fine.'

'I see. And the cupcakes?'

'I didn't get around to trying one.'

'No?'

'No.'

He peers down at Wallace, who's sitting obediently in the footwell, then reaches over and nudges me. 'You know, your mum likes cupcakes. And I wouldn't mind trying one, now I think about it.'

'Dad . . .'

'And you can have one too. My treat.'

'I'd rather not.'

'What? Why?'

I stare ahead through the windscreen. 'It's just . . . Anna and I . . . Well, we didn't part on the best of terms.'

'No?'

I try my best to ignore the raised 'o', then decide *what the hell*. 'When I left. For college. She was here, and I was there . . .' I think how best to explain this without giving him any more ammunition. 'Anyway, so that letter I gave you to give her? It explained every-thing, and . . . Well, she didn't respond. So I guess that was that.'

My dad is looking at me strangely, and I can only think it's because he's disappointed in me. 'You should have talked to her. Face to face.'

'It would have been hard to know what to say.'

'I thought words were your thing?'

'They are. Just . . . on paper. Or so I thought. Because she didn't reply.'

'You should talk to her now. Explain.'

I grip the steering wheel harder. 'What would be the point?'

My dad lets out an exaggerated sigh. 'No, of course. Why waste your time trying to make things right with Anna when you've got a lovely girl like Mikayla waiting for you back in London . . . ? Oh, hang on . . .'

When I don't answer, he cracks open his window and takes a breath of sea air. 'I'll come with you if you like?'

'Why would you possibly think I'd like that?'

'Come on, son. Faint heart never won fair lady, and all that.'

'Just drop it, will you?'

'Okay, okay.' There's a pause, and then: 'Though I'd still like a cupcake.'

I glare across at him. We both know he doesn't want a cupcake. He wants to embarrass me. Or at least try and play Cupid where there's a 'No Firing Arrows' sign quite clearly erected. 'Can't I get you one from Tesco's?'

'I'm sure they won't be as good.'

'Dad . . .'

'It won't take long. Look, we're just around the corner from the shop now. I won't say anything. I promise.'

'But . . .' I catch sight of the pathetic expression he's making, and sigh. 'Okay. But you have to go in and get it yourself.'

'Bit awkward, son, what with the cancer.'

'Didn't seem to affect you when you were digging up the carrots.'

He makes a pained face. 'I think I might have overdone it a bit.'

Luckily – or unluckily, depending on your point of view – there's a parking space right outside Baker's Cupcakes, so I reluctantly pull the BMW into it. From what I can make out through the window, Anna isn't behind the counter, so maybe I'll get away with this if I can manage a speedy exit. 'Right,' I say. 'You stay there. What flavour do you want?'

'They have flavours?' My dad frowns. 'I'll have to come in and choose, in that case.'

'*Dad . . .*'

But he's already heaving himself out of the car, so I run round and remove his wheelchair from the back and help him into it, and two minutes later I'm pushing him in through the door of somewhere that just a couple of short days ago I'd walked out of in shame. Anna's nowhere to be seen, so I quickly wheel him up to the counter so he can get a good look into the glass cabinet. I have to say, the cakes do look good, and I'm almost regretting leaving the two freebies Anna gave me the other day.

'Well?' I say, impatiently.

'I can't decide. They all look so good.'

'Shall we just get one of each, then?'

'Now now, Josh. No need to rush.' He surveys the contents of the cabinet again, then looks up expectantly at the girl behind the counter, but when she says 'Can I help you?', instead of enquiring about the flavours, he does exactly what he's promised not to. 'I think I know the woman that owns this place. Anna Coleman? Though I suppose she's "Baker" now. "A Baker". Oh, that's funny.' As the girl smiles politely, my dad peers towards the kitchen. 'Is she around, by any chance?'

'Dad—'

'Sure,' says the girl, brightly. 'She's just in the back. I'll go and get her, shall I?'

'Would you?' says my dad, as innocently as he can, which – quite frankly – isn't very.

'Right.' I reach down and put the wheelchair's brakes on, wishing I could do the same with his mouth. 'I'll just wait outside.'

'You'll do no such thing,' he says quickly and just as Anna appears from the kitchen, but when she catches sight of me, her face darkens.

'I thought I told you—'

'Anna?' says my dad, in a voice that I'm sure has suddenly become several degrees weaker than normal.

She glances around the shop, trying to locate the source of the sound, then once she's lowered her eyes to wheelchair height, her expression goes through a serious of complicated changes.

'Mr. Peters?'

'Phil, please,' he says.

'Phil,' she repeats, walking round to our side of the counter and kissing him hello. He and Anna always got on. *Like the daughter I never had*, he used to say, then I used to remind him that if that were the case, I'd be done for incest, which would always shut him up. 'I'm guessing I wouldn't like the answer to "how are you?"'

'Cancer,' he says, simply, making the 'what can you do?' face, and at once, even though I'm sure she tries her best to stop it, Anna's hand goes to her mouth.

'Are you . . . ? Is it . . . ?'

'I'm afraid so,' he says.

They stare at each other for a moment or two, then Anna's eyes flick toward me in a 'why didn't you say anything?' kind of way. 'I'm so sorry,' she says, reaching down to rest a hand on his shoulder.

'Thank you.' He pats her hand, then gazes around the interior of the café. It's a million miles away from how it looked when he owned it, and I can't help wondering whether he's upset by the change or is genuinely impressed with how Anna's transformed the shop. 'The old place looks . . . different.'

Anna nods. 'I hope you approve of what we've done to it?'

As I bristle a little at the word *we*, my dad smiles. 'I do. I always hoped Josh would take it over, but . . . Well, I guess you're the next best thing.'

'Thank you.' Anna rubs his arm gently. 'That means a lot.'

'And you're doing well?'

'Yes, thank goodness!'

'Cupcakes selling like hot cakes, eh?' he says, smiling at his own joke.

'They are,' says Anna. 'Though obviously, they're not hot. Otherwise the icing would fall off.'

'I see,' says my dad.

We stand there awkwardly for a moment, then Anna smiles broadly. 'So, what can I get you?'

My dad frowns. 'Well, I heard a rumour that this was the best cupcake café in Derton.'

Anna lets out a short, twinkling laugh, and at the once familiar sound, my heart does a somersault. 'True. Though strictly speaking, it's the only cupcake café in Derton.'

'And what would you recommend?'

Anna points to the glass cabinet in front of her. 'Well, today's special is lemon meringue. I seem to remember you being rather partial to that.'

I cringe. One of my mum's specialities. In the days Anna used to come over for Sunday lunch.

'One of those, then. And . . .' My dad thinks for a moment. 'That red one looks nice,' he says, pointing to the last few remaining red velvet cupcakes.

'Good choice,' says Anna.

'You can always tell. Old shop-keeping trick. Buy the thing there's the least left of. That's the way you know you're getting the good stuff.'

'Aha. But we could just be putting a few out. They may be the worst, so we're using that trick to shift them.' She laughs again. 'Though in this case, you're spot on.' She reaches behind her and picks up a carton. 'How many would you like?'

'One, please.' He turns to me. 'See anything you like the look of, Josh?'

'Come on, Dad. Anna's got other customers to serve.'

My dad winks at Anna. 'Better make that two of them, then.'

As Anna starts to place them carefully in the box, I clear my throat, and I know it's childish, but I can't help myself. 'Actually, I won't have one.'

'You won't?'

I shake my head. 'No, thanks.'

'You used to love cakes.'

'Yes, well, people change.'

'Suit yourself. But I'll take two anyway.' He grins at Anna, then jabs a thumb in my direction. 'He might change his mind.'

'Yes. He does that.'

I stare at the two of them incredulously, then shake my head. 'Well, I'll be waiting in the car,' I say, before flouncing out.

A few minutes later, my dad appears, a box of cupcakes balanced precariously on his lap, wheeling himself carefully through the shop doorway and towards where I'm leaning against the bonnet, and although I know it's not very nice of me, I don't move to help him.

'Well, that was incredibly rude!' he announces.

'What, me?'

'Yes, you!'

'How do you work that one out?'

'Anna was being so nice, and you insult her by turning down the thing she makes her living out of.'

'I just didn't want you to waste your money.'

'I didn't have to.'

'Pardon.'

'These were on the house.'

'What?'

'No charge. Gratis. Free.'

'I know what "on the house" means. Hold on.'

'Where are you going?'

'Back in a sec.'

I head back into the shop. For some reason, the idea of Anna giving my dad freebies just because she now knows he's ill yet still being happy about ripping him off over the shop strikes me as disrespectful, and perversely I find myself not wanting to owe her anything. I march up to the counter (and up to a surprised-looking Anna), pull my wallet out of my pocket, extract a five pound note, and slap it down on the top of the glass cabinet.

'Here.'

'What's this?'

'For the cupcakes.'

'Josh . . .'

I glare at her, doing my best to ignore the fact that her eyes are red-rimmed. 'He doesn't need your charity.'

'Why didn't you tell me?'

'Tell you what? And when?'

'The other day. That your dad was . . . That he had . . . Has . . .'

'Yeah, that would have been nice of me, wouldn't it? *Hi, Anna, long time no see. My dad's dying. How are things in the world of cupcakes?*'

'That's not what I meant,' she says angrily. 'Your dad was always so lovely to me.'

'Which was why you made him such an insulting offer for the shop.'

'What?'

I stare at her in disbelief. Is this really how she decided to get me back – by getting at my dad? Did I hurt Anna that much, that she'd want to take her revenge in such a horrible way? At the time, I'd have doubted she was capable of it, but now? Especially since she went and married Ian.

'I spoke to the agent. He said you came in so far under the asking price it was an insult. And because my dad was worried there was something seriously wrong with him – a worry that turned out to be well-founded – he had no choice but to accept. And now you try and buy him off with a few free cupcakes?'

'Under? But . . . We paid the asking price.'

'You paid thirty thousand pounds.'

'I think you'll find we paid three times that. Ninety thousand. Not that it's any of your—'

'Says who?'

'Says . . .' She stops abruptly. 'Well, Ian. And I certainly didn't know your dad was selling up because he was ill.'

'Well, now you do.'

'I . . .' She shakes her head in disbelief. 'I don't know what to say.'

'Sorry would be a start.'

She sighs. 'I'm sorry, Josh.'

'Not to *me*.' I turn my gaze towards the street, where my dad is sitting in his wheelchair next to the car, feeding Wallace what's probably my cupcake through the window.

Anna gives me a look, though it's hard to decipher, then she walks outside and over to where my dad is sitting and leans down to talk to him. I see her start to cry, and he reaches up and hugs her for a long, long time.

And then Anna's walking back into the shop, and she can't look at me when she passes, but all I hear is her whispered 'Happy now?', which is ironic, because happy is the *last* thing I currently am.

❧

My dad doesn't say much on the drive back, though whether that's because he's still mad at me, or because of something Anna said to him (or because the smells coming from Wallace's rear end as a result of the cupcake he's eaten mean we're having to breathe through our mouths) I can't be sure, and I sure as hell don't want to ask.

When we get to the house, and once I've unloaded the wheelchair, the vegetables, Wallace, and my dad from the car, my mum's nowhere to be seen, then we hear laughter from the back garden, where I'm surprised to find her chatting with someone who I recognise after a few seconds as Mr. Ronson. This is a shock because a) Mr. Ronson is my old English teacher, and b) I haven't seen him since I left school some eighteen years ago but he looks *exactly the same* as he did then, down to the jacket with the patches on the elbows and the knitted tie we always used to joke were the only things in his wardrobe, given how he seemed to wear them every single day. In fact, he looks so much like he always used to that I find myself replying a nervous 'sir' to his 'hello, Josh', which makes both my mum and dad burst out laughing.

'And how's my star pupil?'

I blush. 'I don't know who that'd be.'

'Come on, Josh. How many other people do you think went off and studied English at university after being taught by me?'

I think about this for a moment. If the answer's 'none', then that doesn't exactly reflect very highly on his teaching skills. 'Well . . .'

'And went on to work in publishing . . .'

'Er . . .'

'. . . and then went on to write a book?'

'Yes, well, I haven't got it published yet.' *Or finished it*, I think.

'Well, I'm sure you will,' says Mr. Ronson. He turns to my mum and dad. 'You must be very proud.'

My dad clears his throat awkwardly, but my mum is nodding enough for the both of them. 'Oh yes,' she says. 'And, Josh, guess what?'

I stare at her blankly.

'Mr. Ronson thinks you should go back to St. Martin's.'

'What for? Did I forget to take a GCSE, or something?'

Mr. Ronson laughs. 'No, nothing like that. I'd like you to come and give a talk to year eleven. Sort of a motivational thing. You tell them about your career, lessons you've learned, those kinds of things. It might help them make some choices. Keep a few of them out of dead end jobs. Or even prison.'

'Pardon?'

Mr. Ronson smiles. 'Just my little joke. Well, apart from a couple. There'll be no keeping them from Her Majesty's pleasure. But the rest . . .'

'I'm not sure.'

'Go on. Apart from anything else it'll be good for them to hear that there's a life outside Derton.'

I glance across at my dad, who suddenly seems more interested in something on his shoe, and that makes my mind up for me.

'All right, then,' I say. 'When would you like me to come in?'

16.

But first things first: it's the following morning, and I'm waiting outside a hotel ballroom near Victoria Station, about to audition for *Catch Me If You Can*. While the email telling me I'd been selected came as a surprise (and I'm doing this against my better judgement) we could do with the money, plus it's something my dad's said he'd like to see, and at the moment (like it or not), it's all about him.

Of course, I haven't told my parents where I'm going. These are only auditions, after all, so there's no guarantee I'll get on the actual show, and while the shame of messing up on national television is one thing, the shame of not being good enough to even get picked for the chance to mess up on national television is something else entirely.

Though as I look around me, I have to say I quite fancy my chances. There's a bunch of retirees – not surprising, really, given that the show's aired when most people are at work – plus a few people who look like working is something that's never really troubled (or even occurred to) them. Slightly worrying is the guy sitting opposite me leafing through an atlas, obviously doing some last-minute geography cramming, and I wonder whether I should have a quick flick through Wikipedia on my phone, but what on earth would I look at? I was okay at college, when we pretty much knew the specific syllabus (and therefore what to revise), but on a quiz show where the subject matter is as wide as 'general' knowledge? You can't get much more general than that.

For research purposes, I've watched a few old episodes on YouTube on my way here on the train this morning. Not to try and learn the answers – after all, they're hardly going to ask questions they've already featured, are they? – but to get more of a feel for the show, and in terms of contestants (apart from the obvious swots) it seems like they like people who bring a little more to the party than simply the ability to get the answers right. Some of my fellow auditionees have clearly decided this is the case: in their desire to get noticed, a few of them have dressed up somewhat wackily – one of the women is in a glittering jacket that it's probably dangerous to look directly at, another is wearing a pair of stilettos with heels so high they look like a dare, and one (though it's a woman, at least) is even wearing a tutu. My biggest dilemma this morning was whether to put on a tie, but the fact that I didn't have one with me (and the two my dad owns were so stained a forensics lab could use them for teaching practice) kind of answered that question for me.

At about quarter past nine, we're ushered into the ballroom, where we're handed a sticker with our name on it to fix to our chests and directed to a circle of chairs set up in one corner. Ominously, there's a camera on a tripod set up to one side, and once we've all sat down, a young girl wearing a headset bounces into the middle.

'Morning!' she says, brightly. 'I'm Louisa.'

We all mumble our hellos, and she puts on a pout.

'That wasn't very enthusiastic, was it?'

We repeat ourselves, a little louder this time. Though I'm almost deafened by the woman in the tutu, who's decided to sit next to me and whose name, the tag barely holding on to her ample chest informs me, is 'Devon'.

Louisa smiles her approval. 'I'd like you to start by introducing yourselves to the group. Tell us your name, where you're from, and why you want to be on *Catch Me If You Can*.'

There's a collective groan, though I've seen this on the show, and it's only a ten second introduction, but even the thought of it seems a little too much for some of the people here. And if they're worried about doing it now, how are they going to feel with a camera in their face in an actual studio?

Louisa starts with the person on my left, who nervously tells us his name is Al, and he's forty-four, and from London, and wants to be on the show because he wants to buy a new caravan. Next up is Marian from Maidstone, who looks two decades older than the thirty-five she claims she is and is here because it's her favourite programme after *Countdown*, and it continues in this fashion – people who watch it every day, people who love several of the show's resident know-alls, and even one person who says it's been 'his life's ambition' to go on a quiz show (though he's in his sixties and this is apparently the first one he's auditioned for).

Eventually, it gets to Devon, who looks to her left and her right, takes a deep breath, then announces, 'My name's Devon, and I'm from Cornwall . . .' She pauses so everyone can laugh, and when no-one does, lets out a loud cackle herself. 'I want to be on the show because I'm Lesley's biggest fan, and I'm just desperate to meet him.'

She peels off her cardigan to reveal a t-shirt with Lesley's grinning face on the front, then swivels to her left and right so we can all get a good look. Unfortunately, the position of her breasts and the pointiness of her bra makes Lesley appear as though his eyes are out on stalks, which is probably how he'll *actually* look if she gets on.

Louisa makes a quick note on her clipboard, which I'm sure probably reads 'stalker', then turns to me expectantly, so I clear my throat and take a deep breath. 'My name's Josh, and I'm . . .' – and

I have to swallow hard before I say it, as for some reason, the admission always makes me feel like I'm at an AA meeting – '. . . from Derton. And I want to be on *Catch Me If You Can* because . . .' Then I dry up. Why do I want to be on the show? Everyone else seems to have a reason, and while winning the money would be nice, I can hardly just say that. I'm not a huge fan of the programme, I'm not desperate to be on TV, and I certainly don't want to roger Lesley senseless like Devon evidently does.

Everyone's looking at me, and Louisa is getting a bit twitchy, and I don't want to blow it at this early stage, so I decide *what the hell*. 'Well, because my dad loves the show – he never misses an episode – and he's only got a few weeks to live because he's got cancer, and he's told me it'd really make him proud to see me on it, and as far as I know, he's never been proud of me, so this is, like, my last chance to, you know . . .' I clear my throat again. 'Make him.'

I stop talking and sit back in my chair, because Louisa's staring at me, open-mouthed. The rest of the group are giving me different looks – some of them of contempt, because I've obviously trumped all of their reasons – and even Devon seems to have stopped smiling maniacally for the first time since she walked into the room.

'Right, well . . .' says Louisa eventually, then she makes another note on her clipboard and fixes a smile on her face. 'Thanks, everyone, for sharing' (and she's pointedly not looking at me as she says this). 'Now, it's general knowledge quiz time.' There are more groans, which surprises me even more seeing as we're all here auditioning to be on a general knowledge quiz, then she hands us each a clipboard with a piece of paper attached, along with a pen that has the show's name and a tiny picture of Lesley's head printed on the side, which, given Devon's audible gasp, I know will be ending up as the centrepiece of the 'Lesley' shrine she probably has in her front room at home.

The questions themselves are pretty easy – there are even a couple of obscure 'book' ones that I'm sure I've got right and that I think most of the others might struggle with, which can only count in my favour – and even though I catch Devon trying to peer at my answers a couple of times (like Ian used to do back at school, though then I actually let him), I'm pretty pleased with how I think I've done.

We're then split into two groups where we have to play charades, which goes without incident, apart from when Devon thinks Marian's mime of someone playing trombone in a marching band is a porno movie called *Deep Throat*. After half an hour or so of this, we're sent back outside to wait like naughty schoolchildren. Strangely, no-one wants to talk to each other, as if we're still on trial, or in case showing some friendliness/weakness might jeopardise our chances even now.

Finally, after an agonisingly awkward ten minutes or so, Louisa ushers us back inside. 'Right,' she announces. 'You've all done really well.' Though it's clear we haven't, as the very next thing she says is 'But there are only two of you who made it through to appear on the show. And those two are . . .'

As she pauses for dramatic effect, we stare at her nervously, watching her mouth closely, obviously trying to see whether the word she's about to form starts with the first letter of our names. 'Devon, and . . .'

But we don't hear the second name, mainly because Devon (I'm guessing chosen for entertainment value – either that, or Louisa secretly hates Lesley) has let out such a scream of delight that it's impossible to hear *anything* – and for several seconds afterwards, given how my eardrums are ringing. As the rest of the group stare daggers at her, I have to ask.

'I'm sorry, Louisa. Who was the other person?'

Louisa smiles. 'You, Josh,' she says.

17.

It seems I'm not the only one for whom stardom beckons, as I'm sitting in the shop this morning, willing the numbers on the retro digital clock (£25, but we'll take £20 if you've spotted the slight crack in the glass) on the counter in front of me to count up a little faster, when Gaz appears at the door.

'Michelle here?'

I shake my head. 'Off with her fancy man.'

'I *am* her fancy man.'

'Poor Michelle,' I say, then ignore the rude sign Gaz is making. 'House clearance.'

'Excellent.' Gaz reaches into the carrier bag he's hiding under his jacket and produces a rolled-up poster and some Sellotape. 'Give us a hand putting this up, will you?'

'Sure.' I haul myself out of my chair, grateful to have something to do, and hold the poster as Gaz tapes it to the inside of the window.

'What do you think?'

'It's the wrong way round.'

'You're not supposed to be able to see it from inside the shop.'

'What's it for?'

'Well, seeing as you asked . . .' Gaz beckons me to follow him outside. 'Ta-da!' he says, pointing at a rather grainy picture of four slightly awkward-looking thirty-something-year-old men with forty-something-inch waistlines dressed as if they've raided some teenager's wardrobe. Plastered across the photo, there's a line of vivid red lettering that reads 'F**K THAT! LIVE AT THE SUB-MARINE! SATURDAY 21ST!'

'A Take That tribute band?'

'That's right!' For some reason (though it could simply be the effect of all those capital letters and exclamation marks) Gaz seems quite excited. 'You coming?'

'Why on earth would I want to come to something like that?'

'Well . . .' He grins, then taps the glass in front of the photo, and when I peer a little closer, the face on the left is a face I recognise.

'*You're kidding*?'

'It's just a hobby, really. A laugh,' Gaz says nonchalantly, though he's blushing a little.

'That'll be most people's reaction. Especially when they hear you sing.'

'You've never heard me sing.'

'Can you?'

'A bit. Besides, half of the original group can't.'

'But at least they can dance.'

'You'd be surprised.'

'I already am.'

'You know that song "Moves like Jagger"? That's me, that is.'

'So you dance like a seventy-something-year-old man?' I fold my arms, trying to reconcile the Gaz I know with the photograph in the window. 'How many of these gigs have you done?'

'Including this one?'

'Yes, Gaz.'

'One.'

I peer at the poster again. 'And why did you call yourselves . . . You know, *that*?'

'There was already a Fake That. So we thought . . .'

'And are you any good?'

Gaz hesitates, which – combined with how he's had to sneak into the shop to put his poster up – probably tells me all I need to know.

'So which one are you?'

He jabs a finger at the photo. '*That* one, obviously.'

'Which one of Take That?'

Gaz puffs his chest out, though it's really more a case of raising the bulk of his beer belly upwards. 'Who d'you think?'

When I don't answer, Gaz looks a little offended. 'Gary Barlow, of course!'

'Which one's he again?'

'You know. The—'

'Wasn't he the fat one?'

'The lead singer! And we're not supposed to be lookalikes,' huffs Gaz. 'I'm him because . . .'

'Because you're a Northerner called Gary?'

Gaz looks even more offended, though possibly because I've guessed the right answer. 'So, you'll come?'

'To see a group of middle-aged men poncing about in badly-fitting outfits trying to sing songs that I didn't like when they first came out?'

'Yeah.'

'Gaz, it's a *Saturday night*.'

'And you've got something better to do, have you?'

I open my mouth to say something, then close it again. We both already know the answer to that question.

~

I'm walking back to my mum and dad's when my phone bleeps – a message from Mikayla containing a photo of what I guess is a Sri Lankan beach with the caption 'Wish you were here?' – when I'm nearly knocked off my feet by someone hurrying in the opposite direction.

'I'm so sorry,' I say, as I realise it's a woman I've bumped into and a very solidly built one at that. 'Are you okay?'

'I'll live.' The woman smiles flatly, then she peers at me and her face lights up. 'Josh? Josh Peters?'

'Er . . . Yes?'

'Don't you recognise me?'

'Of course I do. Hi!' I lie, though there is something familiar about her. 'You just look . . . Well, *different*, that's all.'

'I should hope so!' says the woman, indignantly.

'How have you been?' I say, playing for time, hoping a name will pop into my head.

'Never better,' she says, then her face falls. 'I heard about your dad, Josh. I'm sorry.'

I shrug. I've been doing that a lot recently where he's concerned. 'What can you do?'

'What you're doing, I suppose.' The woman smiles grimly. 'So, how's life been treating you since school?'

'Oh, you know.'

'How long are you here for?'

'As long as my dad is,' I say, then realise that sounds a little harsh. 'So hopefully for a while.'

'Great.' The woman smiles again. 'So, we should . . . You know, maybe with Gaz.'

'Yeah,' I say, then wonder if I've just committed myself to some kind of threesome, still no clearer as to who it is I'm speaking to, which is even more worrying, given how much she seems to know about me. And even though she's mentioned school, that doesn't really help, seeing as St. Martin's was a boys' school.

My initial reaction is to wonder whether she's some one-night stand who I probably mortally offended by never calling again, and if I can't remember her name now . . . Well, Derton's too small a town to make enemies of every woman from my past that I bump into, and I've already made one more of those than I need. But then again, I don't remember *any* one-night stands. Mainly because I was too busy standing next to Anna.

Just as I'm in danger of running out of small talk, I have an idea. The new Starbucks is on the opposite corner, and if I remember correctly, it might just help me out of my dilemma. 'Listen,' I say. 'I was just on my way for a coffee, if you fancied one?'

The woman glances at her watch, then smiles at me. 'Sure. Though I might have to drink and run . . .'

I nod across the street. 'We could try the new Starbucks?'

'Ooh, exciting. I've been meaning to give it a go.'

As we cross the road, I half-smile at the idea of a new Starbucks being exciting, but when you live in a place like Derton, I suppose you have to work with what you're given. *Or not*, it suddenly occurs to me, as the distant memory of the other night's drunken conversation with Gaz suddenly raises its hand at the back of my brain, and I almost trip over the kerb in shock. *Andy Wilson has had a sex change*. And this (unless I'm very much mistaken) might well be him (or rather, her).

Trouble is, I've never met anyone who's had a sex change before, and apart from the obvious (and there's no way I'm going to try and check *that*) I can't think of a single way to work it out without asking, and if I was worried about causing offence for not remembering a name, then getting *that* wrong's even worse. He – I mean, *she* – doesn't seem particularly hairy, but then again, thanks to Mikayla, I've seen the wonders that several hours in the beautician's can work. And while s/he's, ahem, somewhat big-boned, Derton's not exactly known (Anna aside) for its selection of delicate, beautiful women. And while I remember reading something about the Adam's apple always being the way you can tell, that's made impossible by the silk scarf that maybe-Andy's wearing around his (sorry, *her*. I'll get the hang of this soon, I promise) neck. Which could be on purpose. Or just a fashion statement. Aargh!

As we reach the opposite pavement, I start surreptitiously looking for clues. Her breasts are obviously false – I could tell that from the collision – but then again, so are Mikayla's, and I'm sure (I hope!) *she* was never a man. Plus she holds Starbucks' door open for me. Though when I think about this, it doesn't really prove anything. If you're forward-thinking enough to go through an operation like that, then maybe gender stereotyping is something you react against.

The other problem with having the door held open for me is that it means I'm first at the counter, and my plan is in danger of failing, unless . . .

'I'd like a grande cappuccino, please, to go,' I say to the barista.

'The same,' says maybe-Andy, and then – and I almost want to high-five myself at the brilliance of my strategy – it happens.

'Name?' asks the barista, looking at me, so I say 'Josh,' which she writes on the side of my cup.

'And?'

I turn round and frown. 'And . . . ?'

'That's right. But with an 'i' now.'

'Pardon?' says the barista.

'Andi,' says Andi (for it is she!). 'With an "i". As in A-N-D-I.'

'Andi it is,' says the barista, scribbling the letters on the side of Andi's cup, and I have to stop myself from repeating the sentence.

I reach into my pocket for my wallet, but Andi waves me away. 'I'll get these.'

'Thanks.'

'You're welcome, Josh.' She smiles. 'It's really good to see you.'

'And you. You look . . .' I dry up, not because I can't think of an appropriate word, but more because I can think of so many.

Andi laughs. 'I'm guessing Gaz told you?'

'About?'

'What do you think?' Andi makes a face, and I roll my eyes at my own stupidity.

'Sorry. Yes. He mentioned something.'

'And at the risk of repeating myself, what do you think?'

I look her up and down. 'I'm amazed,' I say, as the barista calls our names. Which is pretty much the truth.

We carry our drinks to an outside table, and as I follow Andi through the door, I have to admit, she looks *great*. And while that's probably as much due to the confidence with which she's carrying herself as her recent surgery, once we've sat down, I can't help but ask.

'So, the operation . . . Do they just . . . ? Stop me if I'm prying.'

'Not at all,' says Andi. 'Some bits they remove, some bits they, well, *redistribute*.'

'And can you still . . . Well, not 'still', if you see what I mean, but do you . . . ?'

'Oh, it all works.' Andi grins. 'Don't worry, that was one of the first things I asked!'

'Was it painful?'

Andi laughs. 'Not as painful as the previous thirty years trapped in the wrong body, believe me.' She leans across the table and lowers her voice. 'Tell me, Josh. Did you ever suspect?'

'God no!' I say, then catch myself. 'Well, I mean, we knew you weren't the most, you know . . .'

'Manly?'

'Something like that. But not to the extent where . . .' I sip my coffee. 'I mean, there were several kids who you'd have bet might have, you know . . . More so than you. Why didn't you say anything?'

'Yeah, great plan. Because teenage boys are so understanding when it comes to that kind of thing.'

'We would have . . .' I stop talking, and Andi frowns at me.

'What's the matter?'

'I've just remembered. That "tarts and vicars" party we went to at Gaz's.'

'What about it?'

'Gaz and I dressed as vicars. As did everyone else from school. Except for you. And you looked pretty convincing, now I come to think of it.'

Andi pouts at me across the top of her cappuccino. 'What can I say?'

'And how did your parents take it?'

'My mum had always wanted a daughter, so she was made up – though when they first saw *me* made up . . .' She laughs. 'It took my dad a bit longer to get used to the idea – I think he was worried he'd suddenly have to pay for my wedding. Anyway, he eventually came round.'

'It must have been a big decision?'

'Nope. It was inevitable, really. I only wish I'd done it sooner.'

'Well, I'm glad you have.' I pick up my coffee, and 'cheers' it against Andi's cup. 'And that you're happy. Congratulations.'

'Thanks, Josh.' Andi smiles at me, then her eyes flick to somewhere over my shoulder, and she frowns. 'Uh-oh.'

'What's the matter?'

'There. In the car. It's . . .'

But I don't hear the rest of the sentence, because it's drowned out by a deep, throaty exhaust rumble. It's Ian, driving past in an electric-blue Subaru, and as he slows down in front of us, he lowers his window.

'Well, if it isn't, Josh!' he shouts, an idiotic grin on his face. 'With Andy the tranny!'

As Andi blushes, I feel a sudden flash of anger. 'That doesn't even rhyme properly!' I shout back.

It's hardly the greatest of comebacks, but it seems to do the trick. Ian's expression changes, as if he can't work out whether he won or lost that particular exchange, then a car honks behind him, and he accelerates noisily off down the road.

'Thanks, Josh.'

'Hey. Don't mention it.' I reach across the table and clap Andi on the shoulder. 'It's very brave of you, you know?'

'What? Having the op?'

'No – having it and staying here in Derton. I'm surprised you didn't want to go somewhere else. Start again. Where no-one knew you as Andy.'

'Why?'

'Yes. With a "y".'

'No, I meant why would I go somewhere else? Derton's my home, Josh. Everyone I've ever known, everyone I've ever loved, they're all here. And if they can't accept the real me . . .' Andi clicks the lid onto her cup and stands up. 'Well, that's their problem.'

I look up at her in amazement. When I went to London, I'd thought it'd be the best place for me to start again. I reckoned I could lose myself in amongst the millions of people there, and that by losing myself, I might eventually find out who I really was. But then again, I suppose Andi's always known who she really was. Though it's taken her until now to be able to admit that to everyone else.

'So,' she continues. 'Work calls, I'm sorry to say.'

'Yeah? Where are you . . . ?'

'You know the new gallery on the seafront?'

'You work there?' I say, more than a little impressed.

'The pub next to it.' Andi grins. 'So I'll see you around?'

It's a question more than a statement, and while I'm sure she's partly referring to the fact that I won't be here for long, there's probably a part of her that's after reassurance too. And the one thing I'm sure of is that I'm happy to give it.

'Yeah. Definitely. I'll get Gaz to arrange something. It'll be just like old times!'

Andi laughs. 'No, Josh. It won't. Thank goodness.'

We do the same awkward hug/handshake that Gaz and I danced around that first day in Tesco's, then Andi strides confidently back across the road, and as I sit there and finish my coffee, I realise she's taught me a lesson.

Because I came back expecting things here to be the same, and it's beginning to look like the only thing that hasn't actually moved on is me.

18.

My mum hasn't driven for years. She can drive (as she's keen to point out, especially when her newly-renewed licence arrives in the post this morning). It's just that after they got married, she got fed up with the 'tips' my dad would give her whenever she was behind the wheel, and decided for the sake of their marriage it was better if she stopped. Besides, as my dad is fond of quoting, everywhere is within walking distance if you have the time, and in a town the size of Derton, most places are even if you don't.

Anyway, my dad's convinced her it'll be a good idea if she starts again, for 'afterwards', as we've decided to refer to it. Which is why (having left my dad in charge of Wallace, although I'm already starting to suspect it's the other way round) I've driven the Rover to the Tesco superstore's car park and found a space as far away from any parked cars as I can. Though it's been five minutes since we swapped places, and as yet, she hasn't touched the steering wheel.

'Now, you do remember what to do?'

My mum nods as she stares nervously through the windscreen. 'Mirror, signal, manoeuvre, yes?'

'That's right. Although you'll have to actually start the engine before you can do that last one.'

She gives me a sideways glance, changes the position of her seat, checks she can reach the steering wheel, moves the gearstick about a bit, adjusts the mirror, adjusts her hair in the mirror, then reaches down and turns the key, and the Rover's one litre engine coughs into life.

'So, it's accelerator, brake, clutch?' she asks, peering at the pedals. 'A, B, C?'

I pat her arm encouragingly. 'That's right. Though technically it's the other way round.'

'Pardon?'

'C, B, and A. If you're reading from the left. Which is, you know, the way people normally read.'

'Right.'

'So, clutch down, put it into gear, gently press the accelerator . . .'

She mouths the names of the various pedals a few times, then presses the clutch down gingerly and moves the gearstick into first.

'. . . raise the clutch slowly until you feel it start to bite, hand-brake off, and . . .'

'What's that?'

'What do you mean?'

'That violent jerk.'

I peer anxiously through the window, then realise she wasn't referring to Ian Baker. 'We've stalled.'

My mum shakes her head. 'Sorry, Josh. It'll come back to me.'

'No worries.'

She starts the car again, though she's left it in gear and with the handbrake off, so we lurch forward, which means I have to grab the handbrake as the engine stalls again.

'Remember, always check you're in neutral whenever you turn the key.'

'Neutral. Right.' She reaches for the gear lever, slots it into the appropriate position, wiggles it to make sure, and starts the car again.

'Now remember, this time, give it some gas.'

'Gas. Okay . . .' My mum presses her right foot down flat, as if she's preparing to drag race across the car park.

'A bit less . . .'

'Sorry.'

'A bit less . . .'

'*Sorry*, Josh.'

'Right, now . . .'

We lurch forward, but this time she's forgotten to take the handbrake off, so we stall for a third time, and she turns to me in frustration. 'It's just so hard to remember.'

'When was the last time you actually drove?'

My mum thinks for a moment. 'I'm not sure, Josh. Possibly when you left?'

'Well, that's eighteen years ago, so you're bound to be a bit rusty.'

For the next five minutes, it becomes apparent that 'rusty' is a somewhat kind description, as my mum's driving skills are so corroded they'd probably crumble into a cloud of red dust the moment another car came anywhere near her.

'I think it's because you're in the car,' she says, exasperatedly.

'Trust me, I'm beginning to wish I wasn't.' I smile as encouragingly as I can. 'Let me do the handbrake. You just put us into gear, then gently rev the engine, then slowly raise the clutch . . .'

My mum does as told, and the moment I feel the clutch bite I release the handbrake, and finally, as if by some miracle . . .

'We're moving!'

'We are! Now, into second.'

My mum looks down at the gear knob, and frowns.

'What's the matter?'

'I don't have my reading glasses. I can't tell which one is second.'

'Never mind. Just press the clutch down, and . . .' I wait until I see the clutch pedal moving, then I put my hand over hers on the gear knob and ease it into second gear. 'Now, clutch up slowly . . .'

My mum does as told, and the car speeds up, and she looks across at me, beaming with pride. 'This is fun! What now?'

'You might want to try something we in the driving community refer to as "steering",' I say quickly, nodding through the windscreen at a large tree planted, for some reason, right in the middle of the car park, and exactly where we're headed.

To her credit, my mum doesn't miss a beat. 'Which way?'

'Pretend it's a roundabout. Go round it that way.'

'A roundabout. Okay,' she says, though we continue to head towards the tree. 'And that would be?'

'Clockwise, Mum.'

She narrows her eyes, probably trying to picture which way the hands go round on the clock in the kitchen. Unfortunately, we're going at around twenty miles per hour, which means the tree is approaching a little more rapidly than I'd like. Then suddenly, as if it's all coming back to her, she takes a leisurely swing to the left, then pulls the wheel hard right. There's a squeal of protest from the tyres, then a squeal of delight from her.

'Not bad, eh?'

'Well, I don't think Lewis Hamilton needs to be worried, but yes, not bad.' I pat her arm encouragingly. 'Do you want to try third gear?'

'Why not?' she says, after a moment's consideration, and as if I've just offered her a glass of her favourite wine.

As we continue, I take her through the gears, making her speed up and slow down, and practise steering round the tree, a couple of 'Customer Parking Only' signs, and various abandoned supermarket trolleys, all of which she treats as a kind of slalom course. To her credit – and my relief – she seems to be getting the hang of it, and eventually, *finally* – though it's probably only been about thirty minutes – she pulls the car into the space where we started and switches off the engine.

'There,' she says, a satisfied expression on her face. 'Do you think I could drive home?'

I smile. 'I do. Whether you should or not is another matter. I think we might give it a rest for today, don't you?'

'That's probably best.'

'Same time tomorrow?'

'Same time tomorrow.' She opens her door, makes a move to stand up, then turns back towards me. 'Josh . . .'

'What?'

'I can't get out.'

My mind races back to the trip home from the hospital, and I ready myself to give her another pep talk, but before I can think of an appropriate way to start, she breaks into a smile.

'Silly me.'

'What?'

'I'd forgotten to undo my seatbelt!'

I smile back, then reach down and press the button for her, and for the first time, notice the effort it takes her to get out of her seat, and how tired she looks after half an hour's driving. And as I climb into the driver's side, I realise that this is what makes me saddest: my mother, at seventy-two, realising she's got no option but to do these things like learn to drive again, even though she assumed she'd never need to. But I suppose that life does this to you from time to time, and the sad thing is, you've got no choice, and choice was the one thing I always believed I had. Though I'm beginning to suspect that might not be true.

As I start the car, my mum smiles. 'Mirror, signal, manoeuvre, Josh, remember.'

'I shall live my life by those three words.'

My mum lets out a short laugh. 'It's funny,' she says. 'All that driving and we didn't get anywhere.'

I look at her out of the corner of my eye, and see her sitting a little straighter in her seat, a smile on her face, and think that yes, actually, we did.

∽

My dad's still a little frosty with me after the other day's 'Anna' incident, and my mum's a little tired after her driving exploits (and a little miffed that the first thing my dad did when we got back was make me wheel him around the car to check it for dents), so in an effort to restore some sort of peace in the house, I've shut them in the front room with a large glass of wine each while I cook dinner. This is actually quite a big deal, because a) the kitchen is/has always been my mum's domain – and it's a reflection of just how exhausted and stressed she is by everything that's going on that she accepts my offer without the slightest protest, and b) I can't cook.

Though that's mainly because I don't cook. On the nights Mikayla couldn't be bothered to rustle up something from a cookbook written by a chef whose name was a bigger mouthful than the quinoa salads he'd try (and fail) to make tasty (which was most nights), she always preferred to go out to eat, or alternatively, call in at Waitrose to buy something that just needed heating, rather than let me – and I quote – 'blunder my way' round her kitchen. But since Derton doesn't have a Waitrose (virtually a sign of a third-world country as far as Mikayla was concerned) I don't have a lot of choice. Plus, I've spotted the Jamie Oliver *30 Minute Meals* cookbook on the kitchen shelf that I bought my mum last Christmas (though from the looks of it, it's never been opened), so I'm reasoning how hard can 'Easy Spaghetti Carbonara' be?

Though 'quite hard' turns out to be the answer to that particular question, as I soon discover that in order to make any of these meals in the prescribed thirty minutes, you have to have eight pairs of hands. And at least two cookers. And, it transpires, know your way around a kitchen.

Now, I'm a pretty methodical kind of guy. Give me a set of instructions – to assemble an IKEA bookshelf, for example – and like most men, I can follow them (assuming I've bothered to read them in the first place). One step follows another, which makes sense to the way the male brain is wired. But Jamie Bloody Oliver (and trust me, I'm soon calling him a lot worse) seems to assume that we can be sautéing with one hand, dicing with the other, while simultaneously using our teeth to grate the Parmesan, all the while keeping an eye on the kitchen timer to make sure our pasta is 'al dente' – and quite frankly, doing any one of those things on their own is hard enough.

I'm twenty-five minutes in when I realise I haven't a hope of making the thirty-minute deadline, Mikayla's favourite insult ('Why can't men f**k off and die? Because they can't multi-task!') running through my head. Fortunately, my mum and dad seem to be happily working their way through the bottle of wine I've left on the coffee table, so I down the large glass I've poured myself, and soldier on.

Eventually, I get the carbonara part made, and – ignoring the chorus of 'Why are we waiting?' my dad's singing from the other side of the kitchen door – check on the pasta. It looks cooked. It's certainly a lot less stiff than when I put it in the pan, but my mum is the kind of person who keeps pasta in jars instead of its original packaging, so I've no idea how many minutes I'm supposed to boil it for.

Desperately, I grab my phone and type 'how to tell when pasta is cooked' into Google, and though: 'Throw it at a wall. If it sticks, it's ready', seems a bit extreme to me, in the absence of any other strategy (though why it doesn't occur to me to simply *try* a piece,

I don't know) it'll have to do. The wall behind the cooker seems as good as any, so I pull the colander out of the pan, shake the water off, and heave the contents against it.

Too late, I realise I should probably only have thrown one piece, and while it might well be cooked, given the dozen or so bits that stick to the tiles, the rest of it (though that could simply be because it's too heavy) drops back onto the hob. Where I've forgotten to turn the gas off.

There's a sizzling sound as the spaghetti lands on the red-hot burner and begins to turn an alarming shade of dark brown, so I grab the tongs from the pot beside the hob and try and shovel it back into the pan as quickly as possible, a task made harder by the fact that the pasta's decided to stick to the hob. And while I assume that *this* means it's done, I can't help worrying that the words 'to a crisp' could happily follow.

I pour the carbonara in, then turn the gas back on under the pan, and wait for the egg to cook. There are a few burnt bits, but I decide I can probably hide these, or even break them up so they look like bacon. Once I'm sure the egg's 'done' (and I decide not to throw *that* against the wall to check), I artfully arrange the pasta onto three plates, and carry them through to where my parents are waiting at the table.

'Ta-da!'

'Ooh, thanks, love,' says my mum.

My dad picks his fork up, and pokes disdainfully at the steaming pile I've just placed in front of him. 'What is it?'

'Spaghetti carbonara,' I say, in my best Italian accent, in an attempt to distract them from how it looks.

He picks up a piece of blackened spaghetti. 'Well, you've got the "carbon" part right.'

My mum tuts loudly. 'Don't be so ungrateful, Phil.' She scoops up a forkful, pops it into her mouth, and begins to chew. 'Mmm,' she says. 'Delicious,' before swallowing with what looks like a little more effort than she's used to.

My dad looks at her, then at me, then at his plate, then helps himself to the smallest of mouthfuls. He begins to chew, and I force myself to ignore the crunching sound.

'Well?'

'It's . . .' He sprinkles a bit of Parmesan cheese on top, has another taste, then empties the rest of the container over his plate. 'Have we got any more of this?'

My mum stands up. 'I'll see.'

'It's okay,' I say. 'I'll go.'

'Thanks, Josh.' She smiles. 'If it's anywhere, it'll be in the cupboard above the sink.'

I make my way into the kitchen and hunt through the cupboard to try and find the packet, eventually locating it hidden behind several packets of Mingers, and by the time I get back, my dad's plate is empty.

'That was quick.'

He makes a show of putting his knife and fork together. 'Didn't need the extra cheese after all. Thank you.'

'There's more, if you want some.'

He pales a little, then pats his stomach. 'A bit full, actually. Couldn't eat another thing.'

He's acting a little suspiciously, so I glance down at Wallace, who's sitting under the table, licking what looks like cheese off the end of his nose.

'Nor could Wallace, by the look of him.'

My dad holds his hands up in a 'guilty as charged' kind of way. 'I didn't want him to miss out.'

'Well, I like it,' says my mum, though given the way she's pushing her pasta around with her fork rather than eating it, I don't quite believe her.

My dad shoves his plate away. 'Thanks, Josh. Seriously, food like that gives me a reason to stay alive.'

'Really?'

'Mainly because I'd hate it to be my last meal.'

'Say any more and it might just be.'

He laughs. 'I'm sorry, Josh. It's just . . . How do you burn spaghetti?'

'Funnily enough, that was the easy part.'

'Not really your strong point, cooking, is it, son?'

'Why do you always have to criticise me?'

'How can it be criticism if it's a fact?'

I feel the familiar hackles rise, then bite off my answer – after all, I have to concede that my dad's got a point. And I realise that I've got a choice: be offended about something that, quite frankly, he's right about, or stop taking things so personally, and learn to laugh at myself every now and then.

I stare at him defiantly, take a forkful of spaghetti, shovel it into my mouth, and chew slowly, then without another word I pick up my plate and set it down on the floor in front of Wallace, who tucks in gratefully.

'Good boy,' says my dad. Though for a moment, I can't help feeling that he's talking to me.

19.

A funny thing happens at the shop today. I've just finished reading the *Derton Gazette* (breaking news: not very much indeed), and I'm absent-mindedly gazing into the mirrored front of a large oak wardrobe when I see them, or more specifically, their reflections, and straight away I can tell they're not from around here. The woman looks a bit like Mikayla, to be honest – the same tailored-trousers-and-fitted-blouse combination she used to favour, her hair obscuring so much of her face it's a wonder she can see where she's going – but it's him that I can't stop staring at. And it's not the rolled-up-at-the-ankles skinny jeans (you'd be forgiven for thinking he was going for a paddle in the sea, especially given that he's not wearing any socks, though the tan brogues kind of put paid to that idea), or the red-and-black checked shirt, or the two-sizes-too-small tweed jacket I bet he can't fasten, or even the large, tortoiseshell-framed glasses that look like they've got plain glass in the lenses, but it's the *beard*. A mass of ginger whiskers that descend from his chin, covering the top of his chest like a bib, and which rather than being hipster (and trust me, working for a company in Shoreditch, I've seen enough of them to know) puts him pretty much one step away from Tom Hanks in *Castaway*.

Surely no-one's born wanting to dress like that? His kind of style (and I use the word loosely) is something you adopt, a conscious decision. You do it because you're trying to fit in with your surroundings. Because you *want* to. Whereas he looks pretty comfortable, pretty natural (if a bit of a prat), I realise that for me, it'd just be like dressing up. Putting on a costume. And while he *almost* looks like he's trying too hard, I suddenly realise that – when I lived in London – I certainly did.

The shop is fairly dark inside – partly, so Michelle says, because people will have to physically come in to see things, giving us a chance to work our sales 'magic' on them – but mainly, I suspect, so the punters can't see exactly how bad a condition whatever it is they're buying's in, so I take advantage of this to watch them as they point at various things in the window, the expressions on their faces similar to Harrison Ford's in *Indiana Jones* whenever he'd found some priceless relic. This is *second-hand furniture*, I want to remind them. That old desk lamp you're getting so excited about? You'll find one in IKEA for a third of the price, and that one probably works.

Sure enough, the couple come in, nodding hello to me in a cool, disinterested way, then mooch slowly around the shop. They snigger at the Etch-A-Sketch on the shelf (which Michelle's ironically labelled as an 'early version iPad'), then suddenly – as if someone's held a gun to them – come to a dead stop in front of an old chrome fan.

'Look at this!' says the male of the couple, carefully picking it up, and I'm glad it's not plugged in, as any accidental activation would run the risk of snagging his beard, opening us up to all kinds of legal action. 'This would be perfect for our loft in Hoxton.' This strikes me as ironic, because Michelle probably found it in someone's loft around here, but then I remind myself that from London to Derton, words can have very different meanings.

'How much is this?' he calls across the shop, and I stroll over and take the fan from him. Michelle's forgotten to label it, but seeing as most of the things in here have come from house clearances – sometimes where they've even paid Michelle to take the stuff away – I reckon that anything we get for it will be a bonus.

'Six . . . tee . . . ' I think about adding an 'n' to the figure, but decide to chance my luck. 'Pounds,' I add, as if they'll think I mean pence. Which is probably closer to what the fan's worth.

The man frowns. 'Sixty pounds?'

'That's right.' For some reason, it's the first figure that's come into my head, and I immediately worry it's way too high. 'It's vintage,' I add, which gets a knowing nod from the couple.

'Do you deliver?'

I look at him for a moment. The fan would probably fit in the oversized man-bag he's got casually slung over his shoulder.

'I'm afraid not.'

'Right.' The man takes it back from me, checks its weight as if it's a newborn, then turns to his girlfriend – at least, I'm guessing she's his girlfriend, as there's no wedding ring on her finger. 'Babes?'

Babes – and there's a part of me that could believe that's her name – narrows her eyes for a moment. 'I really like it,' she says.

'We'll take it.'

He's said that to her, not to me, and she gives him a smile and a congratulatory squeeze, as if their life has suddenly been made complete by the purchase of this household object. I can picture how they live back in London, in their trendy apartment just off Shoreditch High Street, and all of a sudden I can see Mikayla and me for exactly what we were, which makes me wonder why I was trying so hard to have their life, what it was about living in an apartment with no walls – where exposed brick is a choice rather than a matter to call a plasterer to come round and fix, and where all the furniture's old because that's how it was when you bought it – that held such an appeal. And while I can see that I wanted something different to Derton, I suddenly realise that it was what I wanted then. It isn't now. Though exactly what it is I'm after, I still can't tell.

I ring their money through the till with a satisfied 'ker-ching', and as the couple leave the shop, it occurs to me that neither of them has thought to check whether the fan actually *works*. Though maybe that was never the point. For some people, as long as things look right, it doesn't matter if they work. And for some other people – Mikayla, for example – just looking right *means* that they work.

I stifle a smile, then realise I should be laughing at myself, not them. They're what I've spent the last eighteen years trying to become. And it's only now, back here in Derton, that I've begun to see it might not be such a good thing.

20.

When I get back from the shop today, my dad's sitting in his bedroom, the recently-arrived oxygen mask fixed over his mouth making him sound like Darth Vader every time he takes a breath. He's surrounded by black bin bags, and though I try and sneak past the open doorway, his loud 'Is that you, Josh?' brings me to the door.

'What are you up to?'

He pulls the mask off, then hefts a couple of bags up onto the bed, which makes him a little breathless, and I'm reminded how, at this stage of his disease, even the smallest physical efforts are like climbing a mountain.

'Just been sorting some stuff out while your mum's at the hairdresser's.'

'Stuff?'

'Old clothes, and things. I didn't want you and your mum to have to do it. Afterwards.'

'Oh. Right.'

'Half of them don't fit me anymore, anyway, so I thought I might as well get rid of them. Unless you wanted . . .'

'Why would I ever . . . ?'

My dad looks me up and down. 'Smarten up your look a bit. Make a change from those t-shirts you insist on wearing that look like you've slept in them.'

'Yes, well, it's called "fashion", Dad. Maybe you've heard of it?'

He makes a face. 'Anyway, I thought we could maybe take them to one of the charity shops on the High Street.'

'By "we", you mean "me", right?'

'Right.' My dad grins sheepishly. 'Unless you've got a hot date you need to be getting ready for?'

I bite off my answer. After the other day, we both know I don't. 'Are you sure Mum will be okay with this?' I say, surveying the bags. There must be about ten of them, and while I didn't know my dad owned this many clothes, I've a feeling some of them pre-date even me.

'She'll appreciate the extra space. Your mother always complained I never threw anything away. Well now I am.'

'And you've, you know, left yourself . . . enough?'

He points at the open wardrobe, where a few basic outfits are neatly arranged on the remaining hangers. 'One smart suit for the party – which you can also cremate me in – a couple of casual ensembles . . .' He puts on an exaggerated French accent for this last word. 'And two pairs of pyjamas. Should see me out.' He glances at the bags surrounding him. 'Possibly best to do it before she gets back, though, just in case. And I'd give you a hand, but . . .'

'I know, I know. Cancer.'

'It's a killer,' says my dad, smiling grimly.

With a shake of my head, I collect up as many of the bags as I can and carry them downstairs, though I have to return twice for the remainder. They won't fit in the car as it stands, so I lower the roof and pile them onto the back seat. Once I've loaded the last one, I walk back inside.

'Any particular charity shop?'

'Well, I'd say Cancer Research, but that's a bit like shutting the stable door after the horse has bolted.' He thinks for a second. 'There's not a "struggling writers" one, is there?'

'Ha ha.'

'Just joshing, Josh. Hah! Just joshing! Did you see what I did there?' He starts to laugh, but it quickly turns into a painful-looking cough, and I have to admit a small part of me hopes it feels like it looks. 'No, seriously, what about Age Concern?' he wheezes. 'That's a good cause. Particularly because you're not getting any younger.'

You're not getting any older, I want to say, but even though it'd be giving as good as I get, I still can't quite bring myself to do it.

～

There's a parking space on the High Street outside Age Concern, but then again, there are spaces outside a lot of the shops, mainly because there are spaces *inside* a lot of the shops. Since the Old Town got redeveloped, and the Tesco superstore opened on the industrial estate, the High Street has borne the brunt of everyone moving. Apart from the three charity shops, a Carphone Warehouse, and a branch of WH Smiths that I'm amazed is still here seeing as everyone only ever went in to read the magazines without buying them, there's precious little else to warrant the three-minute hike up the hill from the harbour. Sure, the odd outpost café or restaurant has tried its luck over the years, but they've never lasted.

I climb out of the car, wondering if it's safe to leave the roof down as I unload the bags, but seeing as the only things to steal would *be* the bags, decide it's not an issue. Besides, given the age of the shuffling, limping people making their slow-motion ways along the pavement, I'm sure I'd be able to catch them.

I grab as many of the bags as I can and carry them awkwardly into the shop. As soon as I walk inside, I'm hit by the unmistakeable smell that all charity shops have, somewhere between your grandmother's house and a morgue (I'd imagine), and I can't help but wonder how many of the clothes filling up the racks in here have come from similar situations – though probably post mortem, if you see what I mean. I'm guessing it used to be a hairdresser's, given the mirrors on the walls and the waist-height electrical sockets still visible behind the racks of clothes, though they're the only reminder. There's an old lady standing behind the till at the far end of the shop, so I make my way over to where she's leafing through a box of what I believe my mum and dad would call 'LPs' and clear my throat, and she looks up with a start.

'Can I help you, dear?'

'I wanted to drop these off. They're clothes. My dad's, actually. And I've got several more bags in the car.'

'Oh.' The woman slots the Barry Manilow album she's been admiring back into the box and smiles sympathetically. 'I'm sorry for your loss.'

'He's not dead.'

'Pardon?'

'Yet, I mean. He is dying, though,' I say, suddenly worried that she might not take the stuff, as if death's a condition of every donation. 'We're, well, *he's* having a bit of a clear-out. Beforehand.'

'I see.' She's looking at me strangely, and I'm beginning to regret saying anything. 'Well, you can leave them through there,' she says, directing me to the stock room.

When I walk through the doorway, there are dozens of identical bags piled in the corner, and it's then – and for the first time – it hits me: people *die* here in Derton. A lot of them. And maybe that was one of the reasons I wanted so desperately to leave. My parents – admittedly they *were* old – but they always seemed old before their time. Even Gaz is developing middle-age spread, and he's the same age as me. And I wonder if that's what I've been scared of – going down that same route, getting married, having a family, then waking up one day fat, middle-aged, bald, and wondering how any of that happened. And maybe I wasn't running away from Derton, or running away from my family. Maybe I was running away from Anna, because while I maybe wanted that, I certainly didn't want that then.

But perhaps she didn't either, given the fact that she and Ian never had any kids, which makes me feel that maybe I've been stupid. I could have spent all these intervening years with her, happy, instead of going through a succession of ultimately meaningless relationships that ultimately led me to Mikayla. Or perhaps, led me back here . . .

And the other thing that occurs to me is this: no-one knows how much longer they've got left, or when their time is up. And if things happen for a reason, then my dad getting ill . . . Well, it's brought me back here. Made me reconnect with my family. Catch up with Gaz. End a disastrous relationship with Mikayla. And perhaps, realise what I've been missing with Anna. While I'm sorry that my dad's having to die for any of that to happen, and of course I'd exchange all of those things for a different outcome, it is what it is.

And given that that's the case, I probably need to start paying him back.

❧

My dad's snoring in his armchair when I get back, a repeat of some football game playing on the TV in front of him, but as I reach for the remote control and switch it off, he starts awake.

'I was watching that!'

'Really?' I lift Wallace off the sofa and place him gently on the floor, and he scampers off towards the kitchen, where it sounds like my mum's making some tea. 'What was the score?'

'I can't remember.'

'Well, who was playing?'

'What is this? The Spanish Inquisition?' he huffs. 'Arsenal and Chelsea.'

I click the TV back on. It's Liverpool and Manchester United, and I give my dad a look, but he's already turned his attention to the screen, so I mute the volume, and sit forward in my chair.

'Listen, Dad . . .'

'I'd like to, but it's pretty difficult with the volume off.'

'To *me*, I meant. I wanted to talk to you about something.'

He looks at me suspiciously. 'Oh yes?'

'It's just . . . What with you not being that well, and everything, and me being here, and . . .' I ignore his raised eyebrow. 'I was wondering if there was anything you wanted to, you know, *do*.'

'Do?'

'Before . . .'

My dad raises both eyebrows this time. 'Before?'

'While you still can.'

'Oh. Right.'

'Or anything you wanted full stop. I mean, obviously a Ferrari is beyond me at the moment, but something else?'

He frowns. 'What did you have in mind?'

'It's not what I have in mind. It's what you have in your mind. Unfulfilled ambitions. Things you never got around to doing. It's called a bucket list.'

'A *bucket list?*'

'Yeah.' I gesture towards the TV with the remote. 'So if you wanted to, say, go and see Arsenal and Chelsea . . .'

'It's Liverpool and Man U.'

'. . . for real, or, I don't know, jump out of an aeroplane . . .'

'With or without a parachute?'

I swallow my answer. '. . . I could, you know, *help*. Arrange it. Even do some stuff with you, if you like?'

'Do *you* want to jump out of an aeroplane?'

'Well, no, but that's not the idea. It's more about you, writing down all the things that . . .'

My dad holds a hand up to stop me. 'Listen, Josh, that's very kind of you, but we both know I don't have a lot of time left, and if that's the case, why would I want to spend it doing stuff that could kill me even sooner, or that I've never got around to doing before?'

'That's kind of the point.'

'And *my* point is that I'm already doing what I want to do. Spending my last . . .' He shrugs dismissively. 'Well, however long it's going to be, with my family.'

'Will you just think about it?' I get out of my chair, walk over to the desk in the corner, and retrieve the notebook and pen my mum keeps by the phone. 'Here.'

My dad stares at it, and then at me, as if I'm handing him his own death warrant. 'Just put it on the table,' he says, as if he's afraid to touch it.

'Sure.'

We sit in silence for a moment, watching the game unfold on the screen in front of us, then he clears his throat, an action that seems to take longer, *and* get noisier, by the day. 'So you could get tickets for one of these games, could you?'

'Probably.'

'And you'd come?'

I nod. 'It'd beat the last game we saw.' Derton Town versus Dagenham in the FA Cup. Derton lost six–one. And the 'one' was an own goal.

'*Be* the last game we saw, you mean?'

'Dad, *please*.'

He grins mischievously, then reaches for the notebook. 'Okay. One bucket list coming up.' He uncaps the pen, then – his forehead scrunched up in concentration – scribbles furiously for a minute, before handing the notebook back to me.

'*Sick, wooden, mop, plastic* . . . What's this?'

'What you asked for. A bucket list.'

My dad does his best to keep a straight face, then bursts out laughing at what is quite obviously the best joke he's ever made and quite possibly in his eyes the best joke in the world ever, and after a few moments I can't help joining in, and in that infectious way, we both start to laugh harder and harder until it's almost painful. Then suddenly there's the sound of a pan being dropped in the kitchen and my mum, Wallace hot on her heels, comes rushing into the living room.

'What's going on?' she asks, her hands on her hips like an angry fifties housewife.

'I can't breathe,' gasps my dad.

'What should I do? Do you need an ambulance?' My mum's expression has suddenly morphed from annoyance to panic, but before she can grab the phone, he holds a hand up.

'It's okay,' he gasps. 'It's because we're laughing. Isn't it, Josh?'

I nod, then wipe my eyes on my sleeve. 'He made a joke. And it was actually funny.'

My mum shakes her head in disbelief. 'I thought something bad had happened.'

But as my dad catches my eye and we burst out laughing again, I suspect the opposite is true.

21.

Gaz is having a dinner party. To be precise, Gaz and Michelle are having a dinner party, and I suspect it's more Michelle's idea, as Gaz is the kind of person whose idea of a starter is to order a bag of crisps before his pub meal. I'm guessing that Michelle knows her way around a kitchen given the size of Gaz's belly, though of course, the opposite could be true, and he could have got that size eating take-aways instead of Michelle's cooking, but I'm pretty sure I'm right. You don't invite people round for dinner unless you're pretty confident you can produce the goods, or you have an account at M&S, or, I suppose, access to as much past-its-sell-by-date food as you can carry. Though to be honest, I'm so hungry that any of those works for me.

I've worn an old suit that I've found in the back of my ward-robe, for the simple reason that I'm fed up of only wearing jeans and various t-shirts for the last few weeks, and it's nice to be dressed up again. And while I realise I'll possibly be the only one wearing one this evening – I don't suppose Gaz can still get into the suit he wore for his wedding, and I can't imagine he's had many other occasions here in Derton to need to treat himself to an F&F one – I'm not that bothered. As Mikayla used to say whenever I'd tell her she didn't need to get dressed up just for me, 'I'm actually getting dressed up for *me!*'.

My mum and dad are at home with a takeaway and a bottle of wine. I figured if I was having a night out, then the least I could do was give them a night in, so to speak. And while my dad's order of a triple-meat-feast-stuffed-crust pizza wasn't perhaps the healthiest of options, none of us dared say that it didn't matter.

I check my watch. I'm five minutes early, so I pace up and down the street outside their house, until Gaz sticks his head out of the upstairs window.

'What are you doing?'

'I'm early.'

'You can come in. Michelle's dressed.'

'I was more worried that *you* weren't.'

He gives me a two-fingered salute, then disappears back inside, and a moment later, throws the front door open and shows me through to the kitchen, where Michelle is stirring a pot of something that smells suspiciously like chilli. She's wearing a 'comedy' kilt-patterned apron over a rather nice little black dress, and then I notice that Gaz, too, is dressed rather smartly. And while for Gaz that simply means he's tucked his shirt into his jeans, I start to get a little suspicious.

'Nice of you to make a special effort.'

'Not often we have guests round for dinner.'

'Guests?'

He looks nervously at Michelle, then pretends to be particularly interested in the label on the bottle of wine I've brought. 'Yeah. Didn't I say?'

'Er, no.'

'Right.'

There's a pause, where it's obvious no-one wants to say anything, until I break the awkward silence. 'Anyone I know?'

'Some couple who run the sculpture gallery in the Old Town,' says Gaz, rummaging noisily through the cutlery drawer in search of the corkscrew.

Michelle reaches over and finds it first go. 'They're DFLs too.'

'They're what?'

'DFLs. Down From London.' She hands Gaz the corkscrew. 'Came here about a year ago, and they love it. I thought you might want to meet them. You know, what with you living in London, and them being *from* London . . .'

She's gabbling, and Gaz still can't meet my eyes, so I peer through the hatch at the dining table. There appear to be six places set.

'And?'

Michelle shakes some salt into the pot. 'And what?' she says, stirring the chilli vigorously.

'You and Gaz, me, and this other couple. That's five.'

'Oh, right.'

'Michelle . . .'

'Relax. It's just one of my girlfriends.'

'Is this some sort of set-up?'

Michelle glances quickly across at Gaz, but he's too busy trying to figure out how the corkscrew works to respond.

'Not as such.'

'Gaz?'

The doorbell rings, and Gaz looks as relieved as a condemned man given a stay of execution. 'That'll be them,' he says.

'How do you know?'

'Pardon?'

'Unless you've programmed your doorbell like you can your phone so you can tell who's ringing . . .'

'Well, er . . .' Gaz is looking increasingly uncomfortable, and I'm trying to work out why they might assume Michelle's girlfriend will be the last to arrive, unless they've planned it that way, though why they'd do that is beyond me. I open my mouth to ask more, but Michelle and Gaz have decided it takes both of them to answer the door, so I finish opening the wine Gaz has been struggling with, and I'm just about to pour myself a large glass (I've a suspicion I might need one) when Michelle and Gaz reappear, accompanied by a rather odd-looking couple.

'You must be Josh,' says the man, extending a hand in my direction. He's tall – well over six foot – thin, dressed in a beige polo-neck and matching trousers, and with the reddest hair (and face) I've ever seen, and my first thought is that he's come in fancy dress as a safety match. 'I'm Mark. And this is my wife, Tobi,' he says, introducing the short, no, *tiny* woman next to him, though I only realise that's her name after I've said, 'Oh, congratulations. When's the big day?'

The woman stares at me for a moment, then honks with laughter. 'T-o-b-i. That's my name. We're already married.'

She's wearing some sort of expensive-looking outfit that's either a dress or a very high-waisted pair of trousers, though it's hard to tell, with a cleavage so evidently on display I have to stop myself from staring.

'More's the pity,' says Mark, with an exaggerated wink, and Tobi gives him a long-suffering look.

'Oh. Right. Sorry. I bet you get that all the time.'

'No, actually,' says Tobi, standing on tiptoe and air-kissing me on both cheeks. She looks even smaller given Mark's height, and I can't help myself, but you look at some people and wonder how on earth they have sex, and then you worry they know exactly what you're thinking, so you feel embarrassed.

'You're from London too?' I say, and Mark does a double take.

'I thought you were from here? One of the – what do you call them? Dertoners? Dertonites?'

'Derties?' suggests Tobi, with a snigger.

'Well, yes, I am. Was. Originally. But I live in London now.'

'That doesn't make you *from* London, though, does it?' Gaz points out.

'No, I just meant . . .' I stop talking. To explain any more, given that I'm in a room where the four other people present have made a conscious choice to live here in Derton, might be seen as rude. 'I mean, I'm down from London. Back down, technically,' I add, giving Gaz a look. 'Which I suppose makes me a BDFL.'

'But you're actually *from* there,' says Gaz, to the two of them.

'Oh yes!' exclaims Mark.

'And how do you find Derton?'

'Well, you pretty much drive down the A299, and it's right at the end.' He's obviously trotted out this line on a number of previous occasions, given how Tobi is rolling her eyes good-naturedly, and the polite response is to laugh, even though I'm well aware that laughing probably just encourages him to tell it again on another occasion. For the sake of future dinner party guests I tell myself I shouldn't, but in the end, politeness gets the better of me.

'No, seriously,' continues Mark, just in case we were in any doubt that he was joking, 'we love it, don't we, darling?'

Tobi pauses, just long enough for us all to work out that as far as she's concerned, 'love' is probably too strong a word and that she's still getting used to the idea. 'It's growing on me,' she says, eventually, and Mark beams his approval.

'So, Josh, what brings you down here from *Lahndahn Tahn*?' Mark backs up his funny voice with a little shimmy, as if he thinks he's Dick Van Dyke from *Mary Poppins*, and Tobi rolls her eyes again.

I glance at Gaz and Michelle, who are looking horrified. They obviously haven't briefed the two of them about my dad's situation, and the last thing I want to do is bring down the mood of the evening before it's even begun. And while I know I can't avoid telling people the real reason for my return forever, there's a time and a place.

'I used to live here,' is what I settle for. 'So I'm just visiting my folks.'

'And is it good to be back?'

I smile. 'I'm still getting used to the idea.'

Tobi starts to ask me something, but it's drowned out by a loud 'pop' as Gaz opens the Champagne Mark and Tobi have brought, but he doesn't have any Champagne glasses so we have to drink it out of tumblers, which means Gaz can't quite judge how much to pour, and after he's given Michelle and Tobi what looks like the best part of half a pint each, the rest of us are left with a couple of mouthfuls at best. Though this suits me fine. Champagne's never been my favourite drink, despite the fact that Mikayla always insisted we had a bottle to mark even the slightest of occasions (for example, it being a Friday night (again)), and I'm just helping myself to a glass of the wine I've brought when the doorbell goes.

I glance across at Gaz, who's trying to produce some music from the stereo, though given the unit looks like it belongs in Michelle's shop, I don't hold out much hope. As the bell rings again, Michelle looks up from the stove and smiles at me.

'You couldn't be a love and get that, could you, Josh?'

'Sure.' I put my glass down and walk along the hallway. The fuzzy figure I can semi-make out through the glass looks slim, and blonde, and I'm pleasantly optimistic as I throw open the door, though the feeling lasts for all of a second and a half, as 'one of Michelle's girlfriends' turns out to be one of *my* girlfriends – ex-girlfriends, at least.

Anna takes a step backwards, then double-checks the number on the wall next to the front door. 'Am I at the right house?'

She's dressed beautifully, in a short black dress that hugs her figure so perfectly it takes a real effort to keep my jaw off the floor, and she's carrying a bottle of wine, so I'd guess the answer to her question is 'yes'. Though I'm wondering whether I am.

'I was just . . . Michelle asked me to answer the door . . .'

'On your way out?' It's harsh, and it hits me like a slap in the face, and it hurts, and as soon as she's seen the reaction her words have provoked, Anna's face softens. 'I'm sorry, Josh, I didn't mean . . .'

'Yes you did. Are you on your own?'

She colours slightly, so I don't like to ask any more – or, specifically, about Ian, though I can't help but surreptitiously look to see whether she's wearing a wedding ring, and I'm pleased to see she isn't. She opens her mouth to say something, but at that moment, Michelle brushes past me and grabs her in a hug. 'Anna. Sweetheart. Lovely that you could come.'

And before either of us can say anything more (even if it's just 'goodbye'), Michelle's grabbed Anna by the hand, me (rather firmly) by the arm, and bundled us both inside.

❧

The evening's been an interesting one. Michelle has sat Anna and me next to each other, which I suppose is good in that we don't have to avoid looking at each other for the whole night, and luckily any awkward silences are filled by Mark holding forth on his specialist subject, which turns out to be, well, him.

But that suits me fine, to be honest. Despite the elephant in the room (and that's squeezed itself between Anna and me), it's been fun, and the food's been good, and the wine's flowed freely, and in the presence of the two other couples, though we've hardly said a word to each other, it's been easier for Anna and I to just go with the flow than to take potshots at each other.

By midnight, and with Gaz virtually dropping off at the table, Anna smothers a yawn with her hand, then looks at her watch. 'I'd better be going. Thanks, Michelle, Gaz. It's been . . .'

'Hasn't it?' says Michelle, quickly. 'We must do this again some time.'

There's a murmuring around the table, though when I play Anna's response back in my head, I can't actually hear her agreeing.

'I ought to get off too,' I say. 'Given, you know . . .'

'Of course,' says Michelle, then she glances across at Anna, and smiles at me. 'Josh, you and Anna are going in the same direction, aren't you?'

'Huh?' I frown across the table at her. After the last few hours, it should be patently obvious that we aren't.

'It's just that it's late. And dark. So you should walk her home.'

'I'll be fine,' says Anna, quickly. 'It's not far, and . . .'

'Josh?'

Michelle is glaring at me, and Anna's already on her feet, so I haul myself out of my seat. 'Sure,' I say, unenthusiastically.

'I'll be *fine*.'

'I insist!' This comes from Michelle, not me, and she's not one to be argued with, so we say our goodbyes, and promise Mark and Tobi that we'll call into the gallery as soon as we can, then Michelle virtually pushes us out through the front door together, though the moment she's closed it behind us, Anna stomps quickly off down the road.

With a sigh I break into a jog and catch her up. 'Michelle said I should *walk* you home, not race you there.'

'I'll be fine on my own!'

'That's what I thought.'

'What?'

'Eighteen years ago.'

'Well, I *wasn't*, Josh.'

'I didn't know that, did I? I mean, I wrote to you, then I heard nothing. *Nothing*. What was I supposed to think?'

'I've already told you, I didn't get your stupid letter.'

'But . . .'

190

She's still storming along the pavement at an impressive speed, so I have to jog backwards in front of her to have any chance of talking to her. Though the flaw in this approach is that I don't see the black bin bag someone's left out on the pavement, which I trip spectacularly over.

Anna stares at me for a moment, then all the fight seems to go out of her, and she starts to laugh.

'What's so funny?'

'I always hoped you'd go down on one knee in front of me, Josh. Not your arse.'

I smile up at her, aware that something's changed, and though I don't quite know what, or how, I realise this is my moment. 'Do you think we could start again, and just talk? Forgetting all this stuff in the past, and Ian, and the shop, and my dad . . .'

'What for?'

It's a good question, and it deserves a good answer. Unfortunately, I'm not brave enough to give her the right one.

'For old times' sake?'

She thinks for a moment, then reaches out a hand, and I pull myself up gratefully. 'Come round tomorrow night. I'm at my mum and dad's, if you remember where that is?'

'Your mum and dad's?' I repeat, not because I haven't heard her properly, but more because I need confirmation that she's not living with Ian any more.

'They're at their place in Torremolinos for the summer. I'm sort of house-sitting.'

'Okay. Great.'

'Sevenish? I'll cook something. You bring a bottle.'

I try and take stock of this. Back when Anna and I were together, being in her house when her mum and dad weren't there for even two minutes was a rarity. Now, they're away for two *months*. She's lonely, I'm lonely and probably a bit vulnerable given everything that's going on at home, plus dinner plus wine plus memories makes for quite a combination . . .

I know I shouldn't put myself in that kind of position for a hundred and one reasons, and I take a deep breath and prepare to tell her exactly that. But instead, 'White or red?' is actually what I say.

22.

An uneasy truce seems to have descended on the house. My mum seems to be getting over her resentment of my dad for dying (or rather, for not doing anything earlier when he first fell ill), my dad and I seem to be getting on better, ever since I decided that life's too short (especially his) to take it (and him) so seriously, and in return my dad seems to have toned down his fatalistic optimism. In between the three of us, Wallace struts around like he owns the place (or at least, owns *us*), sensing out the beginnings of any unrest like a tiny, squashed-face UN peace-keeper, defusing any uncomfortable situations with a flash of his big black eyes and the kind of wheezing and snorting my dad's started to make whenever he does anything physically demanding (or wants us to do anything physically demanding for him, like fetch him a glass of wine from the kitchen). In fact, things have got so much better we've decided that today's a good day for that rarest of things in the Peters household – a family day out.

The Derton Contemporary Gallery, the thing that kick-started the town's 'renaissance' (Derton Tourist Board's word, not mine) occupies a spot on the seafront overlooking the harbour. When I was growing up, the Six Bells pub used to be here, but like so many of my old drinking haunts, it's been demolished in the name of 'progress'. Though I suppose I shouldn't complain – even if I do manage to attain the tiniest bit of literary fame, I can hardly see a nostalgic tour of Josh Peters' 'Favourite Derton Pubs' making it onto the list of local attractions.

And the gallery's awful. A waste of money that could have been spent so much more usefully on lots of other things – or at least, that's the view of loads of people here who've never even visited the place, including me – which is why my dad's decided that visiting it will be the first item on his bucket list. As usual, my mum is ready half an hour before our planned leaving time, whereas my dad is still sitting in front of the TV, Wallace by his feet.

'Are you ready, Phil?' she calls from where she's waiting by the front door, and for about the hundredth time.

My dad takes a couple of deep breaths, then removes his oxygen mask and rolls his eyes at me. 'I was born ready,' he says, sarcastically, then he reaches down and pats Wallace on his head. 'Sorry, boy. You can't come. But don't worry. We won't be long.'

'He can't understand you, Dad.'

Wallace licks his nose a couple of times, then lets out a loud sigh and goes to sit in his basket, and my dad gives me a look that says 'Really?'

My mum marches into the front room and looks him up and down – well, down, really, seeing as he's sitting obediently in the wheelchair. 'Is that what you're wearing?'

My dad adjusts his fleece – the one he used to wear for the allotment, until even that simple pleasure was denied him – then picks a piece of fluff from his trouser leg. 'What's wrong with it?'

'You might have made a bit of an effort.'

I wince. Actually getting dressed in anything is enough of an effort at the moment for him, and he bristles a little at the comment.

'We're going to a gallery, woman. I'm not collecting an OBE from the Queen.'

'Josh . . .' says my mum, imploringly, but I have to side with my dad.

'Like he says, we're going to a gallery. People are going to be looking at what's on the walls. Not what he's wearing.'

'Exactly.'

'Did you want to take this?' I say, tapping the side of the oxygen cylinder. 'There's a strap for the back of the wheelchair which . . .'

'For the second time, we're only going to a gallery. Not scuba diving.'

My dad starts wheeling himself towards the door, but there's an armchair to steer round, not to mention the coffee table, and for a second, the briefest flash of frustration crosses his face.

'Here. Let me.' I take the wheelchair by the handles and begin to manoeuvre him through the obstacles and towards the front door, but he waves me away angrily.

'I can wheel myself out of my own home!'

'Phil . . .'

'Be quiet, woman!'

I don't say anything, but just hold open the door, trying to ignore my mum's loud tutting as she follows my dad outside, and as I shut it behind me, Wallace looks glad he's not invited.

~

It's a short walk to the seafront, and a lovely summer's morning, and I have to say, Derton's looking pretty special. The sun is glinting off the rippling sea, expectant seagulls are circling a fishing boat a few hundred yards out, and the beach is full of dog-walkers, tourists, and – even at this hour – the odd drunk. Ahead of us, the gallery looks majestic against the backdrop of the English Channel, and I'm more than a little impressed that Derton Town Council have managed to get their act together to build such a thing.

My mum's a brisk walker, and despite his continuing weight loss, my dad's not light, so it's a bit of an effort to keep up with her as she strides past the arcades and towards the harbour, and by the time we reach the crossing on the corner, I'm out of breath. But I should be grateful, as it's the first exercise I've had in a while, I remind myself, as I push my dad up the ramp that leads to the entrance, then manoeuvre him through the doors and into the gallery's airy reception.

'Good morning,' says the girl behind the counter, cheerily.

'Hi,' I say. 'Three, please.'

'That's two adults and one ch—'

'Thank you, Dad.'

The girl smiles. 'It's free entry.'

My dad makes a play of reaching for his wallet. 'I'll get these, son,' he says, winking at my mum, but she's too busy gazing around the lofty interior to notice.

'It's lovely,' she says. 'So . . . light.'

'So they haven't wasted our taxes, eh, Josh?' My dad's said this loudly enough for the girl behind the counter to hear, but she just smiles patiently.

'So, is there a recommended route, or do we just wander round?'

'Or roll round, in my case,' interrupts my dad.

The girl directs us towards the lifts in the corner, and tells us to start on the first floor (where the 'special exhibitions' are), so we make our way into the biggest elevator I've ever seen (where my dad makes some joke about it being 'Derton-sized', which I don't get until he points out a group of rather large locals wolfing down fried breakfasts in the café), and head up to the first floor as instructed. The view of the sea from the windows up here is even more impressive, and we stand there for a moment, taking it in.

'They don't need any exhibits,' says my mum, nodding towards the seascape in front of us. 'This alone is worth the entrance fee.'

It's rare for my mum to make a joke, and my dad and I widen our eyes at each other, impressed. 'Mind you,' he says, 'that's just as well.' He wheels himself over to a modern art installation on the opposite wall that's made of what looks like old washing machine parts, titled 'A New Spin'. 'I could do better myself.'

'Yes, well, the point is, you haven't, have you? Which is why this is on the wall here, and you've got a shed full of junk at home.'

My dad opens his mouth to answer, then evidently thinks better of it, so we continue the tour in silence, occasionally pausing to 'ooh' and 'aah' (and 'ugh', from my dad) at the works on display, and I have to say, I'm impressed. Growing up here, the only painting you'd see adorning a wall would be graffiti, and even then, it was usually a picture of someone's private parts.

We take the lift back downstairs to where the more traditional pieces are on display and enter the gallery's main room, and in front of us is a sculpture that takes our breath away – especially my dad's, though he doesn't have much to start with. It's a full-size edition of Rodin's *The Kiss* – a man, seated, a woman on his lap, the two of them locked at the lips in a passionate embrace.

My dad wheels himself over and gazes up at it for a while, then he glances down at his chair. 'Come here for a second, Sue.'

As she walks obediently over, he turns to me. 'Josh, have you got a camera on that posh phone of yours?'

'You want me to take a picture?'

'No, it was just a general enquiry. *Of course* I want you to take a picture.'

'Of?'

'Me and your mum.'

I pull my phone out, and my mum goes to stand behind my dad, but instead, he pats his knee. 'No. Like them.'

'Phil . . .'

'No-one's watching.'

My mum casts a wary eye around the room. Given the early hour, we've actually got the place to ourselves, and there's a glint in her eye as she perches on his knee.

'Tell me when you're ready?'

'I was born ready,' she replies, snaking an arm around my dad's shoulder, and for the first time since I arrived back in Derton, I see a flash of their old selves.

'On three,' he says, followed quickly by 'Three!', which strikes me as not the most romantic invitation for a kiss, but my mum's game.

And while their embrace doesn't quite match the grace and elegance of the sculpture, it's quite possibly the most wonderful, beautiful, touching thing I've ever seen.

23.

Anna's parents' house is a modern, two-up (or so I'm assuming, given how I never actually got as far as her bedroom back then) two-down terrace just off the High Street, with the same bright red front door that I remember. Not that I ever thought I'd be walking up this particular path again.

As I ring the doorbell, I can't help wondering how Anna feels being back there (maybe the same as I do at mine, though of course hers are slightly happier circumstances), and what happened with her and Ian to make her move out (I don't buy the 'house-sitting' story for one minute). I also wonder what their marital home is/was like, and whether Ian's currently sitting, sulking, wherever it is they live (lived? Or is that me being presumptuous?). Ian's family were quite well off (he had a car at seventeen when the rest of us were still on our mountain bikes, which was another thing that made him insufferable, especially when he used to drive alongside and try and knock us off as we cycled home from school), so I'm guessing this is a bit smaller than she might have become used to. I'm feeling a bit mean about only spending a fiver on a bottle of wine (though it was reduced from seven ninety-nine in Tesco's), but when Anna opens the door and I hand it to her with a mumbled apology, her face lights up. She's looking good, dressed in a simple white-t-shirt-and-faded-jeans combination that's possibly the sexiest outfit I've ever seen.

'How lovely. My favourite!'

'Sauvignon Blanc?'

'No, just white wine full stop, really.' She smiles mischievously. 'Come on in.'

She steps back from the door, but she's holding it open with one foot, so I have to shuffle awkwardly past her in the cramped hallway rather like I did at Ziggy's the other day (though it's much more of a pleasant squeeze), but by the time I've plucked up the courage to lean in for a kiss hello, she's already turned and shut the door behind me.

'Something smells nice.'

'Thanks. It's Nina Ricci.'

'Great. I love Italian food.'

Anna frowns, then breaks into a grin. 'Oh, you meant *dinner*. I thought you were referring to my perfume.'

'No. Sorry. Not that you don't smell nice too . . .'

She makes a 'yeah, right' face that suddenly transports me back nearly two decades, then shows me through to the front room. It's different to how it used to be (though I guess that's not surprising after so long), open-plan to the kitchen now, and sparsely furnished: just the one sofa, which I note with interest, given that it means that later there'll be none of that awkward 'if you sit on the sofa and I sit on the armchair, then how do we get together?' issue that two- or three-piece suites mean. There's a small dining table in front of the window that's already set for the two of us, and a half-empty bottle of red wine on the kitchen surface, and I wonder whether Anna's needed a drink to calm herself. Or, possibly, she's just needed it for cooking.

'I like what they've done with the place.'

'What was it my mum always used to say? *It's not much, but it's home.*' She smiles. 'A bit like you used to say about Derton, I seem to recall.'

'Anything I can do to help?'

Anna shakes her head. 'Almost done,' she says, bending over to peer through the oven door, giving me a perfect view of her (still) perfect behind. 'Perhaps you could open that wine you brought? It might need to breathe.'

As do I, I think, reluctantly averting my eyes. 'Sure. What are we having?'

'Fish pie. With a rocket salad. And rhubarb crumble for afters.'

'Ah. Right.' I swallow hard. Anna couldn't have listed a worse menu as far as I'm concerned, given that fish, rocket, and rhubarb are my least favourite things in the entire world. Maybe she *is* torturing me, and for starters (no pun intended) she's going to make me sit here and force down . . . I look up to find her shaking her head at me.

'Got you! It's lasagne.'

'My favourite.'

'I remember.'

'As opposed to those other . . . things.'

'I remembered that too.'

'Thank you.'

She holds eye contact with me for a little longer than strictly necessary – not that it's unpleasant – then she passes me the corkscrew, which I fiddle with for a moment until I work out that the bottle's actually got a screw-top, so I open it with a little 'ta-da' to cover the noise that breaking the seal makes, which is a bit pathetic if you think about it. But Anna doesn't seem to notice, so I pour us both a glass, and we 'cheers' without actually saying what we're cheering to, and I don't give my glass of wine the chance to breathe even the once before I've inhaled most of it, and it does its job, and I sit down at the breakfast bar and watch Anna finish her preparations.

And as she does so, she tells me all about what she's been up to in the preceding eighteen years, which of course includes getting married to Ian ('My big day,' she says, 'which was ironic, because it was the thinnest I've ever been'), and that they'll soon be divorced (a piece of news I have to physically restrain myself from leaping up and punching the air in celebration at), and going to catering college before working in Greggs on the High Street. 'It's where . . .' – then she names some celebrity chef – '. . . started,' she tells me, as if worried I'm about to accuse her of selling out, and I think about telling her my 'Salman Rushdie' anecdote, but decide I'll save that for another time. About Ian buying my dad's old shop ('Wasn't that a coincidence?' she says, though she apologises again for Ian's stinginess and promises she'll never forgive him for lying to her about how much he paid) and turning it into a cupcake café just as the new gallery opened and the Old Town smartened itself up, and how she absolutely loves running her own business (High point: serving a union-jack-iced cupcake to the Queen during her royal visit last year. Low point: she didn't eat it).

And I tell her about my job (leaving out the 'losing it' part), and London (leaving out the Mikayla part, because I'm worried that both being with her and then being dumped by her will show me in a bad light), and about my dad, and when she asks what the prognosis is I tell her he's dying, and soon, and – in a sharp contrast to Mikayla on the phone the other week – she puts her hand on my arm, and asks me if there's anything she can do, anything at all. And it's at that point, with her hand on my arm, and her face (her concern making cute furrows in her forehead) just a foot or so from mine (though for no other reason than the stools we're both now sitting on don't have very comfortable backs, so we've both leaned forward and rested our elbows on the narrow breakfast bar), that I decide I absolutely, categorically, one hundred percent want her back, starting *now*. Which, of course, is why the oven timer decides to ring at that exact same moment.

Then, after we've eaten (High point: the lasagne. Low point: in my haste to eat it and get on with the 'good' part of the evening I burn the roof of my mouth), we're both sitting on the sofa, and we've had a bit of wine, and (as far as I can tell), we've been getting on fine. Great, even. And while (like most men) I'm useless at reading those body language signs that are supposed to tell us, for want of a better phrase, that we're 'in there', like women absent-mindedly playing with their hair, or licking their lips, or even the more blatant – and yes, this has happened to me and I've let it pass me by – telling me it was time for bed (and me therefore thinking I had to leave instead of join them), if I didn't know better, I'd think that it was safe to say I was.

Trouble is, I don't want to blow it. What if I *have* misread the signs? What if Anna is just being friendly? The last thing I want to do is ruin my chances completely by going in for the kill too early. Besides, I'm not sure I *want* to sleep with her tonight. For a start, I'm too nervous, and a little drunk, and I haven't had sex for a while, and any one of those factors on their own would be enough to . . . shall we say, *influence* any between-the-sheets action (and that doesn't even take into account the eighteen-year foreplay period).

But we're both in our thirties now, so I can't really expect her just to want to – to use the horrible American phrase – 'make out', like we used to do. Back then, the kissing was all about leading to something else – trying to get my hand up her jumper, or even other places, so now, to just kiss? It seems wrong, somehow. A bit disrespectful, as if that's all I'm after. Why *wouldn't* I want to sleep with her? What possible reason could I give to justify leaving it at the kissing stage, particularly if – as I remember all too well, Anna's rather good at this kissing lark, meaning that I'll be very unlikely not to show my appreciation in other ways, if you know what I mean?

Then it hits me: I'll go. Just thank her for a nice evening, peck her on the cheek, and say I'll see her later. That I have to get home. For my dad. After all, isn't that how the old showbiz maxim goes – always leave them wanting more? So if I play it cool, maybe exchange the peck on the cheek for something a little more lingering, then leave . . . Well, surely she'll be desperate to see me again?

Convinced it's a top plan, I drain the last of my wine, then smile broadly. 'Well, that was a wonderful dinner.'

'Thanks.'

Anna's not giving much away, and not for the first time, I wish I'd paid more attention growing up. Back when Anna and I first went out, our first kiss – and I remember it as if it was yesterday – happened as so many do, at a slow dance at some friend's party. And slow dances were always good for that, giving you carte blanche to actually put your hands on a member of the opposite sex, hold them close, sway about a bit (all the time trying to think of something else so you wouldn't get visibly turned on in public), and all this with your face a few inches from theirs. Kissing, when it happened, was the easiest thing to do, involving a movement of the tiniest order, and giving the recipient the chance to ignore it by simply turning their head. But right now the chasm between us on the sofa seems as wide as the Grand Canyon, and there's nothing at all I can think of to bridge the gap without a) lunging, b) doing it by stealth, or c) asking politely – and I'm sure as hell not brave enough to do c) and risk a 'no' in return.

Then again, I tell myself, Anna might not be expecting me to kiss her. She might not even be *wanting* me to kiss her. And the more I think about it, the more it becomes an issue, so by the time I'm desperate to do it, I start to doubt if I can even remember *how* to do it, worried I'll be a mess of teeth and tongues.

And I realise the problem is this – that there's so much riding on our first (well, *second* first) kiss, that I'm too scared I'll mess it up.

And like a penalty-taker in extra time who needs to score to win the cup, I'm suddenly convinced I'll blast it over the bar.

As I try and make sense of all of this, I realise Anna is looking at me strangely, a fact reinforced when she says, 'Are you okay?'

'Me? Yes. Why?'

'You've got a funny look on your face. And you keep licking your lips.'

Ah. 'I'm sorry. I think I burned my mouth. On the lasagne.'

'Oh no. Let me see.'

She leans in towards me, and I suddenly, *foolishly* conclude that this is her way of initiating the kiss, so I lean in towards her too, and it's possibly the longest lean of my life, and halfway through I realise that I'm actually sitting too far away from her to actually make lip contact if I keep on this trajectory, so I stand up a little so I can edge along the cushion towards her, but Anna seems to have realised exactly the same thing, so she gets up too, and the action of us both getting up at the same time means she head-butts me right on the tip of my nose, painfully enough to make my eyes water.

'Josh, I'm so sorry . . .'

'Don't worry. My fault.' I wipe my eyes with the back of my hand, try and block out the pain, and lean in again, but before I can get anywhere near kissing territory, Anna leaps off the couch.

'What's wrong?'

'Your nose.'

'What about it?'

'It's bleeding.'

'What?' I reach up, and my fingers come away bloody.

'Don't move.' Anna rushes into the kitchen and returns with a roll of paper towels. 'Here,' she says, balling one up and handing it to me. 'Put your head back.'

'I'm okay. Honestly.'

'Is it broken?'

I press gingerly on the bridge of my nose. To my relief, nothing moves that shouldn't. 'I don't think so.'

I think about moving in for a final try, but the look on Anna's face suggests she might recoil in horror, and besides, now I'm not convinced she was moving in for a kiss in the first place, so I clamp the tissue to my nose and make for the toilet, cursing my bad luck.

When I eventually emerge, having cleaned the last traces of blood from my nostrils, Anna's in the kitchen clearing up.

'How is it?'

Though my nose may not be broken, the mood certainly is. 'I'll live.'

'Josh, I'm so sorry.'

'Don't be. It wasn't your fault.'

'I didn't see anyone else head-butt you in the face.'

'True, but . . .' I shake my head. If I wasn't still in pain, I'd almost find this funny. Ever since I've been back in Derton, I've been worried that Ian's going to give me a bloody nose, and it's actually Anna who finally did it.

She puts a hand on the side of my face. 'Does it hurt?'

'I'll get over it.'

'Not emotionally, Josh.'

'It feels a little bruised.' As does my ego. 'So I'd better, you know . . .'

'Sure.' Anna walks me to the door, and then stands up on tiptoe and kisses me softly, carefully on the cheek, which makes my head spin, though that could be a combination of the wine and the blood loss. 'It's been lovely.'

'Yes,' I say. 'It has.'

'And I'm glad we could talk.'

'Me too.'

'Friends?'

Anna holds a hand out for me to shake, and though 'friends' is the last thing I want to be, 'friends' is what I say.

'So I'll see you around?'

'Definitely.'

Though as I'm walking back through the chilly night air, my mind is racing. Do I really want Anna and me to even be friends, knowing where that might lead? She has a business here, and here's the last place I want to be. And after my dad's . . . Well, when my mum's here on her own, how long do I really see myself staying? How long is it going to take before she's okay enough for me to leave? And given my dad's situation, is it really fair for me to be – to borrow one of his phrases – 'off gallivanting' while he's going through what he's going through?

Besides, maybe Anna's just on the rebound – God knows I am. Her homicidal soon-to-be-ex is still around, and he didn't like me in the first place. Plus I haven't told her about Mikayla, or my work situation, both of which (literally, in Mikayla's case, given that she should be flying back from Sri Lanka about now) are still up in the air . . . And if there's one thing life has taught me, none of these on their own are circumstances in which you should be making any kind of decision about your future, let alone when they're all happening together. No, I tell myself, Anna was right, we'll be better off seeing each other as 'just friends' for the time being – though how I'm going to cope with that is beyond me.

Which is why I take the coward's way out, and for the next week or two, I don't see her at all.

24.

Today is a bad day. I can tell this as soon as I get up – and I'm getting up early nowadays, seeing as my mum's alarm goes off at six o'clock most mornings. She says it's because she doesn't need the sleep, though really I suspect it's so she can spend an extra hour with my dad every day. The kitchen's below my bedroom, and the combination of the noise as she clatters around, and the smell of bacon (my dad's favourite breakfast, and the one thing he's asked for every day until, well, we don't see him at breakfast) is impossible to sleep through. And while my mum's been defining days as either 'good' or 'bad' since my dad got ill, I've never actually understood just what 'bad' meant until I get downstairs this morning, rub the sleep out of my eyes, and see the look on her face.

'Is he . . . ?' I start to ask, automatically assuming the worst, then feeling stupid as I realise she'd hardly be making up a tray for him if he had actually died in the night. 'I mean, is everything okay?'

'Your dad's having a bit of a bad day.'

'Right.' For a moment, I wonder if it's simply the effect of the whole box of past-their-sell-by-date After Eights he found when he was clearing stuff out for the charity shop, and polished off last night. 'Should I call Doctor Watson?'

My mum sighs. 'No point, love. I've given him his tablets. We just have to wait until they kick in.'

We look at each other for a moment. One day they're going to stop 'kicking in', and none of us are looking forward to that.

'Anything else I can do?'

She places a cup of tea on the tray next to the bacon sandwich. 'You could take this up to him?'

It's a question as much as a request, as if she's worried I won't want to go and see him like this, and I know that she'll gladly do it, but she's looking tired. 'Sure. Are *you* okay?'

'Sometimes it all gets a bit much when he's like this, but . . .' My mum shakes her head. 'I married him for better or for worse – although I'm sure it doesn't get much worse than this.' She forces a smile. 'And I know he'd do the same for me, if the tables were turned.'

Wallace has hauled himself sleepily out of his bed, and he's stretching alternate legs by my feet in that way pugs do, as if they're ballet dancers about to embark on a high-kicking routine, so I reach down and scratch the top of his head.

'Don't worry. You have a cup of tea. I'll take it up. C'mon, Wallace.'

As Wallace looks at me, then at the stairs, then back at me disdainfully, as if I've just suggested a quick Everest summit attempt, I take the tray from my mum and trudge up the stairs, then knock softly on my dad's bedroom door, and when there's no response, push it gingerly open with my foot and walk quietly inside. He's lying on his side on the bed in the foetal position, groaning softly into the oxygen mask that he seems to be wearing more often than not nowadays, and for a moment, I'm too shocked to move. I've only ever seen him in pain once before, when a rare game of football in the back garden ended with me sending a penalty attempt square into what – with his eyes watering – he'd described as the 'family jewels', and judging by the look on his face and the sounds he's making, this seems to be almost as painful.

'Dad?' I say, then 'Dad!' a little louder, and he opens his eyes and focuses on me.

'Josh,' he says, weakly.

He tries to sit up, though I can tell the effort's too much for him, so I hurry across the room and deposit the tray on the bed-side table.

'Is it . . . bad?'

He looks at me in a 'silly question' kind of way, then slides the mask down and forces a smile, though it looks more like a gri-mace. 'Sorry, son. Sometimes it just . . .' But before he can finish the sentence, he winces again, and turns even paler, so I wait there, not knowing what to do, until a bit of colour returns to his cheeks. 'The doc said this'd . . . Happen occasionally. Just have to . . . Grin and bear it, I suppose.'

'You're not doing a lot of grinning,' I say, helping him into a sitting position. 'I brought you some breakfast.'

My dad's gaze settles on the tray, his eyes widening a little at the sight of the bacon sandwich, but then I know how bad a day it is, because he passes. 'Maybe later, Josh. In fact, you have it. Or give it to Wallace.'

'Okay. Anything else I can get you?'

My dad doubles over again, and instinctively I put a hand on his back, and he looks up at me with tears in his eyes, though I know they're from the pain and not some sudden great emotional connection we're having. After a moment, he shakes his head. 'Go and keep your mum company,' he wheezes. 'I'll be down in a bit.'

'Sure?'

'Sure.'

I lay him back down, and make sure the duvet's covering him, his pillow's plumped up enough, and his mask is on comfortably, and all the while, it occurs to me that this is coming way too early. I'd always kind of thought that in fifteen or twenty years I might be having to tend to him like this, but doing it now just seems so . . . wrong. Unfair, if you like. Though I realise it would be a little churlish for me to complain.

I give his arm a gentle squeeze, pick up the tray, and make for the door. 'Just shout if you need anything,' I say, and he nods imperceptibly, and it tears me up inside, because what he actually needs, neither my mum, nor me, nor anyone can give him.

25.

My mum comes into the shop at lunchtime, and my first thought as I leap out of the extremely comfortable battered leather armchair I've been in danger of nodding off in (and that I'm seriously considering asking Michelle if there's a staff discount on) is that something's happened.

'Everything okay?'

'Relax.' She reaches down and strokes Wallace affectionately, and he snuffles approvingly. 'He's feeling a bit better. I'm just popping to the seafood stall round the corner.'

'Really? Sounds fishy to me.'

I nudge her, but my mum just shakes her head. 'You've been spending too much time with your father.'

'What's he up to?'

'I'll give you three guesses.'

Given that it's Wimbledon fortnight, I only need one. 'Watching the tennis?'

'Exactly.' She straightens up with a bit of difficulty. 'Will you be home for dinner tonight? I'm making shepherd's pie.'

'In that case, definitely.'

'Lovely.' She casts an eye round the shop's dim interior, taking in the lack of customers, then suddenly turns to me, a sympathetic expression on her face. 'Oh, Josh, I know this wasn't how you saw things going.'

I fix my mouth into a grin, and shrug as nonchalantly as I can, though both of those things take more than a little effort. 'Hey, don't worry about it. Just doing my bit. And at least it's not, you know, *forever*.' My mum grimaces a little, and immediately I feel guilty. 'I'm sorry. I didn't mean it like that.'

'Don't worry.' She gives my arm a squeeze. 'See you later.'

'See you later,' I say, and then the worst thing possible happens. As my mum is leaving the shop and crossing the road, Anna comes out of the cupcake café opposite (well, it's not the worst thing possible, in that she's not knocked down by a speeding car or anything, but you know). They stare at each other for a moment or two, then Anna makes a 'how nice to see you' face and envelops my mum in a massive hug.

I take a couple of steps closer to the window so I can observe them a bit better from behind Gaz's F**k That poster, and though I can't hear anything, it's easy to tell from their body language what's being discussed. Anna points back to the café, and my mum nods, and Anna looks like she's apologising, and my mum puts a conciliatory hand on her arm, then they talk for a moment, and Anna's face falls, and she hugs my mum again. Then my mum says something, and – and I don't know why I don't see this coming – jabs a thumb back in my direction.

I see Anna mouth 'Josh?', her frown making it seem like a question, then she peers over at Second Time Around, so I duck out of sight, but not before my mum swivels round and – and I'm sure she's doing it innocently, rather than the way my dad would – waves.

Anna stares at the spot where I've just been standing for a moment, then she turns back to my mum, makes the 'how nice to see you' face again, gives her yet another hug, then starts crossing the road towards the shop, and at once, I panic. I've successfully avoided her for the best part of two weeks, and now, thanks to my mum, all of my good work is about to be undone.

213

The shop does have a back door, but it's padlocked shut, and I don't have time to crawl over to the front door and slide the bolt and turn the open/closed sign around, which leaves me only one other option . . .

'Josh?'

I peer through the crack between the doors of the wardrobe I'm hiding in, which gives me the narrowest view of Anna as she strides past. She calls my name again, then walks to the back of the shop, then I hear her footsteps get closer, and she says, 'Hello, gorgeous', so I assume my number's up, and I'm just about to emerge, shame-faced (though I'm rather chuffed at the compliment) from my hiding place when she follows it up with 'What's your name?', and the snuffling sound I hear in response makes me realise she's not talking to me.

I curse under my breath. If there's one thing that's going to give the game away, it's Wallace. And what on earth am I going to do if he leads Anna to where I'm hiding? Tell her I got locked in accidentally, or that I'm cleaning it, or trying it for size?

'Are you here all on your own?' she says, then Wallace's snuffling grows louder and louder, which means he's standing right outside the wardrobe.

I shrink against the back, my heart hammering. The last time I hid like this was (ironically) at Anna's house, years ago, when her dad had come home unexpectedly. That didn't end well, and I've a sneaking suspicion this won't either.

'Josh?' she repeats, and then – and this is typical of Anna – she knocks lightly on one of the wardrobe doors. But then again, I suppose, she has no idea who (or if anyone) is inside here, and walking into a shop staffed only by a pug she's never seen before who's started sniffing at the door of a large wooden wardrobe (£199, in case you're interested) must be a bit spooky.

I have two choices, I know: stay in here and hope Anna goes away, or come out with some story that'll explain what on earth it is that I'm doing, and seeing as I can't seem to think of one, I decide on the first option. Unfortunately, Anna doesn't seem to want to play along, as a moment later the door begins to slowly open.

'Hi, Anna,' I say, weakly. She's got Wallace (lucky dog) cradled against her chest, a 'what were you thinking?' expression on his face. And while I'd try and describe the expression on hers – as a writer, you'd think it'd be easy – there are no words that fully encapsulate the way she's looking at me. Though amusement, disbelief, and quite possibly pity might just about go some way to summing it up.

'Josh.'

'Er . . .'

'Dare I ask?'

'Well, I . . .'

'Were you *hiding* from me?'

'Me? Hiding? From you? Ha ha! No. Why on earth would I do something like that?'

'I don't know. Why would you?'

It's a good question, one I'm regretting suggesting, and not one I can easily think of an answer to. Then Wallace snuffles again and buries his face into Anna's cleavage, and I have an idea.

'I was hiding from Wallace. We were playing a game.'

She glances down at Wallace, who looks up at her as if to say 'No, I don't know either.'

'A game?'

'Of hide and seek.'

'I guessed it wasn't chess. And what happens when he finds you? Is it his turn to go off and hide?'

'No, it's . . .' I shake my head. 'I'm sorry. As you can see, we don't get many customers. So sometimes it gets a bit boring in here.'

Anna stares at me in disbelief. 'And you didn't think to say anything when I was calling out your name? Or did you think that was just an elaborate ruse by . . .'

'Wallace.'

'. . . Wallace, barking your name in a female voice to get you to come out?'

'They're very clever dogs, pugs.'

'Really.' Anna places him carefully back on the floor. 'So you haven't been avoiding me?'

'Avoiding? Me?'

'Avoiding *me*, Josh.'

Quite sensibly, Wallace scuttles off to hide behind my chair, and I realise I'm on my own here. 'Not really, no.'

'No? How long have you been working here?'

'Um . . .'

'I'm only over there,' she says, pointing at her café through the window. 'And you didn't think to just pop across the street and say hello? Especially after the other night. I thought we were friends?'

'We are.' I know I owe her an explanation, but how do I tell her that I can't *be* just friends? And then there's the Ian factor. He made my life a misery at school for years, and he's still doing it, given how he short-changed my dad over the shop. And it's shameful to admit, but I'm still scared of him, even though every part of the adult me knows I shouldn't be. And like my feelings for Anna, that kind of thing just doesn't go away. 'But Ian . . .'

'What about him?' She shakes her head. 'I'm mystified, Josh. Ian doesn't own me.'

'Well, he used to own me. And seems to think he still does.'

'He's not as bad as you think he is. And besides, we're not sixteen anymore.'

I am, I want to say. In fact, most men are. And maybe even a couple of years younger than that, in their heads and especially emotionally. Which is probably why Ian's going to be so pissed off with me if he even finds out I'm talking to Anna, let alone anything else. But instead, and immediately I hate myself for it, I lie.

'It's not just that,' I say, and at once her face crumples, though my 'It's my dad too' rescues it a bit. 'I just feel really bad about having such a nice time with you again when he's . . . I mean, while he and my mum are going through such a tough one. And it's not fair on you to put you through it too.'

'I don't mind.'

'And that's what makes you so lovely. But I just . . . can't. Not right now.'

Anna looks at me for the longest moment, then leans in and gives me a brief kiss on the cheek. 'I understand,' she says, and all of a sudden I want to be honest with her, and tell her the real reason I'm scared to spend any time around her has nothing to do with my dad or Ian, and in fact, it's pretty simple.

What if we fall in love? What am I going to do then?

∾

When I get back that afternoon, my mum accosts me almost as soon as I walk in through the front door.

'Did you have a nice chat with Anna?'

'I'd rather not talk about Anna, Mum.'

'Why not?'

'Just because . . .'

'Because what?'

'Because . . . I don't want to.'

My mum looks at me as if I'm five years old. Not unreasonably, probably. 'Josh . . .'

'Mum, just drop it, will you?'

'No, I will not "drop it", Joshua. You need some cheering up. And Anna's perfect for that. She's perfect for you, in fact. And forgetting all this other stuff that's going on, you're allowed a little fun . . .'

She's used my full name, so I know I'm in trouble. 'Mum, *please*.'

'I didn't mean it like that! Though now you mention it, you're both young and single . . .'

'Well, I can't.'

'Why ever not?'

I take a deep breath. *Because I'm not staying around* is what I should be saying, but I can't bring myself to admit it, so instead I take the coward's way out. Again.

'Because of Ian, Mum.'

'Ian Baker?'

'That's the one. Anna's husband?'

'I thought he and Anna were separated?'

'They are. I know that, you know that, Anna knows that. Trouble is, Ian doesn't seem to. Or at least, he doesn't seem to want to accept it.'

'Right.' She marches into the hallway and grabs her coat, and I feel a sudden panic rising up inside me. I know lying isn't good, and that it usually comes back to bite you in the arse, but I wasn't expecting it to happen so quickly.

'Where are you going?'

'Somewhere I should have gone years ago.'

I'm hoping she means she's going round to Anna's, but I think 'to see Ian' is a more likely destination. 'Don't you dare!'

'Why not?'

'Well, because . . .' I stop talking. How do I explain that a seventy-something woman going to confront a thirty-something charmer who's actually a thug might not be the best idea in the world? How do I say that I'm thirty-six and I don't need my mum to fight my battles, when it's quite clear that I'm no good at fighting them myself? And more importantly, how do I tell her that I'm using Ian as an excuse not to ask Anna out, when the real reason will leave my mum even more disappointed in me?

'We knew Ian was making life uncomfortable for you at school, Josh. I wanted to speak to his parents about it, but your dad said not to. He said you had to find your own way of dealing with it. And even after all this time, it's quite evident that you haven't.'

'Mum, *please*, I'm begging you . . .'

'No, Josh. This needs to be sorted out,' she says, heading out through the door, and while Ian's house is quite possibly the last place on earth I want to go, I can't stop myself from following her.

∽

The guest house that Ian's parents used to run is only a few streets away (though it's flats now – they live on the ground floor, Ian above them, and the others are on the market for 'a fair bit', my mum tells me on the walk here in that small-town 'everyone knows everyone else's business' kind of way). There's a large sign in front of the building advertising 'Luxury Apartments for Sale', and three cars in the parking space behind it – the his-and-hers Mercedes (Mercedeses? Mercedi?) which must belong to his parents, and the obnoxiously loud Subaru that Ian roars around town in. I've only been here the once before – for Ian's thirteenth birthday, when he took the greatest pleasure in convincing everyone to give *me* the bumps instead of him – and the memory's still as fresh as it was the next shame-faced day at school.

My mum gives the building a quick once-over, her hands on her hips, then marches up to the front door and rings the bell, and after a few seconds, Ian's mum answers. She's a tiny, elegant, grey-haired woman, and the idea that someone as big as Ian could have come from her womb is even more of a shock now than it ever was.

'Sue,' she says. 'This is a pl . . .'

'Is that son of yours home?'

Mrs. Baker's expression changes to one she's probably made a thousand times before in front of other parents, or schoolteachers, or policemen. She doesn't say anything; instead, she just glances at the Subaru, then reaches over and presses the buzzer for the upstairs flat. There's a pause, then a gruff 'What?' emerges from the speaker.

'Ian? Can you come down here for a moment? There's someone at the door for you.'

'Who is it?'

Mrs. Baker doesn't answer. Instead, she just takes a step backwards and folds her arms until Ian comes ambling down the stairs, looking as if he's just got up, which, I suppose, is possible. He peers at my mum, then at me, and he seems like he's about to say something snarky when he perhaps remembers what I've told him about my dad.

'Sorry, Mrs. Peters,' he says. 'You know, about Mr. Peters.'

'Thank you, Ian. And?'

'Er . . .' Ian frowns. 'And what?'

'Is there something else you want to apologise for?'

'Probably,' says Ian's mum. She's glowering at him, and obviously assumes he's done something even though she doesn't know what.

'Um . . . Sorry about the shop. The money, and everything. It was just business. Honest.'

'And?'

Ian looks genuinely mystified, and I actually feel a little sorry for him.

'What?'

My mum folds her arms. 'Don't you have someone else you need to say sorry to?'

'Sorry, Mum?' he says, though it's obvious he's clutching at straws.

'Not to *her*, Ian,' says my mum. 'To Josh.'

'To Josh? What for?'

'For bullying him all through school. And for making him feel bad about being back.'

'Sorry, Josh,' he mumbles. 'Really I am. I had no idea. About anything.'

I'd be enjoying this if I still wasn't a little bit scared, and I want to say 'That's okay', but even after eighteen years, I still can't forget everything that went on between us. Which means I've got even more admiration for Anna, for wanting to be my friend after what I did to her.

Ian reaches out a hand, and I regard it warily, then give it the briefest of shakes, and when he doesn't try and crush my fingers, I can't help but regard this as progress. But just when I think we've gotten away with it, his mum reaches out and pats him on the arm.

'See, Ian?' she says, as we turn and leave. 'If you'd been that nice all along, maybe Anna wouldn't have left you in the first place.'

And given the thunderous look on Ian's face as his mum closes the door, I can't help feeling we're back to where we started.

26.

I'm up at ridiculous o'clock this morning to catch the early train up to London for the filming of *Catch Me If You Can*. I've told my mum and dad I've got to go up for a work 'thing', and though they both know I don't have any work that there might be 'things' for, they haven't asked any questions. To be honest, I think they're happy to have me out of the house – I've been moping around since the Anna/Ian incidents a few days ago. Even Wallace is getting fed up with my hang-dog expression.

I suppose I should look on the bright side. I've checked every time I've left the house and there are no bright blue Subarus revving their engines waiting for me to cross the road, which means Ian doesn't seem to be stalking me, so maybe he's too embarrassed (as I am) after my mum accosted him to do anything. As to whether I'll ever hear from Anna again . . . Well, what would be the point? Which is good, I suppose – now I can just get on with this thing with my dad, then get back to London, and get on with my life. And luckily, even though Derton's a small town, it's pretty easy to avoid her. I just need to be careful when (and where) I walk Wallace, keep to my current timings with the shop, and I should be okay. Or at least, that's the theory.

The filming's taking place at a studio on the South Bank, and I'm surprised they want us there so early given they record it in advance, but I don't work in TV, so maybe this is par for the course. In any case, they've laid on breakfast, which is why I'm sitting next to Devon and a couple of other people called Harry and Sally, which seemed to set them both off into peals of laughter (and I'm sure they've been put together on purpose) when they were introduced to each other.

Anyway, we're all eating bacon sandwiches, except for Devon, who's announced that she's some strange brand of vegetarian who eats fish, but only if it doesn't actually *look* like a fish (though why she needs to fill us in on the details of this is beyond me, as it's not as if I'm ever going to be buying her dinner), and who's polishing off some unappetising-looking cereal-like substance she's brought in a Tupperware container. I'm on my third cup of coffee (unlike Devon, who won't even touch decaff as it 'makes her hyper', and if this is what she's like in 'normal' mode, that's probably a good idea) while Louisa explains the rules of the show, which pretty much seem to be: 'Don't blurt out the answer before pressing the button'. Lesley's still nowhere to be seen, which seems to be making Devon more and more anxious, and I worry that she'll burst when she finally does meet him. At least she's not wearing her 'I heart Lesley' t-shirt. Though I wouldn't vouch for her underwear.

'Have you got any questions?' says Louisa, once she's finished her long summing-up.

'I thought you supplied those,' I say, which sends Harry and Sally into gales of laughter again, but Louisa just stares at me.

Then we have a couple of practice run-throughs, though sitting round a table it seems a lot easier than I'm sure it will be when the cameras are in our faces, then it's elevenses (and again, Devon produces another container full of some brown mush that makes me glad I've still got my caveman tendencies), after which we're ushered into a screening room to drink more coffee and watch old episodes of the show. Finally, we're shown into make-up, where a pretty young girl stuffs tissue paper down my shirt collar and proceeds to dab some brown stuff all over my face and neck, and when I open my eyes and see my reflection in the large mirror on the wall in front of me I tell her I'm worried I look like one of the Oompa-Loompas from Willy Wonka's chocolate factory, but the girl gets a bit huffy, and assures me it'll look fine on TV.

After a quick spray of hairspray (which almost blinds me when I get a puff in my eye, and I have a sneaking suspicion she's done that on purpose to get me back for my Oompa-Loompa comment), I'm ready, so I walk back through to the 'green' room (which I'm guessing is so called because that's the colour Devon's turned, such are her nerves at meeting Lesley, let alone being filmed for TV in less than ten minutes). Then, finally, we're led through to the set.

In truth, it's a little disappointing. The multi-coloured lights and ladders that on screen look like something from *The Matrix* are somewhat smaller (and wobblier) than I'd expected, as is Lesley, whose appearance causes Devon to excitedly jump up and down on the spot so vigorously that a couple of the floor staff have to rush and steady the set.

As Lesley sidles over to introduce himself, she grabs him in a bear hug so firm it requires the same floor staff to come and prise him from her grasp. He looks a little shell-shocked, as does Devon, who – thanks to his liberally-applied make-up – has an almost perfect imprint of the side of his face on the white blouse she's wearing.

As she's sent off to change it, Lesley calls Louisa over. 'Who was that?'

'Devon. From Cornwall,' says Louisa, flatly.

'Ah. Of course.' Lesley pulls a small mirror out from his jacket pocket and inspects his face. 'I need a touch-up,' he says, waving the make-up girl over.

Louisa smirks. 'I think you've just had that.'

He glares at her. 'Just keep that one away from me, will you?'

'Yes boss,' says Louisa, saluting smartly, before changing it into a V-sign when his back's turned.

Devon reappears, and is ushered to her spot – as far away from Lesley as possible, I note – then the curtains are drawn back, revealing an audience of around a hundred or so, and what seems to be a mix of mainly pensioners and students. Finally, Louisa winks at us, then begins the countdown.

'Remember,' says Lesley, beaming at us, his teeth still Day-Glo white even as the spotlights dim. 'Have fun.'

The familiar music starts, and I feel my stomach lurch. I've never been on television before, and now, with my usual impeccable good timing, the doubts are starting to surface. What if I dry up, or can't remember any of the answers? I'm here to make my dad proud, yet actually seeing me on here might give him a heart attack. But at the same time, I realise it's probably too late to do anything about it.

'Hello, and welcome to *Catch Me If You Can*,' says Lesley, to camera. 'Can our four contestants beat our resident know-all and go home with a cash prize? We'll find out in the next half hour. But first – it's time to meet them.'

This is it. Our big moment. I know how it'll go – first the camera will focus on Harry, and he'll introduce himself, then it'll be Sally's turn (they've stood them together for comic effect – Lesley's already been primed to make the joke), then it'll be Devon, then me. My mouth is dry, I'm suddenly desperate for the toilet, but I remind myself why I'm here. I've been doing a lot of that recently.

Harry and Sally do their bit, the audience titter as expected, then it's Devon's turn. There's the slightest flicker on Lesley's face, then his smile clicks on. 'So, contestant number three. Tell us who you are, and where are you from?

'I'm Devon,' says Devon. 'From Cornwall,' which (much to Devon's evident relief) actually gets a laugh.

'And if you win tonight, what will you do with the money?' asks Lesley.

Devon frowns. 'Spend it,' she says, as if she's just been asked the most obvious question in the world.

As the audience laugh again, Lesley opens his mouth as if to ask, 'On what?', then obviously receives a prompt via his earpiece to tell him to move on. Quickly.

I swallow hard, then hope the camera (or microphone, given how Devon's looked round at the sound) hasn't caught it, and as Lesley turns to face me I fix a smile on my face.

'And last, but by no means least, it's our final contestant. What's your name, and where are you from?'

'I'm Josh,' I say. 'From Derton.'

'Derton?' Lesley frowns. 'Where's that?'

Exactly, I'd normally say, but given all that's happened in the last few weeks I'm past the point where I want to diss my home town. 'Kent,' I say, then I'm suddenly mortified that I've mispronounced it, and in doing so voiced the worst insult possible on television, but instead of looking all offended and saying 'I only asked', Lesley smiles.

'The garden of England,' he says, affably. 'And tell us, Josh, why do you want to be on *Catch Me If You Can*?'

I've promised myself I won't repeat what I blurted out at the audition – after all, it's unlikely they're going to go easy on me for sentimental reasons – and besides, while the 'make him proud of me' line was fine in front of a group I'll never see again, this time people I know might be watching. And because me being on here isn't actually about me, I decide to go with the truth.

'Because my dad's dying of cancer, and he loves the show – never misses it, in fact – and I thought him seeing me on here might cheer him up a bit.'

Lesley stares at me, and I'm conscious we're experiencing what I understand from Louisa's earlier briefing to be 'dead air'. What I was worried about has happened, and I've overstepped the mark. Maybe they're going to have to start again. Or at least re-do my bit.

Then the audience begin to applaud, slowly at first, then faster and faster. A couple of people even whoop, at which Lesley holds a hand up. 'Steady on,' he says, jokingly. 'We're not in America.'

As the audience settle back down, he turns back to face me. 'Well, I hope you win tonight, Josh, I really do,' he says. 'What's your dad's name?'

I frown, and go completely blank. What *is* my dad's name? I can hardly say 'Dad', can I? How embarrassing is this? And it's hardly a good omen for the questions later.

Suddenly, fortunately, it comes to me. 'Phil,' I blurt out. 'Phil Peters.'

Lesley smiles reassuringly at me, then turns to the camera. 'Well, Phil, if you're watching, and I gather from Josh here that you probably will be, best wishes from everyone on the *Catch Me If You Can* team. Now . . . Let's play.'

As the camera switches back to long view, Lesley gives me a thumbs-up, and I swallow the huge lump in my throat, grateful to have at least got through this part of the show. Because while dying on TV would be embarrassing enough, crying on TV might be even worse.

Harry's up for his questions first, so I relax a little, confident I've got ten or so minutes before the spotlight's back on me. He does okay – six questions right in his allotted thirty seconds – all of which I would have got, and a couple of his wrong ones too. Then it's Sally's turn, and she scores seven, and I'm good with those as well, and by the time Devon gets up, I'm alternating between thinking I'm going to get all of mine right and worrying that they've already asked the questions I know the answers to so the ones I'm going to get will be impossible. And I'm so worried about this that I don't concentrate at all on how Devon's done, and it's only as she's walking back to her seat, a mortified look on her face, I realise she's only scored two points.

Then it's my turn, so I walk nervously out from behind the desk and position myself on the cross on the floor we've been directed to. Lesley is standing behind his lectern, and it's only now I can see – though the camera can't – the box he's standing on so he appears to be taller than the rest of us.

'And the final contestant is Josh, from Derton,' he announces to camera, then he flashes a smile at me. 'So, Josh, the current top score is seven, by Sally. Think you can beat it?'

I shrug. 'I'll give it a go.'

'Great. Your time starts . . . Now!' He glances at the first card in his hand. 'What's the capital of Italy?'

I shout out 'Rome' a little too loudly as my nerves get the better of me, though I'm thankful that they always start with an easy one, but even so, the relief I feel when Lesley says, 'Correct,' is incredible. From there, it's an easy question about films (because surely everyone knows Francis Ford Coppola directed *The Godfather*), followed by one on wine ('What country does sherry come from?', and even though the only sherry I know is Harvey's Bristol Cream, I'm pretty sure the answer isn't 'The West Country', so I guess at Spain and get it right), then there's one I don't know because it's about cricket, and I hate cricket, so I randomly choose a county and get it wrong, wincing internally as I know my dad will be shouting the correct answer at the TV, then I recover with a question about Picasso, which I get right because Mikayla has the exact same picture on her wall, and then the rest go by in a blur, and sooner than I think, my time's up.

'And at the end of your turn, Josh, you've scored . . . Eight points.'

There's a burst of applause from the audience, and as I walk back to my seat I detect a slight scowl from Sally, as my score means I'll be going last – which is usually the best position to play from – and what's more, by my calculations (which are really no more complicated than multiplying the number of correct answers I've given by a thousand) I've got a chance to convert those eight points into eight thousand pounds. Then Lesley turns back to the camera and announces that we're going to a commercial break, the floor manager counts us down, and we all breathe a sigh of relief.

As a make-up girl rushes over to Lesley and dabs some stuff on his face from a tin of what looks like brown shoe polish, Louisa walks over to where we're all nervously waiting.

'Well played, everyone. And especially well done, Josh. How are we all feeling?'

We look at each other, nod, and mumble 'Fine,' except for Devon, who looks like she's going to burst into tears at any moment.

'Right,' says Louisa. 'We'll be going again in a second. Have fun – and try and look like you're enjoying yourselves.' This last comment is directed at Devon. 'And good luck!'

We mumble our thanks again, someone else checks we're all sitting in the right places, there's another countdown, and then Lesley is illuminated in the centre of the set.

'Welcome back to *Catch Me If You Can*,' he says. 'Now it's time to meet today's know-all. The one who's going to try and stop our plucky contestants going home with the total cash jackpot of *twenty-three thousand pounds*!'

There's an 'ooh' from the audience, then a doorway opens at the top of the set, and through a cloud of dry ice marches a very fat man in a tight-fitting black suit. I don't recognise him but judging by the way my fellow contestants' faces have just dropped, he's going to be a toughie.

I lean across to Devon and nudge her. 'Who's he?'

She turns and stares at me incredulously. 'The Terminator?' she says, as if I've just asked the dumbest question in the world, and I'm sure she has to stop herself adding 'duh' to the end of the sentence.

'Ah. The Terminator. Right. Of course.'

It doesn't take me long to work out how he's got his nickname, as Harry lasts approximately a minute before he's sent scuttling off to wait behind the cameras. The guy is brutal – there's not an answer he doesn't seem to know. If Google and Wikipedia ever got together and had a son, this is what he'd probably be like.

Sally is dispatched almost as quickly, and by the time it's Devon's turn, she almost has to be forced into the hot seat – even the lure of standing next to Lesley isn't enough. To give her some credit, she lasts longer than either Harry or Sally, but that's possibly because The Terminator seems to be enjoying torturing her.

Finally, it's my turn, and for some reason, a Zen-like calm descends on me. Whatever happens, I tell myself, I'm here for my dad. He's given some advice, and I've taken it. He'll be sitting at home watching proudly (hopefully), and all I have to do is go out there and do my best. So as long as I don't fall flat on my face on the way to the hot seat, or say something stupid . . .

Of course, now I've thought about falling, I have to walk extra-carefully over to the chair just to make sure I don't trip over my own feet, which makes me look like some sort of *Thunderbirds* puppet. And what's worse is as I sit down, a siren goes off and the studio lights begin to flash.

Alarmed, I leap up out of the chair, only to feel Lesley's hand on my shoulder easing me back down.

'Relax, Josh,' he says. 'That's the bonus buzzer. And you know what that means?'

My blank expression makes him do a quick double take, but ever the professional, Lesley just flashes his over-white teeth at me. 'That's right,' he continues, despite my lack of an answer. 'The chance to play for . . .' He points at the screen behind him, where a series of figures flash up in seemingly random order, before finally settling on '£50,000'.

'Fifty, thousand, pounds,' announces Lesley, for the benefit of anyone who might not be able to read.

There's another 'ooh' from the audience, and I look round to see my fellow competitors glaring at me jealously.

'So, Josh, would you like me to remind you of the rules?'

'Yes, please,' I say, given that 'remind' isn't the most appropriate word.

'Well, you can play the normal round for eight thousand pounds if you like, or we'll reduce the time you have to answer each question to ten seconds, you can take one step closer down the ladder towards our know-all . . .' He pauses, so the camera can switch to The Terminator, who's wringing his hands for effect. '. . . but if you manage to get home, you'll win *fifty thousand pounds*!'

Now, admittedly, I've only watched the programme a few times (and most of those times were earlier today just before we came on), but thinking about it, I have seen this random bonus round once. The contestant has less chance to win, hence the higher cash prize, though if there's one thing even my limited viewing has taught me, it's that it's hard enough to beat the know-all even under normal circumstances.

'Did you want to consult your team?'

I nod, and swivel round in my chair, where Harry, Sally, and Devon are already shaking their heads frantically. What's more, Devon's also giving me the thumbs-down. With both thumbs.

'So, Josh. What's it going to be?'

My mind is spinning. Fifty thousand pounds would make a huge difference to my mum, plus there's no guarantee I'll win the eight, so surely it's worth the gamble? Then again, it's The

Terminator, and don't I want to give myself the best chance of at least walking away with something?

I think of my dad, watching this – assuming he survives that long – when it airs in a couple of weeks. Even though he knows it's not live, he'll probably be shouting at the screen right now, telling me to play it safe. Not to take the risk. To go for the eight. Given our situation, I don't suppose I've got a choice.

'Well, Lesley,' I hear myself saying, 'I'll go for the fifty.'

27.

I'm sitting numbly on the train back to Derton, staring at the cheque I've propped up on the small, crumb-strewn, slightly sticky fold-out table in front of me. I still can't quite believe I went for the big prize, but that's me, I'm beginning to realise. Always looking for something better. And there are times that it pays off.

Unfortunately, though, this wasn't one of them, and while I'd like to report that I managed to escape The Terminator in a way that'd make Sarah Connor look like an amateur, sadly that wasn't the case. Still, the television company have been good enough to refund my train fare, and I got breakfast, so it's not been a completely wasted morning. Though my dad may have a different opinion when he watches the programme.

I miserably pull my phone out of my pocket and nervously check my messages. Every time I see the voicemail icon appear, I assume it's my mum to tell me my dad's died – but instead, it's a curt message from Marty, asking me to call him back. Reluctantly, I dial his number, and ask to be put through.

'Well, well, well, if it isn't Josh Peters,' he announces. 'The man who came up with "A touching novel" for *Lolita*.'

'Please, Marty, now's not the time.'

'Don't you want to hear what the client said?'

'Not really,' I say, praying the train will go through a tunnel and the call will cut off. I've had all the humiliation I can take for one day.

'No? Well, that's a shame. Because they LOVED it.'

'What?' He's almost screamed this down the phone, and I have to move the handset to my other ear. 'I thought it was "too controversial"?'

Marty sighs theatrically. 'That's what people want nowadays. Conventional is boring. You need something that's going to get you talked about.'

'That's what I—'

'You're *back*, Josh. With a vengeance. And speaking of "back", when are you?'

'I'm not sure, Marty. My dad's still . . .'

'Alive?'

'Yeah,' I say, trying to ignore the disappointment in Marty's voice.

'Oh. Right. Well, keep me posted. And in the meantime, whizz me over an invoice and I'll pay it. And let me know when you've had some more thoughts about *The Blind Masseur*.'

'Right. Although I—'

'Great. Laters.'

'Laters,' I say – though it pains me to do so – but Marty's already ended the call.

༄

When I get to the house, my mum and dad are having an afternoon nap in the front room, so I quietly collect Wallace and take him out to the seafront while I try and work out how (or rather, if) I'm going to tell them about *Catch Me If You Can*. While Marty's call was a bit of unexpected good news, I've still got a long way to go before I can make up the rest of even the eight thousand pounds I didn't win. And short of coming up with another blinding (if you excuse the pun) idea for *The Blind Masseur*, spending another seven-hundred-plus hours at a tenner an hour working in Michelle's shop is looking like my only alternative.

When Wallace and I get back my mum is waving frantically at me through the kitchen window, and when I see the look on her face my heart skips a beat.

'What's happened?'

She nods towards the front room. 'In there.'

I unclip Wallace's lead and he trots off ahead of me along the hall, but two seconds later he's coming back even faster in the opposite direction. With a heavy heart, I make my way down the hallway and into the lounge, but instead of the sight I've been expecting – my dad lying slumped in his chair, or flat on the floor surrounded by medics – something more chilling awaits me. Because he's sitting at the table, a bemused expression on his face, and opposite him, perched on the sofa, is Mikayla.

'Hello, Josh.'

'What are you doing here?'

'It's nice to see you too,' she says, then she unfolds her impossibly long legs from underneath her and stands up. 'Come and give me a hug.'

'But . . .' I stay where I am. 'You should have called.'

'I wanted to surprise you.'

'Well, you have. Seriously, you should have called.'

Mikayla pads over to where I'm standing and drapes her arms around my shoulders. She's tanned from her holiday, and wearing the shortest of dresses – probably so she can show it off.

'I missed you.'

'I guessed that. Seeing as you *haven't* called. At all. For the past three weeks.'

'Oh, *Josh*,' she says, in a way that's supposed to be playful, but ends up sounding patronising. Then she tries to kiss me on the lips, but I turn my face quickly to one side, and quick as a flash she turns it into a couple of little air kisses so as not to look silly.

There's an anxious growling from somewhere behind me, and Mikayla lets me go. 'And who is this?' she asks, kneeling down and holding out a hand to Wallace. He's poking his head nervously round the door and looking even more scared than when he met an amorous Alsatian on the beach earlier.

'It's Wallace,' says my dad.

'Oh. Like the clothes shop?'

My dad and I exchange glances, and I hear my mum unsuccessfully try and stifle a laugh in the kitchen.

'Yes,' says my dad. 'We were going to name him Dorothy Perkins, but decided that would be too embarrassing in the park.'

'Does he bite?'

'I think he's wondering the same thing.'

Mikayla stands back up quickly. 'I was just telling your father how well he was looking. You know, for someone who's . . .'

'Dying?' suggests my dad. From the sound of him, he's been having to entertain Mikayla for too long already – even though it's possible she's only been here a few minutes.

Mikayla lets out an awkward little laugh. 'Well, yes. And he's been filling me in on how well you've been looking after him.'

'He has?'

I perhaps sound more surprised than I should, and my dad looks up sharply from his chair.

'And how you've been catching up with your old friends. Like Baz.'

'Gaz.'

'No, I'm sure your dad said his name was Baz.'

This is another of Mikayla's traits. Telling people who actually know something that her mis-remembered version is the right one.

'It is. But everyone calls him Gaz.'

'Uh-huh,' says Mikayla, her expression suggesting she's not interested enough to ask why.

'So . . .'

We're standing there awkwardly, my dad watching us anxiously, though I know he's probably just impatient to get back to his Sky Sports. My mum's still hiding in the kitchen, and even Wallace is looking like he's desperate to be out of here. Which suddenly gives me an idea.

I lean down and clip his lead back onto his collar, and clear my throat. 'So, listen, Wallace needs his daily constitutional, so if you wanted to join me . . .'

'I thought he'd just been for a walk?'

'Oh no. We were only halfway through. I always like to pop back in and check on Dad mid-way.'

'Oh. Right.' Mikayla looks over at my dad, who mimes dying, and for once I'm grateful for his black humour, then she finally twigs that I'm trying to get her out of the house. 'Well, okay, then. Where shall I leave this?'

For the first time, I notice Mikayla has an overnight bag slung over her shoulder, and I start to panic. 'Give it to me,' I say, taking her bag in one hand, Wallace's lead in the other, and steering Mikayla along the hallway and out through the front door.

'Why are you bringing that?' she says, nodding towards her bag (which is as heavy as I remember, and I hope Nino isn't asleep in there) once we've reached the pavement.

'You can't stay. And certainly not here.'

'Why ever not?'

Mikayla's evidently struggling to keep up – and not just with the conversation, as Wallace is pulling me along at a fair pace. 'Hello? My dad's ill?'

'I wasn't planning to bunk in with him.'

'Well, we don't have a spare bedroom.'

'I could snuggle in with you, silly.'

Something about the way Mikayla says 'snuggle' makes my skin crawl. 'I'm in a single bed.'

'Ooh. Cosy.'

'Mikayla, what do you want?'

'Like I said, I missed you, Josh. And I was thinking that when this is all over, perhaps we could think about getting back together?'

I stop in my tracks, nearly throttling Wallace in the process. 'When this is *all over*?'

'That's right.'

And this is Mikayla's problem – or rather, the problem I have with Mikayla. Because the kind of person I want to be with is the kind of person who wants to be there while 'this' is all going on. And if Mikayla can't see that . . . Well, it just reinforces the fact that she's not for me.

I start walking again, aiming for the station now. Wallace seems to sense where I'm going – he's straining even harder at his lead to speed us along. And Mikayla follows me, and it's cruel, but I know she will, because I've got her bag, and she can't survive more than five feet away from her make-up.

'Come on, Josh. The least you could do is give me five minutes.'

'Can't we talk while we walk?'

'I've had a long and difficult journey down here . . .'

'It's an hour and a half on the train.'

'. . . and I need a coffee. Assuming they've heard of the stuff here.'

'Of course they have,' I say, feeling strangely defensive about Derton. 'We've got a Starbucks . . .'

'Yuk.'

'Well, there's a café in the station. Or even better, a buffet car on the train.'

'Are you trying to get rid of me?'

'Um . . .'

'How about that place?' she says, pointing at Baker's Cupcakes on the far corner.

'What? No! We can't . . .'

'Well, I'm going in there. So unless you want to hang around here with a woman's bag around your shoulder and a rather effeminate dog on a lead, which I suspect might not be the best of ideas in a town like this, you'd better join me.'

With that, she marches across the road and into the café, and though I know it's possibly the stupidest thing I can do, I follow her inside.

❧

Of course, these things never go well. Because for it to go well, Anna would have to be on her lunch break, or taking the day off, instead of standing behind the till when we walk in. And when Mikayla marches right up to the counter with me and Wallace (and a handbag) in hot pursuit, she instinctively knows something's up.

'Josh?'

Mikayla peers at Anna, particularly at what she's wearing, because that's what's important in her world, then frowns at me. 'A friend of yours, Josh?'

I attempt some sort of simultaneous nod/shrug, trying to convey that Derton's a small town, and that everyone knows everyone here, but given the expression that flashes across Mikayla's face, I don't get away with it for a second.

'Hi,' she says, holding her hand out to Anna, as if she's allowed to know everyone I know by right. 'I'm Mikayla. And you are?'

'Anna,' says Anna, suspiciously.

'And how do you two know each other?'

'I'm sorry? Who are you, exactly?'

'Mikayla,' repeats Mikayla, and even though I'm repeating *don't say it* to myself over and over again, I'm just not that lucky. 'Josh's girlfriend.'

'Josh's . . .' Anna looks at her in disbelief as she visibly pales, then her eyes flick across to me, and at once, I'm filled with regret. Regret that I didn't come clean with Anna the other night, regret that I followed Mikayla in here just now, but on top of everything, regret that Mikayla's shock appearance is in danger of messing everything up.

'Didn't he say he had a girlfriend?' Mikayla is obviously enjoying the moment.

'No. No, he didn't.' Anna can't look at me, though that's actually something I'm grateful for, then with what seems like the greatest of efforts, she regains her composure. 'So, what can I get you?'

'What's good here?'

Anna smiles. 'Everything.'

Mikayla makes a face that can best be described as 'I doubt that'.

'Josh? Sweetie? Have you tasted Anna's cupcakes?'

I glare at her. Mikayla's never called me sweetie once in all the time I've known her, and I'm not pleased at her attempt at innuendo either. 'I thought you just wanted a coffee. Before you went back to London. On your own.' I enunciate that last bit as carefully as I can, trying to imply that it's a fleeting, even *final* visit, but by the look of Anna's expression I've a lot of ground to make up.

'That's right. I do. Not good for the old waistline, I suppose, are they, Anna?' Mikayla looks her up and down disdainfully, then her gaze settles on the coffee machine behind the counter. 'I suppose a decaff latte's out of the question?'

'No, we can do that,' says Anna, flatly. 'Josh?'

'Nothing for me. And can we have that coffee *to go*?' I say, desperate for Anna to understand that Mikayla's not staying. That she shouldn't even be here. That I don't want to share a coffee with her, because I'm not sharing anything with her. I tap my watch exaggeratedly, but Mikayla smiles sweetly back at me.

'So, how do you two know each other?' she asks Anna.

'He used to be *my* boyfriend.'

'Well, it's nice you have something in common,' I say, pointedly, and although I've said it to get the message that Mikayla and I are finished across to the two of them, I perhaps haven't thought this through, because they both round on me.

As I cower against the onslaught, I can't help but wonder how this has happened? I'm here to look after my dad – which is a good thing, surely? – and through, what, Mikayla's bloody-mindedness, and Anna's mistaken assumption, I've found myself being painted as the devil incarnate. And I could stand here and take it, as I've taken it for the last few years from Mikayla, and as I took it all those years ago from Ian, or I can stick up for myself for once. Which is what I decide to do.

'I'm sorry, Mikayla, but you don't belong here – in Derton, or with me. And it's taken me being back here to realise it, but we haven't belonged together for a while. And I don't know what you're doing here now, but you dumped me, remember, because I chose to come and look after my dying dad, rather than go and spend a couple of weeks sunning myself on some tropical beach with you.'

'But you don't even *like* your dad!'

I'm guessing Mikayla's said this for Anna's benefit, perhaps even hoping to get her on her side, and that angers me even more.

'You're wrong, Mikayla. I *love* my dad. It's you who's not particularly likeable. And, Anna – I fell in love with you the moment I first saw you. Twice, in fact. But the first time, you decided you loved Derton more than me, then to add insult to injury you married the guy that made my life hell. And then, while I was away, you and your husband screwed my dad . . .'

'Eew . . .' says Mikayla.

'Not like *that*. And now, just when I think I've got a chance to make everything okay again with my dad before it's too late, and make sure my mum's fine, and keep my boss happy, and look after Wallace, and not embarrass myself on television, and all the while, while I'm trying not to hurt you again, you treat me like . . .' I struggle to find the appropriate phrase. 'Like *I'm* the bad guy. Well, I'm not. In fact, I'm the opposite. I'm the good guy,' I add, just in case she hasn't got it.

And then, like the big girl's blouse that I fear I've become, I hand Mikayla her bag, pick a bemused-looking Wallace up from the floor, turn on my heel, and flounce out through the door.

28.

It doesn't feel good being back at school, even some eighteen years later when I'm coming here voluntarily. The place doesn't seem to have changed much. The iron gates still look like something you'd see guarding the entrance to a maximum-security prison (which was how it felt to me back then), the playing fields are more mud than grass, and the general standard of teachers' cars in the car park is a sad reflection of just how little the government seems to value this most important of professions. Either that, or they're scared to drive nice ones for fear of what the kids might do to them.

As I walk in, I'm annoyed to find myself still checking the bike sheds on my left where Ian Baker and his gang used to hang out (and often chuck whatever they had to hand – empty Coke cans, conkers, some of the smaller first year kids – at me as I'd cycle in). To be honest, I'd rather not be here after yesterday's debacle – though I'm not sure which out of *Catch Me If You Can*, Mikayla's visit, or blurting out to Anna that I loved her was worse – but people are counting on me. And I've let too many people down recently to want to make a habit of it.

I look at my watch. Mr. Ronson has told me to meet him at eleven, and it's five to already, so I get a move on up the once-familiar stairs, standing back as a tsunami of scary-looking teenagers rush along the corridor and into the assembly hall (where it sounds like a riot is taking place). I knock on the staffroom door, and it's opened by a pretty teacher who barely looks older than the kids I've just seen.

'Can I help you?'

I peer over her shoulder. Instead of the smoky fog that always used to pour out of here back in the day, there's actually some music playing, and I'm surprised to see a Nespresso machine.

'I'm here to see Mr. Ronson.'

'Aha. So *you're* Josh Peters.'

'That's right.'

As I wonder what I've done that's made me one of the famous 'old boys', the woman smiles. 'The one who's doing the careers session with year eleven.'

'Uh-huh.' Most times, if you knocked on this door, you were probably in some kind of trouble, and given the look she gives me, I can't help worrying the same thing's true today.

'Good luck with that,' she says, but before I can ask her what she means, a grinning Mr. Ronson appears at her shoulder – though he seems a little surprised that I've actually turned up.

'Josh! I'm so pleased you're here! Thanks again for agreeing to do this.'

'No problem.'

'They're all waiting for you in the assembly hall.'

'The *assembly hall*?'

He nods. 'I thought we'd get them all in.'

'And how many is "them all", exactly?'

Mr. Ronson looks round at me reassuringly as he leads me back along the corridor. 'A hundred or so. Assuming most of them haven't skived off for the afternoon.'

'A *hundred*?' I swallow hard. I've never been good at public speaking. It's one of the reasons I like being a writer – you're in a room on your own, and you get a chance to revise your words a thousand times before anyone else so much as hears one of them. This, however, is the complete opposite. I'm heading towards a room full of people (well, kids), all of whom are desperate to be somewhere else – including (now) me. And – as it soon becomes obvious when Mr. Ronson leads me in through the double doors and up onto the stage – all of whom are looking at me with the kind of contempt that suggests that I'm the person keeping them from exactly that.

'Settle down,' says Mr. Ronson, followed by 'Settle down!' in a somewhat louder voice, and gradually, the room quietens. 'This is Josh Peters,' he announces, as a hundred pairs of eyes shift their disgruntled gaze to me. 'He's an old boy.'

'You're telling us,' someone shouts, and there's a ripple of laughter around the hall, which only stops when Mr. Ronson says, 'See me afterwards, Mason.'

'Now,' he continues, 'Josh has very kindly agreed to come here and tell you about his experiences as a writer.' There's a collective groan, though I can't blame them, as if it's anything like my days at St. Martin's, most of them would struggle to write their own names. 'Josh was one of my star English pupils here. Then he went on to read English Literature at London University.'

'As opposed to just looking at the pictures, sir?' comes the same voice.

'It's your own time you're wasting, Mason,' says Mr. Ronson, sternly, though strictly speaking it's mine too, and I'm beginning to suspect this whole exercise might be a waste of everyone's time.

'Sorry, sir,' says Mason, weakly.

'Now he's writing a novel, and he works in publishing, with a lot of famous writers . . .'

I think about saying that strictly speaking, I work for someone who has clients who work in publishing, and that the famous writers I work with are often dead, but don't want to take the sting out of what's just been said, mainly because at the word *famous*, half of the kids have actually woken up.

'So, who wants to start?'

Mr. Ronson leans across to me. 'We normally do these things as a kind of question and answer session. It stops them from getting bored.'

By the looks of the audience that ship's already sailed, but all of a sudden, a hand shoots up from the back of the room.

'Yes, Simons,' says Mr. Ronson.

'Are *you* famous?'

I want to say that no, I'm not, and that the fact that he has to ask that question makes it somewhat rhetorical, though by the looks of Simons, he won't know what *rhetorical* means. 'Not many writers are famous. I mean, how many can you name?'

There's a collective silence, then a few hands go up.

'Yes?' I say, pointing to a spotty kid in the back row.

'Harry Potter.'

'He's not a writer, is he?' says Mr. Ronson. 'Come on – who wrote about him?'

'Don't you know, sir?' shouts someone. 'I thought you were supposed to be an English teacher?'

Mr. Ronson rolls his eyes. 'Yes, yes. Very funny. Let's have some proper questions, shall we?'

There's silence for an interminable amount of time.

'Come on,' says Mr. Ronson, crossly. 'Josh has given up his morning.'

Eventually, a hand is tentatively raised, a bespectacled boy at the front.

'What's the name of your book?'

'It . . . It doesn't have a title yet.'

'Why not?'

'You'd hardly give your child a name before it was born, would you?'

'My mum did,' says a voice from somewhere in the middle of the room.

'Yeah,' shouts someone. 'Bastard.'

'And what's it about?' asks someone else, once the laughter has died down, which takes a while.

'Well, it's . . .' I take a deep breath. 'It's about someone who grows up in a seaside town . . .'

'Is it Derton?'

'No, it's not Derton. Though there are parts of it that are loosely modelled . . .'

'And what happens?'

'Well, like I said, this person . . .'

'Is there any sex in it? Like in those Filthy Sheds?'

'*Fifty Shades*. And no.'

'Why not?'

'Are you gay?'

Mr. Ronson leaps to his feet. 'Wilson, you can see me afterwards as well. Go on, Josh.'

I swallow hard. 'So, this person hates where he's growing up. And . . .'

'Why?'

Well, there's not much to do, and he doesn't get on with his father, and . . .'

'Why not?'

'Well, it's complicated, but . . .'

'Does his dad try and shag him?'

Mr. Ronson leaps to his feet again. 'Right, Wilson, go and wait for me outside the staffroom. And the rest of you. Sensible questions please, or we'll all stay here over lunch.'

Wondering whether that punishment will include me, I peer expectantly around the hall, but the rest of them don't seem to have any sensible questions – or any questions at all, for that matter. So instead, I tell them about going to college, and what fun it was, and about my job, and what fun it is (and I have to use all my creative powers on that one). And despite my best attempts to engage them by seeing if they can guess what books I'm talking about by their taglines (though I decide not to try my latest *Lolita* one on them), then asking them what they like to read (nothing, apparently), or what they like to do in their spare time (same answer, closely followed by Playstation or Xbox), it's clear they'd rather be anywhere but here. And by that, I mean 'here' as in 'school', rather than simply listening to me.

And I can't help wonder whether it's Derton that's done this to them. Were we like this, back when we were sitting where they are now? Is it the lack of opportunity that creates the lack of ambition, or has that always existed? Most of them must have parents who work, or who studied, and who of course want the same thing for their kids. But how do you find that in a town where the major achievement was always seen as escaping it?

Eventually Mr. Ronson clears his throat and stands up. 'Well, if there are no other questions?' he says, and there aren't, though I suspect it's the first thing everyone's in agreement about. But as the room begins to make what we back in the day would call 'general packing up noises', I tentatively raise a hand.

'Yes, Josh,' says Mr. Ronson, to a loud grumbling from the rest of the hall.

'So, what do you lot want to do?'

There's an awkward silence.

'Okay, what do you want to be?'

'Famous,' says someone, eventually.

'A footballer,' says another.

'A famous footballer,' says a third.

'What about normal jobs?'

The kids are looking at each other anxiously, as if the prospect of actually having to do some work at some time in their lives is too terrible to contemplate.

'No-one wants to be a writer?'

A bout of giggling circles around the hall.

'Why not? Writing's cool.'

'Yeah, right,' sniffs a big kid at the back.

I peer at him. He's not unlike Ian used to be, sitting there as if he owns the assembly hall, an entourage of smaller kids surrounding him. 'Okay, well what about *Game of Thrones*? Is that cool?'

There's a general murmur of approval, and sensing I'm onto something, I plough on. 'Well, that was based on a book.' I stare at the sea of blank faces. 'Which was written by someone. A writer. Like me.'

'But not actually you, yeah?' says the big kid.

'No.' As he gives me a smug smile, I have to stop myself from adding *do you think I'd be wasting my time with you lot if it was?* 'But everything you watch on TV, every film you see at the cinema . . . Someone wrote it. A writer.'

A few of the kids have strange expressions on their faces, which, after a few seconds, I recognise as comprehension.

'So how many of you want to go to university?'

There's a pause, then a couple of kids sitting in the front row tentatively put their hands up, to a chorus of boos, and an avalanche of missiles, some of which seem to be coming in my direction.

'And the rest of you? Aren't you desperate to do something with your lives?' I ask, to a sea of blank faces. 'Something worthwhile? There's a whole other world outside of Derton, you know?'

Then the big kid pipes up again. 'So what you doing back then? If Derton's so shit?'

Mr. Ronson flinches at the swearword, though he's wearing the expression of a man who's long ago given up trying to stop this kind of thing.

'He's come back to speak to you ungrateful lot.'

'Nah, seriously,' says the kid, who I'm beginning to dislike.

'Derton's not so . . .' I glance across at Mr. Ronson, but he just gives me a 'whatever' look. 'Shit.'

'Yes it is,' says the kid. 'If it wasn't, why did you leave?'

'Well, back then, it didn't have what it has now. You know, the gallery, and . . .' I think quickly – I can't really list Starbucks and Baker's Cupcakes as major attractions. 'Well, and the retro vibe. Retro's cool nowadays. Especially to people from London. And sometimes, you have to leave a place before you can see what it's really like. Because it's only then you've got something to compare it to.'

'So you're back because Derton's cool?'

There's a muttering round the room, and a few of the kids are actually sitting up a bit straighter, as if my sudden endorsement of the place where they live has actually hit home. All eyes are on me, and while I don't want to depress them, I don't want to sugar-coat things either. 'Well, actually, mainly because my dad's not very well, so . . .'

'What's wrong with him?'

'That's enough, Atkins,' says Mr. Ronson, but I hold my hand up.

'No, that's okay. He's got cancer, actually.'

This shuts them up. Because 'cancer' is one of those words that everyone appreciates the seriousness of. Back when I was at school, it was almost acceptable to make jokes about all other diseases or disabilities except this one, perhaps because it's touched most of us (or because we've all seen *Breaking Bad*), and everyone knows just how shit (to borrow recent terminology) it is.

'Is he dying?'

'Yeah,' I say, quietly. 'Yeah, he is.'

The big kid – Atkins – frowns. 'And this is the dad who, in the book, you don't get on with?'

I colour slightly. 'No, I told you, the book's a work of fiction.'

'But it's based on Derton, right? And so the main character, he's probably based on you, yeah?'

'Well, perhaps there's a little bit of me in him . . .'

There's a lot more sniggering this time, and Mr. Ronson rolls his eyes again. 'Minds out of the gutter, please.'

'So why did you come back?' Atkins is just like Ian used to be, not letting anything go, sensing a chink in the armour and working away at it, and it's what makes the most successful bullies. Not only are they bigger than everyone else, but they're pretty smart – although they do their best to hide it. 'If you don't get on with your dad?'

'Because it's what you do, isn't it?'

Atkins shrugs. 'I wouldn't.'

'Well, perhaps that's the difference between you and me,' I say, levelly, wishing I'd been able to say that kind of thing to Ian's face all those years ago. But Atkins – and he could do with following his namesake's diet, though I decide not to tell him that – won't let it go.

'What's going to happen when he dies? Are you going to stay here in Derton, or go back to London?'

'Well, that depends.'

'On what?' asks Atkins, just as the bell rings to signal the end of the session.

On my mum, and Anna, and Wallace, and my job, and a million other things, is what I want to say. But as the kids stampede out of the assembly hall as if the school's just hit an iceberg and is beginning to sink, I realise it's a lot simpler than that.

It's whether I've got anything to go back for.

29.

There are no pictures of the three of us in the house. Not that my mum's a 'photographs up' kind of woman, or the type that would include a recent family snapshot along with an update whenever sending out Christmas cards (thank goodness!), but the photo I took in front of *The Kiss* has – like Rodin's other famous sculpture – got *me* thinking that the fact that there's not one photo of us all together is perhaps something that a psychologist might have quite a bit to say about. Until recently, I've never thought this odd – after all, everything's digital in my world – but this isn't my world, as my dad points out when I mention the fact. And when I flick through the dusty family albums he's brought out this morning, their fading Polaroids barely held in place by the slightly gummy, plastic-covered pages, it's evident that there are very few family photos at all.

'All of them. It's just me and Mum. Or you and Mum.'

My dad frowns as he leafs through the album. 'Well, someone had to take the photo. And seeing as there are only three of us . . .'

'Didn't it bother you? That there wasn't a single family portrait from the last twenty years?'

'It didn't. But it does now. For obvious reasons.'

'Right.' I place the album carefully on the shelf, then pull out my phone and dial Gaz's number. It rings twice, and then:

'Mate.'

'You busy?'

'That depends.'

'On what?'

'Whether Michelle wants to have her wicked way with me.'

'So you're not, then?'

'Not especially. What's up?'

'I need you to take some photos.'

'Of Anna? I've got just the camera, with a good enough zoom that . . .'

'No, of us. And *what*?'

'Nothing,' says Gaz, quickly. 'But why d'you want photos of you and me?'

'*Us*, Gaz. My mum, dad, and me.'

'Ah. Right. Give me ten minutes.'

I turn to my dad. 'Gaz says he can get here in ten minutes?'

'Tell him to hurry,' he says, in his weakest possible voice.

❧

I find my mum in the kitchen and explain what's happening, and as she rushes upstairs to get changed, I head back to where my dad's sitting.

'Right. Shave time.'

My dad rubs his chin. 'Do I have to?'

'Yes. Unless you want people to wonder why Mum and I are having our photo taken with Gandalf?'

'Point taken.'

I wheel him outside, find him a spot in the sun, then go and locate a towel and the electric clippers.

'Right.' I drape the towel round his neck, stand back, and try and decide where to start. 'Keep still.'

'With you with that dangerous device in your hand? Don't worry. I will.'

It seems silly to say, but I've never shaved anyone else before, and it's actually quite difficult, like on those programmes where someone has to shear a sheep for the first time. I also haven't been this close to my dad for quite a while, so we're both more than a little uncomfortable. Especially when he keeps wincing.

'What's the matter?'

'You keep cutting me.'

'That's physically impossible. These are electric clippers. With a plastic guard.'

'Well, something hurts.'

'Sure it's not just your pride?'

Eventually, I'm finished. And while it's hardly the kind of close shave you see in Gillette adverts (and there are a few tufty bits I haven't managed to tame), it's the first time I've seen my dad looking relatively normal for a while. And while his cheeks may have sunken a bit, and his complexion isn't the healthiest, at least he looks a little like he used to before all this started.

'How's it looking, son?'

'Not bad. Less *Lord of the Rings*, anyway.'

'Well, that's a good thing, I suppose.' He reaches a hand up and gingerly rubs it across his face. 'Still got all my features, too.'

'You're welcome,' I say, sarcastically. I undo the towel from around his neck, and shake the not inconsiderable amount of hair onto the floor. 'Now, what are you going to wear?'

My dad looks down at his jogging-bottoms-and-sweatshirt combination. 'What's wrong with this?'

'Apart from the fact that they don't fit? And you can see last night's dinner down the front of them?'

'Ah. Well, you took all of my clothes to the charity shop, remember?'

'They wouldn't have fitted you anyway,' I say, a bit miffed at being blamed, then try and remind myself that I need to stop being so sensitive. That was as easily a statement of fact as an accusation. I look him up and down, and it occurs to me that we could take a trip to Tesco's for some of Gaz's F&F clothing, but without wishing to sound harsh, that would be a waste of what little money my mum and dad have left. There's always what he's been referring to as his 'death-day suit', but that strikes me as a little macabre.

As I stare at him, I have an idea. 'Wait there,' I say, then head inside and upstairs to my room. My dad appears to be about my size now, and the suit I wore to Gaz and Michelle's the other night might just do the trick. I look it out, along with one of my white work shirts, then go back downstairs to find he's wheeled himself back inside.

'Here.'

'What's this?'

'Like I said. Something for you to wear.'

'Are they clean?' he says, inspecting the trousers closely.

'Of course they're . . . Just put them on, will you? Or do you need a hand with that?'

'No fear.'

He stares at me for a moment.

'What?'

'At least turn round.'

I shake my head as I do as instructed, then have to listen to his sighing, grumbling, and grunting as he eases himself into the outfit. Though when I finally turn back round, I'm more than a little shocked at what I see. And even Wallace, who's just sauntered into the room, seems a little confused.

'What?'

'Nothing. It's just . . .' I shake my head. For the first time, I can even see we look a little alike. 'It suits you.'

My dad smooths the front of his shirt down self-consciously. 'Not in bad shape for seventy-three, eh?' He says. 'Apart from . . .'

'The cancer.' I smile at him. 'I know.'

The doorbell rings, and I go and let Gaz in, passing my mum in the hall, then trying not to laugh when I hear her sharp intake of breath at seeing how my dad looks.

'Thanks for coming, mate.'

'No worries.' Gaz lowers his voice. 'How is he?'

'As you'd expect.'

We walk into the lounge, and Gaz does a good job of hiding his surprise at my dad's appearance.

'Mr. Peters.'

'Gary.'

'Mrs. P.'

'Hello, Gaz.'

Gaz holds his camera up. 'So, where would you like this?'

I take a look around the room. 'In front of the fireplace?'

I wheel my dad into position, and my mum stands next to him, but just as Gaz is about to start shooting, my dad shakes his head.

'What's the matter?' I say, just managing to stop myself from adding the word *now*.

'I don't want my last photo to be in *this* thing,' he says, hauling himself out of the wheelchair. 'Though I don't think I can stand for that long.'

'Here,' I say. 'Put one arm around Mum, and the other round my shoulders.'

'What about Wallace?'

'He's too short to hold you up.'

'He should be in the photo.'

'Fine.' I reach down and pick Wallace up. 'Ready when you are, Gaz.'

'Okay.' Gaz takes a pace back, then tweaks one of the buttons on the front of his camera. 'Right. Smile, everyone.'

'You too, Wallace,' says my dad.

As Wallace gives me a look that seems to say 'will this take long?', Gaz starts snapping away, until my dad can't stand (or stand it) any more.

'Are we done?' he asks, collapsing back into his chair.

'Pretty much,' says Gaz, flicking through the photos on the screen on the back of his camera. 'Anything wrong we can fix. I mean, you know, with Photoshop . . .'

My dad grins. 'I know what you meant, Gary. Thank you.'

Gaz hands me the camera, and I take a quick look through the photos. It's hard to tell on the small screen, but one thing's obvious despite my slightly strained smile, Wallace's lolling tongue, my dad's unhealthy demeanour, and my mum's long-suffering expression: stood together like this, my dad's arms round my mum and me, we look like a family.

30.

I've been here for a month now, and today I have my first stroke of luck. According to the email I wake up to from Louisa, my episode of *Catch Me If You Can* is being screened this lunchtime, and unbelievably, my dad's funeral party is happening at *exactly the same time*. This is a good thing, because even he won't be rude enough to ignore his guests for half an hour so he can watch it, which means I might just get away with my disastrous performance. Especially since everyone who's likely to tell him I'm on it will be at the party too. And it's not that I'm embarrassed about losing. Just that I know he'll disapprove of my gambling for the big prize – just as he has done for most of my life. And the last thing I want is my dad's 'I told you so' ringing in my ears for the rest of the day.

My mum and I have spent most of the morning hoovering, tidying, and (me) on constant errands back and forth to Tesco's to make sure we've got enough plastic cups, paper plates, serviettes, and disposable cutlery. We've had a grand total of around thirty positive RSVPs (or RIPs, as my dad insists on calling them), which out of a total of fifty-seven invitations isn't the biggest turnout. But then again, none of the guests know it's actually a big 'goodbye'.

And though we haven't had a party here – garden, or otherwise – since my sixteenth, I'm pretty confident today's going to go well. My dad's invited Gaz and Michelle, so at least I'll have someone to talk to. And though at the last minute my mum tells me she's invited Anna too, I'm pretty sure she won't turn up. Especially after the other day's Mikayla incident (as it's become known).

At least my dad seems happy. He's been supervising operations all morning, much to my and my mum's annoyance, and with the first guests expected at around eleven we're pretty much ready: there's enough Marks and Spencer finger food to feed three times as many guests (and Wallace for the rest of the week), and the alcohol supply works out at around a bottle of wine per person. I've made a Spotify playlist of my dad's favourite seventies numbers – not that we're expecting dancing (though the garden furniture's been moved to one side 'just in case'), and I've set up the hi-fi speakers to point out of the kitchen window to provide, in my dad's words, 'house music'. And while my mum's worried about disturbing the neighbours, we have in fact *invited* the neighbours. Debbie and Martin from number twenty-two are away (but my dad doesn't like Martin much anyway, ever since an incident involving creosote twenty years ago that my dad still can't talk about), but Pete (he of always-wears-shorts fame) and Sylvia from number eighteen are coming, and in fact are the first to arrive.

'Aye aye,' says Pete, handing over a bottle of red wine so dusty I sneeze when he hands it to me. 'Are we the first?'

'Someone has to be,' says my dad, affably. He's dispensed with his oxygen mask for the day and is wearing his best (only) suit, and I'm sure he'd be pleased he can still get into it if it wasn't for the fact that his dramatic weight loss was caused by his illness. I've got a suit on too, my mum's in her best summer dress, and even Wallace (though I give it five minutes, given how he's fussing at it) has a plastic bow tie fastened to the front of his collar, and you can tell Sylvia's a bit narked at Pete.

'You might have dressed up,' she hisses at him, as they make their way into the garden.

'I did,' he hisses back. 'These are new shorts.'

As per my dad's pre-party briefing, I go and wait behind a large table loaded with glasses and bottles of wine – the reds on the table, and the whites mingling with several cans of beer in a large paddling pool full of ice at my feet (this week's 'special buy', procured specially for the occasion). Gaz, bless him, is the next to arrive, Michelle on his arm, struggling to hide her shock when she sees my dad.

'Christ, Josh, I had no idea,' she says, hurrying over to the drinks table and gulping down the glass of wine I hand her. 'How are you doing?'

'Oh, you know. It's not me I'm worried about, though.'

She's got a tear in her eye, and I'm hoping it's not from the cheap wine. 'It's a bastard, that cancer,' she says. 'How is your mum?'

'She'd appreciate someone asking her.'

'Of course,' says Michelle, heading over to where my mum's standing.

A few more guests arrive: Barry and Billie, who used to own the shop next to my dad's, followed by old Mrs. Wilson from the house opposite, who's been about eighty ever since I was a child. Then, it's as if the floodgates have opened, though I quickly realise it's because my dad's written 'eleven o'clock sharp' on the invitation, and everyone here is of an age where punctuality means something (either that or they're keen to appear, drink up, and get back in time for their Sunday roasts). It's beginning to get busy, and without a word, Gaz steps round to my side of the table and helps me serve drinks, and that simple gesture puts a lump in my throat.

Fifteen minutes later, from what I can tell, everyone's arrived. Everyone except Anna that is, though I'm not sure how I feel about that. After all, this is my dad's day – not a time for me to be pining after my ex-girlfriend. And he seems to be having a good time – shrugging off the shocked looks people are giving him, enjoying the company of friends he hasn't seen in a while, and even my mum looks relaxed. For the first time since I arrived.

My dad catches my eye, and gives me the signal to nip inside and turn the music down a touch (which pretty much consists of him waving me over and asking me to do exactly that), then he wheels himself to the end of the garden and – at the second attempt – hauls himself out of his chair and clears his throat.

'Thank you all for coming,' he says, his voice stronger than we've been used to the past few weeks. 'I just wanted to say a few words. First, to thank Sue and Josh for organising this little get-together.' There's a murmured 'cheers' in our general direction, and my dad starts speaking again. 'Now, I know some of you are aware that I haven't been that well recently. The rest of you may have guessed that from seeing me today . . .' A couple of people say 'nonsense', but we all know it isn't. '. . .but the real reason I'm so pleased so many of you could be here, is so I can say . . .' He reaches out and takes my mum's hand, though I'm not sure whose benefit it's for. 'Goodbye.'

'We've only just got here!' shouts Pete, to a smattering of nervous laughter.

My dad smiles. 'That's not what I mean at all. Stay as long as you like. Because, well, this'll be the last time I see most of you, because I've got cancer, and I'm dying. There's nothing they can do, apparently.'

A hushed silence has fallen over the garden. No-one knows what to say, and it's obvious people can't meet each other's eyes, so my dad soldiers on.

'But what can you do? I had the choice of going out with a whimper, or with a bang. And a party like this seemed . . . Well, I'm not going to have a funeral, so I'm having today instead. And I'm just so pleased you could all be here with me and my family.' He waves over at where I'm standing. 'Josh? Come here and join me and your mum, will you?'

A few heads have turned to look at me, and it's all I can do to ignore them and keep staring at my dad. For some reason someone in the crowd has started applauding – and I suspect it's Michelle – then everyone else joins in, so I fix a smile on my face and do as instructed.

'Now,' continues my dad. 'Some of you will know that Josh and I haven't always seen eye-to-eye. Those of you who are fathers will know what it's like.' There's a murmur of agreement from the male voices. 'But I want you to know I'm grateful, Josh, for everything you've done. Especially coming back to Derton to look after me and your mum. I'm proud of you, son. More than you'll ever know.'

My dad reaches over and hugs me, and after a few stunned seconds I hug him back. And while I'm shocked by how thin, how frail he feels in my arms, and I'm embarrassed at this rare public display of affection (and can't remember the last time he's so much as ruffled my hair), I never want this moment to end. He's proud of me. *Proud*. Of *me*.

And just as I'm thinking that I needn't have bothered going through all that *Catch Me If You Can* bollocks, he whispers in my ear that he loves me, so of course I burst into tears in front of everyone, then push through the crowd, past Gaz, past Michelle, and past Anna, who's been standing in the corner all along, and run upstairs to my bedroom to hide.

As if by magic, it's my sixteenth birthday party all over again.

31.

It's the day after the party, and all's calm again. Gaz had eventually fetched me – red-eyed and red-faced – back downstairs, but instead of everyone laughing at my ridiculous disappearance, all I'd had was sympathy. *It's tough, losing your dad* seemed to be the common response, and for the first time since I've arrived back in Derton I'm beginning to appreciate that yes, actually, it is.

Anna, of course, had gone by then, and while I know she'd probably only shown up for my dad, a part of me had hoped she might have been there for me too. But then again, why should she, given how I've behaved towards her recently? And that I haven't been there (that is, here) for her for the past eighteen years.

As is par for the course, we've not mentioned my disappearance, though that's partly because my dad's looking particularly tired after yesterday. And while I've suggested he might want to skip today's walk Wallace/swift pint at The Lobster, he's not having any of it.

'Cheer up, Wallace. It might never happen.' This has become his standard line, and while admittedly Wallace has the kind of face that makes you think he's the most miserable pug in the world, I understand from Google images that all pugs look like that. 'Mind you,' my dad continues wryly. 'It is going to happen. And I'd hate to think what his face will look like then. Probably turn inside on itself, like a . . .'

'Dad, please.'

Wallace chooses that moment to stop and sniff at a nearby lamp-post, meaning my dad has to stop too, since he's got Wallace's lead tied round one of the wheelchair's armrests, which in turn means *I* have to stop, seeing as I'm the one pushing my dad's wheelchair. We must make quite a sight, although I've long since stopped caring what other people think.

Not that we're going far – these walks (weather permitting) usually only take us as far as the pub now, and while I suspect my mum knows this is exactly where we're going, I also suspect she's glad of a little quiet time.

'Uh-oh.'

'What?'

My dad nods down at Wallace. 'Someone's doing his business.'

'Can't you just refer to it as . . . ?' I stop talking. Despite my use of the word in front of Mr. Ronson the other day, I still can't bring myself to swear in front of either of my parents. I reach into my pocket for the little bone-shaped plastic bag carrier, and my dad grins.

'Thanks, son. I'd do it myself, but . . .'

'I know, I know.'

'Still, could be worse.'

I hold my breath as I do my best to gather up as much of Wallace's 'business' as I can, cursing the fact that the leftovers from yesterday's party that my dad's been feeding him don't seem to have done much for his consistency.

'How, exactly, could it be worse?'

'You could be doing this for me. If I was ninety, like. So thank your lucky stars you're being spared all that.'

'For this barrel of laughs instead? I've won the lottery.'

My dad rolls his eyes as I knot the little plastic bag and toss it into the nearest litter bin. 'You know,' he says, and I brace myself for another of his observations. 'If an alien came down to earth, and took a snapshot of this little scene, you know what they'd conclude?'

'That I deserve a medal?'

'That dogs are the rulers of the earth, not us. The fact that we walk around behind them, picking up their . . .'

'Mustn't be late for the pub,' I say, quickly grabbing the chair's handles and making hastily for The Lobster. And then I see someone doing exactly the same thing (well, not exactly – she's pushing a stroller, not a wheelchair, and there's a baby in there with a dummy in its mouth rather than an old man wearing an oxygen mask, and the huge dog she's got attached to the stroller's handle looks like it could probably pull the two of them at great speed along the pavement, but you get the picture), so I nod and smile at her as we draw level, and she nods and smiles back in the same way that people who drive the same kind of classic cars acknowledge each other. But it's not until we're sitting in the pub, the usual beer and crisps in front of us, that I realise she was probably my age – younger, in fact – and she's got a baby, and no doubt a partner (though there was a time in Derton when that usually wasn't the case). And I don't.

'You ever thought about starting a family, Josh?' says my dad, as if reading my mind.

I help myself to a Quaver – crisp make number twelve on my dad's 'try every crisp type/flavour at The Lobster' bucket list item. 'I don't think I'd be very good at it.'

'Like father, like son, you mean?'

'I didn't say that.'

'Yes, well.'

We sit in silence for a while, then he re-positions the mask over his face, takes a couple of deep breaths, and clears his throat. 'No-one teaches you how to be a dad, you know? I thought I was doing the right thing, working all those hours, to provide for you and your mum.'

'Don't worry about it.'

'Seriously, Josh. You asked me the other day about my bucket list. If I had any regrets. If there was anything I wanted to do? Well, this is one of them.'

'Eating crisps?'

'Well, yes. But also spending more time with you. Quality time. We should have done this more.'

I catch sight of our reflection in the mirror behind the bar, the two of us sitting, miserably staring into pint glasses. If this is 'quality' time, then I don't hold out much hope for my future.

'Seriously, don't worry about it. In fact, you probably did me a favour.'

'How so?'

'Listen, this may sound funny coming from a thirty-six-year-old man who's currently living with his parents, but you taught me to be independent. To stand on my own two feet. And surely that's the best lesson any parent can teach their kids?'

'Maybe.' My dad nods sagely, then he suddenly looks up at me. 'Actually, no.'

'What do you mean, no?'

'It's a sense of family, Josh. The fact that you're here now . . . It must mean I did something right?'

He's looking up at me with the same expression of desperate expectation that Wallace wears whenever he hears his dog food tin being opened, and while I could tell him that actually I'm here because he did nothing right, I'm here for my mum, his wife, who he's about to leave in the lurch because of all the stupid decisions he's made, I know I can't do it. And not just because he's dying, but because it's not my dad's fault he wasn't the dad I wanted growing up. Just like it's not his fault he got cancer. Blaming other people for the situation you find yourself in is just a waste of time. And besides, what's he going to learn if I tell him a few home truths?

'Listen, Josh,' he continues. 'I've never been one of those dads who was good with words, you know? Ask your mum – she'll tell you. But like I said yesterday, I am proud of you. Everything you've achieved. Everything you've ever done. Especially this.'

'Thanks, Dad.'

'And there's one last thing . . .'

'I'll look after Mum, I promise.'

My dad laughs, and even that seems to drain him nowadays. 'Thanks, Josh, but your mum can look after herself. I'm more concerned about you. We both are.'

'*Me*?'

'When you went to London, we knew it was more about escaping this place than anything else. And we could understand that – Derton wasn't the town me and your mum moved to when you were born. But now . . . Maybe you could be happy here, if you give it a second chance.' He starts to cough, and I lean in anxiously and reach for his mask, but it's just from a bit of Quaver that's gone down the wrong way.

'Yes, but you've got to keep moving forward, don't you?'

'True. But sometimes you find your path gets blocked, and you have to take a step back – back home, even – *to* move forward.' He smiles. 'Listen, son, I'm the last person to tell you how to live your life. I mean, look how mine's ended up.'

'That's hardly your fault.'

'Listen, all I'm saying is . . . I don't know what I'm saying, apart from that not everyone gets another bite at the cherry. So if you do, if someone offers you a second chance . . . Well, you've got to take it, haven't you?'

It's the longest speech I've ever heard from him, and quite frankly, I'm a little taken aback. I haven't even told my mum about my actual feelings about Anna, and I'm sure Anna hasn't said anything.

'I was lucky with your mum.' My dad picks his glass up, and I notice his hand is shaking. 'I had my share of girlfriends, but never quite met someone who I thought I could spend my life with. And then, just when I was giving up hope, I met her, and we just . . . clicked.' He raises and lowers his eyebrows like a ventriloquist's dummy. 'In all departments.'

'Dad, please, too much information.'

'What was your phrase earlier? I'd won the lottery. Though of course, it was the football pools back then. I was lucky that she turned out to be the one for me. And it's the same for you – you've been out and . . .' He frowns as he searches for the right example. 'Well, do you remember when you were younger, and after you'd helped me out in the shop every Saturday, I used to tell you that you could choose something from the shelves? Anything you wanted.'

'Yeah. Though actually paying me might have been better.'

'And do you remember how you used to stand there for ages trying to make your mind up?'

'Well, I didn't want to pick the wrong thing, did I? There were so many to choose from.'

My dad sits back in his chair. 'Well, now you've had a chance to taste all the sweets in the shop, haven't you? So I think you're in a pretty good position to decide what your favourite is.'

'It's not that simple, Dad.'

'Yes it is, Josh. It's the simplest thing in the world.'

And then he reaches into his pocket, pulls out an envelope, and hands it to me, and I hesitate before I take it, puzzled by the fact that Anna's name is written on the front, and from somewhere far away I recognise my teenage handwriting and notice how the envelope looks old, maybe eighteen years old, and then I understand what it is. And while I know I should be angry, I can't be. Not just because he's ill, but because I realise he *knew*. All that time. That she was – is – my *one*. Then, and now.

I stare at him for a moment, then stuff the envelope into my jacket pocket and drain the rest of my beer. I don't want to admit anything – about Anna, or how I feel about being back in Derton, or how I feel about how he's done as a dad. But most importantly, perhaps because it's a conversation I'm saving for when he needs it the most, I don't want to admit he might be right.

32.

I'm not working today, so after a leisurely breakfast, I retrieve Wallace's lead from the coat rack in the hallway and jingle the metal end, but there's no sign of him. Puzzled, I make my way into the kitchen, where my mum is already making a start on lunch, but he's not in (what's become) his usual place under the kitchen table, waiting for her to 'accidentally' drop the odd scrap.

'Have you seen Wallace?'

My mum peers down at her feet. 'Not since I gave him a bath this morning, now I come to think of it.'

'You gave him a bath?'

'He was getting a bit whiffy, so I used some of that posh shampoo of yours. I hope you don't mind?'

'My *Molton Brown*?'

'That's the stuff.'

'Mum, that's . . .' I stop short of saying 'expensive' as I don't want to appear tight-fisted. 'Not really for dogs.'

'No, he didn't seem to like the smell much. His coat looks lovely, though.'

I think for a moment. He's unlikely to be upstairs – he doesn't quite have the legs for them – so I hurry into the front room.

'Wallace?'

My dad looks up from where he's reading the paper at the dining table, and gingerly removes his oxygen mask. 'No, I'm your dad,' he wheezes. 'Honestly. Nearly forty years, and you still don't . . .'

'Have you seen him?'

'Not since breakfast. Have you asked your mum?'

I nod, then peer out of the window into the back garden, but there's no sign of him there, though it's then I notice the back gate is open. Hurriedly, I grab my jacket, slip his lead into the pocket, then run out into the street.

From what I can tell, there aren't any squashed dogs at the side of the road, but even so I start to panic, remembering stories I've read of pets whose families have moved houses and not taken them with them, so one day they set off on epic journeys and manage to find their way home. Wallace is a rescue dog, after all, so maybe my mum washing him with that shampoo triggered some memory in him, and he's gone back to his original home – though on second thoughts, he can just about make it to the beach and back before exhaustedly collapsing for the rest of the day. But maybe it's more sinister than that. Maybe he's been dog-napped. You hear about this happening, pedigree dogs pinched and either ransomed back to their owners, or even worse, sold to unsuspecting punters at the other end of the country. Or restaurants . . .

I tell myself to relax. He's probably just decided to take his walk on his own. After all, I was a little late this morning, and dogs are creatures of habit – or at least this one is. And perhaps he thinks today's a work day (though I realise I might be giving his calendar-reading abilities too much credit), and if that's the case, maybe he's gone to the shop.

I decide there's nothing for it but to retrace our normal route, so I run back inside, explain to my parents what's happened, then head into town. Fortunately, Derton's not known for its busy roads, and I've seen Wallace react to cars, so I'm pretty sure he won't have run out in front of one, but you never know.

Just in case, I peer between every parked car on the way, but there's no sign of him (or bits of him), and when I arrive at the shop, hoping he'll be waiting in the doorway, he's nowhere to be seen. Desperately, I run up to the window and peer inside, though Michelle's not there yet, and I've got the only other set of keys, and he's a little bit chunky to have made it through the letterbox.

I know it's probably silly, but I can't help thinking the worst. How long is it going to be before I get an envelope pushed through the door, with a picture of Wallace, a ransom demand below spelled with cut-out-and-glued letters? Though I already know, however much they want, I'll pay it.

I look frantically up and down the street, then notice the door to Baker's Cupcakes is open. Perhaps Anna's there. Maybe she knows something. And even though I'm still trying to avoid her, it's the only thing I can think of to do.

I run across the road and push the door open nervously, and at the sound of the bell – my dad's bell – Anna looks up from behind the counter.

'Well, look what the cat dragged in. Or should I say "dog"?'

'Have you seen him?'

'Seen who?' she asks, innocently.

'Wallace. He's missing.'

'And you thought I might have had something to do with it? Well, thanks a lot.'

'No – he's escaped. And I know he likes cupcakes. So I thought . . .'

Anna raises both eyebrows, then she smiles. 'Listen,' she says, and when she doesn't continue, I realise she's actually asking me to listen, rather than giving the next thing she says dramatic effect. I cup my hand to my ear, then hear a familiar snuffling sound.

'Wallace!'

I make my way behind the counter. On the floor by Anna's feet, Wallace is licking the wrapper of a large vanilla cupcake, the remains of which are plastered across his face.

'He was waiting outside when I got here,' explains Anna. 'He seems to have enjoyed his cupcake.'

'Well, he demolished that one the other day. They're like crack cocaine. For dogs, I mean. I imagine. Not that I've ever tried it. Or given any to Wallace. Anyway . . .' I reach down and lift him up to my eye level. 'I thought you might have been hit by a car.'

Wallace gives me a look, as if to remind me that all pugs look like this, then wriggles impatiently. I put him back on the floor, where he returns to his wrapper.

'Thank you.'

'What for?'

'For looking after him.'

'He's no trouble at all. Unlike his owner.' Anna kneels down and scratches him between his ears, and he licks her fingers enthusiastically. 'And he smells lovely too.'

'It's Molton Brown,' I say, then remember what happened the last time he ate a cupcake. I doubt even an £18 bottle of shampoo could mask those smells. 'And speaking of which, I should get him out of here. In case what he's just eaten makes him do something. You know. Molten. And, um, brown.'

Anna makes a face, then stands back up. 'So . . .'

'So . . .' I take a deep breath, and prepare to launch into the apology I've been rehearsing since yesterday's chat with my dad, but the bell on the door jingles again, and I don't really want to have this conversation in front of the group of old ladies making a beeline for the counter. 'Can we go somewhere and talk?'

'What have we possibly got to talk about, Josh?'

Everything, I want to say, *and nothing*, but the look on Anna's face suggests that I'm not going to get the chance any time soon.

With a sigh, I reach into my pocket to find Wallace's lead, but I'm trying the wrong one, and instead, there's only an old envelope.

Hang on . . .

'This,' I say, putting it down on the counter between us. 'And I'm sorry it's eighteen years late, but my dad ran a sweet shop, and not a Post Office.'

Anna stares at the envelope, then her expression softens. 'The Submarine? One o'clock?'

'It's a date,' I say.

And as I pick Wallace up, peel the cake wrapper off his face, and carry him out of the café, a part of me really hopes it is.

❦

There's an ambulance driving away from the house when Wallace and I get back from the extended walk I've taken him on in an attempt to minimise the effects of what he's just eaten, but (once I've run inside in a blind panic) although he doesn't look it, my dad insists he's okay.

'Your mum phoned 999,' he says, weakly.

'Yes, well, you were having a bit of trouble breathing,' says my mum, defensively. She's watching anxiously from the doorway as my dad adjusts the straps on his oxygen mask, and looking paler than he is.

'You and me both,' I say, shepherding a rather gassy Wallace out into the garden. 'Why didn't you call me?'

'I did.' My mum points to the coffee table, or more specifically, my mobile on the coffee table.

'Ah. Sorry.' I pick my phone up and slip it into my pocket. 'How are you feeling now?'

'Fine,' says my dad, and I know it must have been bad if he can't come up with a joke, then he taps his oxygen cylinder. 'Turns out I was running on empty.'

'You and me both,' deadpans my mum.

My dad forces a smile, then peers out through the window at Wallace, who's lying in a sunny spot on the patio. 'You found him then?'

'He'd gone to see Anna.'

'You see?' he says, in between breaths. 'That dog knows a good thing when he sees it. It's just a shame his owner . . .'

'I thought Wallace was *your* dog?'

My mum opens the patio door, and Wallace comes running up to me. 'He seems to have made his choice. Besides, in the absence of any grandkids . . .'

'Mum, *please*. And it's just cupboard love with Anna.'

'I think you mean "puppy love".'

My dad grins. 'Are you talking about Wallace, or Josh?'

'Wallace. And it's only because you fed him that cupcake the other day.' I shake my head. 'Now will you both please just drop all this "Anna" stuff?'

'Sorry, Josh.' My mum pats me on the shoulder. 'Are you staying for lunch?'

'Er . . . No.'

My dad raises an eyebrow. 'No?'

'I'm meeting someone.'

'Who?'

'An—' I don't want to give them the satisfaction. 'An old friend.' Which is true, if you think about it.

～

Anna's nabbed us a table by the window, and she looks so pretty, so . . . Well, so out of my league that I almost lose my nerve. But then I remember my dad's lecture about second chances and walk in through the door, and at once I know I've made the right decision, as her face lights up when she sees me.

'Sorry I'm late,' I say, ordering a pint from the barman. 'My dad . . .'

'Is he okay?'

'It's hard to tell nowadays.'

'You look tired.'

'I'll live.' I shake my head. 'I just wasn't expecting this. Not now. Not so soon. I mean, back when you and I . . . This kind of thing seemed an age away.'

'Sometimes an age goes by before you know it.' She pulls out a chair for me. 'I've always expected it with my mum and dad. Even back then.'

I suddenly remember Anna's dad's been living with a heart condition for years, though whether that's better or worse than what my dad's going through, I'm not sure. 'Even so . . .'

'We were both only children, Josh.'

'Yeah, but we're older now. We shouldn't have to . . .'

'No, I mean we were *only* children. Didn't have any brothers and sisters. So of course the responsibility was going to fall on us to look after our parents. You must have known it would happen?'

I shrug. 'Maybe. Although not quite so soon. But now I don't know what to do. Or what my mum's going to do on her own here after my dad dies.'

Anna smiles sympathetically. 'Derton's not such a bad place to be, Josh.'

I raise my eyebrows at her. I'm beginning to realise that. 'Did you always know you'd stay here?'

'I think so.' She pulls the letter out of her pocket and places it on the table in front of her. She's opened the envelope, so I guess she's read it. 'Besides, as far as I knew back then, I didn't have any better offers.'

I make a guilty face, then lean back as the waiter deposits my drink, and a plate of what looks like sushi on the table. 'Is that . . . ?'

'I know. Sushi. In Derton. Who'd have thought?' Anna grins mischievously as she picks up her chopsticks. 'I ordered us some.'

'Trying to convince me the place has changed?'

'No, actually, I thought you might be hungry,' she says, picking up a California Roll and dabbing it into the bowl of bright green wasabi.

'Be careful. That stuff's hot.'

She shoots me a look. 'I have eaten sushi before, you know? Derton's a fishing village, remember? We practically invented the stuff.'

'Only because fire didn't arrive here until . . .'

Anna reaches over and pokes me in the ribs with a chopstick. 'Very funny, Mr. DFL. But you're right. The place has changed. I can see how it's been a shock for you. But it wasn't as bad as you think. Remember what fun we had growing up here?' She smiles wistfully. 'It's always been a great place for kids, with the beach, and Funland, and everything.'

'So why didn't you and Ian . . .' I immediately feel I've overstepped the mark, as Anna looks down at her lap. 'I'm sorry. I don't mean to pry.'

'No, that's okay. We just . . . I kind of got the feeling he wouldn't be a very good dad, you know? He was always too interested in pleasing himself.'

I shake my head to get rid of the rather disturbing mental image that phrase has just created. Anna looks at me and makes a horrified face, as if she's read my thoughts.

'Not like *that*. And I wanted to do more with my life than just be a stay-at-home mum.'

'And you thought you could do that here?'

'I *am* doing it here, Josh. In case you haven't noticed, I have my own business – or at least, it will be when the divorce comes through. And it's doing pretty okay.'

I look at her with a new admiration. I remember what Ian was like, how manipulative he could be, how domineering, and yet Anna seems to have emerged from their relationship relatively unscathed.

'How about you?'

I think for a moment. 'I guess I never really thought about kids – perhaps because I never felt all that grown up myself. But I can't say my own experience was the best, with my mum and dad being so much older, and feeling like I wasn't wanted . . .'

'Surely that's not . . . ?'

'Wasn't *planned*, then. And that kind of influences how you feel about wanting them.'

'Why?'

'You worry you need to be doubly sure about it. Then you worry you'll make the same kind of mistakes. Then time kind of passes, and then you meet someone who's hardly ideal parent material . . .'

'Like Mikayla? Now there's a girl who lights up a room.'

'By leaving it.'

Anna laughs. 'Maybe that's why I never wanted kids with Ian. Because I didn't want to inflict him as a dad on them – didn't want them to turn out anything like he turned out to be. And he didn't seem that bothered. Which I guess proves I made the right decision.'

'Unlike when you married him?'

Anna pokes me again. 'I don't regret it. He was there, and he was nice to me, and I'd just had my heart broken, and he said all the right things. I thought I was making the right decision at the time, and as long as you can say that . . . And it's all a learning experience, eh? What doesn't kill us makes us stronger and all that.' She smiles. 'How about you, Josh. Do you have any regrets?'

Anna's gazing through the window at the sea as she asks this, so I lean back and pretend to consider the question, when what I'm actually doing is (just like on our first ever date) looking at her out of the corner of my eye. And she's beautiful, and strong, and confident, and just as funny and smart as I remember, and more than ever I want to kick myself for leaving all those years ago, because I've missed out on spending those years with her. And I want to tell her that while I don't regret leaving here at eighteen, I regret leaving *her* at eighteen. Not standing up to Ian at school. Never finishing my novel. Pretending I wanted someone like Mikayla as my girlfriend – or rather, trying to convince myself that someone like Mikayla was right for me. Not insisting my dad get medical help sooner. Not being a better son.

'Maybe one or two.'

'And what are you going to do about them?'

I puff air out of my cheeks. 'I don't know.'

'What do you think your dad would say?'

'My dad?'

Anna turns to face me. 'He's not so stupid, you know?'

I stare back at her. Because I know exactly what my dad would say. That life's too short. Especially now. And while it's perhaps one of the biggest clichés ever, given how the last few weeks have whizzed by, I can start to see how it might be true.

'Learn from your dad, Josh. Because what happens if the same thing happens to you? He's pretty contented with his lot, right? Doesn't seem to want to put much on this bucket list you've tried to get him to write. Could you say the same, if someone came up to you and told you that you were going to die soon?' She takes a sip from her glass of wine. 'What's that Dalai Lama quote? Something about "the longest journey starting with just a single step"?'

I smile, because she's pronounced it '*daily* Lama'. 'Something like that.'

'Well, sometimes, that's what you have to do. And trust me, I know taking that first step can be tough, but once you've done it – well, the others don't require quite as much effort.'

She's probably referring to the day she left Ian, but a part of me is hoping she's hinting at the two of us getting back together. Perhaps she's asking me to ask her out again? Does she want me to lean across and kiss her? I'm suddenly transported to the other night, pre-head-butt, and wonder if this is how it's always going to be. You pass seventeen, you can drive a car. Eighteen, you get the vote and can legally buy alcohol. Twenty-one . . . Well, I'm not sure exactly what you get then, but essentially, all these age milestones are your path to adulthood. But even at thirty-six I still don't seem to be getting any nearer to the point where asking a girl out, even one you've already done that to (though admittedly a while back), gets any easier.

Anna stands up suddenly, and I'm worried I've missed my chance. 'Are you going?'

'Just to the toilet.'

'Oh. Right.'

She smiles at my apparent panic, then slides the plate of sushi towards me. 'Help me eat this, will you? Before it gets cold.'

'It's already . . .'

Anna gives me a 'got you' look, then makes her way to the Ladies, so I pick up my chopsticks, and I'm just about to help myself when I become aware of someone standing over me, and when I look up I feel a sudden knot in my stomach. Because judging by the scowl on Ian's face, he's not at all pleased to see me.

'Well, well, well,' he says, like some comedy policeman. 'Look who it isn't. And having a cosy little lunch with my wife.'

'Well, I haven't eaten anything yet, so technically, we're not actually having lunch.'

'Mind if I sit down?'

I'm guessing it's a rhetorical question, as he's already squeezing himself into the chair opposite. But I don't want to start arguing with him today. Not with Anna here.

'Actually, I was just leaving.'

Ian's eyes flick towards my barely-touched pint. 'Doesn't look like that to me. Though that is what I wanted to talk to you about.'

'What?'

'You leaving.'

I'm puzzled. Does he mean 'the pub', or 'Derton', or – and I'm guessing this is the right answer – 'Anna alone'? Though thinking about it, it's probably all three.

'Listen, Ian, I—'

'We're getting back together, you know?'

'Who?'

'Me and Anna.'

'Does she know that?'

Ian ignores me. 'So the last thing she needs is you hanging around her.'

I'm having a hard time believing any of this. I mean, fair enough, this sort of thing used to happen at school when we were young and marking our territory, flexing our still-growing muscles. And while I had my share of fights back then – won two, lost two, of which one was a questionable draw due to my mum's intervention, which technically counted as a loss – it's been a long time since I've so much as raised my voice at another person, let alone a fist.

The pub's too nice for a fight – not in the least because I don't want to get barred. But Ian's looking like he's spoiling for one, and while I've taken the odd boxercise class with Mikayla in London, that hardly qualifies me to defend myself against someone his size. Then again, you read about boxers who abstain from sex and it makes them fight harder, and if that's true, given the last few weeks I should be able to dispatch Ian within the first round. Besides – and I realise this is a sentiment I might come to painfully regret – with everything that's happened in the last few weeks, there's really only one appropriate response.

'And what if I don't? Leave, that is.'

Ian stares at me in disbelief, obviously not used to having his 'authority' questioned.

'Pardon?'

I think quickly, trying to remember what it is I've read about bullies. That they're all mouth and no trousers, and the moment you stand up to them, they back down. 'What if I don't leave? Or leave Anna alone? Because I'm not sure I can.'

Sadly, Ian doesn't seem to have read the same thing I have – either that, or he's been watching too many episodes of *EastEnders*. He leans across the table, his face so close to mine that I can smell the beer on his breath, and picks up the bowl of wasabi.

'Then you'll be finished. Like this guacamole,' he says, scooping the bright green lump of red-hot paste into his mouth with his fingers.

'Ian, that's . . .' But I don't get any further, as Ian suddenly turns a striking shade of red.

'What the f—'

'. . . wasabi.'

I start to laugh, even though I know it's probably a mistake, but I can't help myself, particularly when Ian starts looking desperately around for something to drink. Too late, I realise I've still got most of my pint left, and as I grab my glass, Ian tries to wrestle it from me, spilling half of it over himself in the process.

'Give me that,' he gasps.

'Or?'

'Or you'll be sorry.'

I'm already sorry. Sorry that my dad's got cancer. Sorry that I've had to turn my life upside down and come back to a place that I thought I'd seen the back of. Sorry that while I thought we'd all grown up, that's proving not to be the case. And sorry that Anna – *my* Anna – has had to spend even five minutes of her life married to someone like Ian – something that's possibly my fault. And the combination of all this, plus the fact that Ian feels he can threaten me even now, is too much.

'Right. Outside,' I say, barely able to contain my anger.

Ian stops fanning his open mouth with his hand. 'What?'

'You heard me. Outside. Now!'

The rest of the pub has gone quiet. People are watching us with interest, and while I don't want to make a scene, I think we're a long way past that point now.

'You're serious?'

I nod and realise that I am. That actually, I've been waiting for a chance to do this for half my life. And I'm so looking forward to it that I actually crack my knuckles, haul myself to my feet, and start to do a couple of shoulder stretches in a 'limbering up' kind of way.

Trouble is, I have no idea how to actually *start* a fight. Obviously I know the mechanics once you're involved, but to actually kick off proceedings without looking like a bad version of something from the first *Bridget Jones* film is trickier than it looks. But just as I'm squaring up to him, Anna chooses that moment to return from the toilet.

'What's going on here?'

'Your *ex* . . .' and I can't help but emphasise the word '. . . and I are going outside,' I say. 'For a chat.'

'What? This is ridiculous. You're two grown men.'

'One of us has grown a bit more than the other,' I say childishly, glancing at Ian's stomach.

'Ian?'

'Joth thtarted ih.' Ian's desperately trying to scrape the remains of the wasabi off his tongue with his fingernails, something I'd find funny if I wasn't so angry.

'What?'

'Josh started it,' Ian says, more carefully this time.

'Oh, yes, very mature.'

'But . . .'

'Go home, Ian,' she orders. 'Now!'

There's a muted booing from somewhere in the pub, and as Ian slinks out of the door, she turns to me.

'What were you thinking?'

'I wasn't. I was just sitting here, minding my own business.'

'Well, you shouldn't have risen to it. Just been the bigger person.'

'That's quite hard when you're not actually the bigger person. And I didn't start it. Honest.'

Anna shakes her head, though she's hiding half a smile. 'What did he want?'

'For me to leave you alone.'

'And what did you tell him?'

'That I couldn't.'

And though Anna's still mad with me, given the speed at which her expression softens and the way her hand goes to her open mouth, I can tell that after all this time, I've (finally) said the right thing.

33.

My stuff arrives this morning, courtesy of Mikayla (or rather, UPS), all neatly packaged up in seven Topshop cardboard boxes that she must have broken a nail or two (and, unusually for Mikayla, quite possibly a sweat) struggling home with on the Tube. Perhaps not surprisingly there's no note, but at least she hasn't cut the arms off my suits, or sprayed the insides of my underwear with pepper spray, or done any of the things I've been reading about recently in my mum's *Daily Mail* that scorned women sometimes do. I haven't heard from her since I abandoned her in the café – though perhaps 'abandoned' is too strong a word – and though I suppose that's not much of a surprise, and I'm still feeling terribly guilty for some reason, at least I feel I've gotten some 'closure' out of it. Said my piece. Told her how I felt. And maybe, just maybe, made her think twice about how she conducts her relationships. (Though I doubt it.)

I have a quick rummage through the contents but don't bother unpacking and instead just stack them against the far wall of my room. After all, I've survived with the little I've brought with me so far, and besides, what's the point if I might have to pack them all up again soon? When I come back downstairs and walk into the front room, my dad's watching me anxiously.

'You okay, Josh?'

I think about his question for a moment, and realise that, actually, I am. 'Yeah. Saved me a job, I suppose. And a potentially awkward encounter.'

'That's the spirit.' He peers through the patio doors and into the garden, where my mum, Wallace at her feet, is inspecting her plant beds with the same intensity with which a drill sergeant might inspect his troops. 'And your mum?'

I shrug. 'I guess so. She and Mikayla were never that close, so . . .'

'No, I mean is she okay *generally*? With . . . everything.'

'You know Mum.'

'I do. Which is why . . .' He reaches into his pocket, and pulls out a rather crumpled ten-pound note. 'Here.'

'What's this for?'

'I thought you might want to take her out for a coffee. Maybe a cupcake too?'

'Don't start that again! Anna and I . . .'

'Not because of *that*. Just to give your mum a break. So the two of you can have a chat. See how she's feeling. Take Wallace with you.' He waves the ten-pound note at me. 'My treat.'

I look down at him, then take the money. 'And how do I get her to go?'

'What do you mean?'

'What excuse do I give her?'

'She's your mother,' says my dad, as if I've asked a really stupid question. 'Why would you need an excuse?'

෴

'This is nice,' says my mum. 'We hardly ever do this, you and me.' And she's right. We do hardly ever do this, and it *has* been nice, spending a bit of time when we don't have a chore to take care of, or some shopping to do, or my dad to run around after. Not that we've minded doing any of those.

We're sitting at an outside table at Baker's Cupcakes, sipping cappuccinos, a half-eaten cupcake on a plate in front of us that an expectant Wallace at our feet – even though he can't see it – knows is there, and knows couldn't have his name on it any more clearly than if it actually had 'Wallace' iced across the top. And while coming here was – surprisingly – my mum's idea, when I'd suggested she might want to walk Wallace with me, she'd leapt at the chance.

'Isn't it?'

'It is.'

She smiles at me, then reaches down to feed Wallace a piece of cake, glancing at her watch as she does so.

'Mum . . .'

'I'm sorry, Josh.' She sits back in her chair and gazes around the Old Town. 'So listen. Your dad wanted me to talk to you about something.'

I frown at her. 'That's funny.'

'What is?'

'He wanted me to talk to you about something too.'

She reaches into her purse. 'You'll be telling me he gave . . .' She stops talking, as we both put crumpled ten-pound notes down on the table.

'Snap.'

My mum laughs. 'What do you suppose he's up to?'

I shrug. 'I think he's just trying to stop us from moping around the house. Either that or he wants to raid the leftover wine from his funer— I mean, party.'

'Knowing your dad, it's quite possibly both.'

We sit in silence for a moment, then I smile across the table at her. 'And how are you doing?'

'Is this you or your dad asking?'

'Both.'

She sighs. 'Fine, I suppose. In one way, I just want this to be all over. But at the same time, I don't. Do you know what I mean?'

I nod, because in a funny way I feel the same. I know my dad's suffering, and it's natural to want that to stop – for all of our sakes. 'It's funny,' I say. 'When Doctor Watson told us he could give my dad something to manage the pain, I didn't think to ask him how we were going to manage ours.'

'Oh, *Josh.*'

She looks like she's about to cry, and at once I worry I've overstepped the mark.

'Have I said something wrong?'

'Quite the opposite, actually.' My mum reaches over and squeezes my hand. 'Have I told you that I'm glad you're here?'

'Only about a million times.'

'Well, I am.'

'Me too,' I say, and I mean it.

My mum breaks off another piece of cake for Wallace, and I find myself glancing up at Derton's clock tower at the other end of the seafront before I remember the clock hasn't worked for ever, although it's 'still right twice a day', as my dad is fond of saying. And I realise I'm looking at the time not because I'm not enjoying being here with my mum, but more because I'm missing out on spending time with my dad. I'm already afraid the last days of his life are a film I'm skipping through on fast forward, rather than watching at a normal speed, and I'm just about to suggest that we ought to get back when I'm aware of someone standing behind me, although when I swivel round nervously in my chair, it's Anna.

'How are you both doing?'

For a moment, I wonder whether my dad's given her a tenner too, then when she adds, 'Or should I take the fact that you're feeding them to Wallace as a bad sign?' I realise she's talking about the cupcakes.

'They're delicious, love,' says my mum.

Anna beams with pride. 'Coming from you, that's a great compliment.'

'We all think so. Don't we?'

Wallace's mouth is too full to answer, so I nod. 'Just like my mum used to make.'

Anna smiles again, then she looks as if she's had an idea. 'Do you still do much baking, Sue?'

'From time to time,' says my mum. 'Though Josh's dad doesn't quite have the appetite he used to.'

'It's just . . .' Anna pulls up a chair, and sits down. 'One of my suppliers . . . Well, what's happened isn't important. But alongside the cupcakes, we do a 'cake of the day' – old favourites like Victoria Sponges, and gingerbread, and fruit cakes. They're very popular. Anyway, we've got a vacancy.'

'Shouldn't that be a "cake-ancy"?'

Anna ignores my admittedly poor attempt at a joke. 'So if you were interested? I'd pay, obviously.'

'I don't know, love,' says my mum, hesitantly.

'Go on,' I say. 'You can knock them up in your sleep. Though obviously,' I add, for Anna's benefit, 'she wouldn't.'

'Well . . .'

'I won't take no for an answer,' says Anna.

My mum smiles, and so do I. Because where Anna's concerned, that'll be my philosophy too.

∽

When we get back, my dad looks like he hasn't moved from in front of the television, though the glass of red wine on the table next to him that he instinctively tries to hide from my mum would suggest otherwise.

The unmistakable intro music from *Catch Me If You Can* is playing, so my mum joins him on the sofa, and while I'd normally be tempted to sit and watch with them, my experience the other week hasn't exactly made me the biggest fan of the show. Instead, I unclip Wallace's lead, and as he runs over to sit under my dad's legs I slip into the kitchen to put the kettle on.

But it's not until I'm splashing some milk into my cup (and contemplating stealing a Minger) that it occurs to me to wonder why the show is on a couple of hours later than usual, and why – to my horror – I've just heard a familiar voice announce that she's 'Devon, from Cornwall'.

Nervously, I tiptoe to the door and peer through, just in time to see a long-distance shot of the competitors, then curse under my breath. Only my dad would record a quiz show that's on every day.

My mum and dad exchange glances, then lean towards the TV to get a closer look, so I duck back out of sight to consider my options. The fuse box is in the cupboard under the stairs, right next to where I'm standing. I could fake a power cut, then get them out of the room somehow, wipe the recording and pretend there's been some technical problem. But the effort of getting my dad out of the room is pretty intense, and it's hardly fair of me just to spare my embarrassment. Besides, when I hear Lesley say, 'And our final contestant is . . .' I realise it's too late. Particularly when there's the sound of a saucer being dropped on the floor in shock.

'Josh?' calls my dad, though my name's a bit muffled by his oxygen mask.

'Just a minute . . .'

I realise there's nothing for it and walk miserably into the lounge, where my parents have paused the recording and are staring accusingly at my frozen, gormless face up on the screen.

'Why didn't you tell us?' says my mum.

'I wanted to surprise you.'

'We might have missed it,' says my dad.

'You might wish you had, in a minute.'

'How exciting!' My mum shifts along the sofa and pats the cushion next to her. 'Come and watch it with us?'

'But don't shout out the answers,' says my dad.

'Do I have to?'

'Yes,' says my mum. 'You do.'

Reluctantly, I sit down between the two of them. I know what's going to happen. My dad will answer the questions I don't get right, then tell me off for going for the big prize and *losing*, and all our progress in the last few weeks will have been for nothing. But at least when my dad presses 'Play' again, and hears Lesley wish him all the best, he beams as proudly as I've ever seen him.

And then, although I can't watch, they're caught up in the excitement of the show. Even Wallace seems to know there's something going on, and while I don't think he's recognised me on screen, he seems a little confused every time he hears my voice coming from the television, though not too confused to prevent him from joining in. Lesley: 'What was the name of the decorative lace adornment the Elizabethans used to wear round their necks?' Devon: 'A doily?' My dad (excitedly): 'What is it, Wallace? What's the answer, boy?' Wallace: 'Ruff!' Which makes my dad almost pass out from laughing, so much so we have to pause the programme for a good five minutes while turning his oxygen flow up to maximum.

After an excruciating twenty minutes, we reach the final round, and when it's my turn, and the bonus buzzer sounds, my dad almost falls off the sofa in excitement. But as Lesley asks me what I want to play for, I reach over, grab the remote, and hit 'Pause'.

My dad frowns at me. 'What did you do that for?'

'Can we just . . . not?'

'It's just getting to the good bit.'

'No it isn't.'

My mum pats me on my knee. 'Come on, Josh. It's exciting.'

'For you, maybe.'

'For everyone.' My dad points at the screen. 'You never see anyone from Derton on TV.'

'Except for on *Crimewatch*, maybe,' suggests my mum.

I force a smile, and reluctantly hand him the remote. 'Okay.
But promise you won't get angry?'

'Why on earth would we get angry?' asks my dad.

Ș

As the end credits start to roll, my dad switches the TV off, then
sits there staring at the blank screen. Even Wallace can't look at me.
Eventually, my mum hauls herself up from the sofa.

'I'll go and put the kettle on,' she says. 'Bad luck, Josh.'

'Thanks.'

My dad and I sit in silence for a moment or two, then with not
an inconsiderable amount of effort, he swivels round to face me.

'You had to go for it, didn't you?'

'Pardon?'

'You're never just happy with what's in front of you.'

'That's hardly . . .'

My dad sighs. 'I'm not having a go at you, Josh.'

'That makes a change.'

He pulls the mask from his face. 'Will you just let me speak?'

'Sorry.'

'It's just . . .' My dad shakes his head slowly. 'I never understood
why you always wanted to go off and do something different. Why

292

the shop wasn't enough for you. Why *we* weren't enough for you. And for a long time, I resented it. Resented you. How ungrateful you were, I thought, to turn your back on your mum and me. And for a long time, I thought it was *us*.'

'It was never you, Dad.' I smile. 'How does that saying go: *it's not you, it's me*? Well, that's true, in my case. It *is* me. And it's not that I always think the grass is greener. I just want to go and walk on that grass. Take my shoes off and feel it between my toes.'

'That's what I'm trying to tell you, son. I know that now – that it's you. Always looking to improve yourself. To do something different.' He clears his throat noisily, painfully. 'It's taken me a long time to realise it. I know you had some exploring to do. Had to make your own mind up about stuff. And recently, rather than tell you what to do – and we both know how successful *that* approach has been – well, I've been trying to help you.'

'Help me?'

'See for yourself. Or rather, find out for yourself.'

'Find out what?'

'What it is you want, Josh. If it's the last thing I do. Even though it might well be.'

I stare at him for a moment, feeling stupid – though not quite as stupid as I felt after my final round on *Catch Me If You Can*. I've missed what's been staring me in the face ever since I got here – that everything he's done, from us spending time together, to family trips out, me and my mum bonding again over her driving lessons (or even just over a cupcake), Wallace, family photos, and yes, even forcing me to see Anna that day . . . Everything's been designed to get me to see things in a different light. To see *Derton* in a different light. To challenge my preconceptions. To get me to try new things, in the hope that I might like them. Or rather, that I might realise they're different to how I once thought they were.

And right now, more than ever, I can see how things – and people, and perceptions – can change. Because I used to think my dad was pathetic. Selfish. An embarrassment. And now I can see he's the bravest, smartest, most selfless person I know.

34.

It's the following Sunday, and I'm out walking Wallace along the seafront when Gaz texts to see if I fancy a quick drink, and seeing as it's an hour till my mum – assuming she's finished whatever cake she's making for Anna – will be putting dinner on the table, I decide that I do. Then it occurs to me that I better check with Wallace, but fortunately, I've discovered that anything said to him in an enthusiastic-enough voice gets a happy snort and a wag of that stubby little tail of his, so he seems happy enough to come along.

The Submarine's only five minutes away, and they positively welcome dogs, giving Wallace a bowl of water before they've even asked me what I'm drinking. Gaz turns up and we chat about nothing over a couple of pints, and I'm relaxed because I don't have to leave till five to six because I only live five minutes away, and again I'm reminded how easy it is living here. In London, the chances of arranging an impromptu beer were pretty much zero – in fact, arranging any drink usually involved several days' planning ahead, negotiating on the location, and then (once you'd forked out a small ransom for a bottle of obscure German lager and a glass of wine so large you'd normally expect to find a goldfish swimming in it) a desperate attempt to find a seat in the 'so loud you can't hear yourself think' venue you've chosen. And 'after work' would always mean 7 or 8 pm at the earliest (given how no-one in London does the nine-to-five any more out of fear of losing their job), plus a cramped, sweaty Tube ride, then another less-cramped but full-of-drunks/muggers one home while desperate for the toilet, or paying the big fortune a black cab would cost (though you'd pay anything to spare you from the horrors of the night bus).

And Wallace is free to roam the pub and sniff what he likes (though he actually seems happiest when he's within a two-feet radius of my two feet), without the landlord complaining or someone trying to dog-nap him, and people I've never met before even come over for a chat (though usually *about* Wallace, or actually *to* Wallace), and there's space to sit – inside, *or* out – without feeling that you have to spread out and guard your table to stop a loud gaggle of secretaries on a hen night muscling you out. Plus the landlord's asked me if I want to run a tab despite only having seen me a couple of times before, and he doesn't ask for my credit card (or my first born) for the privilege.

And while I know it's not all about the pub (for me, at least), these things are starting to seem important. The cashiers in the supermarket who talk to me (though that's taken a bit of getting used to) and ask how my dad is. People on the pavement who nod (or even – shock horror! – *say*) hello as I pass. Drivers who let me out of a junction even though I'm driving a BMW – a car that in London is guaranteed to produce a sneer of disdain and confine me to edging out of that side road for what feels like forever. Neighbours who actually pop in or talk to me over the fence, instead of ignoring my very existence.

Don't get me wrong – I know places like Derton have their downsides. But when you live like most people in Derton seem to, quite honestly, they don't seem so important, and after a few weeks of this I must admit I can see the attraction of Derton life. It's not that people here are lazy, or unambitious, or backward, as I used to (shamefully) think – they've just chosen to do things a different way.

Opt out of the rat race (which might actually make them smarter than everyone else, if you think about it). And while they might not make as much money, they don't have to spend as much money either – on their houses, or their beer, or on their commute to work. Which kind of evens out in the long run, I suppose.

I'm quite enjoying this dog lark too. Wallace is a real character and fortunately (post-cupcake incidents aside) doesn't seem to have the same kind of flatulence problem that Ziggy demonstrated, either because he's good at saving any particular gas grenades until we're out of the house, or because the dog food from the discount supermarket is as impressively good as the rest of their stuff seems to be. And while my mum hasn't quite bonded with him in the way my dad was obviously hoping, that's okay – to be honest, I'm appreciating our walks, and he's company at the shop, especially on the days when we don't get many customers. Which is most of them.

As for Anna – well, it's impossible to avoid anyone in a town the size of Derton, especially if you plan your dog-walking schedule around when she's likely to be opening up the café, or just happen to be rearranging the furniture on the pavement outside Second Time Around when she's heading out for her lunch break. And while it's also been impossible to avoid Ian, my standing up to him the other day (or possibly Anna's lecturing, though I'm telling myself it's the former) seems to have made a difference. Though I still double-check for electric-blue Subarus every time I'm about to cross the road.

All in all, it's fair to say that life's a little strange at the moment. Every morning I'm woken by what I know is my mum trying to tiptoe along the landing to quietly open the spare bedroom door to see if my dad's died during the night and to wake him up for breakfast if he hasn't. And while I've thought about explaining to her that, for either of those scenarios, there's no need for her to be so quiet, I haven't, mainly because I can't imagine what must be going through her mind during the few seconds before she opens the door.

Then, because I generally can't get back to sleep, it's up, shower, check on my dad (who generally seems as pleased as punch to have made it back for another day), and (on the days I'm not working) walk Wallace to the beach and back. And though I haven't quite got used to picking up after him, I remind myself it's good training for nappy-changing. If and when that ever becomes a possibility.

After breakfast, if I *am* working, it's the short, five minute walk to the shop – and given how we hardly have customers banging on our door first thing – a leisurely opening up, which pretty much just involves switching on the kettle, making myself a cup of coffee, checking Wallace has some water in his bowl, and sitting down with the newspaper. I don't need to tidy, or dust (mainly because Michelle says it adds to the authenticity) or straighten anything on the shelves (because most of the shelves aren't straight). And because we don't get many customers (and because they're not my ex-classmates trying to nick sweets, which is what I had to put up with *all the time* when I worked in my dad's sweetshop), I'm genuinely pleased whenever someone comes in, even if it's just to browse. And this must show, because quite often they buy something, which makes me happy, and Michelle happy, which means work's actually, well, *rewarding* (apart from in the financial sense).

Plus it's funny to see the reaction on people's faces when they come in and see things – the old phones, for example – that remind them of days gone by, and give them such a warm feeling that they even pick the handsets up and on occasion (and this always makes me smile) speak into them, as if they find it so quaint to remember a world in which you took a call where you answered it, mainly because of the coiled piece of wire anchoring you to where the phone was plugged in. And though nowadays things have changed, and we're free to roam wherever we want, keeping in touch even when we're nowhere nearby, I'm starting to suspect that's not always a good thing.

And while I find it hard to imagine that in, say, fifty years' time, people will come into shops like this to buy old iPhones, or laptops, or e-readers, I know they're doing it now not because the old is better (it wouldn't have become 'the old' if it was), but because there's a real affection, or nostalgia, or even *love* for this old stuff. Perhaps because it's familiar, perhaps because it's what we grew up with. And that makes me think.

Because for most of my childhood, I hated Derton. Found it boring. And although my mum always used to tell me 'only boring people get bored', if you were fourteen (or fifteen, or sixteen, or seventeen, or even . . . well, you get my point) it was the worst place in the world, with absolutely nothing to do, even though it had a beach, and amusement arcades, and a funfair, because to a fourteen-year-old boy (or fifteen, or sixteen, yada yada yada) that kind of stuff *is* boring, once you've done it the once or twice. We want *new* stuff. Different stuff. Stuff that's going to challenge us. And I guess that's why we were so desperate to meet girls too. Because they were new. Had different 'stuff'. And boy, did they challenge us.

But the funny thing is, I'm beginning to see that Derton isn't quite as boring any more. Sure, it might still be to my fourteen-year-old self (or my fifteen-year-old self, or my sixteen-year-old self . . . okay, okay). But to my thirty-something self, I can see that actually, nowadays, there *is* stuff to do (or rather, stuff *I* want to do to do). There's the Derton Contemporary and the refurbished pubs, bars, and restaurants. There's the new Old Town (if you see what I mean), with its retro and vintage shops and cool art galleries and buzzy cafés (and yes, I include the cupcake one in that). They're even refurbishing Funland and reopening Derton's only other tourist attraction – a museum so obscure (seashells!) it should be in a museum itself. And because of all this new stuff, there are new people in the town, both running the new stuff and coming down from London to see the new stuff. And that's good, because on a sunny day like today, the place comes alive. This morning there's even a farmers' market in the square, and while there are a few of the older Derton residents wandering around with bemused looks on their faces at what it is the stalls are selling (sample conversation: 'What's that funny-looking bread?' 'Focaccia.' 'I only asked.'), for the rest of us, whether we're locals or tourists (and I'm still not quite sure what camp I fit into just yet), more and more of this can only be a good thing.

Maybe it's living back at my parents' house, or perhaps going back to school, but somehow, surrounded by all these reminders from my past, in the middle of all the stuff I grew up with, with the people I grew up around, I think I'm finally beginning to understand what 'home' means.

35.

I help my dad into his wheelchair, set Wallace gently down on his lap, then slot the oxygen bottle into the strap on the back and fix the mask round his face, though by the time we've reached the allotment gates, I could do with one myself. Gaz and Michelle are already there, waiting by the shed, and my dad's pleased to see them. They do a convincing job of not appearing shocked at how much worse he looks since his party, and then my dad hands me his key ring, and (after I've eventually found which of the several hundred keys he seems to have on there actually fits the padlock) I unlock the shed and hand the tools out.

The three of us stand there and stare at the waist-high weeds, clueless as to where on earth to start, so my dad directs Gaz and me towards the far end of the plot and tells us to 'Get rid of pretty much anything that looks dead – except me', which is a little close to the bone, but we laugh good-naturedly, and it seems to make sense (though it includes pretty much *everything* we can see – including him). So I take the strimmer and (when I've eventually managed to start it) start strimming everything (including the toe-caps of my new-ish Adidas Stan Smiths), reducing the foliage down to just above earth level, which Gaz and Michelle gather up in huge arm-fuls and pile in the centre of the plot.

I've already checked we're allowed to have a bonfire (although the irony of burning something isn't lost on any of us), and after close to three hours of back-breaking work (it's a mystery to me how my dad managed to keep the place so tidy and productive for so long) we've built the kind of bonfire that wouldn't look out of place in *The Wicker Man*. And while the rest of the plot is looking pretty bare, at least it's not the jungle it used to be.

Then my mum arrives with flasks of tea and a packet of biscuits (and a cold six-pack of beer for Gaz, two of which he downs in quick succession), and she breaks into a smile when she sees what we've done and gives Gaz and Michelle a huge hug, then goes to stand with her arm round my dad's shoulders as we light the bonfire. As we stare into the flames, several of the other allotment-holders stroll over and compliment us on our fire as if we're cavemen, then chat briefly to my dad, and as they leave a couple of them seem to have something in their eyes, though it could of course just be smoke.

Eventually, once the flames have died down, we're done – though Gaz looks like he's done in, so much so that my dad offers him his chair.

'I'm okay, Mr. Peters.' Gaz sits down on a paving stone. 'I didn't think it'd be such hard work.'

'An allotment's a bit like a woman, Gary. You've got to keep on top of it regularly. Otherwise it can run away from you.'

'I heard that,' says Michelle, from where she's cleaning mud off a sharp-looking fork. 'And I hope you did too, Gaz.'

Then we put everything away, and Gaz and Michelle say good-bye, and my mum says she has to nip off to the shops, but as I'm getting ready to push my dad down the path after her, he asks me to wait.

'You're sure I can't tempt you, Josh?' he says, once the others are out of earshot.

'This place?' I smile down at him. 'Bit of a long drive every Sunday, don't you think?'

'It's two minutes from the house.'

'From London.'

'Ah. You not staying, then?'

For what? I want to say, but I don't, because I don't want to hear his reply. 'Dad, *please . . .*'

'So what did we do all this for this morning?'

I ignore his use of the word *we*. 'Well, for you.'

'And there was me thinking it might have been for you. Oh well. But then again, I suppose there's no point starting what you can't finish.'

'No, Dad. There isn't.'

'Fair enough.' There's a pause, and then: 'But you'll still come and see your mum?'

'Of course. Whenever I can.'

'Good, good.' My dad takes a final look around the allotment, then looks up at me with red-rimmed eyes. 'I'm ready to go now, Josh,' he says.

And it's only later that I wonder exactly what he meant.

∽

The Submarine's pretty full – though that's probably simply because there's not that many other places to go on a Saturday night round here, rather than Gaz's enthusiastic plastering of any spare wall or window in Derton with posters advertising the show. I'm sitting at a table with a nervous-looking Michelle – though an even more anxious Gaz is with the rest of the 'band' in the back room.

'What are you worried about? That he's going to embarrass himself?'

'That he's going to embarrass *me*.' Michelle makes a face. 'Derton's a small town.'

'How bad can it be?'

'You obviously haven't seen them rehearse.'

'I wouldn't worry.' I nod at the crowd hanging around the bar. 'Everyone's had a few drinks . . .'

'As has Gaz. More than a few.'

'Ah.'

As if on cue, the lights go down. Gaz and the other three emerge through a side door and make their way to the stage area by the toilets at the back of the pub – not that anyone seems to have noticed – so Michelle lets out a whoop and starts applauding, then nudges me to join in, and the rest of the drinkers reluctantly swivel round to see what's going on.

'Ladies and gentlemen,' says a voice from the loudspeakers. 'Please welcome, for one night only . . .'

'Thank God,' whispers Michelle.

'. . . F**k That!' Which gets a laugh, because they've bleeped out the middle part of 'f**k', then Gaz and the other band members line up behind a row of microphones, the opening bars of 'Pray' begin, and . . .

And they're *terrible*. Gaz is off-key – though maybe it's stage fright affecting his voice – none of them can dance, and it's debatable whether any of them have actually heard the original version of the song they're murdering. It's bad karaoke. In fact it's worse than that. But like a car crash, or those YouTube videos of people falling over and hurting themselves, it's impossible not to watch.

Michelle doesn't seem to know whether to cover her eyes or her ears, I'm wondering whether I should set off the fire alarm just to spare them further embarrassment, and then a funny thing happens. The audience – who I'm guessing are about the right age to know all these songs – begin to sing along. And maybe it's the group effect, pulling Gaz and the band up with them, or the fact that the audience are singing louder than they are so we can't hear them, but as they sing Gaz seems to get more confident (and more in tune), the other three guys seem to relax a little, and by the time they've moved on to 'Could It Be Magic', while the word *tribute* would still be stretching it, at least they've escaped being done for murder.

As they run through their playlist I realise I'm having a good time and even find myself joining in. It's impossible not to – there's something about a roomful of people singing along to the chorus of 'A Million Love Songs' at the tops of their voices that warms your heart – and by the end of the song Michelle and I are even adding harmonies. The crowd are great. There's no cynicism, no shame, no animosity – they're remembering, or maybe *celebrating*, their youth. A time gone by. Either that, or they're just drunk.

After a few more numbers, a somewhat sweaty Gaz glances over in our direction, then he holds a hand up, and the audience quietens down obediently. 'Ladies and gentlemen,' he puffs into the microphone. 'We have a very special guest here tonight. Someone who left us a while ago, to go and make it big on his own . . .'

I start to get an uneasy feeling and glance across at Michelle, though she's nodding encouragingly at the stage. But surely Gaz wouldn't put me on the spot? Not like this. Not *now*.

'. . . and now he's back. Hopefully, he's *back for good*.'

As the opening guitar chords of the song of the same name begin, I get to my feet and peer around anxiously, looking for an escape route. Gaz serenading me in the middle of a packed pub is the last thing I want, but given the number of people crammed into this tiny space, making for the fire exit will take a while. Plus I've just spotted Anna standing by the door, and she's the last person I want to see me doing a runner.

Michelle tugs at my sleeve. 'Where are you going?'

'Toilet,' I say, quickly.

'You'll miss the best bit.'

'You knew about this?'

Michelle makes a face. 'I've been with Gaz for nearly twenty years. I know about *everything*.'

'So,' continues Gaz, 'please give a huge Derton welcome – or should that be "welcome back" – to . . .'

Of course, now that I'm standing up a few faces have turned towards me, and I debate whether to sit down again, but I do actually need the toilet. And because I don't want to insult Gaz and whatever announcement he's got planned, I reluctantly make my way towards the back of the pub.

'. . . Robbie Williams!' shouts Gaz.

There's a loud cheer from the audience, and a man dressed in a similar style to Gaz bursts in through the pub door, elbows me out of the way, and joins the other four on stage.

And as the band launch into the song's chorus, I suspect there's probably a lesson here, but it'd take a smarter person than me to work out what it is.

∽

I'm on my way back from the toilets when I bump into Anna. Or rather, she bumps into me. Spilling the best part of her glass of rosé down my white shirt.

'I'm so sorry. I . . . Josh.'

'Evening.'

'How's your dad?'

'Fine, considering. Not getting any better, of course.'

'And how are you?'

'Pretty much the same, actually.'

She gives me a look, then nods towards the stage, where the band are finishing 'Back for Good' to rapturous applause. 'They're not bad.'

'I suppose not. Listen, Anna, I . . .'

But I don't get a chance to say anything more, because Gaz has taken the mic again and asked for quiet.

'So this is our last song of the evening,' he says, then he waves away the chorus of disappointment from the crowd. 'And I'd like to dedicate it to my lovely wife Michelle, who's . . .' Gaz peers into the crowd, finally locating her 'trying to hide under that table in the corner.'

'Sorry,' she says sheepishly, as she reluctantly re-takes her seat. 'Dropped something.'

'Anyway,' continues Gaz. 'This is for you, *babe*. It's our song. "Babe",' he adds, just in case anyone hasn't got it.

As Gaz begins crooning, and Michelle smiles through gritted teeth, Anna steers me towards the bar. 'Come on. Michelle looks like she needs a drink. And so do I now, unless you want to take your shirt off and wring it out into my glass?'

'I'll get them. Did you want to join us?'

Anna thinks for a moment, then she nods and goes over to join Michelle at the table, so I push my way to the front (a task made a lot easier given how people move out of the way when they see my soaked shirt) and get a round in. By the time I get back to the table, Michelle has her head in her hands.

'Make it stop,' she says, as I squeeze in between the two girls and deposit three drinks on the table.

Anna smiles. 'Is that really your song?'

Michelle shakes her head. 'It's actually "It Only Takes a Minute Girl", but he was too embarrassed to admit that in case people thought he was referring to his sexual performance.'

Gaz finally finishes singing, so Michelle gives him a 'cheers' with her glass, then (mercifully) the 'boys' look to be taking their final bows. Or not, as it turns out, because despite no-one calling for more, they re-take their positions and ready themselves for an encore.

I turn to Michelle in disbelief. 'There can't be any Take That songs left?'

'There's one,' she says, as the music starts for what's hopefully the final time, then she leans across so Anna can't hear her. 'And I think it's meant for you.'

'For *me*?'

As Gaz honks 'Everything changes, but you . . .' at the top of his voice, I sit back in my chair and smile to myself, because given everything that's happened over the past few weeks, that's patently not true.

And then the only thing that can't change happens. My dad dies.

36.

It's not dramatic, or shocking – one minute he's alive, the next minute he isn't, it's really as simple as that. And it's different to how you see it in films or on television – much less action, but much more drama. My mum is holding his hand as he sits on the sofa, and it looks like he's sleeping, he opens his eyes briefly and focuses on her, flicks his eyes across to me, then he closes them, and he doesn't open them again.

And we don't notice his breathing stop, but we're suddenly aware that it has – the increasingly laboured rattle that's been the soundtrack to our lives these past few weeks (and that's become almost unbearably loud these last few days) just isn't there anymore. So my mum whispers his name, almost as if she doesn't want to wake him, then she looks at me, so I reach over, pull the mask from his face and check his pulse like I've seen Doctor Watson do on so many occasions, and I can't feel anything, anything at all, and even before I've tried his other wrist, we both know.

So I get up and leave the room, not because I can't stand to see it, but to give them a few moments alone together, and it suddenly occurs to me that I don't have a clue what happens now, so I get out my phone and Google 'what to do when someone dies at home', and I'm on the phone to Doctor Watson when my mum comes out of the room, and she walks past me and briefly rests a hand on my shoulder, then she goes into the kitchen and puts the kettle on.

'Who were you speaking to?' she asks, when I've finished the call.

'Doctor Watson.'

'I don't think he'll be able to do anything, love.'

'No, you . . . You kind of have to. To, you know, get him certified.'

My mum forces a smile. 'He should have been certified a long time ago,' she says, and I do my best to force the corners of my mouth up, but instead I burst into tears, and she comes over and hugs me for a long time. 'Do you want some tea?' she asks, eventually, and when I sniff, and nod, she rests a hand on the side of my face. 'Why don't you go in and see him?'

I look at her, horrified, my first response *what for?*, but then I realise it's probably not a bad idea. Before all the fussing starts and the undertaker arrives, it's my chance to say goodbye. Nervously, I walk back along the hallway, then reach the door that my mum's pulled to, and I'm just about to knock on it when I almost laugh at the absurdity.

I've never seen a dead body before, and I assume he's just going to look like he's asleep, but it's not like that at all. At the risk of stating the obvious, there's something missing: while it looks like my dad (albeit a thinner, greyer version of the one I grew up with), it also *doesn't* look like him. The spark (and boy, did he have a spark, I've come to realise these past few weeks) is gone.

Wallace has jumped up onto the sofa and is resting his head on my dad's lap, his eyes impossibly big, and though it's one of the saddest things I've ever seen, I can't bring myself to shoo him off.

I watch him for a while, then tentatively reach a hand down and touch his stubbly cheek, trying manfully to prevent the massive lump in my throat from turning back into tears. I'm expecting him to be cold, or clammy, and the fact that he's neither takes me by surprise, so much so that I find myself staring at his chest just to make sure he's not breathing.

'It'd be just like him,' says my mum, from the doorway. 'Make us think he'd gone, then "Boo!"'

'We should be so lucky, eh?'

I call Wallace softly, and he leaps down off the sofa and follows me into the kitchen, where there are three cups set out on the table.

'Mum,' I say, 'it's just the two of us now.'

'I thought you said Doctor Watson was coming?'

'Oh. Right. Of course.'

As if on cue, there's a knock on the door, and Doctor Watson lets himself in.

'Thanks for coming so quickly,' I say.

'Where is he now?'

It strikes me as a rather deep question. I mean, I don't believe in heaven or hell, but surely . . .

'The living room,' says my mum, matter-of-factly, then she blanches as she realises what she's said.

'Second door on the left,' I say.

It takes Doctor Watson no time to certify that my dad's dead, and I wonder how *he* feels. Derton has loads of old people, and he must have done this a thousand times, maybe it's even a daily occurrence for him, and whatever you do that regularly – if it's this, or drive a Ferrari, or sleep with a supermodel – surely it becomes routine?

But when he walks back into the kitchen he seems genuinely concerned and even a little upset, and even though he glances at his watch a couple of times – those ovens don't turn themselves off, I suppose – he accepts my mum's offer of a cup of tea and (although I can't bring myself to eat one) a Minger gratefully.

And my mum, being as organised as she is, has already got the number for the undertaker, so I phone them, and when they arrive an hour or so later to collect him, she goes out into the garden and tends to her plants while they load my dad into the back of their van. And it is a van – a white, unmarked one, and while he'd surely have made some joke about 'white van man', this is the saddest part of the day. The moment my dad leaves his home. *Their* home. And it's no wonder my mum asks me if I'd mind signing the paperwork to confirm the arrangements, because if I was her, I wouldn't even be able to breathe.

37.

I've driven past Derton Crematorium a hundred times, though only because it's right next door to the council refuse tip, but I've never had cause to turn in through the large iron gates and drive along the path that leads to the building itself. And I don't know what I was expecting, because it looks quite modern. A bit like a church, though I suppose the chimney in place of the spire is a bit of a giveaway as to what kinds of services actually go on here. My mum's in the car with me (though I've turned down her offer to drive), and we've left an out-of-sorts Wallace at home, though I get the feeling that neither of us wants to be here either.

'Is this it?' says my mum, peering through the windscreen.

'I'm guessing so, given the chimney.'

My mum grimaces, and I want to kick myself. 'Sorry.'

She pats the back of my hand, then points out a parking space in between two funeral cars, and I pull the BMW into it. It's a hot day, so I've got the roof down, which I suddenly realise might not be that appropriate, though at least the car is black so we don't look too out of place.

'It's smaller than I thought it would be.'

I don't know how to answer, not wanting to think how big a crematorium needs to be, because I'd then have to think about what happens inside, and that's the last thing either of us wants to consider. There's a family coming out, all black suits and dresses, and smoking like, well, chimneys, which strikes me as ironic.

'Shall we go in?'

I look at my watch, then nod, sure that we're both keen to get this over with as soon as possible. That we've managed to get a 'slot' so quickly is a bit of a miracle – the crematorium has had a cancellation (and I can't even begin to imagine how that's come about) – but even so, the past few days have been surreal, my mum and I hanging about an unsettlingly empty house, competing with Wallace as to who's wearing the most miserable expression. Though on balance, my mum would be the winner.

We walk in through the heavy swing doors and up to the desk, where I mumble 'Peters' to the stern-looking woman sitting there, and she directs us into a room at the far end of the corridor. We're a few minutes early, and – mainly because we haven't invited anyone – there's no-one else there. Except for my dad, that is, in a plain wooden coffin, on a table at the front.

'Is that him?' says my mum.

'I guess so,' I say, though we'll have to take their word for it, given that the lid is closed.

I hang back as she slowly approaches the coffin and tentatively rests a hand on it, as if there's still a tiny part of her that expects my dad to fling it open and shout 'Surprise!' Then there's the sound of someone clearing their throat from the doorway, and a man in a smart grey suit (and with a complexion the same colour) approaches us with a solemn 'Morning,' and I say 'Yes, we are,' because I think he's said 'Mourning?', which seems to confuse him a little.

'Are you the Peters party?'

I look around the featureless room. It's the last place I'd want to hold a party. 'I suppose so.'

'Are there many more coming?'

'There aren't *any* more coming,' I explain. 'We've already had the funeral. A couple of weeks ago.'

The man looks at me with a 'does not compute' expression.

'It's a long story,' I tell him.

'Right,' he says, and then, with the air of someone who's keen to get this over with as quickly and painlessly as possible, he touches my mum sympathetically on the shoulder. 'Shall we begin?'

My mum nods.

'Did you want to say anything?' says the man, and my mum shakes her head vigorously. I can tell she's trying desperately to hold it together, and I'm not so far off that myself.

'Josh?' she squeaks, and I shake my head too. Summarising a ninety-thousand-word book in a few words is easy compared to trying to do the same for a seventy-odd-year life. What can I possibly say that'll sum up what I'm feeling, or describe what the last few weeks have been like? How can I possibly tell him what he meant to me? And even if I could, it's not as if he can hear me. And besides, in this miserable place that my mum and I are keen to leave as soon as we can, anything that delays the proceedings seems like a bad idea.

'Ah, here's someone else, at least,' says the man, with more than a little relief at not having to keep dealing with two people who don't seem to be following the party line.

I hear a clicking of heels on the stone floor and swivel around, preparing to tell whoever it is that they're at the wrong funeral, and that it isn't a funeral at all – more of a disposal, really, but then I recognise the woman in the fitted black dress, and my heart does a double back-flip.

Anna hugs my mum quickly, then turns to me. 'I didn't think it was right, the two of you having to go through this alone,' she whispers.

'We're not alone,' says my mum, grabbing my arm tightly. 'But thanks, Anna. It's really . . .'

But then her voice begins to crack, so the three of us sit down on the uncomfortable wooden chairs, and Anna takes my hand, and I take my mum's hand, and the man looks at us, opens his mouth as if to say something, then thinks better of it and just presses a button on the side of the table. And as my dad disappears off through the curtain at the back, I get the crazy impulse to leap up onto the coffin to try and stop it, as if to say *this is all too soon*, because I'm suddenly desperate for another chance to do it all over again, not just the last few weeks, but the last eighteen years – no, scratch that, the last thirty-six – and the feeling is so strong, so overwhelming, that I can't stop my shoulders from shaking and my heart from pounding and my chest from heaving, and before I know it I'm doubled over, sobbing like a baby, with Anna trying to comfort me on one side, my mum doing the same on the other.

Eventually, and it takes a while, I manage to regain some level of control – though I've gone through most of the packet of Kleenex my mum always has with her – and we're conscious that the next group are waiting to come in, so we troop miserably back out to the woman at the desk, and Anna asks (because neither my mum nor I can form coherent sentences), and apparently it takes a couple of hours for my dad's ashes to be ready, and there's nowhere really to wait, and even though the woman tells us we can come back and pick them up tomorrow if we'd prefer, my mum turns this plan down as she doesn't want to leave him in a place like this – 'No offence' – overnight. So Anna suggests we go and grab some lunch at The Submarine, and when I hear the word *we*, I realise something's changed.

So I drive us there, Anna following in her car, and when we get to the pub, the waitress tells us they've got artisan bread on the menu today, and that it's 'oven-baked', then she spots that we're all dressed in black and starts to apologise, but my mum tells her not to worry.

'I think we've had enough of ovens today, Josh, don't you?' she says, and then, to her credit, my mum starts laughing, and I can't help but join in, and eventually we're clutching each other we're laughing so hard, and then the laughter turns into tears, and Anna sits there patiently until we're finished. Which takes a while.

Over lunch, the three of us chat about everything and anything, but nothing about my dad, and I see what Anna's doing: trying to take my mum's mind off things. On what's possibly the saddest day of the whole process – the day when the reality of the last few weeks has probably finally hit home – Anna's talking to her about her garden and answering questions about cupcakes and trying to guess her favourite flavour (red velvet, as it turns out, though I'm beginning to believe that's everyone's favourite flavour).

Then after lunch, when it's time to collect the ashes, Anna says she should really get back to work, so my mum gives her a hug, then climbs wearily back into the car, and I finally see the toll all this has taken on this strong, proud woman, and there's a strange feeling in my chest that I suspect is nothing to do with earlier events.

'Thanks for coming,' I say as I walk Anna across the street.

'Even though I wasn't invited?'

'You know what I mean. And I'm sorry.'

'What for?'

'Everything. Being an emotional mess.'

'You mean today? Or the last few weeks?'

I smile guiltily. 'Both.'

'Josh, I'm hardly going to judge you because of how you behaved while your dad was dying.'

'Thanks.'

'Though how you behaved eighteen years ago . . . Well, that's another matter.'

'Right.' I make a face, and glance over towards the car, where my mum's watching the two of us with interest. 'Well, I'd better . . .'

'Okay.'

'So . . .' I stay where I am, not quite knowing what to say next.

'What are you going to do now?'

'Well, we've got the ashes to pick up, and Wallace will need a walk . . .'

'*After* all that, Josh.'

I shrug. 'Go home, I guess.'

She leans across and gives me the briefest peck on the cheek, and tells me to give her a call when I know when that is.

But it's not until later, when we're driving back to the house, my mum cradling the urn containing my dad's ashes like a newborn on her lap, I realise Anna's actually said 'where that is', not 'when'.

38.

It's funny how it's taken me until now to realise there is something I've missed about Derton – the sea. And it's what the town has, if you think about it, what brought everyone here in the first place and what brings them back again, in the summer months at least. The Victorians used to come here and 'take the waters' to cure themselves from whatever ailment they were suffering from, and while nowadays a swim in the English channel is more likely to have the opposite effect given the stuff those foolish enough to go for a dip will frequently see floating past their noses, on a sunny day (and from the safety of the beach) you can see the attraction.

And while London has its parks, and its buildings, and that large brown/grey watery thing called the Thames flowing right through the middle, it's just not the same. This is the *sea*. It's what makes us an island. Separates us from the French. Stopped us all from speaking German, as my dad always used to say, though for some strange reason, in a German accent. And while Derton's half a mile of coastline (or 'the front', as my mum insists on calling it) hasn't changed much since I was a kid (although I'm beginning to suspect it's the only thing that hasn't), the basics – a sandy beach, and the sea – are pretty much all you need.

And I've been sea-ing a lot of it recently (ha ha – see what I did there? Or should that be 'sea' what I did? Anyway . . .) on my walks to work, on my walks with Wallace, and also on my walks to work with Wallace. And I'm sure it's a lot different in the winter, with the wind howling in from the north and the rain whipping horizontally into your face, but in June, the summer just about starting, the sun almost hot enough for me to leave my jacket at home, the sky such a clear blue I'm confident I don't need my umbrella, it's actually quite pleasant. London would be sweltering round about now, but here? I can understand why people like it so much.

I mention this because I'm standing with Michelle and Gaz at Michelle's brother Martin's 'surf' concession on the main sands, staring out at the water. And while Derton's waves are generally more laughable than surfable, he does a good enough business renting equipment to drunken tourists so they can pose *Baywatch* style at the water's edge before realising that actually, perhaps taking them out to sea is more hassle than Hasselhoff. We're here because Martin's just taken delivery of a couple of what I'm reliably informed are known as paddleboards, which a quick Google search has told me are large surfboards that you stand up on and (perhaps not surprisingly, given the name) *paddle*, and which – given that none of us owns a boat – are the best way we can think of to sprinkle my dad's ashes at sea.

Gaz finishes zipping up his wetsuit, which makes him look more like an overweight seal than the surf god he's been aiming for, and picks up his board. 'You ready?'

I reach over and take the urn from my mum, then wink at her. 'I was born ready.'

'Hold on . . .'

I look around to see Michelle standing there, her phone poised to take a photo of the two of us.

'What do you want to do that for?'

'Just so I've got something to show to the lifeboat that'll be coming out to look for you both.'

'Yeah. Very funny.'

I slot the urn into the rucksack I'm wearing back-to-front, reach a finger into the neck of my wetsuit in a vain attempt to loosen it, then tell myself that if I can't even get a finger in there, then I'll get no water in there either. Not that I'm planning to go into the water at all.

Martin lays my board down, hops onto it and shows us the correct paddling technique, which seems to consist of just sticking the paddle into the water and paddling.

'Looks easy,' says Gaz, sarcastically. 'On land.'

As I bend down and pick up my board, Martin looks out to sea, where thankfully the water's as flat as a pancake. 'You'll be fine.'

Gaz and I exchange glances, then grab our paddles and head nervously for the water, though I almost stop when I get ankle-deep.

'What's the matter?'

'It's cold.'

'Wuss,' says Gaz, though I laugh when I see him slow down too.

We place the boards on the water's surface, step on gingerly and begin our wobbly paddle out to sea, and while it's *not* easy, it's amazing how not wanting to fall into the chilly water focuses my technique. We're both doing pretty well, until a passing fishing boat sends up the only wave we've encountered all day (apart from the ones that Michelle's doing to attract our attention from where she's filming us from the beach), and while I manage to ride it out by turning my board head-on into it, Gaz isn't so lucky, performing a perfect cartoon wobble along the board, before falling head-first into the water.

I nearly fall off myself given how hard I'm laughing, though by the look on Gaz's face, he's not quite sharing my amusement. He hauls himself back onto his board, then after several failed attempts to stand up, looks apologetically up at me.

'I'm heading back in.'

'Not got your sea legs?'

'I didn't know seals laid eggs.'

'What?'

'Never mind. In any case, I need the toilet.'

'Just go in your wetsuit.'

'Not that kind of toilet.'

As Gaz lets the tide take him in, I paddle out a bit farther, then carefully steer the board through a hundred and eighty degrees and look back at Derton. I don't think I've ever seen it from this far out to sea before, and it's funny, like when you see somewhere you know from an aeroplane, to look at the various landmarks from an alternative viewpoint and realise how different it is, how small it seems. There's the rollercoaster in Funland, once the tallest structure in town, now dwarfed by the ugly block of flats next to it. The clock tower. The shelter where Anna and I spent many a weekend afternoon. The parade where my dad's shop was (and if I squint a little, I can just read the sign that says 'Baker's Cupcakes'). The bus stop where I used to get on and off every day on my way to and from school, hoping Ian wouldn't be flicking my ears from the seat behind me. The arcades where I'd lose most of my pocket money on the fruit machines. And while it's hardly a Lion King 'circle of life' type epiphany, I suddenly realise it's here that my fondest memories are from. Everything major I've ever done, every person who's ever really mattered to me, was here. *Is* here, in fact, although with one recent exception. Which reminds me.

I reach into my rucksack, retrieve the urn, and unscrew the top, then after checking the wind direction – after all, the last thing I want is a face-full – shake my dad's ashes onto the water, and as I watch them slowly sink, I feel strangely calm. Me, being here now, doing this – it's what he would have wanted. Finally, and for the first time ever, I'm sure I'm not disappointing him.

And then I peer back towards town and see that Anna's joined Michelle and my mum on the beach, and she waves at me, and I wave back just as a wave hits me, and – just like every time I see her – I fall spectacularly.

∾

Michelle's waiting, a towel in one hand, her camera in the other, when I eventually return to dry land.

'Please tell me you didn't get that on film?'

'I'm uploading it to YouTube even as we speak.'

My mum puts Wallace down onto the sand, and he immediately jumps up onto Gaz's discarded paddleboard, either to demonstrate just how easy it is, or because the sun-baked sand's a little warm for his paws. 'You were doing well, up to that point,' she says, patting me proudly on the shoulder. 'Wasn't he, Anna?'

Anna gives me a look over the top of her sunglasses. 'I suppose so.'

'Did you . . . ?' My mum nods towards my now-soggy rucksack, so I unzip it and hand her the urn.

'Mostly. Here.'

'Mostly?' Puzzled, she unscrews the lid, then peers at the handful of my dad's ashes I've left in there. 'What's that for?'

'Funland.'

She widens her eyes. 'He told you?'

'Well, he said something about your life being one long roller-coaster ride . . .'

For a moment, I think she's going to burst into tears, but instead, she breaks into a huge smile, and even though I'm still in my damp wetsuit, gives me a hug that almost squeezes the breath out of me.

I take her arm and lead her down to the water's edge, and we stand and listen to the waves lapping around our feet. The beach is pretty busy – small children charging excitedly into the water then screaming as they beat a retreat from the waves; several West Indian families camped happily behind vividly-striped windbreaks; an old lady next to us, her feet in the water, sucking happily on an ice lolly; large-bellied men in football shorts stretched out on too-small towels, turning a shocking shade of pink in the midday sun; and out there, my dad . . . Well, he's probably fish food by now. But that's payback, I suppose, given his regular takeaways from The Codfather on the High Street every Friday night for the past thirty-odd years.

As I make a mental note not to order cod and chips for the next few weeks *just in case*, my mum gives me a squeeze.

'Thanks, Josh. For everything.'

'Are you going to be okay?'

'I think so. I miss him, though.'

'We both do.'

We stare out to sea, watching a brightly-coloured beach ball drift past us in the shallows. Behind it, a small boy is swimming as fast as he can, though each time he tries to grab the ball, he only succeeds in pushing it farther away.

My mum lets go of my arm and turns to face me, shielding her eyes from the sun with one hand. 'So, what are you going to do now?'

I smile as the boy finally catches his ball, then look back over my shoulder. Gaz is struggling with the zip on his wetsuit, looking like he (and it) is about to burst. Michelle is shaking her head in a 'he may be an idiot, but he's my idiot' kind of way. Anna has Wallace – a look of utter bliss on his face – cradled against her chest, and though I'm sure she's pretending not to watch us, I manage to catch her eye. I've still got a lot of work to do where we're concerned, but this is one job I'm happy to do on spec.

'How do you mean?'

'Are you going back to London? Back home?'

'What do you mean?' I take a deep breath, and the familiar tang of the sea air triggers a welcome feeling of nostalgia that I hope I'll never lose. 'This *is* home.'

ACKNOWLEDGEMENTS

Thanks: To Emilie Marneur and Jenny Parrott, for editing, rather than 'ed-hitting'. To Sana Chebaro and the rest of the Amazon team, for everything else that turns my writing into an actual book that people can read. To the usual suspects (Tina Patel, Tony Heywood, Lawrence Davison), the lovely Chris Manby, the wonderful authors at Notting Hill Press, and – of course – the Board, for keeping me sane, entertained, and supplied with material*. (*not really)

And lastly, as ever, to my fantastic readers. It's always a pleasure to meet/talk to you on Facebook and Twitter, via email, and sometimes (shock horror!) even in person. If you didn't keep reading, reviewing, and recommending my books, I couldn't keep writing them. So it's your fault!

ABOUT THE AUTHOR

Photo © 2014 Cassandra Nelson

British writer Matt Dunn is the author of nine (and counting) romantic comedy novels, including *A Day at the Office* (a Kindle bestseller in the UK in 2013) and *The Ex-Boyfriend's Handbook* (shortlisted for both the Romantic Novel of the Year Award and the Melissa Nathan Award for Comedy Romance). He's also written about life, love, and relationships for various publications including *The Times*, the *Guardian*, *Glamour*, *Cosmopolitan*, *Company*, *Elle*, and *The Sun*. Before becoming a full-time writer, Matt worked as a lifeguard, a fitness-equipment salesman, and an I.T. headhunter.